W9-CLE-677

PRAISE FOR *THE PERFECT CHILD*

"A mesmerizing, unbearably tense thriller that will have you looking over your shoulder and sleeping with one eye open. This creepy, serpentine tale explores the darkest corners of parenthood and the profoundly unsettling lengths one will go to to keep a family together—no matter the consequences. Electrifying and atmospheric, this dark gem of a novel is one I couldn't put down."

—Heather Gudenkauf, *New York Times* bestselling author

"A deep, dark, and dangerously addictive read. All-absorbing to the very end!"

—Minka Kent, *Washington Post* bestselling author

THE PERFECT CHILD

THE PERFECT CHILD

LUCINDA BERRY

This is a work of fiction. Names, characters, organizations, places, events, and incidents are either products of the author's imagination or are used fictitiously. Any resemblance to actual persons, living or dead, or actual events is purely coincidental.

Published by Thomas & Mercer, Seattle

www.apub.com

ISBN-13: 9781542040549 (hardcover)
ISBN-10: 154204054X (hardcover)
ISBN-13: 9781503905122 (paperback)
ISBN-10: 1503905128 (paperback)

Cover design by Rex Bonomelli

Printed in the United States of America

First edition

To my readers, who have been with me since the beginning

CASE #5243

Interview: Piper Goldstein

"Is this your first homicide case?" he asked in a clipped voice, all business. His chest bulged with muscles underneath his blue collared shirt.

No matter how many times I was questioned by the police, it never got easier. My nerves jumped into high gear automatically. They always made me feel like I was lying, even when I was telling the truth.

I cleared my throat. "I've been on other cases."

I wished I lived in a world where I didn't know violence intimately, but I'd seen more than my fair share, given the work I did. I'd just never expected the Bauers to be involved in anything so awful.

"How did you find out there'd been a break in the case?"

I glanced at the two-way mirror behind us. Even though we were the only two in the room, I knew we weren't alone.

"Claire told me."

He raised his eyebrows. "Claire?"

"My coworker," I responded quickly.

It was hard to believe it'd been less than an hour since Claire had walked into my office. We were always the first ones in in the morning, and I'd assumed she was stopping by to ask how my date had gone the night before, since she got more excited about them than I did. She had been married for twenty years and liked to live vicariously through me, but her married life must have been pretty boring for her to get so excited about mine. My dating life was nothing to get worked up about.

The officer's eyes drilled holes into me. He wanted more from me, but I didn't want to say too much. He rested his elbows on the table and leaned forward. "What did she say when she told you?"

He had to be new, because I'd never seen him before. In a town as small as Clarksville, even the police had familiar faces. He'd told me his name when he'd come into the waiting room, but my head had been swimming with shock, and it had never registered.

I shrugged, anxiously twisting my hands underneath the table. "She didn't say much, but I could tell something was wrong as soon as she came into my office."

I had just logged on to my computer and had been organizing my files for the day when Claire had stuck her head through my door before I'd even finished my first cup of coffee. "Jeez, girl, why don't you just go on my dates for me?" I had joked, but my joke had fallen flat when I'd seen the look on her face.

All semblance of playfulness had been gone, replaced with her most serious expression. All of us had it. The face we wore when the case was so horrible we knew it would keep us up at night and infiltrate our dreams after we finally found a way to fall asleep—the cases that made the social workers with kids hold them tighter.

"So you just knew?" His tone suggested he wasn't sure if he believed me.

I hated when we weren't on the same team. You couldn't be on the other side of the law and not feel like a criminal. It was impossible.

"I knew something serious had happened, but I didn't have any idea what it was or who was involved." I glanced down at my phone for the third time, willing it to vibrate. It wasn't like I was under arrest. I could leave anytime I wanted, but there was no way to leave without looking like I was hiding something.

"What did you think when you found out it was the Bauer family?"

I swallowed past the emotions pushing their way up my throat. "I hoped that it would finally provide them with some answers. They're like family to me."

He glanced down at the open file spread out before him. "It says here that you were the original social worker assigned to the case?"

I nodded, then quickly remembered I was being recorded. "Yes."

"What was that like?"

How could I describe what the last two years had been like? It was the most complicated case of my career and had ended with the worst possible outcome. I'd doubted myself at so many different points, wondering if I'd made the right decisions for everyone involved—what if I'd been wrong? What if I was partially responsible for all this? I took a deep breath, trying to clear my thoughts.

"You couldn't have asked for a better home for Janie. I've been in children's services for over twenty years, and there are plenty of bad foster homes. A lot of foster parents just do it for the money, so they run their families like businesses, but the Bauers were one of the good ones. All they wanted to do was help." My eyes welled with tears, and I couldn't hold them back, even though I tried. I wiped them away quickly, embarrassed to look so soft in front of him. "I'm sorry. This is all just happening so fast."

"I understand," he said, but I knew he didn't. In all my years, I'd never seen a cop cry. He waited a few beats before continuing. "Would it be easier for you if we started at the beginning?"

It didn't matter where we started. Nothing about this was going to be easy.

ONE

Hannah Bauer

"I wouldn't let that fly. I'd ignore him until he apologized," Aubrey said in the righteous, uncompromising way all unmarried people do, without even looking up from her phone. I forgot she was there half the time because her eyes were glued to her phone from the moment we all walked into the hospital break room, her fingers gliding across the screen with manic speed.

Stephanie and I rolled our eyes at the same time. Stephanie had just spent the last ten minutes unloading her pent-up frustrations with her husband—things ranging from leaving his dirty socks all over the house and forgetting to take out the trash to not cleaning up his wiry black hairs in the sink after he shaved. She'd called him out on it, which had led to the age-old argument of her being a nag and him not carrying his weight in household responsibilities that anyone who'd been married for over a decade knew well. Their argument had ended in a major blowout.

"He's so manipulative when he's angry. He leads me on these wild trails, trying to put all this stuff back on me, and before you know it, I'm the one apologizing. I fall for it every time. It drives me crazy,"

Stephanie continued, shoveling bites of reheated pasta in her mouth while she talked.

"See, that's what I was saying last night—we need a girls' weekend. It's been way too long," I said. Last time we'd checked ourselves into the Four Seasons for the weekend and done nothing but drink wine next to the pool and bliss out in the spa. I loved their papaya facial peels and was long overdue for one.

"Totally. Just say when," Stephanie said.

One of our other coworkers, Carl, stuck his head in the door. "We need you guys."

We jumped into action, and within seconds, we'd picked up our mess and were squirting antibacterial foam on our hands as we walked out the door. The nurses' station buzzed with activity and anticipation, everyone on heightened alert. Stephanie shifted into nurse-manager mode and made a beeline for Dr. Hall. The two of them ran the emergency department like a well-oiled machine.

I leaned into Carl. "What happened?"

He shrugged. "Not sure. Only know that it's a lost kid or something, and she's in really bad shape. Ambulance is bringing her in with a police escort."

My stomach churned. Treating sick kids was one thing. Treating hurt ones was another, and police presence always signaled serious injury. It was the part of my job that had never gotten easier. I glanced at the board, seeing how many of my assigned rooms were open, and breathed a sigh of relief when I saw that all my beds were full. The call button on bed 8 blinked, and I headed in to see what Eloise wanted.

She was one of our frequent flyers. She was a widow and often came into the emergency room because she was lonely. There was never anything seriously wrong with her. She was one of the healthiest eighty-one-year-olds that I worked with, but she came in every few weeks convinced that she was dying. This time, she complained of throbbing leg pain and was terrified she had a blood clot.

She smiled up at me from bed, wrinkles moving underneath her eyes. She motioned for me to come closer. I leaned in to give her the customary hug she'd grown to expect from me. The familiar scent of vanilla musk and baby powder filled my nose. She squeezed me tightly before pulling away to arm's length while still holding on to my forearm. "Hi, dear. I don't mean to keep bothering you, but do we have any of my results back?"

I shook my head and moved above her bed to adjust the drip on her IV. "We're still waiting to get them sent down from the ultrasound tech. Sorry. It's probably going to be a few more minutes because we're pretty slammed tonight."

As if on cue, the sound of police scanners interrupted our conversation. Eloise peeked around her curtain, trying to catch a glimpse of the police. "What's going on out there?"

I smiled. "You know I can't tell you that."

She leaned forward, trying to get a better view. "There are just so many officers. Why are there so many? Am I in danger?"

"You're fine. I'd never let anything bad happen to you." I patted the top of her hand. I could tell by the doughy feel of her skin that she was dehydrated again. "And you, Miss Thing"—I shook my finger at her playfully—"need to drink more during the day. How many times have I told you that?"

She hung her head but couldn't hide the smile tugging at the corners of her lips. I checked her vitals, noting them in her chart. "I'll keep my eye on your reports and let you know as soon as I know anything. Deal?"

"Deal." She crossed her arms on her chest, settling in comfortably. She closed her eyes, and some of the lines in her face relaxed. She had told me once that she didn't sleep well by herself and spent hours each night terrified of someone breaking in to her house while she slept. It was no surprise that her hospital visits were only at night. She didn't even open her eyes as she spoke. "And see if you can find out anything about what's going on with all the police officers."

"I will," I promised as I headed out to check on my other patients, knowing I wouldn't be able to tell her even if I did.

The night grew busy as it wore on, and I didn't get a chance to sit down until after four o'clock. I poured myself a cup of coffee and logged on to the computer, eager to get started on my notes while I had a brief reprieve. Stephanie grabbed a chair and slid down next to me. "Did you hear anything about what happened?" she asked.

I'd forgotten all about the officers earlier. I shook my head. "I haven't had time to even breathe. We ended up doing a lumbar puncture on bed 6." I pulled up my first patient and scrolled through their blood type results, searching for the one I needed in my report. "What'd I miss?"

"The police brought in an abandoned toddler. She's pretty beat up. They found her wandering around a parking lot. She was only wearing a diaper and some kind of weird collar thing around her neck. How sad is that?" She talked fast, eager to get out the story before she got called to the next crisis. "She wouldn't let the police anywhere near her. It took three officers to coax her into the car. She's filthy, has blood all over her hands and arms, but we can't clean her until they've gathered all the evidence that might be on her. They have no idea who she is or where she's from."

The angry knot of unfairness lodged in my stomach. Why did the universe allow people who hurt kids to have them? Why couldn't it give them to people like me, who wanted them?

My husband, Christopher, and I had tried to get pregnant for years, but it was one disappointment followed by another. We got a second opinion after our doctor diagnosed me with an inhospitable uterus, but he agreed with the first doctor—birthing a child of my own was impossible. I swallowed down the bitterness. Some days it was better than others. Today wasn't one of those days.

"Do they have any leads on her parents?" I asked.

"Nope. Not a thing. They think either she walked over there from the trailer park across the street or she was dropped there by someone."

She wrinkled her face in disgust. "She's so skinny, looks like she hasn't eaten in days."

"Poor thing. Hopefully, they'll find her parents, and it'll turn out to be some weird accident or misunderstanding."

Stephanie raised her eyebrows. "Misunderstanding? What kind of misunderstanding leads to your toddler being lost in a parking lot wearing only a diaper? And blood. Did you forget that part?"

"Someone's got to be an optimist."

I wished I were as optimistic as I pretended. I used to be. Not anymore.

Stephanie burst out laughing and squeezed my arm. "That's what I love about you," she said before hurrying off.

Christopher was waiting for me with a cup of chamomile tea when I got home. He held his cup of morning coffee in one hand and my favorite mug in the other—the one that said **Pug Life** on the front even though I'd never owned a dog. I'd been working swing-shift overnights for the last two years, and he worked days unless there was an emergency, so we were on opposite schedules, but it worked for us. It gave us an opportunity to miss each other, and sometimes you needed that in a relationship even when you loved each other as much as we did.

I grabbed the mug from his hands while I slipped off my shoes and followed him into the living room. I plopped down on the sofa beside him and sank into it, the down feathers contouring around my body. It was the piece of furniture we'd fought over the most when we had decorated the house shortly after we'd bought it. The living room was one of the first rooms you saw when you came inside, and he had thought we should have a formal couch so that it would look pristine and nice. But our house was too small to have another main living area, so I'd known we'd spend all our time there and wanted it to be comfortable. In the end,

I had won, and he'd said on more than one occasion that he was glad I had because he couldn't imagine coming home to a stiff couch.

He sat on the other end, and I stretched my feet onto his lap. He peeled off my socks and started massaging my feet. When I'd first told my sister about his foot rubs after work, she'd been sure it was only because we were newlyweds, but he was still doing it after all these years. If he was there at the end of my shift, he rubbed my feet. Period. It didn't matter if he'd been in surgery for twelve hours.

"Well?" He raised his eyebrows, questioning.

You couldn't practice medicine and not be affected by it. Over the years, we'd grown into each other's therapists. We understood what it was like to be responsible for other people's lives in a way nobody outside the profession could.

"Eloise was in again tonight."

"What was it this time?"

"Blood clot."

"And?"

"Negative."

He smiled. His dark hair was combed straight back, a few strands stretched flat over a thinning spot in the back. He was self-conscious about his hair loss, but I didn't care. I loved the weathered look, and as far as I was concerned, he grew more handsome with age. Men were lucky that way. Even his wrinkles were cute.

"What's your day look like today?" I asked.

"Two surgeries. Three consults."

Christopher was an orthopedic surgeon at Northfield Memorial, the same hospital where I worked. Northfield was the largest regional hospital in Ohio, and we'd met in the cafeteria while he was a first-year medical student back when he used to work all day and study all night. He'd been so focused and goal driven that he almost hadn't noticed me, but his work ethic had paid off. It had landed him a residency followed by a specialty placement.

"Anything interesting?" I asked.

He shook his head. "Oh, before I forget to tell you, make sure you read the email from Bianella. She wants us to go to a seminar next weekend on international adoption. There's supposed to be a panel of parents talking about some of the hidden challenges in international adoptions," he said.

Bianella was our adoption specialist. We had connected with her after our fertility doctor had sat us down and explained the grim statistics for the final time. Christopher and I had always wanted kids, so adoption was a logical choice for us, and we'd dived into researching facilities immediately, not wanting to waste any more time than we already had. I had been almost forty at the time, and neither of us had wanted to be older parents. I had thought adopting a child would be easy in the same way I had thought getting pregnant would be easy when I'd first started. We'd already had one failed adoption, and it had hurt as bad as any miscarriage.

"I'm still on the fence about going the international route," I said.

"I know. Me too. Just read it, and let me know what you think." Christopher slid my legs off his lap. "I've got to get getting."

He headed to the kitchen to put his mug in the dishwasher, and I was walking toward the hallway leading to the bedroom when I suddenly remembered.

"Hey, Christopher," I called out.

"What?"

"I did forget to tell you one thing that happened tonight." I paused to make sure I had his attention again. "The police brought in an abandoned toddler."

TWO

Christopher Bauer

I'd just gotten back to my office after a grueling six-hour reconstructive hand surgery that had turned out to be more complicated than we'd expected. I was making a cup of coffee when Dan, the chief of surgery, walked in looking upset.

"Can I talk to you?" he asked, shutting the door behind him.

"You want to sit?" I pointed to the chair in front of my desk. We rarely had closed-door meetings, so it had to be serious.

He shook his head, running his hands through his dark hair. His forehead was lined with stress. "What the hell is wrong with people? Really, how can they be such monsters?" He paced across my office as he spoke.

We'd worked together for years, and I'd never seen him so unnerved. "Are you sure you don't want to sit down?"

"No, no, I'm good. What I really want is a drink." He laughed bitterly. "A toddler girl was brought into the ER last night, and her case is awful. I've never seen anything like it. Never." He wrestled with his emotions, probably thinking of his own three daughters, whose pictures lined the desk in his office. "I can't imagine someone doing that to a child. I just can't."

"Just what are we talking about here?" I asked, my curiosity getting the best of me.

"You might want to be the one to sit down," he said, only half joking. "She was brought in by the police and child services. Apparently, she was found in a parking lot over on the west side down by Park's Station. You know which one I'm talking about?"

I nodded. Everyone knew Park's Station and the trailer parks that lined the streets behind it. It was where the town's meth habit grew and flourished. You only went to that part of town for one thing.

"Her entire body is covered in old scars and bruises. She must've been abused for a long time." He struggled to gain his composure. "She's severely malnourished and dehydrated, so she looks like those starving orphans you see on TV. You know the ones I'm talking about?" He didn't wait for me to respond before continuing. "There're weird rashes on her legs like she might have some kind of septic infection. Her x-rays show multiple fractures all over her body. Some of them are old. Others are relatively new. She's probably never seen a doctor, so who knows what we'll find once we start looking." He cleared his throat. Cleared it again, shifting into project-management mode. "There's going to be a huge team on this one, and we need all of our best people on it, which is why I want you to take her case. We're going to convene first thing tomorrow morning, so I need you to cancel your morning."

"Okay, sure. I can have Alexis rearrange things." I pulled out my phone and quickly tapped out an email to my receptionist before slipping it back in my pocket.

"Come on, let's go." Dan headed toward the door, and I followed him out. He talked as we walked. "This is going to be a complete media circus as soon as the word gets out. So far, nothing has leaked. We're trying to protect her privacy for as long as possible, but seriously, it's only a matter of time before they get wind of it. You understand the limits of confidentiality on this one, right?"

"Of course." I nodded, even though I'd never had any sort of high profile case before. We didn't get high profile cases in a town of our size, and most of the kids I worked with were victims of car accidents or sports injuries. I was excited about being involved in something so unusual, but I couldn't admit that.

We stepped into the elevator at the end of the hallway. It was packed with people, so we stopped talking as we rode to the third floor. Dan held the door open and motioned for me to step out.

"What's she doing down here?" I asked. The third floor was the neuroscience ward, where stroke and heart attack patients stayed.

"No one will think to look for her here," he said.

"You mean the media?"

"We're not too worried about the media. They're easy to keep out. They're trying to keep her safe just in case whoever did this to her comes looking for her. They don't know who hurt her or if she's still in danger. They don't even know who she is yet. She said her name is Janie, but who knows. She could've just made up the name. She might have even been kidnapped. We'll know more about her as the case unfolds."

Dan nodded to the nurses scurrying around the station as we walked by. Two uniformed officers stood outside a door in the middle of the hallway. Dan strode up to them and flashed his hospital ID. I did the same. He turned to look at me before opening the door.

"Prepare yourself," he said.

He pushed through the door, and a wave of sadness washed over me as I stared at a small child lying on the bed. Nothing could've prepared me for her. Dan had said she was a toddler, but the child on the bed looked like she was barely over a year old. Her arms and legs were frail, like they wouldn't be able to support her if she stood. Her stomach was distended, and her head was massive in proportion to her tiny body and too big for her fragile frame to hold. She was nearly bald. There were only short tufts of blonde where hair should've been. She turned to look at us with the palest blue eyes I'd ever seen.

"Hiya." Her lips spread into a shy smile, revealing a rotten tooth in the front.

"Hi, Janie." Dan walked over to her bed and bent down to get closer to her.

She reached her arms up. "Hug?"

He leaned over and wrapped his arms around her delicately, afraid to hurt her. She clung to his lab coat. Dan looked uncomfortable.

"I like your smell," she said in a small voice, barely above a whisper.

She refused to let go, so he turned to look at me, motioning me over. I stepped around one of the nurses and into her view.

"Hi, Janie. My name's Christopher. I'm going to be one of your doctors," I said, choosing my words carefully. "I'm going to help take care of you."

She let go of Dan and reached out to grab my hand. Her nails were long, caked with dirt. Her fingers were so bent they couldn't coil naturally around mine.

"Hi," she said hesitantly. "Are you going to fix me?"

I nodded. "I am, sweetheart. I promise."

THREE

Hannah Bauer

I was in the kitchen packing my lunch for my shift when the front door opened, signaling Christopher's arrival. "Hey, honey, I'm in here. I still haven't finished getting my stuff ready for tonight. I got caught up in some stupid documentary."

He came up behind me and wrapped his arms around me. He kissed the top of my head and let out a deep sigh. I dried my hands on the towel next to the sink and turned around. Sadness clouded his face.

"Did you lose a patient?" I asked. He rarely lost patients, but sometimes it happened when they had other complications.

He shook his head. "I met the abandoned girl."

"You did?" I motioned for him to sit down at the table.

"That poor little girl. She's so beat up and starved." His voice caught in his throat. "People treat their pets better than she was treated."

"It's that bad, huh?" I asked.

He nodded.

I prepared a tumbler full of his favorite scotch and took the seat across from him. He took a small sip, then fingered the top of the glass as he stared out the window above the sink. I reached across the table and took his hand in mine, rubbing the top of his palm with my thumb. I understood his sensitivity toward children. Neither of us had had it when we first married, but years of infertility problems had made us emotional about almost everything involving kids, especially young ones.

"Her name is Janie, and she's adorable. She has these massive pale-blue eyes that blow you away." He took another drink. "I reviewed her notes before I left, and she's been starved for so long her body started eating itself. She has so many old breaks that went untreated and never healed right, so some of the bones fused together. There wasn't a part of her that went untouched." His eyes flashed with anger. "Who would do such a thing?"

We both knew the answer to his question—a monster. It went without saying.

"She's going to need surgery on her elbow. It was a complicated break and healed into almost a ninety-degree angle because it was never set properly. Lots of her bones have fused together from other untreated breaks and injuries. Dan and I are coming up with a game plan first thing tomorrow morning."

"You've got this," I said. We sat in silence, enjoying our brief time together before I had to leave for my shift. "By the way, I read through all the information Bianella sent us about that seminar you told me about. I even watched the videos. I think we should go," I said after a few more minutes had passed.

"Really?"

I nodded. "No matter which direction we go, there're going to be challenges, and we're going to need the advice of other people who've done it before. Just think how helpful our RESOLVE meetings have been."

After our third round of failed IVF, our doctor had suggested attending a support group for other parents going through similar challenges. Nobody understood the dramatic highs and crushing lows of infertility unless they'd been through it too. Christopher had balked at the idea at first because he hadn't liked the thought of baring our souls in a room full of strangers, but he'd gotten used to it. A few of the couples had grown to be some of our closest friends, and we went out for dinner and drinks on a regular basis.

"Do you want me to sign us up, or are you going to do it?" he asked.

"I can do it on my break tonight. Why don't you just relax and prepare for tomorrow?"

"Janie isn't in the ER anymore," he said, reading my mind before I could ask the question.

I breathed a sigh of relief.

"They moved her to the third floor. She's tucked in with all the geriatric patients to keep her safe."

I raised my eyebrows. "Do they really think someone is going to come looking for her?"

He shook his head. "I think they're just being extra cautious. I can't imagine that someone who dropped their kid off in a parking lot in the middle of the night would show up to claim her later, but you never know."

CASE #5243

Interview: Piper Goldstein

"When did you first meet Janie?" The first officer had been joined by a former detective turned private investigator who'd introduced himself as Ron with a firm handshake. He tried to play himself off as a fellow cop, but his civilian clothes were a dead giveaway. I had no idea why he was so critical to the case.

"On her third day in the hospital."

"Is that how long it usually takes for a social worker to meet their client? I thought social workers were required to speak with the victim at least twenty-four hours after the incident."

I hated when they asked me questions that they already knew the answers to. "They are, but she wasn't stable enough for me to see her." The bad fluorescent lighting was starting to give me a headache. I rubbed my temples, trying to stave it off for as long as possible.

"She was that sick?" the officer, Luke, asked. Ron had clued me into his name. They both wore the same close-cropped haircut.

I shook my head. "Not sick—starved. Did you know you can't just feed a starving person or you can actually kill them?" I didn't wait for an answer. "I had no idea that could happen. She went into cardiac arrest a few hours after being admitted because they fed her too much. It took two days to stabilize her, so I didn't get a chance to meet her until she'd been there for almost three days."

"What did you think about her when you met?"

"She was a complete surprise," I said.

"How so?" Luke cocked his head to the side, eyeing me quizzically.

I didn't know how to explain Janie. It was difficult to put into words unless you'd been there at the time and seen how she looked. Thankfully, they'd seen some of the crime scene photos, so the responsibility of a perfect description didn't fall on my shoulders.

"I'd expected to find a really frightened and traumatized girl, but Janie was talking and smiling with her nurses when I walked into the room." Her room had been an explosion of color that day, filled with balloons and stuffed animals donated by the hospital staff. Everyone who had met her had brought something with them, and I was no different. I'd come with a small teddy bear holding a heart in its paws. She'd sat in the center of the room perched on her bed while the nurses took turns trying to coax smiles out of her. "She wasn't incapacitated with fear like I'd expected. People had made her sound like she was some kind of feral child, but she wasn't."

I'd worked hard at hiding my shock over her emaciated figure. The outline of her skull had been clear underneath her pale skin, so translucent that purple veins showed through. Her cheekbones had jutted out, and her pale-blue eyes had bulged out of her sunken sockets.

Ron nodded at me, signaling me to continue, but it was hard to just talk freely without them asking me questions. I knew what was expected of me with their questions. Talking freely and open-endedly could result in me saying something I wasn't supposed to. Nerves twisted my stomach.

"It was hard to connect with her at first, but it's always like that. Nobody likes social workers, even the people we're trying to help. I wanted to talk to her alone, but she looked terrified when I asked the nurses to leave, so I let them stay," I said. "We still didn't know the circumstances of her case—didn't have any clue about her parents or guardian or who was responsible for her and if they'd been the ones to hurt her. The police were interviewing all of the people in the trailer park behind the store for potential leads, but they hadn't gotten anywhere yet. As far as I knew, anyway. The police aren't always the best at letting me know what they know." I stopped short, realizing what I'd said. "I'm sorry. I just—"

Ron dismissed it, waving me off. "I get it. No need to apologize." He looked at Luke pointedly. "We could all do a better job of working as a team." He held his gaze before looking away and directing his attention back to me. "Did you have any concerns about her mother? Was anyone worried she might be in danger?"

I hung my head, embarrassed. "I know we're always supposed to keep an open mind and not jump to any conclusions until we have all the facts about the case, but everyone assumed Janie's parents were the ones who hurt her. Or some really sick psycho. It never crossed anyone's mind that someone else might be in trouble. I wished it would've. Maybe then things would've ended differently."

FOUR

Christopher Bauer

"I meet with Janie for her surgery consult on Tuesday, and I was wondering if you'd come with me to help make her feel comfortable." I visited with all my patients before surgery if possible. I liked us to know each other because surgery went better when we had a connection. It wasn't the first time I'd asked Hannah to help me with a patient. Sometimes I came across too clinical when I was nervous, and she was the kind of person who put people at ease without even trying.

She shook her head. "You know I can't do that."

Janie's presence at the hospital hadn't stayed a secret for long. As soon as the police had started asking questions around town, her case had spread like wildfire, and everyone was obsessed with finding out the story about the abandoned girl. Police stood guard twenty-four seven at her hospital door, and no one was allowed to see her unless they were on a special clearance list. It was highly unlikely anyone would try to sneak in to see her, but everyone was protective of her privacy and care.

"I got you added to her list," I said.

"Really? Stephanie told me they were being super strict about it."

"They always make exceptions when I tell them I need the most talented nurse in the world by my side." I winked at her.

She rolled her eyes. "I'm trying to stay as far away from that one as possible. You already know that."

She wasn't the only one. There were interns and residents who excused themselves from rounds during Janie's updates. Child abuse was horrible, and some people couldn't handle dealing with it, but Hannah had never been one of those people. At least, not until recently.

"Pretty please?" I begged, even though I knew how unlikely she was to change her mind once it was made up.

"It makes me too sad. I'll be an emotional wreck, and we both know that won't be helpful to anyone," she said, shaking her head.

I didn't press her further and met with Janie by myself on Tuesday. She was huddled against the wall behind her bed when I arrived. She gained weight every day but still looked so small. She wrapped her arms around her legs and pulled them up to her chest, glaring at the nurse, who was busy entering notes into the computer next to her bed, tapping on the keys angrily. What could've happened to make her so angry? The tension in the room was thick. I glanced back and forth between the two, wishing I'd come at a better time.

I stepped closer to Janie's bed, but not too close, as I wanted to respect her space. I cleared my throat. "Hi, Janie. I'm Dr. Christopher, but you can call me Dr. Chris if you want. Do you remember me?"

She nodded without looking at me, her gaze fixed on the nurse.

The nurse pushed the computer aside. "Janie is having a difficult time right now because dinnertime is over, and she doesn't like when dinnertime ends."

I bristled at one of my biggest pet peeves—talking about patients in third person while they were in the room with you.

"I'm still hungry," Janie said. Her lower lip quivered.

I reached into my lab coat pockets, feeling for the protein bar I'd nibbled on earlier. I held it out for the nurse to see. "Can she have this? It's chocolate chip."

The nurse glared at me. "She's on an eating schedule for a reason."

"That's why I asked. I was hoping she might be able to have a tiny piece."

She rolled her eyes. "Really? A protein bar?" She turned on her heel and stomped out.

Hannah never would've acted that way. I didn't think that just because she was my wife. I knew a good nurse when I saw one, and I'd seen Hannah in action numerous times over the years. She was one of the good ones—going the extra mile, cleaning up food trays that were the nutrition staff's responsibility, staying with patients to talk when her job was done, helping relatives after they'd heard terrible news, and doing the things everyone else avoided, like cleaning up vomit.

I put the bar back in my pocket. I'd been pretty sure it wouldn't be on her list of acceptable foods, but it had been worth a try. "Sorry, hon." I smiled down at her, hoping she could tell I was sincere. "I wanted to come see you so that we could talk about what's going to happen tomorrow." She stared up at me. I couldn't tell if she was hanging on my every word or didn't understand what I was saying. "Do you remember what you and Dr. Dan talked about?"

"Yes." Her voice was quiet, unsure.

"Well, I am the doctor who is going to fix your bones. Tomorrow Nurse Ellie is going to wake you up very early. You're still going to be sleepy when they bring you to me. Then one of my doctor friends is going to make you go back to sleep and have wonderful dreams about all your favorite things. I'm going to fix all your bones while you sleep." It was a complicated surgery. Multiple bone grafts were never easy, but I planned on doing everything within my power to make sure I fixed it all so she didn't need additional surgeries.

"Will it hurt?" she asked, her lower lip trembling again.

I shook my head and pointed to a spot on the bed next to her. "Can I sit here?"

She nodded. I perched on the edge.

"Surgery is not going to hurt because you will be asleep the whole time, but I'm not going to lie—your arm will hurt when you wake up. I'm sorry, sweetie. I wish there was a way we could do it without any pain."

I would've given anything not to hurt her any more than she'd already been hurt. I didn't like having to break the bones of a child who was already so broken, but we didn't have any other choice if she was going to use her arm.

A lone tear slid down her cheek. I reached out and wiped it with my thumb. I wanted to pull her onto my lap and hold her but was worried it might scare her. "Hey, now, it's okay, sweetheart. You're going to be okay."

"Promise?"

"I'm going to make sure of it. We're going to get you magic medicine, and it'll help your pain feel so much better. Do you know what color the magic medicine is?" She looked at me, wide eyed and curious, waiting. "It's going to be red. Do you like the color red?"

She shook her head.

I faked surprise. "You don't? How can you not like red?"

"I like purple," she said.

"Hmmm . . ." I scratched my chin, pretending to think. "I can't do anything about the magic medicine. It has to stay red, but I'll tell you what—why don't we make your cast purple? Would you like that?"

"Purple?" she asked again, like it was too good to be true.

"Yep. And I will come check on you every day after your surgery to make sure you're getting better."

She squealed, beaming. She crawled toward me, and I opened my arms so she could crawl onto my lap. She cuddled up against me. I wrapped my arms around her tiny frame. I'd never felt so large. I didn't want to move too much because I was afraid of accidentally hurting her. She was as delicate as any newborn I'd ever held.

I was just as nervous to perform her surgery as I had been for my first solo surgery during residency. I wanted it to go perfectly. Feeding experts flew in from around the world to consult on her case. They assured me she was stable enough to go under, but it did nothing to ease my worry. I didn't want her to go through any more than she'd already gone through. I burned with anger every time I thought about the person who'd hurt her. The police weren't any closer to finding out who'd done it than they'd been a week ago, but I refused to entertain the possibility that they wouldn't find the person who'd hurt her. Someone had to be punished.

Janie was clutching her favorite dinosaur to her chest when I came into the preoperating room. She gave me a big smile when I walked in, recognizing me even in all of my surgical gear. She had a gap-toothed smile now. They had removed her rotten tooth in front a few days ago. "Dr. Chris!" Her face lit up.

"Hey, sweetie. I see you brought Fred." I leaned over and planted a kiss on her forehead. Normally, I wouldn't think about kissing a patient on the forehead, but none of the regular rules applied to Janie.

"I wanna keep Fred." She hugged him close to her chest.

"Of course Fred can come." I jiggled one of his arms dramatically. "I think he has a broken arm too. We have to do something about this."

She giggled. It was the first time I'd made her giggle, and my heart melted.

"Do you have any more questions for me?" I asked, even though it'd been less than twelve hours since we'd been through it.

She shook her head, holding Fred just as tightly. I planted another kiss on the top of her head. "You're going to do great. I'll see you in a little bit."

I'd never performed surgery with an audience, but the adjacent room was filled with residents and interns. It went better than I had expected. She tolerated the anesthesia, and the break to her elbow was clean, without any of the splintering I'd been nervous about. I reset it the way it should've been done the first time. I fused and grafted the four places where her muscles and tendons had calcified together. It was over before I knew it, and they were wheeling her into the recovery room. I wrapped Fred's arm in a matching purple cast and brought him with me into recovery.

I leaned over her bed and placed my hand on her forehead. Her eyelids fluttered as she struggled to wake up. "Look who I brought." I held him up so she could see him better. She was still disoriented from the anesthesia. A smile slowly spread across her face. She grabbed him and brought him to her face. "See, he had surgery just like you. I made his cast just like yours so you guys match."

Another hazy smile. Her eyes looked funny. Her body heaved, and yellow liquid spurted from her mouth. I grabbed the green basin and quickly sat her up. I held her while she dry heaved into it. There was nothing in her stomach, since she hadn't been able to eat anything the night before surgery. "It's okay, sweetie. It's just the medicine making you sick."

I took off her soiled gown and covered her up with a fresh new blanket. I rubbed her arm softly. "You're doing great, sweetheart. Just great."

She closed her eyes and drifted back to sleep. She opened her eyes every so often to make sure I was still there. Normally, the nurses sat with kids in the recovery room, but I wanted her to have a familiar face looking back at her when she woke.

I pulled a chair next to her and propped my legs up on the end of her bed. She looked so peaceful, lost in her world of dreams. Stillness enveloped her, and Janie was never still. She moved constantly, always fidgeting. It was so nice to see her at rest, even if it was from the drugs coursing through her system. I couldn't pull myself away from her. I closed my eyes, and it wasn't long before I fell asleep beside her.

FIVE

Hannah Bauer

Where was Christopher, and what was taking him so long? He was the one who'd booked the dinner reservation and sent it to all our calendars, so there was no way he'd forgotten about it. I glanced at my watch for the third time in ten minutes. It was so unlike him to be late and not let me know something had come up. I'd already pictured him in a car accident on Highway 12 more than once.

My sister, Allison, reached over and poured me a glass of wine, fingernails perfectly manicured, glowing pink. I didn't know how she found the time to get them done with how busy she was. "Don't worry. He'll be here soon."

Of course Christopher's tardiness wasn't a big deal to her because her husband, Greg, was always late. Whenever Christopher and I needed them to be somewhere at a specific time, we told them it was thirty minutes earlier than it was, and even then, they still managed to be late sometimes. In fact, Christopher was so late tonight that Greg was already here.

Greg was uncomfortable being at dinner with just Allison and me, though he wasn't doing or saying anything to let on that he felt that way. Allison had told me he'd said that being alone with us was like being the awkward third wheel on a date. He was right. It was hard for anyone to get a word in when the two of us got going, but that was what happened when you grew up only eleven months apart. We were more like twins than sisters.

"Should I try to get ahold of him?" Greg asked, rubbing his chin. He had a scruffy layer of light facial hair all the time—never clean shaven and never a full beard. He directed his question at Allison like he needed her permission more than mine.

Allison flicked her hair over her shoulders and rolled her eyes dramatically. "He's not ignoring her because he's mad. Not like someone I know."

"Like I'm the only one who uses that tactic," he snapped back.

They had no problem fighting in public, and I'd told her how uncomfortable it made me, but she never listened. Christopher rushed up to our table right before they stepped into a full-fledged argument. I breathed a sigh of relief—both to see his face and because I wasn't going to have to listen to Allison and Greg fight.

"I'm so sorry I'm late." He bent to kiss me, and I turned my head so it landed on my cheek instead of my lips, my worry instantly replaced with annoyance.

"It's totally fine," Greg said. He pointed to the full drink in front of Christopher's place setting. "I took care of you."

Christopher laughed and slid into his chair. "Thanks."

"So where were you?" I asked, not willing to let him slide that easily.

"I fell asleep after Janie's surgery," he said.

"You fell asleep after her surgery?"

"I know, right? Pretty unbelievable. I don't even know how it happened. One minute I was sitting next to her bed watching her sleep, and the next second I was out." He reached underneath the table and squeezed my knee. "Don't be mad."

Allison reached across and slapped my hand. "She's not going to be mad. We don't get to see you guys enough for her to get mad and ruin our night."

"Fine, but only because she's got a point. For the record—I'm still mad at you." I stuck my tongue out at him.

"How'd her surgery go?" Allison asked.

Even though we couldn't see each other as much as we wanted, Allison and I texted constantly so that we stayed current with whatever was going on in the other's life. I'd been filling her in all week with the details of Janie's case as they came forth. Initially, police investigators had thought she was a neglected toddler, but the wounds on her body told a more painful story. The marks on her neck and wrists were consistent with being tied up, which elevated her case to another level of severity, as if it weren't already bad enough.

Allison was obsessed with finding the person responsible. She scoured missing-children databases and even had Google alerts set up on her phone notifying her when a new missing-child case occurred. It reminded me of what she'd been like in law school. Sometimes I thought she missed it, though she'd never admit it, since she swore staying at home with her boys was the best job she'd ever had.

"Everything went smoothly. Perfect, really." Christopher beamed. "I'd gone over her x-rays so many times it was like taking my boards."

"How'd the fusions go?" I asked. They were the part he'd been most worried about. He'd pored over those scans for hours.

"Better than I could've expected. Some of it was impossible to cut through because her bones are so small. It was like working on a model. I'm glad that part is over with. Now we just hope she heals okay." He took another drink. "You're never going to guess what we found out." He looked around the table, making brief eye contact with each of us. "Janie isn't a toddler—she's actually six years old."

"What?" Allison said. "Seriously?"

"How do you know that?" I asked.

"No one has ever been sure about her age. Dan thought it'd be a perfect opportunity to measure all the gaps between her growth plates while she was under, so we did. Every single one. Turns out she's six years old."

"Wow. How does that change things for her care?" I asked.

"It's going to be interesting. The progression of a—"

Allison interrupted him. "Okay, this is where I'm stopping the conversation because I know you're about one step away from getting all medical on us. No more work talk tonight. Seriously. Just fun from now on."

I laughed and grabbed my glass, raising it to hers. If anyone needed a night out, it was Allison. We'd been raised like twins, but Allison had actual twins. Caleb and Dylan were my nine-year-old nephews and kept her busier than any full-time job I'd ever had.

"I'm so glad Janie's surgery went well," I said to Christopher later that evening as we turned down our comforter and climbed into bed. "Now maybe you'll be able to relax a little."

He'd been so tense all week. He'd spent all of his free time studying her case. He'd fallen asleep with his notes on his nightstand, the last thing he'd looked at before bed.

"I don't know, but it's weird. I'm actually more committed to her than I was before." He pulled me close, and I snuggled against his chest. I loved when we got to go to sleep with each other at night. It was the best part of the weekend. "Like I'm kind of bummed that I don't get to do more for her."

I'd felt the same way with my first child abuse case. You never forgot your first. Mine was a ten-year-old boy brought in by his mother with a bloodied and broken nose. His mother had kept trying to convince us that he'd fallen, but something about his demeanor had sparked everyone's suspicions. We'd kept him in the hospital until the social worker could talk to him, and he'd finally confessed that his stepfather had punched him in the face after the boy had accidently spilled his beer. For weeks, I'd thought of excuses to call him so I could check on him until my supervisor made me stop. I didn't have any choice but to let it go. It would probably take Christopher even longer to let go of Janie.

"It's not like she'll be going anywhere anytime soon, and you'll still have to follow up with her postoperative care," I said, rubbing his arm.

"I just wish there were more for me to do, but so much of her care is centered on her eating issues. There's nothing I can do there." He shook his head in frustration. "Nothing."

"How's the oven timer working?" I asked.

One of her nurses had brought in an old-fashioned oven timer so Janie would have an idea when she could eat again. The idea was to use the clock as a cue for her in hopes that it would calm her.

"She watches it constantly, but I'm not sure it helps much. They put her meal times on the whiteboard too," he said. He was quiet. For a minute I thought he'd fallen asleep, but then he said, "I think I'm going to stop at Target tomorrow before work and pick up some markers so people can sign her cast and she can color on it if she wants to."

"Oh, that's so cute." I scooted up and gave him a big kiss, wrapping my arms around his neck. "You're going to be a great dad. The best. I just know it. Things have been busy lately, but now that they're settling down a little, we can start looking at profiles again."

CASE #5243

INTERVIEW: PIPER GOLDSTEIN

"We hadn't considered Janie a reliable source of information when we thought she was three, but all that changed when we learned she was six. She broke open the case." My supervisor had finally called me back. She'd spoken with our lawyers and told me I should help the officers in any way I could, that I didn't have to hold back. Despite the lawyer's permission, I still wanted to be careful about what I said. "We started asking her real questions, probing into what happened before she got to the hospital. We pushed her further than we'd pushed her before."

"How did she respond?" Ron asked.

It was just the two of us in the room now. Luke had gone to get us coffee. We'd been sitting in the room for over an hour, and we all needed a pick-me-up. I should have told him to grab me something from the vending machines too. I hadn't eaten since breakfast.

"During the times we met before, I only asked her yes-or-no questions, so I brought my iPad with me because I thought I'd need to use the TAP program with her. It's a program that helps me communicate with nonverbal autistic children. Even though she was six, we figured her language was probably way behind. But I didn't need it. She was able to answer all my questions. Once she opened up and started talking, I couldn't believe how well she spoke, since she'd probably never been to school."

"She provided you information about her mother?" His interest was piqued again.

I shook my head. "Sorry." I hadn't meant to mislead him. I needed to be more intentional with my words. "She still refused to talk about her mother, or any person for that matter, but she opened up about where she lived."

"She described the trailer?"

"Almost perfectly, even down to the black garbage bags on the windows."

Investigators had always suspected Janie was from the trailer park, and they'd gone door to door with her picture, but nobody had reported seeing her. It had been Janie's description of two dogs tied up in the front lawn next to a dilapidated bird feeder that had led them to the correct place—the last trailer on the left side of a dead-end street. Officers had expected to find tubing running through glass jars and odd-size bowls, since meth was what the trailer park was most known for, but they had found a ransacked trailer reeking of urine and spoiled food instead. It was clear from the holes in the walls and dried blood on the floor that there'd been a struggle. Maybe more than one. But it was the closet in the back bedroom that had shocked everyone the most.

Ron splayed out the pictures of the closet on the table like he was laying down his hand at a poker game. He pointed to the picture with the zip ties and dog collar. I hated that one even more than the blood-marked walls. I was glad he had the pictures, though. It was something you couldn't describe in words unless you'd seen it, and I'd thought I'd seen it all.

"Did she describe this?" he asked.

"No. She wouldn't talk about the back bedroom."

"Understandable. Hard to imagine any kid ever wanting to talk about that."

I forced the images from the closet out of my mind. "But her information about the trailer gave us a physical address that led to a name."

"Becky Watson?"

"Yes."

The trailer had been rented to Becky Watson for the last four years. Nobody else was on the lease. The police had spoken with the manager at the park, and he hadn't remembered her at all, said she must've kept to herself. The only personal thing he could tell us about her was that she had always paid her rent on time, but he had given us an even more valuable piece of information anyway—her social security number. It wasn't long before we had Janie's birth certificate and confirmation that Becky Watson was her mother. It had also confirmed Janie was six and not three.

"What led you to the GoFundMe accounts?"

"Once child-protection investigators had a name and started digging online, they discovered Becky had been pretending Janie had cancer and creating fake GoFundMe accounts to get people to donate money for her medical expenses. It was why Janie's head was shaved. She had seven fake accounts for Janie posted under various names with different cancer diagnoses, all of them with pictures."

They'd traced the GoFundMe accounts to the computer in the trailer. Becky's account history showed the transfers from PayPal into her personal checking account, and the bank had her on camera cashing all the donation checks. There hadn't been any activity since the day before they had found Janie.

"And the blood in the trailer?" Ron asked.

"It matched the blood that was on Janie."

I didn't know why he was asking questions he already knew the answers to. Maybe it was some kind of test. The police at the initial scene in the parking lot had thought Janie was injured because of the blood on her hands and shirt. It wasn't until after they'd gotten her cleaned up at the hospital that they had discovered the blood wasn't hers. She had had plenty of old wounds and scars covering her body, but nothing fresh.

"The blood belonged to her mother?" he asked.

I nodded.

SIX

Christopher Bauer

I dashed down to the third floor to hang out with Janie whenever I had spare time during my day. The more time I spent with her, the less sorry I felt for her and the more amazed I was at the capacity of the human spirit to overcome unimaginable horrors. There was this part of her that was still innocent and untouched despite what she'd been through. I saw it in her eyes whenever she looked at me.

Janie's entire day was structured around different therapies and meeting with various doctors. Everything she worked on in the hospital had a specific purpose and goal, so I took it upon myself to teach her how to have fun. Go Fish was the first game I played with her, and she loved it.

"Go fish, Dr. Chris! Go fish!" she'd squeal, bouncing on her bed like it was a trampoline.

I let her beat me because her reaction was one of the best parts of my day. I even started skipping my lunch breaks so I could spend them with her instead.

"What are you going to do once she's not here?" Dan had asked after I'd raced back upstairs just in time to see a patient after one of my visits.

I didn't like thinking about when she left, even though more and more of her case consultations shifted to discussions about potential discharge dates and her outpatient medical care. I wanted Hannah to meet her before she was gone. She hadn't wanted to before, but she might want to now, since it would be her last chance.

"I really want you to meet Janie," I said that evening as she and I sat in the living room working on our latest jigsaw puzzle. We'd been competing with Allison and Greg for years over who could find the most difficult one. We were constantly trying to stump the other couple. The one we were working on now was a series of cats with no edges. Greg had said it had taken them over three weeks to complete. So far, we were two weeks into it and not even close to finishing.

Hannah was hunched over the table, searching for a piece. Her fiery red hair was pulled into a ponytail with runaway strands trying to escape that she constantly brushed off her forehead while she studied the puzzle. She didn't bother looking up.

"You should see how much she's changed. She gets better every day. It's really inspiring," I said, remembering how she'd shown me how one of the nurses had taught her to write her name. She'd been so focused as she'd painstakingly drawn each line and so proud of herself when she'd finished. "There's something really amazing about watching someone transform before your eyes. It's like witnessing a small miracle. I don't want you to miss it."

She finally raised her head. "Christopher Bauer, I would say you are officially smitten."

I laughed. "I can't help myself. That's why you have to meet her. Just wait until you do. You'll see exactly what I'm talking about."

SEVEN

Hannah Bauer

The following day, Christopher led me down Janie's hallway for the first time. I didn't know what to expect after all the stories he had shared with me. He'd told me in one of our previous conversations that she decided whether she liked you the first time you met, and apparently, it was impossible to recategorize yourself afterward no matter how hard you tried. What would I do if she didn't like me?

I heard her screaming from the nurses' station. Primal screams unlike anything I'd heard before. There weren't any words to accompany them. Only tortured sounds. I stopped in my tracks. "Maybe this is a bad time?" I looked toward Christopher, expecting him to agree with me and say we needed to come back another day, but he was already pushing through the officers outside her door and running into her room. I handed my badge to the officer, and he pulled my name up on her visitor log.

"You might not want to go in there," he said as he handed it back to me.

I swallowed the fear in the back of my throat and stepped inside. Janie writhed on the bed like she was in the throes of demon possession, her eyes wild. She wailed like a wounded animal. Her bedding lay crumpled on the floor. Blood spotted the mattress. Two nurses scuttled around her bed, trying to grab her without hurting her. One of them held a syringe. Christopher lurched into action.

"Janie. Janie, honey," he said tenderly as he took cautious steps toward her bed. "It's Dr. Chris. I'm here. Honey, you need to settle down."

She continued screaming incoherently. He tried to reach for her, but she was too quick. She dodged his grasp and tumbled onto the floor, her cast making a loud crash when she hit the floor. Christopher knelt beside her.

"Janie, it's Dr. Chris, and I'm here to help you," he said softly.

She just kept screaming.

"Janie!" This time he yelled. "It's Dr. Chris!"

It was as if a light switch went off inside her. She stopped midfit, blinked, and turned to look at him. "Dr. Chris!" A relieved smile spread across her face.

He crawled over to her and scooped her into his arms. She curled her head against his chest. He rocked her back and forth as she relaxed into him. "It's okay. You're okay now. I've got you, honey, I've got you."

I stood watching, stunned. A second ago she'd been in the midst of a psychotic episode similar to the ones I'd seen schizophrenic patients throw when they were dragged in from the streets. There was nothing that could calm them down except drugs, but just the sound of Christopher's voice had stopped Janie. I didn't know what to think. I looked at one of the nurses, the one wearing SpongeBob SquarePants scrubs. She smiled at me and shrugged her shoulders.

The blood on Janie's mattress was from where she'd ripped out her IV, and Christopher held her close while they put it back in place. She clung to him like he was her favorite teddy bear, and he whispered to her as they stuck her with the needle. She didn't even flinch. Christopher wiped her tears away with the back of his hand after they'd finished.

"I'm proud of you, sweetie. That wasn't so bad, now, was it?" he asked.

She shook her head, eyes watery and red rimmed. He carried her over to me while the nurses remade her bed. I hadn't moved from my spot in the doorway. She was so small. It looked like he was holding an oversize doll.

"Janie, I have someone I want you to meet," he said. He motioned for me to come closer. "This is my wife, Hannah. She's a nurse here too. She's been waiting to meet you."

She kept her face buried in his chest.

I stepped toward them. "Hi, Janie. It's nice to meet you," I said. I placed my hand on her back. She flinched. I took a step back.

"Would you like Hannah to come back at another time?" he asked.

She grabbed his head and pulled it down to her mouth, cupping her hand around his ear so she could whisper into it. He nodded at whatever she was saying and then turned to me. "Why don't we try this another time? I don't think she's ready."

Christopher felt awful about how my introduction with Janie had gone, but it wasn't his fault we'd come after one of her feeding times. It didn't help that it was with one of her least favorite nurses. I was determined to make our second visit better than our first. I spent hours at the bookstore thumbing through the latest children's books. There were so many to choose from, and I had no idea what Janie liked. Was she into princesses? Animals? Fire engines? Did she even have any clue what those things were? Had she ever been outside the trailer and exposed to life? I settled on a wide assortment of books ranging from Dr. Seuss to *Fancy Nancy*.

Christopher wanted me to meet with her by myself, but I asked him to come with me again so she'd be comfortable and relaxed. I didn't want to push myself on her and overwhelm her any more than she already was. This time, Christopher scheduled our visit after one of her physical therapy sessions, since she tended to be in a good mood after them.

She was sitting on her bed chattering away with one of her nurses when we walked in. Her face lit up when she saw Christopher. The transformation that had taken place in the month since she'd been admitted to the hospital was astounding. She looked like a different child than the one he'd described to me. She was still very small for her age and looked much younger than six, but her stomach no longer distended from her body. She'd gained seven pounds, and her body had filled out. Her eyes were a light blue, so pale you could almost see through them. She'd grown into a sweet, cherub-faced little girl with a head full of wispy blonde curls.

"Hiya, Dr. Chris!" She waved at him. Her hand still curled despite all the work in physical therapy.

"Hey, sweetie," he said, walking over and planting a kiss on top of her head.

"Sit! Sit! Sit!" she ordered, pointing to a spot next to her on the bed.

He motioned for me to come over. "Janie, do you remember when Hannah came to visit the other day? She came with me again today."

"Hi, Janie," I said.

She stared at me blankly—no sign of recognition.

I stepped toward her cautiously, holding the books out in front of me like a peace offering. "I brought some books. Do you want to read a book with me?"

She looked at Christopher, searching for his approval.

"Why don't we read together?" he asked.

This time, she nodded. Christopher pointed to the spot next to him on the bed, and I sat, the plastic mattress crunching underneath my weight. Janie scampered up on his lap. I fanned three books out in front of her. "Which one do you want to read?" I asked.

She studied them carefully before pointing to *The Day the Crayons Came Home*.

"Good choice," I said. "This is one of my favorites."

I opened it and started reading. She was hooked from the first page. She strained to get a better look from her spot on Christopher's lap. He slowly edged her in my direction until she was wedged between us, sitting on one of each of our legs. Christopher looked over at me and beamed. My heart swelled.

EIGHT

Christopher Bauer

Piper Goldstein's name flashed on my cell phone screen. She was Janie's social worker. Dan had given me her number, and I'd left a message earlier in the day. Hannah and I had read with Janie twice in the last week, and yesterday Hannah had suggested taking her out of the hospital. I loved the idea and had started figuring out the logistics immediately. I hurried into my office before answering the phone, shutting the door tightly behind me.

"Hello?" I said.

"Hi, this is Piper Goldstein returning your call."

"Thanks so much for getting back to me, Piper." I didn't waste any time getting down to business. I had a consultation in twenty minutes that I needed to prepare for. "I wanted to talk to you about Janie. I—"

She cut in. "I'm sure you already know this, but before you get started, there are certain things about Janie's case that I won't be able to share with you because of the limits of confidentiality or because they relate to the ongoing criminal investigation."

I had limits of confidentiality with my patients, so I understood exactly what she meant. I'd expected as much given the nature of Janie's case. "Of course," I said.

"Okay, as long as we're clear on that before we get started."

"Definitely." I cleared my throat. "I've been on Janie's medical care team since she was admitted. I'm the orthopedic surgeon who performed her surgery, and I've provided her postoperative care, but at this point, I'm more of a friend than anything. We spend most of our time playing Go Fish—"

She interrupted, "You're that Christopher?"

I laughed. "I guess."

"Janie's nurses have wonderful things to say about you."

"Thanks. I can't say enough good things about them either. She has some great people taking care of her." I'd never seen a patient with such a strong support team. She had so many people rallied around her. It reminded me why I had fallen in love with medicine.

"What can I help you with?" Piper asked.

"My wife is Hannah Bauer, and she's a nurse at Northfield Memorial. You should be able to look both of us up in the directory. Anyway, we would like to take Janie out of the hospital for a few hours."

Hannah left for work early every evening now so that she could read to Janie at bedtime each night. They both loved it. This morning she'd suggested taking Janie to the park down the street from the hospital. I hadn't thought of it before, but it was a great idea. I'd promised her I'd figure out the protocol and see if we could get permission to take her on an outing.

"Wow. Janie sounds like she's in great hands," Piper said, but I sensed hesitation in her voice. "But I'm not sure that's a good idea."

I tried not to be insulted. "Can I ask why?"

"Trust me, I know how badly some of these cases can tug at your heart, but you have to be careful about getting too involved."

"I wouldn't call taking her to the park getting too involved. She's been in the hospital for almost five weeks, and I'm pretty sure that she's only been in the prayer garden with her occupational therapist. How much fun do you think that was?" I gave her a second to think about it before adding, "We're just trying to give her a few hours to feel like a regular kid."

Her voice softened. "There's a lot of variables in this case that you don't know about. There are—"

"I understand it's a complicated case. We're not trying to get involved in any of that. We just want to give her some time to run around in the sun."

"Again, there are risks involved with her case, and you might be putting yourselves in danger."

I wasn't worried about anyone coming back for Janie. I never had been. Whoever they were, they'd given her up because they didn't want her. All you had to do was look at her body to see that.

"I appreciate your concern, but we'll be all right. I just need to make sure it's okay to take her outside the hospital and to know if there's any red tape I need to complete." I had called her out of courtesy, not to ask permission.

She dropped her voice like someone might be listening. "Listen, I shouldn't be telling you this, but you are obviously a good person, so I feel like I should warn you."

"Warn me about what?"

"Janie's mother."

No one knew anything about her mother or father. At least that's what I'd been told.

"They've identified her mother?" I asked.

"They have." She gave me a moment to let it sink in before continuing. "Janie's mother is dead, and the police suspect foul play."

"Did you tell Janie?" My head swam with sadness for her. Kids loved their parents no matter how badly they treated them. It wasn't fair. None of this was fair to her.

"I did." Her voice thickened with emotion. "I told her this morning."

Janie hadn't said anything about her mother when I'd seen her this afternoon. Nothing was off or different. She was really happy today, asked to learn a new game. Maybe she was still in shock, or maybe it was her way of coping with things. I couldn't begin to understand her behavior after everything she'd been through.

"Do they think whoever killed her mother was the same person who hurt Janie?" I asked.

"Like I said, I'm limited in what I can share because it is an ongoing criminal investigation, but the police are pursuing all possible leads at this time." She waited a few beats before continuing. "Now do you understand my concerns?"

—

I'd spent most of the night filling in Hannah about my conversation with Piper, but she was too distracted by Dylan and Caleb fighting over whose turn it was on the iPad to give me her full attention. We'd been having the boys overnight every month since they were babies to give Allison and Greg a break. A few years back, Greg had told me they'd never actually gone anywhere when the boys were infants. They'd drop them off at our house and go home to sleep.

"I can't believe how big they're getting. It seems like every time I see them, they've grown another few inches," Hannah said. Being an aunt was one of her favorite things in the world.

She watched them, but I stared at her, still mesmerized even after all these years—the way her porcelain skin shone and the tiny freckles sprinkled across her nose. I stretched my legs out on the coffee table. She'd given up telling me to keep my feet off of it. The battle wasn't worth fighting. "Not an inch, but technically, their bones grow nine millimeters per day, so they are taller."

She slapped my arm. "Do you have to be such a nerd all the time?"

"Isn't that what you love the most about me?" I threw my arm around her shoulders, and she settled comfortably onto my chest. I breathed in the smell of her.

Caleb turned around; a miniature Greg stared back at us. "Dylan won't let me do this level. It's my turn."

Dylan was hunched over the iPad, gripping it like it was gold. Caleb eyed it hungrily.

"Dylan, give Caleb a turn now," I said. Allison and Greg were sticklers when it came to Dylan and Caleb's screen time. At first, I'd thought they were being too overprotective, but we'd seen firsthand what it did to them. They acted like it was a drug they couldn't get enough of. I turned my attention back to Hannah.

"What happens to Janie now?" she asked.

"Piper didn't know. Apparently, Janie's case is a legal nightmare. She said normally the Department of Children's Services would put her in foster care until they determined a permanent placement, but there are lots of additional steps since her mother is dead and they have no idea who the father is or any relatives. For now, they filed something called an emergency protective order that gives the Department of Children's Services temporary guardianship while they try to figure this mess out."

"Can you imagine all the paperwork involved?" Hannah asked with one eye still on the boys.

I shook my head.

"I still don't understand why they're keeping her mother's death a secret," Hannah said.

I lowered my voice so the kids couldn't hear. "She said they don't want whoever hurt Becky to know that she's dead. I guess they think maybe someone will come forward if they think she's still alive? Or trip up in some way?"

She eyed me nervously. "Do you think we should still go?"

Our plan was to take Janie to the park behind the grocery store. It was six blocks from the hospital, and we'd chosen it because it was small and private. I'd spoken with Janie's psychologist at the hospital to see if she thought it would be too overwhelming, and she'd thought it was a great idea but that we should keep it simple and as low key as possible.

We'd chosen the park with that in mind since it stayed empty most of the time and because being around other kids was probably too much for her right now. But even though it wasn't a busy place, it was still in public. I didn't want to put us in any danger.

"Piper said if we decided to do it, they'd probably send an unmarked squad car to the park just to keep an eye out for anything unusual or suspicious."

The concern left her face. "Well, if that's the case, then I don't think we have anything to worry about. Nothing is going to happen with them there."

We stared at Dylan's and Caleb's backs as they played together, listening to their giggles and squeals interspersed with the occasional mad shout.

"It's all so unfair," I said. It was the one thing that struck me over and over again about Janie's situation. None of it was her fault. All she'd done was be born, and we didn't get to choose our parents.

"It really is," Hannah agreed.

Both of us came from great families. I was an only child, and my parents had given me everything. Dad had worked full time as a civil engineer, and Mom had stayed home to raise me. We'd never struggled financially. The worst thing that had happened to me in my childhood was when our Little League team had lost the state championship in eighth grade. Hannah had had an ideal childhood, too, except she also had a sibling. We'd talked about it all the time during our engagement. It was one of the main reasons we stayed in Clarksville, Ohio—we wanted our kids to grow up with the same innocent childhood we'd experienced.

But neither of us had done anything special to have such easy lives. We'd just been born into them in the same way that Janie hadn't done anything to have such a hard one. All I could think about when I spent time with her was how she'd done nothing to deserve what she'd been through. Who was going to make it up to her?

NINE

Hannah Bauer

"Janie, can you put these on your face like this before we leave?" I asked.

Janie had limited sun exposure because she hadn't been allowed outside the trailer and the windows had been covered. The doctors had given us special sunglasses since her eyes were so sensitive to the light. I showed her how to put them on before handing them to her. She twirled them around in her hands like she was still unsure what to do with them. Finally, I just helped guide them onto her face. The sunscreen was next, and Christopher lathered her with so much that we couldn't rub it all in, but we weren't taking any chances with her getting a nasty sunburn.

She plodded along in flip-flops between the two of us, holding on to our hands as we walked out the back entrance of the hospital. She still had a hard time walking upright despite all the work with her physical therapist. She wanted to walk on all fours even when you held her hands, so it felt like we were dragging her along, and I was glad Christopher had brought our car around earlier. Janie waved and smiled at all the nurses we passed, excited to leave the hospital even if it was only for a few hours. I was glad we'd stuck with our plan rather than letting fear make the decision.

One of the valets was waiting by our car when we got to the east exit. He hurried to open the doors when he spotted us. Allison had lent us an infant car seat because Janie was too small for a booster seat. Christopher had taken it to the fire station the previous Saturday to make sure it was installed properly.

"No! No! No!" Janie screamed, shaking her head wildly when I tried to set her in the seat. She arched her back and kicked defiantly. I tried to hold her down, but she bucked against me. I didn't want to use force because I was afraid of hurting her, so she easily wiggled free from my hold. She toppled onto the sidewalk, howling. Christopher and I knelt beside her. I reached out to touch her, and she jerked away.

"Honey, we really want to take you to the park and play, but you have to get in the car." Christopher's voice was calm and steady. He pointed to the back seat. "That is a car seat, and all kids ride in car seats. It's the safest way for them to ride in the car."

She scowled at us.

"Do you want to go to the park?" I asked. I felt like such an idiot for not considering how hard it might be for her to be restrained given her history. I made a mental note to be more conscientious about her past in the future.

She nodded.

I reached out and rubbed her arm briefly before putting my hand back passively at my side, not wanting to frighten her any more with my touch. "I bet it's really scary for you to be locked into a car seat." Her lower lip quivered. Tears filled her eyes. I reached forward and grabbed the passenger-side seat belt. I gave it a sharp tug, pulling it toward us. "See this belt? Everyone in the car has to wear one." I pointed to myself as I spoke. "I'm going to drive the car, and I have to put my seat belt on too. How about if Christopher sits in the back seat with you? Would you like that?"

She shook her head, but Christopher ignored her protests. He crawled over her car seat and sat in the spot next to it.

"See, it's not so bad," he said, patting the car seat. "Why don't you let Hannah put you in your seat? I'll be here with you the whole time. We can ride together."

She looked back and forth between us. We stood there in silence for a few more minutes before she finally got in. I clipped her into her seat and jumped into the driver's side, eager to leave before she threw another fit. She stuck her lip out in an angry pout, but after a few blocks, her face transformed as she stared out the window. She pointed to everything. "What's that? What's that?" she called out as we drove. She did the same thing whenever I read to her. I loved giving her words for the new world she lived in. Christopher and I took turns trying to figure out what she was pointing at while we drove.

The park was only a short drive from the hospital, so it wasn't long before we pulled into the parking lot. Christopher worked on getting Janie out of the car while I grabbed the cooler and bag from the trunk. I'd never been on a picnic with so little food. Usually I packed way too much, and half the food ended up going back home with us, but we could only give her safe foods, which meant our picnic was limited to greek yogurt and pureed peas. I'd gotten her menu approved by her dietician. We'd brought along our own spoons to eat the yogurt and pureed food with her so she wouldn't feel different. Christopher had come up with the idea, and I thought it was brilliant.

"Janie!" Christopher suddenly yelled from in front of me.

She was headed through the parking lot and straight for the street. He took off running faster than I'd ever seen him move. He scooped her up in one swift movement and cradled her next to him as he walked back through the parking lot. He was still breathing hard when he got back to me. She buried her face against his shoulder, cradling herself in the nook of his collarbone. He looked petrified. I rubbed her back.

"I only took my eye off her for a second," he said breathlessly.

I rubbed his shoulder with my other hand. "It's okay. It happens. Remember what it was like with the twins?" The boys had been full of so much energy when they were toddlers and had had no sense of danger. They'd always been taking off—and never in the same direction at the same time.

"If we can handle the twins as toddlers, we can definitely handle her," he said, trying to sound convincing, but we both knew this was completely different than the twins.

I motioned for him to take her to the playground equipment. "Go play with her. I'll set this up."

I found a shaded spot underneath a tree and spread out the blanket, enjoying being outside. Spring was so unpredictable, but it was perfect weather for a picnic in the park. I sat on the blanket, taking a minute to soak in the sun. There was nothing better than the feel of the sun on your skin after a long winter. The winters got harder the older I got, and each year, I understood more why people moved out of the Midwest after retirement.

I watched as Christopher went down the slide with Janie tucked between his legs and his arms wrapped around her. She squealed with delight. He'd been right about how amazing it was to watch her. She was beaming with happiness, the crisis from moments ago already forgotten.

"Again! Again!" she shrieked at him each time he pretended to be too tired to play anymore.

I'd never seen Christopher look so childlike. For the thousandth time, I felt the pain of everything I couldn't give him. He had always done such a good job of being there for me—holding me while I cried, bringing me flowers, and assuring me that we were still a family even without children—but I knew it hurt him too. He wanted kids as much as I did. He'd never understand how hard it was for me not to be able to give it to him even though he tried to be strong at all times for me. I pushed the thoughts aside. No need to spoil a beautiful day.

Playing with Janie at the park was so different than playing at the park with Caleb and Dylan. She had no idea what anything was and took it all in, wide eyed. She moved like a young toddler, unsure of her footing, and her balance was always slightly off. She didn't know how to climb anything, and we helped her through most things. Christopher had said that her physical therapist gave positive reports on Janie's progress and was working hard at rebuilding and strengthening her muscles, but she had a long way to go.

What would happen to her? Would she be able to make up for the important things she'd missed in her development? Were there other kids like her? Did traumatized kids ever recover? I couldn't help but share Christopher's sense of responsibility to Janie. How would we know she went to a good home after she left the hospital and not one of those awful foster homes I'd read about in the news? Or what if she was too difficult for a family to handle and ended up becoming a kid who was raised in the system, shuffled around from home to home? What if she became a drug addict or prostitute?

We couldn't let that happen to her. There had to be something more we could do.

CASE #5243

INTERVIEW: PIPER GOLDSTEIN

"What did you think of the Bauers when you met them in person?" It was Luke's turn to ask questions now. Ron had pulled a chair into the corner and was leaning back against the wall, arms crossed on his chest, staring at me.

I folded my hands on the table in front of me. "It was obvious from my first meeting with them that Chris already had a tight bond with Janie. She never left his lap and didn't speak to anyone except him. She whispered the answers to my questions in his ear, and he acted as her interpreter."

"We've heard from others that he was very good with her. Is that true?"

I nodded. "He's a pretty huge guy—over six feet tall—but he handled her like she was a teddy bear. It was clear he was her favorite person."

Christopher was one of those guys you would never fall for when you were a teenager because he was so nice, too sweet. There wasn't a semblance of a bad boy in him. He was the guy you permanently placed in the friend category when you were young. But when you got older? He was the kind of guy you wanted to marry and build a life with.

"What about Hannah? What were your initial impressions of her?" Luke asked.

"She seemed more anxious than Christopher over the situation, but she was as eager to get Janie home as he was."

"Did you discuss the potential challenges they might be up against if they were responsible for Janie's care?"

"Absolutely."

I'd always been honest and up front with them about Janie's challenges. It didn't do any good for there to be a mismatch between a foster parent and the child, so I made sure everyone knew what they were up against and could make an informed decision. It was my policy for every family.

"What kinds of things did you share with her? Could you please be more specific?" Luke smiled at me.

I was going in the direction they wanted me to go. They were only polite and nice when you were doing something they liked or giving them something they wanted. I'd been fooled before. I wasn't going to be fooled again.

"They'd officially diagnosed Janie with child abuse syndrome. People always assume sexual abuse is the worst kind of abuse that a child can endure, but it's not. It doesn't have the kind of lasting effects that you see in kids who've been severely neglected. Don't get me wrong. Sexual abuse is terrible, but the type of neglect that Janie experienced? That affects brain development."

Ron eased his chair off the wall, returning all four legs to the concrete. "How did Hannah respond when you told her?"

"Hannah didn't go into the situation blindly, not like Christopher did. He was convinced love would heal all Janie's wounds, but Hannah was more realistic. She understood you couldn't go through what Janie went through and come out unscathed. She walked into the situation with her eyes open and ready for any of the challenges Janie presented."

"And what about Christopher? Did you ever present this information to him?"

"Of course."

"But he wasn't as receptive to it?"

"How do I explain this to you?" I took a minute. "He was fully aware of her potential difficulties and problems. He just didn't care."

It was what I loved the most about him. But it was also what had gotten him into the most trouble.

TEN

Hannah Bauer

I only had ten minutes to fill Allison in on everything before she had to pick up Caleb from soccer practice, so I talked fast. "Do you think we're crazy? It's only temporary, until they find a permanent placement for her, but we thought it'd give her the extra time she needs to heal while they get everything else figured out."

I'd just finished telling her how Christopher and I had applied to be emergency foster parents for Janie. It meant she would live with us after she was discharged until they found a family to adopt her. Neither Christopher nor I could stomach the idea of her going into foster care, getting settled with a new family, and then having to be ripped from that family to go live with her adoptive family. Staying with us would seem like a logical extension from the hospital and was the way we'd present it to her if our application was approved.

"You're not scared?" Allison asked.

"Of course I'm scared. It's going to be hard, but I think it's something amazing we can do for her."

Allison shook her head. "That's not what I'm talking about."

"You mean her situation?" I dropped my voice low so no one could hear. "Like whoever killed Becky coming back to kill Janie?"

"Or you and Christopher."

"It does freak me out." Christopher and I had spent hours going through different possible scenarios. We'd already made an appointment to get an alarm system installed in our house. "They still have no idea who killed her. Well, at least that's what they're telling us."

I liked Piper as a person, but she wasn't the best at keeping us updated on all the case details, and sometimes it felt like she was purposefully trying to keep things a secret from us.

"How do you know for sure that whoever hurt them won't try to finish what they started?" Allison asked.

"We don't, but she's not going to be with us for that long. It's not going to be more than two weeks—probably even less than that." I leaned across the table and whispered, "And honestly, I think the police or FBI, something, is following us anyway."

Her eyes grew big. "Are you serious? What makes you think that?"

I shrugged. "I just get this feeling, like I'm being watched. I don't really know how to explain it. But it's more than a feeling. Both me and Christopher have seen random unmarked cars following us and parked outside our house."

"That doesn't freak you out?"

"No, because I'm pretty sure it's the good guys following us." I smiled at her, trying to ease her worries. I would've felt the same way if the roles had been reversed. "And besides, it's not like the investigation is going to end just because she gets out of the hospital. Who knows: they might catch whoever did this before she's discharged, and all this time spent worrying will have been for nothing."

"I think what you're doing is really honorable." I could still hear the hesitation in her voice. "But aren't you afraid of getting too attached? What's going to happen to you once they place her with a family?"

"I'm obviously going to get attached. I mean, we already are, but leaving the hospital is going to be her first step into the real world, and we want to make sure it's a good one. She deserves that. What if she ended up in one of those messed-up foster homes and they screwed her up even more? At least this way, we know she'll be as prepared and secure as possible until she goes into her permanent home." Christopher and I had taken her to the park again yesterday, and it was everything we could do not to tell her that we were trying to bring her home with us for a while, since she was becoming more and more obsessed with seeing our house. Christopher had taken pictures of every room in it and shown them to her. But of course we couldn't tell her until it was a sure thing. "I knew Christopher was going to be the best dad. You should see him with her. It's about the most adorable thing I've ever seen."

"I know exactly what you mean. I fell in love with Greg all over again when I saw him with the babies. There's something about watching them be fathers that makes you love them in a completely different way."

"Totally. He's probably going to have a harder time than me when it comes to saying goodbye because the two of them are already so close, but we can do it. She deserves to have a safe place to recover until they find her a home that's a perfect fit," I said with determination.

"I don't know. I'm just going to be honest—it makes me a little worried."

I held back the urge to laugh. Everything made Allison worry. Always had. She was the only kid I knew who had had an ulcer in elementary school.

"We're going to be fine," I assured her.

I was calmer than I imagined I should be, but we were doing the right thing. Christopher had been shocked when I had proposed the idea to him a few nights ago. I couldn't blame him. I wasn't usually that impulsive.

"Why not?" I had smiled. "Maybe it's just what we need right now. A break to think about someone else for a little while and take our minds off of ourselves."

"Theo would be so proud of you." Christopher had laughed.

Theo was the leader of our infertility support group. He had a twelve-step background, so he was always saying that the best way to fix yourself was to get your mind off your own problems and help someone else with theirs. I couldn't think of anyone who needed our help more.

"Really, though. We can let her stay in a cocoon a little while longer before she's thrust into the world. We'll give her an extra step of healing and care she wouldn't normally get."

"I'm totally up for it if you are," he had said, his face filled with excitement.

ELEVEN

Christopher Bauer

Becoming Janie's emergency guardians wouldn't be as simple as we thought it'd be. I called Piper and let her know we were interested. She informed us we'd have to go through a home study as part of our petition for guardianship. The first part meant meeting with us in person, and we agreed to meet at the hospital the following day.

She strode into Janie's hospital room with quiet confidence, dressed in jeans and a T-shirt, a bag strapped across her chest. Her chestnut hair was slung into a messy bun, graying at the roots. "Hi, everyone. I'm Piper." She shook hands with Hannah first. Janie was tucked on my lap and hid her head when Piper spoke to her. "Hi, Janie."

Janie didn't move or respond. Piper had warned me that her previous meetings with Janie hadn't gone well, so I wasn't surprised when Janie didn't speak to her. She liked most people, but there was something about Piper that Janie didn't like.

"Can I get you some water or coffee?" Hannah asked. She was twisting her hair around her finger, something she only did when she was nervous or upset.

Piper held up a travel mug with the Starbucks logo printed on the side. "Thanks, but I'm good. Today's visit is basically just for us to sit down and get to know each other better. You're going to see lots of me in the next few days. You might think I'm coming to live with you, too, but I promise I'm not."

We all laughed nervously, trying to ease the tension. She didn't waste any time getting started. The next hour was like a grueling job interview focused on our childhoods, any past abusive experiences, our views on discipline, and any history of domestic violence. We filled out questionnaires on our medical histories, education, and employment.

There were specific guidelines the state required for all foster parents, and a home inspection was mandatory for anyone in our situation. Hannah took it all in stride, but she was really nervous for the home visit with Piper. So nervous that the night before she was still up scrubbing bathroom floors at midnight, even though she'd already been over them once. She'd spent the last three hours cleaning our house like an obsessive-compulsive person. Our house hadn't been that clean since we had bought it. It wasn't like we were messy people, but our house definitely looked lived in. The last thing either of us wanted to do when we got home after a long day at the hospital was vacuum the floors or do the dishes.

I stood in the doorway, watching her bent over on the floor with a bucket and washcloth as she furiously attacked the tiles. "Honey, I think that's enough. There's no way there's a speck of dirt anywhere on that floor. We haven't even walked on it since the last time you washed it."

She turned to look at me, the sheen of perspiration on her forehead. She brushed the hair off her face with the back of her arm. "I just want everything to look perfect."

"Well, you've pretty much turned our house into a museum, so if that's what you're going for, then I'd say you've succeeded."

She threw her rag at me. "You're terrible. Everyone knows that women are judged by what kind of a house they keep. I don't want her to think I'm some kind of slob."

"Slobs are good people too."

"Shut up!" She laughed. "You're not making me feel any better."

"Come on, let's call it a night." I walked over and grabbed her bucket. "Sink or tub?"

She pointed to the tub, and I poured the rest of the water down the drain. I held out my hands and pulled her up, then brought her against me and rubbed her back. "It's all going to work out okay."

"You're not nervous at all?" She raised her head to look at me. Worry lined her forehead.

I shook my head. "I know it's meant to be." I pulled out her hair tie and let her hair fall down her shoulders. I loved when she wore it down, but most days it was pulled into a tight ponytail. I ran my fingers through it.

"I'm just nervous. What if—"

I put my finger up to her lips, shushing her midsentence. "Everything is going to be fine. You'll see."

CASE #5243

Interview: Piper Goldstein

"You couldn't have asked for a better home for Janie. I've been in children's services for over twenty years and met my share of foster parents. Believe me, they're not all good. I wish people became foster parents because they have big hearts and want to help children, but sadly, that's not usually the case. A lot of the parents I work with look at foster care like a job. They do it to get a paycheck, and their families run just like a business. I'm not saying all the business foster families are bad. Some of them are actually good, but there's just not a lot of love and caring that goes on in them besides meeting the child's basic needs. Don't get me wrong—for many of the kids in the system, it's way better than where they came from, so I don't complain too much."

"And the Bauers?" Luke asked.

I took another sip of my coffee. He'd forgotten my cream, so I was drinking it black, even though I knew my stomach would protest later. "Like I told you before, they were one of the good ones. Good foster homes are the ones where they really care about the kids they take in. They do it out of love versus any kind of monetary gain. They're the homes where children thrive, and the Bauers were certainly one of them. No question."

Therapeutic foster homes were better equipped to deal with Janie's issues and had more experience working with high-risk children and might have been a better fit. The Bauers hadn't had any history dealing with kids with special needs and definitely not the kind of needs that resulted from kids being severely abused. It took special skills to live with kids who were emotionally disturbed, and there was never a doubt in my mind that Janie was emotionally disturbed, given her background and my interactions with her. But that didn't mean that someone couldn't learn how to do it, and the Bauers had been willing to learn whatever they needed to. It wasn't just that, though. They had already loved her, and Janie had loved them. Well, she'd loved Christopher. She'd still been warming up to Hannah.

My mind had been made up the day I'd walked into Janie's hospital room for a scheduled meeting with her and found Christopher cuddled up with Janie on the bed, both of them fast asleep. He'd been dressed in his green scrubs, like he'd run to her room after surgery. He'd lain stretched out on her bed, his long legs reaching the end. Janie's head had rested on his chest, and his arm had been protectively curled around her small body. Her tiny toes had peeked out from underneath her knitted blanket—the one Hannah had made for her. His other hand had clasped her fingers in his. Her face had been perfectly still and calm. She'd looked peaceful. Truly peaceful. In all the times that I'd seen her, I'd never seen her look peaceful. Janie was never still. Every one of her muscles needed to move, and she was an endless stream of chatter, her words running over each other.

I hadn't even considered waking them up, even though we'd had a scheduled visit, because the moment had been too beautiful to ruin. Instead, I had sat down in one of the chairs, pulled out my laptop, and started typing up the report to submit to family court. I had recommended that Janie be placed in emergency foster care with the Bauers.

TWELVE

Hannah Bauer

We were thrilled when we got the call from Piper that our application had been accepted and the judge had granted us temporary guardianship as Janie's foster parents. She'd been in the hospital for six weeks, and the plan was to use the next two weeks to transition her into outpatient care. Christopher scoured Amazon, overnighting books to the house so we could take a crash course in working with traumatized children. Piper wanted us to start having home visits with her immediately because of the short timeline, and I was so excited the night before the first one that I barely slept.

This time Janie got into the car easily and without a struggle. I couldn't help but smile at the small victory. It wasn't long before we reached our house, since we didn't live far from the hospital. It was the main reason we had chosen the house. When we'd considered buying it, we had talked about how we could bike or walk to work if we wanted to, but we'd been in the house for six years, and so far neither of us had done it.

I turned the car off and twisted around in my seat. "This is our house, Janie. Christopher and I live here."

I expected her to be hesitant and shy when we walked into the house, but she embraced it all without fear. She was always surprising me with her fearlessness. She took Christopher's hand as he led her from room to room in the house. I walked beside them. I was careful not to push myself on her. Christopher was always trying to force our physical interactions, but I wanted her to do things in her own time and come to me when she was ready.

The tour abruptly stopped at the kitchen. She let go of his hand and dashed into the room. She spotted the refrigerator and scampered to it with a huge smile on her face. She tugged on the door and frowned when it wouldn't open. She pointed at it. "Dr. Chris, help me. I want food."

He shook his head. "It's not eating time."

She stomped her foot. "I'm hungry. Wanna eat. Now!" She yanked on the door again, but it was useless since it was locked tight. Her doctors had told us to lock all the refrigerators and cupboards because if we left them unlocked, she'd probably sneak into them and gorge on all the food until she got sick. It was still dangerous for her to eat too much.

"Honey, do you want to go outside?" I asked, moving to stand beside her, hoping I could distract her. It seemed torturous not to feed her, but the doctors had assured us that keeping her on her schedule was the best thing for her.

She glared at me and shook her head, pointing to the refrigerator again. This time she smacked it. "Food! I want to eat!"

We were one step away from a full-on meltdown. Suddenly, Christopher broke into a goofy dance and scooped her into his arms before she had a chance to protest. He swung her around. "Whee!"

She looked longingly over her shoulder at the fridge, but he twirled her again.

"Whee!" I exclaimed this time. "Look how fast you're going!"

Slowly, a smile spread over her face. Christopher kept swinging her. Finally, she started giggling and stopped trying to look at the refrigerator. I let out the breath I'd been holding. We'd just passed our first parenting test.

But things didn't go as smoothly during our visit the next day. We were sprawled out on the living room floor coloring when she suddenly started screaming. They were angry, violent screams. Not scared screams—rage screams. There were no tears. She wouldn't let us get near her. Every time we inched closer, she screamed louder.

"It's okay, Janie. There's nothing to be afraid of," Christopher said.

His words had no effect on her. It was like she couldn't hear him; she was somewhere else. She panted like she couldn't get enough air. Christopher reached out to bring her close to him, and she sank her teeth into his forearm. He yelled and jerked back instinctively, pushing her away. She howled.

I crouched in front of her. "Honey, it's—"

Her spit hit my face before I finished my sentence. I wiped it off with the back of my hand and turned to Christopher. He looked as lost as I felt.

She flipped herself onto her back and beat her fists against the wooden floor manically. Before we knew what was happening, she flung her head back and smashed it on the floor. It made a loud crack.

"Oh my God!" Christopher grabbed her and wrestled his arms around her to hold her in a tight bear hug. She let out another wail and head-butted him in the nose. He let her go, and she threw herself back down on the floor. Within seconds, she was banging her head again.

"She's going to knock herself out," I said. "You get behind her and hold her. I'll grab her legs."

He held her from behind so she couldn't head-butt him again. I held her legs down with my arms. She fought against us, her small body rigid with rage, but we refused to let go. I was afraid she was going to pop her hips out of socket with the way she tried to kick me again and again. It felt like hours before she stopped fighting and her body went limp. It was finally over, but we were afraid to let go. It took another few minutes before we released our hold, and she burst into tears immediately, her body shaking with heaving sobs.

I ran to the bathroom down the hallway and grabbed a washcloth, running it under the faucet. I held it on her forehead like she was feverish, hoping the coolness would alleviate some of the heat flowing through her body. We tried everything to comfort her, taking turns holding her and rubbing her back. Christopher tried distracting her with videos on his phone—the ones with gorillas that usually made her laugh—but nothing worked.

She cried until the visit was over and we had to take her back to the hospital. She wailed the entire drive and was still carrying on when we left her in her room.

"Wow, that was so intense," Christopher said as we drove away. Perspiration marks lined the armpits of his favorite T-shirt.

"Have you ever seen her like that?" I asked.

"I've seen her freak out before, but I had no idea it could last for so long. The nurses talk about how long she screams sometimes, but they never said it went on for hours. Do you think it's too much for her too soon?" he asked. He was obviously shaken.

I reached out and grabbed his hand. "I think it's going to be a tough transition for her, and this is probably just the beginning."

"I don't even know why she freaked out. I mean, one second we were coloring, and the next minute, she just freaked out for no reason. I didn't even tell her no or anything." His eyes were filled with questions, searching for answers.

I squeezed his hand. "There's probably a lot going on inside her that we don't even know about."

"It's just that I can usually calm her down. What's going to happen if I can't calm her down?" Worry flooded his face.

"Thankfully, we don't have to do this alone." Janie went to so many different therapies each day I didn't know how she had time for anything else. Each of them had given us a detailed summary of her care.

"Rhonda told me she's going to give us a bunch of sensory toys that she uses with kids who've been severely abused. She says they work great at helping them learn to self-soothe. She's got stacks of other resources for us too. All kinds of different therapeutic games and books." Rhonda was the chief psychologist at the hospital, and she worked with Janie for two hours every day.

"Do you really think they'll help?"

"Absolutely," I said, trying to be strong for him despite the fear gnawing in my gut.

CASE #5243

Interview: Piper Goldstein

The sun hit my eyes, making me squint, but I didn't care. It felt good to be outside, even if it was only going to be for five minutes. For a second, I wished I smoked. At least then I would have had a valid reason for asking them to let me step outside for a minute. Instead, I'd just looked shady when I'd asked if I could get some air. They'd looked at me suspiciously, but it wasn't like they could say no.

"Let's make it quick, though, so we can finish this thing up," Ron had said, as if we were almost finished. I hoped we were, but I doubted it. We hadn't even gotten to any of the hard stuff yet. They'd spent way too much time on the Bauers' first home visit.

Hannah had called me afterward, worried and frazzled, wondering if they'd gotten in over their heads. I hadn't told the officers that, but they hadn't asked the question either. Besides, I knew what they'd think if I told them, and it wasn't even like that. She had just been concerned. She was always so much more practical about Janie than Christopher.

"Is there anything we can do to make things better for her?" she had asked that day.

"Just keep doing what you're doing, but honestly, it's going to take a long time for the psychological and emotional healing to happen. That part isn't going to start until she's settled in a more permanent home. Even if she's not consciously aware of it, at some level, she still doesn't feel safe. No kid feels safe when they don't have a home."

"How are the prospects looking?"

"There are a lot of people who want her." I had rubbed my forehead just thinking about the hundreds of pages of paperwork I had to go through. "But it's a good problem to have."

"Still no luck tracking down any of her family members?"

"Nothing worth reporting," I had said.

It wasn't exactly a lie—telling her about visiting Becky's mother in jail would have served no purpose except to upset her more, and nothing good had come out of our visit anyway.

We started with family members whenever we needed a permanent placement for a child, and Becky's mother, Sue Watson, was the only relative we'd found. She had a criminal record spanning the last two decades and was in Fodge County Jail awaiting her trial after pleading not guilty to her third DUI charge and reckless driving. I'd gone to see her last week.

Sue was so obese her folds had slid over the aluminum chair, since her fat was the loose kind. She had worn the characteristic orange jumper. Usually women swam in them, but hers had hugged her body tightly. Her hair had been a frizzy mess, long and bushy, like it'd been years since a brush had passed through it. She had wrapped her arms around her wide chest and glared at me. "Who are you?" Her teeth were as rotten as Janie's had been.

"I'm Piper Goldstein. We spoke on the phone? I'm the social worker who's been assigned to your granddaughter, Janie's, case?"

"What's Janie need a social worker for?" she'd asked, eyeing the other visitors in the packed room like they might be able to hear, but there hadn't been any reason to worry; visiting hours were short, and nobody cared about any other visit but their own.

"The courts assign a social worker when a child is in need of protective care," I'd explained like I'd done the first time we'd spoken on the phone.

"What's that got to do with me?"

I'd hated to even bring it up, but I hadn't had a choice. The state insisted we pursue family care if at all possible. Sometimes it worked, but more often than not, it didn't. Dysfunctional parenting usually spanned generations, and most of the time, the family member didn't do any better than the parents. In Janie's case, I'd known she wouldn't stand a chance with any of her extended family because Sue had been arrested more times than Becky.

"We're trying to determine the best placement for Janie and thought you might be able to help us find the information we need to do that."

She'd leaned forward on the table. "What kind of information you looking for?"

"Anything you might be able to tell us about Becky and Janie."

She'd snorted. "I haven't seen that child in years."

"Janie or Becky?"

"Both."

"Did you use to see them frequently?"

"I raised Janie."

I'd picked up my pen. This had been new information. "Can you tell me more about that?" I had asked, sounding just like a reporter.

"Becky never wanted that baby. Only reason she even had her was because she waited too long to go in and get it taken care of."

"What about the father?"

Sue had burst out laughing. "Father? Becky can't keep her damn legs shut. Who knows who that baby's daddy is? Definitely not Becky.

She don't have a clue." She'd snorted. "I brought them two home from the hospital to stay with me. I thought I'd give Becky another chance. Maybe give her time to get off that nasty junk, but I should've known better." She'd rolled her eyes. "She was back smoking within three weeks. Didn't even last a month with her baby. Took off one night and never came home. Left me with the damn baby to take care of."

"How long was she gone?" I'd asked.

She'd laughed again. This laugh had been so deep that it had shaken her belly underneath her jumpsuit. "She didn't come back until Janie was almost two."

"And Janie was with you that entire time? Nobody else?"

She'd nodded.

"Why did Becky come back for her?"

"She'd gotten herself clean. Been in some kind of program for six months. I gave her Janie, but there's no way I was letting that girl back in my house."

I had scribbled down the timeline. "What was Janie like when she was a baby?"

"She never slept. Ya know how they always be saying babies sleep all the time? Not Janie." She'd shaken her head. "She came into the world woke, and she stayed woke."

"You mean she was colicky?"

She'd looked puzzled. "What's that?"

"It's when babies cry a lot. Babies with colic usually don't sleep much."

"Oh, hell no. That ain't what she was like. She never cried. She just stayed woke. Like I said. She just laid there staring at the ceiling. She didn't want nuthin' to do with me. Didn't even care I was her grandma. How you s'pposed to care about a baby who don't care nuthin' for you?"

"I don't know. That must've been really hard for you."

She'd shrugged. "Oh well, I just figured you can't pick babies. Sometimes ya just get a bad one."

"So what'd you do?"

"I just let her do whatever she want till she got bigger, but then she turned even worser."

"What do you mean?"

"Couldn't get her to do anything you wanted her to. She freak out if you told her no. That girl would kick me. Try and bite me. If she couldn't bite me, she'd bite her own self. Craziest thing I ever seen." She'd nodded her head, agreeing with herself and gaining momentum as she spoke. "Then she start taking off her diaper and peeing all over everything. Not just in the room. Everywhere in the damn house. She drop a dookie whenever she feel like it. Get all mad and make herself throw up. I was like, nuh-uh. Ain't no child gonna act all crazy like that, messing up my house. That's when I had to start whooping her good. That's what I did with all my kids." She'd locked her eyes on mine pointedly. "I had a right to whoop my children when they got out of hand just like Becky got a right to do the same to Janie when she was getting out of hand."

Everyone who beat their kids had an excuse, and it was usually because they thought it was their right to do it. People even used Bible verses to justify beating their children. I couldn't count the number of parents who'd quoted the "Spare the rod, spoil the child" verse to me. I hadn't bothered trying to change her mind. She'd be locked away from children for a long time.

"Were you concerned that there was something wrong with Janie?"

She'd leaned forward again and lowered her voice, whispering like we were best friends. "You ever looked in her eyes? Those eyes turn black as night. Sometimes, I just had to smack her upside the head just to get her eyes look blue again. You know what I mean?" She'd laughed, but I was pretty sure she was serious. "I woulda just got rid of her. Believe me, I thought about it. But then Becky came back. She'd gotten herself clean and wanted Janie again. I was like, 'Hell yeah—take her.'"

"When was the last time you saw them?"

Her forehead had creased as she'd tried to remember. "Two years? Maybe three?"

"And what was Becky like then?"

"Crazy as ever. Strung out again and talking about taking Janie to church so she could have the pastor pray over her again."

"I know you said that you didn't know who Janie's father was, but were there any men in Becky's life?"

We had to track down the biological father or any other male figure who might have custodial rights. Even if they weren't around, we had to give them an opportunity to take Janie. I'd never seen it happen. Deadbeat dads didn't resurrect themselves to show up for their kids when they needed it. It was just another box I had to check off my form.

"No idea."

"Were there any men who'd hurt Becky in the past?"

She'd raised her eyebrows. "Were there any who didn't?"

THIRTEEN

Christopher Bauer

I was so excited to bring Janie home, but the sheer magnitude of the task at hand pummeled me when we walked through the front door, and I froze. The entryway stretched out in front of me, leading to our rustic living room with the burnt-orange accent wall I'd insisted on. The sun from the bay windows drenched the room in light, illuminating every piece we'd so thoughtfully and lovingly designed, but nothing felt safe or familiar. Everything looked different, even the artwork. Suddenly, all this time opened up in front of us. Hannah and I had each taken three weeks of vacation to be with Janie until they matched her with a family, but now that we had her home, what were we supposed to do with her?

Hannah took one look at my face and read what I couldn't say.

"Why don't we all get something to eat?" she asked. Even though food was a touchy issue with Janie, it was the one thing guaranteed to make her happy, and we'd purposefully scheduled our arrival to coincide with her snack time. Hannah stretched her hand out to me, and I grasped it, grateful for her lead. We filed into the kitchen.

The rest of our house was homey and inviting, filled with our down-to-earth style and lived-in looks, but the kitchen was a different story. It was set up with purpose and function in mind. The kitchen was supposed to be the heart of the home and the place people spent the most time, but not with us, since both of us hated to cook. I would be perfectly content ordering takeout every night or heating microwave meals, but Hannah insisted on cooking, so it was all designed to make things easy for her. There was open shelving so that she knew exactly where everything was, and it was easy to grab.

We had set up a whiteboard on the refrigerator so Janie could see when she was going to eat, just like at the hospital. Her timer was on the kitchen island. We had bought the same one the nurses had used. Our goal was to keep everything like the hospital so we could maintain her routines. We hoped her adoptive parents would do the same.

Hannah unlocked the refrigerator. Janie let go of my hand and ran to it. Her eyes grew big as she took it all in. She'd probably never seen a full refrigerator before, and ours was stacked. It was all neatly organized and labeled in storage containers.

"Janie, I want you to know that this is your food." Hannah waved her hand around, pointing to each shelf. "All of it. You will always have enough to eat in our house. We are always going to feed you, okay?"

She was too busy eyeing all the food and fingering the Tupperware full of colorful sliced fruit—Hannah's work—to respond. She pointed to the strawberries. "That. I want that," she said.

Hannah pulled out the strawberries.

"And that. And that. And that." She pointed so quickly it was hard to tell what she was pointing at.

Hannah laughed and pulled out some cheese along with a few slices of salami. "How about we put some of these on crackers?"

Janie's smile grew even wider, and I finally felt like I could breathe. I took a seat at the island. I had only sat on the stools when we were deciding which ones to purchase, because we rarely ate in the kitchen. We usually carried our meals into the living room to watch whatever show we were currently bingeing on. A smile tugged at the corners of my mouth as Janie crawled onto my lap. Maybe we didn't spend time in the kitchen because we'd never had a reason to before. Hannah lined the island counter with food and pulled the other stool closer to us. I reached over and rubbed Hannah's back as she stared at Janie in awe. Janie shoveled food in her mouth. Hannah flashed me a smile, her eyes filled with happy tears.

All my nerves had been for nothing. It had been an amazing day. It'd gone better than I could've expected. The three of us were snuggled on Janie's bed reading books together. We'd been in the same position for over an hour.

"One more," Janie said after Hannah finished the book. She loved reading. It was one of her favorite activities.

"You promised you'd go to sleep if we read *Whistle for Willie.*" Hannah closed the book and gave her a pointed look. We'd already read it three times. It was past ten o'clock.

She stuck her lower lip out. "I don't wanna sleep."

"Christopher and I are going to be right outside your door if you need us, okay?"

"If you need anything, all you have to do is call us, and we'll come," I said, rubbing my hand across her cheek.

She nodded obligingly. We each gave her a kiss on the forehead. Then we laid her down on the bed, pulled the covers up to her chin, and tucked her stuffed animals around her. She smiled up at us. "Good night," she said sweetly.

"Good night, Janie," we sang back in unison.

We left her door open a crack and plopped down on the couch in the family room outside her room. The glow from the night-lights edging the hallway cast shadows on the wall. I put my feet up on the coffee table and let out a deep sigh. We'd no sooner settled on the couch when Janie bounced out of her room carrying her dinosaur.

"Hiya," she said. "Whatcha doing?"

I looked at Hannah, and we both tried not to laugh.

"We're resting. Just like you're supposed to be doing," I said. I took her hand and led her back to her room, where I tucked her in like we'd just done.

It wasn't so funny when she popped out of bed as soon as I sat down again. We repeated the routine for the next two hours. Hannah and I took turns bringing her back to bed and laying her down. It grew more and more difficult each time, and eventually, we were practically dragging her there. By one o'clock, we were both exhausted.

"Why don't you just lie down with her?" Hannah asked. "She'll probably go to sleep if you're in there with her."

"I know, but Piper was adamant about not sleeping with her."

Piper had stressed the importance of letting her sleep alone because otherwise it would be harder for her to leave when it was time. We were trying to facilitate a smooth transition, not make it more difficult.

"The first night isn't going to hurt anything, and she's clearly not going to go to sleep in there alone," Hannah said.

I shrugged. "I guess it can't hurt."

Hannah gathered blankets from the linen closet in the hallway.

"What are you doing?" Janie asked, coming out of her room again.

"Christopher is going to sleep on the floor of your bedroom. Will that help you sleep?" she asked. She tried to keep her tone light, but I could hear the exhaustion in her voice.

Janie clapped, her face beaming with excitement. "Yes!"

I helped Hannah carry the blankets into her room, and I made up a pallet on Janie's floor while Hannah went and grabbed a pillow from our bedroom.

"Janie, lie down and go to sleep," I said.

She flopped down on her bed without a word.

“Good night,” Hannah whispered, handing me the pillow before tiptoeing out of the room and turning off the light.

I lay on the floor waiting for my eyes to adjust to the darkness. Slowly, her room came into view. Her small twin-size bed was pushed up against the wall on the right side, and we’d put a rail on the other side of it to keep her from falling out. The comforter was bright yellow with huge pink flowers stamped all over it. Her favorite stuffed animals from the hospital lined her bed. A circular rug with purple and blue stripes filled the center of the room. There was so much we’d wanted to get her, but it didn’t make sense to fill her room with stuff when she was only going to be with us for a short time.

I strained to hear the sounds of her breathing and listened for the weird clicking sound she made in the back of her throat whenever she slept. It seemed like forever before I heard it, but I finally did, and my body slowly relaxed. I closed my eyes and fell asleep immediately.

A sharp smack to my forehead jolted me awake. My eyes snapped open. Janie hovered over me, holding one of her toy trains in her hand. I rubbed my head. There was a lump forming where she’d hit me.

“Janie, did you hit me with your train?” I asked with surprise. My head throbbed in the spot where she’d hit me. Her face was blank, emotionless, an expression I’d never seen her wear before. “You cannot hit me. It hurts when you hit me.”

She just stared at me in the dark. The night-light cast an eerie shadow on her face. She raised her arm like she was going to hit me again. I grabbed her arm. “Give me the train,” I said.

“No!” she screamed and pulled her arm free.

“Janie, give me the train. You can’t hit people with your toys.” I kept my voice steady.

She shook her head.

“You need to get back in your bed, and I don’t want you to take your train with you because you hit me with it.”

Her eyes narrowed to slits, her pint-size body full of challenge. In one swift movement, she threw the train at me and took off, bolting out the door. I threw off my blankets and chased after her. She ran into the family room and tore the cushions off the couch, screaming at the top of her lungs.

Hannah raced out of our bedroom. "What's going on?" she asked as she watched Janie tear through the room.

"I think she had a nightmare," I said.

Hannah ran toward her as she grabbed the candles on the coffee table and smashed them onto the floor. "Janie, stop!"

Her face was contorted in rage. She ripped off her clothes, shaking in her diaper. Her fists clenched at her sides. She eyed the room, looking for something else to destroy. Hannah stepped cautiously toward her like Janie was a feral cat. She crouched down in front of her.

"It's okay, honey. You're okay," she said softly. She grabbed Janie, encircling her small body with her arms. Janie kicked and screamed against her. Suddenly, she plunged her teeth into Hannah's arm just like she'd done to me before. Hannah yelled and instinctively let go. Janie took off again, this time running into the kitchen.

We followed her. She had flipped over one of the barstools and was standing in front of the refrigerator, pounding on it. She grew even more frustrated when the refrigerator wouldn't open and threw herself down on the floor. She flipped around, and before we knew it, she was bashing her head violently against the floor. We rushed to her side. Rhonda had instructed us on the importance of keeping her from hurting herself during her tantrums and shown us some holding techniques.

"Grab her," Hannah said, lurching into action. She tried to grab Janie's legs, but Janie writhed and moved around, making it almost impossible to grab her and keep her still. It was easier for me to grab her upper body and twist her arms behind her back the way we'd practiced with Rhonda.

Janie strained against us. She growled and grunted, alternating between screams. It was hard to believe we weren't hurting her, but Rhonda had assured us it was a safe hold. We stayed in our position for an hour before she was finally still. Not asleep but still. The fight had left her body. I scooped her up and carried her to her room. I placed her on the bed, and she lay there motionless, staring at her ceiling.

"Do you think she's all right?" Hannah asked. "Should we take her back to the hospital?"

I eyed the clock. It was four thirty. "I don't know."

Hannah rested her hand on Janie's forehead. "It's okay, Janie. You're safe."

Janie didn't move or respond. It was as if she hadn't heard her. We crawled onto the bed with her, resting against the wall. I took one of her small hands in mine and held Hannah's hand with the other. We sat that way until the sun came up.

FOURTEEN

Hannah Bauer

Allison waved to me from a spot in the corner, and I made my way through the crowded coffee shop over to her. She jumped up and hugged me before sitting back down and sliding my latte across the table. "Okay, you have one hour to tell me everything. Go."

Janie had been with us for five days, and I hadn't talked to Allison since her first night. We'd texted, but even that was minimal. I didn't even know where to begin. I took a sip of my coffee.

"I'm pretty sure this is the first time I've rested since we brought her home." We'd assumed that if we mimicked the hospital structure, Janie would respond to it in the same way that she'd done there, but it hadn't been the case. She screamed and cried for hours. Most of our days were spent trying to console her. Her doctors and therapy team had warned us about her episodes, but it was different once you were in them yourself. "She has fits every day, and they can go on for hours—I'm not even exaggerating when I say hours—and there's nothing you can do to calm her down. I'm continually amazed at how much rage can come out of such a little girl. She's got that frothing-at-the-mouth kind of rage, and you just have to sit with her during it and restrain her if she starts banging her head. I hate holding her down, but we have to do it to keep her safe."

"What gets her so upset?"

I shrugged. "We never really know what triggers her. Certain things are a given, like taking away her food or being told no, but most of the time we have no idea."

Allison's face filled with sadness. "That sounds terrible."

"It's pretty awful for her right now. She gets overstimulated really easily, and she's hyperaware, so she jumps and plugs her ears every time a car goes by. Tuesday was one of her worst days since it was trash day. Most of the day was spent trying to coax her out from underneath the bed. Oh, and she's decided she doesn't want to wear clothes anymore. She scratches and claws at them like they're burning her skin. We spent the first two days getting her dressed over and over again because she kept ripping them off." I laughed. "Now we just let her run around in her diaper."

"Her diaper?"

"I thought I told you she wasn't potty trained?" I could've sworn I had. They had put her in diapers in the hospital, and she'd been content running around in them ever since. She wasn't bothered by her soiled diapers even when they were packed with feces. If it weren't for the smell, we wouldn't have noticed because she never complained about it or told us she'd gone. Urinating was the same way; she'd sit in her mess all day.

Allison shook her head.

"Yeah. She has no idea how to use the toilet. At least she's good about changing her diapers, though. She lies right down on the floor and raises her legs for one of us to change her. There're so many things she doesn't know how to do. Like she doesn't know how to hold silverware. Isn't it weird that holding silverware is a learned skill?"

Allison laughed.

"What?"

"It's not all that weird when you have kids." Her eyes widened in horror. She reached across the table and grabbed both my hands. "I'm so sorry, Hannah. I'm such an idiot. It just came out of my mouth. I wasn't even—"

I interrupted her. "Stop. It's okay. Really, it is." I gave her a convincing smile. "You know how you used to say motherhood was a world of conflicting emotions?" She nodded. "I get it now. I mean, I said I did before, but now I do in a way that I don't think you can understand unless you have kids yourself. Like last night after the dinner battle finally ended, we were all exhausted and frustrated, but as soon as we got Janie in the bath and started splashing around with her toys, it was all forgotten."

Allison took a bite of her muffin, chewing quickly before talking. "You're going to have such a hard time when she leaves."

"Thanks for the vote of confidence." I smiled, tossing a napkin at her.

"You are, and you know it." She shook her head.

"Of course I'm attached—I'm not going to deny that—but it's actually been good for me. It really has in a lot of ways."

She tilted her head at me, skeptical still. "How so?"

"Before Janie, I was thinking about giving up on my dream of being a mother. I didn't tell you that, but I was. As much as I wanted to be a mother, I didn't think I could stand to get my hopes up another time and end up disappointed, but Janie's made me realize that I don't want to give up on it. I can't ever give up because no amount of disappointment is worth giving up on what it feels like to be a mom. She gave me a taste of it, and I know I'll never be satisfied until I get to enjoy the experience."

FIFTEEN

CHRISTOPHER BAUER

I watched as the man, Carl, squeezed Janie's cheeks playfully.

Don't do that. She doesn't like her face touched, I wanted to call out. It was so hard not to say anything. All of this was so painful to watch, but I couldn't walk away. I couldn't just leave Janie with a stranger. I didn't care if the stranger had been screened and thoroughly investigated by the Department of Children's Services.

His wife, Joyce, stood next to the bookshelf in the living room talking to Hannah, but Hannah's eyes were glued to Janie and Carl just like mine. She didn't trust him any more than I did. It didn't matter that they looked harmless in their worn jeans and tucked-in T-shirts, but they weren't doing things the way Janie liked. They weren't in tune with her. Carl still hadn't noticed that she flinched each time he spoke because it was too loud. Janie looked back and forth between Hannah and me, chewing on her thumbnail, something she only did when she was uncomfortable.

"Janie, sweetie, do you want to come over here and talk to Joyce?" Hannah said, right as I was about to create a similar diversion. I grinned. She wanted to rescue Janie as badly as me. Janie nodded and quickly walked over to Hannah. Joyce knelt in front of her before she reached her.

"Do you like playing outside?" Joyce asked. She was in her early fifties, slightly on the heavy side, and wore a long red cardigan despite the heat today.

Janie froze.

It'd been like this for over an hour, and I wasn't sure how much more I could take. These people might have looked good on paper, but they were not good with her in person. Hannah scooped Janie up, and she laid her head on Hannah's shoulder.

"I think she's overtired today," Hannah said, looking apologetic. "Maybe we should set up a visit for another time."

Joyce huffed, clearly offended.

I shook Carl's hand. "It was nice to meet you."

"Likewise. I'm sure we'll be in touch," he said.

He seemed like a nice-enough man, just not the right match for Janie. I walked over to Joyce and put my arm around Hannah's shoulders. "It was nice to meet you as well, Joyce."

"It really was," Hannah said. It sounded genuine if you didn't know her like I did.

I excused myself and headed to the backyard, where I walked to the far corner. I didn't want to take the chance of someone overhearing me. I called Piper, pacing back and forth as I waited for her to answer. Relief washed over me at the sound of her voice.

"That was awful," I blurted out, skipping all the small talk. "They looked like they walked out of a car-insurance commercial."

Piper laughed. "Really? They were that bad?"

"Yes. Janie froze every time they talked to her." She'd been that way from their first hello. She'd refused to move from her spot behind me during introductions. It'd taken over ten minutes just to get her to show her face.

"In their defense, she probably would've done that to anyone regardless because she really likes you guys."

The next set of prospective parents was even worse. The woman had terrible breath, and Janie plugged her nose every time she came near her. Her husband had shifty eyes, and I didn't trust anyone who had trouble with eye contact. I stepped out to call Piper like I'd done before.

"Where do you find these people?" I asked.

I expected her to laugh again, but there was silence on the other end. It was a few more beats before she spoke. "I think you need to lower your standards for parents."

I was taken aback. "What do you mean? Neither of these couples was a good fit for her. It was obvious immediately. They had no clue how to interact with her."

"You've seen two of the best sets of parents we have."

"You're kidding, right?"

"Nope."

This time the silence came from me.

"What if I said we were thinking about becoming her permanent foster parents?"

It wasn't exactly true. I hadn't even considered it until I blurted it out, but I realized as soon as I did that I meant it. I wanted to be her dad. What if she was the child we'd been waiting for all along? Maybe this was the reason things had worked out the way they did.

SIXTEEN

Hannah Bauer

I gripped the edge of my seat and glared at Christopher. "Are you serious? How could you? How could you possibly make that huge of a decision without asking me first?"

His eyes widened in shock. "I didn't . . . I just . . ."

"Spit it out. What? What were you thinking when you told Piper we wanted to keep Janie?" I stood up, my chair slamming into the wall behind me.

"Keep your voice down," he hissed. "She's going to hear you."

I worked my jaw back and forth, too furious to think straight. "How could you assume you knew how I felt about something like this?"

I watched as the realization hit him. He dropped his voice to a whisper. "You don't want to keep her?"

He looked like he was going to cry, and Christopher rarely cried. I'd only seen him do it a handful of times in all our years together.

Shame washed over me, making it hard to speak around the lump of emotions in my throat. "I just . . . I mean, I know it sounds silly, and I get that we'd be great parents for her, but I . . . I want a baby."

I couldn't look at him. I stared at an imaginary spot on the tiled floor instead.

During our infertility journey we had agreed to stop trying once I reached forty and accept our childless fate because neither of us wanted to raise children when we were older. We wanted to be able to run freely after balls and play tag with bodies physically fit enough to do it and didn't like the possibility of not being able to see our grandchildren grow up. We'd celebrated my forty-first birthday this past year and decided we'd stretch our limit to forty-three. Janie was going to take years of work to stabilize. There was just no way to make it work.

He waited a few minutes before speaking. "I understand that you want a baby, and I've always felt the same way, but I think we need to really think about this before we say no to it. For years, all we've wanted is a baby. It's consumed us. And now?" He lifted my head up with his fingers so I would look him in the eye. "It's like the universe had a special plan all along and just dropped her in our lap. You don't feel that at all?"

"I do." Every part of me wanted to help her, to give her a perfect home and wash all her pain away, but adopting her meant giving up my dream. I would have to say goodbye to the possibility of ever having a baby to hold in my arms. I'd already let go of carrying a baby and having one that was our biological child. Could I give up another piece of my heart?

I didn't know if I could. I wanted the tiny fist wrapped around my fingers and the new baby smell. I longed for the experience of cuddling my child against my chest as I fed him or her and the joy of every first.

"What about the father?" I asked, grasping at straws.

"There's no record of a father on her birth certificate."

"I already know that. That's not what I'm talking about. Her father is somewhere out there, and we know nothing about the guy. What if it was him? What if he comes back for her?"

"Her dad isn't coming back for her. He probably doesn't even know she exists."

"You don't know that. What if years down the road he decides that he wants her and comes looking for her? The only way I can do this with Janie right now is because it's temporary, so I don't allow myself to get attached like it's permanent. But if I thought we'd be her forever parents? Everything would be different. Everything." My voice cracked.

He took a strand of my hair and tucked it behind my ear. Concern was written all over his face. "I understand your fears. All of them. Look, it's been a really long day. Super emotional. Let's just give it a rest for the night and not make any big decisions, okay?" He rubbed my cheek with the back of his hand. "Just think about it. No pressure. I'll be okay with whatever decision you make."

And for the next few days, he tried to be patient. He left me alone, never even brought it up. But I knew it was eating away at him. He wanted Janie as much as I wanted a baby, and he was right—we were the perfect parents for her. I couldn't argue with him about that. She was going to need ongoing medical care for a long time, and no one could manage it better. Social services wouldn't find a better match.

I grieved the loss of my faceless babies. I did it alone because Christopher didn't understand. It wasn't his fault. No man understood what it was like for a woman not to have a baby to hold. I didn't like to cry in front of other people, so the shower had always been my sanctuary. I'd spent hours crying in it after my miscarriages, and it wasn't any different now. I let the torrent of sobs rip through me as the water pounded against my bare flesh, turned up so hot it left red marks on my body when I was done, like I'd broken out in a bad case of hives.

I brought it up the following night since Christopher grew more anxious with each passing day even though he still hadn't mentioned it again. I couldn't stop thinking about adopting Janie either. It was the first thing on my mind when I woke up and the last thing I thought about before I went to bed.

I waited until Janie was engrossed in a movie so we could sneak into the kitchen without her noticing our absence. She hated being alone, especially at night. I took a seat on one of the barstools, and Christopher quickly did the same, knowing we only had limited time before Janie lost interest in whatever was playing on the screen. She'd been with us for almost two weeks and hadn't made it through a full movie yet.

"I'm ready to talk about adopting Janie again," I said, not wasting any time. His face lit up. He was bursting to say something but held himself back, letting me go first. "Being Janie's emergency foster care placement is one thing, but becoming her parents is entirely different. Our whole life is going to be disrupted, and I'm not sure you've given thought to all the problems she's going to have. Look at what we've already seen, and I'm sure that's only the beginning." I took a deep breath, choosing my words carefully. "Sometimes I think you let your emotions with Janie cloud your thinking, and I just want to make sure you're thinking about this rationally."

He jumped in as soon as I paused. "Of course she's going to have problems, but that's exactly why she'd be such a great fit for us. We have the time and the resources to help her in ways nobody else probably can. Any new family would be up against a steep learning curve trying to figure out her medical issues, but I've been on her case from day one and followed every piece. We'd be able to make sure everything got followed up on and nothing was missed. It'd be a seamless transition for her services. Plus, she would have our undivided attention because she wouldn't be in a foster home with other kids running around."

"But what about her emotional issues? We have no idea how child abuse syndrome plays out over time. Piper said her case is one of the worst that she's ever seen."

"I don't expect her to be able to function like a regular kid any more than you do. It's going to take time, but think about it, Hannah—she's still so young and has so much time to heal. There's going to be a ton of work initially, but there might come a day when she's totally normal."

I raised my eyebrows. "Do you really think she could be normal?"

Christopher reached over and took both my hands in his. "I do. Look at how well she's done in such a short period of time with only a little bit of love and attention. Imagine what she could do in a real home with two parents who loved her and were willing to do whatever they could do to support her. We could take our family leave time like we planned to do when we got a baby and put all our focus on helping her adapt and adjust."

It made sense, and there was something beautifully poetic about it. That wasn't lost on me. But my heart still ached.

"I don't know, Christopher. How is this any different than what we talked about with the foster-to-adopt kids?"

We'd spent most of our evenings this past year cuddled up next to each other on the couch with our laptops open, flipping through hundreds of pictures of kids and reading their stories. I'd had no idea there were so many kids up for adoption. There were kids who had been in foster care for years, sibling groups begging to stay together and not be separated. Other children with severe physical disabilities or who had been abandoned. No matter what their stories, they had one thing in common—all of them were searching for their forever families, and their stories were heart wrenching.

Kids in foster care came with a host of problems that we didn't want to deal with. Most of the kids were drug addicted or exposed, had been medically neglected, or had pretty significant disabilities. We didn't want to be saviors. We just wanted to be parents.

"But we never met any of those kids. Maybe if we had, we would've felt differently."

"Maybe," I said, but I wasn't convinced. The closer I got to saying yes, the further away my dreams of a baby went. "Have you even considered the danger we are putting ourselves in if we become her parents? We don't even know what happened to her. Isn't it a huge risk if someone comes back? Do you want to always be looking over your shoulder? Are you ready for all that?"

He nodded. "Of course I've thought about all of that, and yes, I'm willing to take the risk."

"Even if it means putting me in danger?" It came out without thinking. I was desperate.

He balked with offense. I quickly added, "I'm sorry. I shouldn't have said that."

"I would never knowingly put you in danger, Hannah," he said, swallowing his anger to avoid a fight. "If I really thought someone was going to come after Janie again or do something to hurt you, I wouldn't consider it, but I don't think that's the case. I've always believed the police are going to catch whoever did this to her and put them away. I still think that. They just haven't found the person yet. That's all."

"It might not be that simple." I sighed. Janie giggled from the living room, and my heart flooded with warmth like it did each time she laughed or enjoyed something. I couldn't deny how much she already meant to me. "I need more time to think about it."

He jumped up from his chair and stood in front of me. "Hannah, that's just it—we don't have time. They've already scheduled another family to come meet with Janie on Tuesday, and they have another one on the calendar for next week if that one doesn't work out. What if this is our chance to have a beautiful family and we never get another one?"

"Can you at least give me a few more days?" I asked.

He nodded, searching my face to see if his argument had moved me. I struggled to keep my face natural and maintain my composure.

"I'm going to take a shower," I said.

I headed to our bathroom before he could say anything else and turned on the shower. I couldn't hold my tears back any longer, and they slid down both cheeks as the room filled with steam. I stepped inside, sliding the glass door shut behind me. I had never met a child who needed a home more than Janie. There wasn't a kid in any of the profiles Christopher and I had looked at who needed love more than her. I knew what I had to do, what I wanted to do—but it didn't make the pain of what I was giving up any less.

—

I had told Christopher to take Janie for a walk until I texted him to come back home. He'd looked at me strangely but had gone without question. I'd been rushing around the house trying to get everything set up as quickly as I could ever since. I decorated the living room with balloons and draped a banner over the fireplace that read **CONGRATULATIONS—IT'S A GIRL.** I ordered our favorite sesame chicken and set it on the dining room table. I placed a fresh bouquet of daisies in our best vase in the center of the table. It was perfect.

I texted Christopher:

You can come home now.

I flung open the door when I saw them walking up the sidewalk. Christopher was giving Janie a piggyback ride.

"Hi, guys. I missed you," I said.

"Been like this for the last ten blocks," Christopher said. He was trying to pretend he was annoyed to be carrying Janie, but his eyes smiled.

I took Christopher by his arm and led him to the living room. He scanned the room, taking it all in. It took a second for the words on the banner to register. His eyes grew huge.

"Are you serious?" he asked. He set Janie down on the floor. She looked around curiously at all the balloons and eyed the banner, trying to decipher the letters.

I nodded. "I am."

He threw his arms around me and lifted me off my feet, twirling me around as he shrieked with laughter. "Really? This is so amazing! We're finally going to be parents!"

I smiled as he danced me through the living room. It was just like I'd imagined he'd react when I showed him a pregnancy stick with two red lines in the window. Maybe this wouldn't be as different as I'd thought.

He cupped my face in his hands and kissed me slowly. "I can't believe we're doing this."

I leaned into him, his arms encircling me. "Me either."

CASE #5243

Interview: Piper Goldstein

It'd taken me over three months to grow my nails out beautifully and only a few minutes to chew them back down to nubs. It was so nerve racking. Why did they insist on asking me questions that they already knew the answers to? I took a deep breath, hoping I'd give them what they needed this time.

"I did a home visit with them the day after their hospital visit."

"Which hospital visit?" Ron asked.

"The first one," I said. Janie had gotten into the bathroom during her third week with the Bauers and swallowed a bunch of shampoo. They'd pumped her stomach and kept her overnight for observation. "And yes, I did suggest respite care then because I was shocked at how tired Christopher and Hannah looked."

Respite care was a break for foster parents. Another foster family took your child for the weekend so you could rest. It would've been horrible for Janie, but I had considered it because the two of them had looked awful. They hadn't even looked like the same people.

Christopher had been bleary eyed and unshaven. His clothes had been wrinkled and unkempt, like he might have slept in them the night before, which was completely out of character for him. He had always looked like he'd just stepped off the golf course, with his polo shirts tucked into his pressed khaki pants. He had sat slumped in the upholstered chair next to the fireplace in the living room. Hannah hadn't looked any better. She had bustled around the living room with frenetic energy like if she stopped moving, she might fall asleep on her feet. There had been heavy black creases under her eyes.

"And they refused respite care?" Ron asked.

I didn't like his tone. "Lots of family don't use respite care, but I always offer it," I said. "We sat down and had a discussion about learning to take care of themselves and developing a support network for all the challenges that would present themselves as time went on. Janie had an entire team helping her with her issues, but they didn't have anyone. Lots of parents forget about themselves."

"What sort of things did you discuss?"

"They'd been keeping themselves fairly isolated inside the house. I stressed the importance of getting their family and other trusted people involved so they could have help caring for Janie. When you're dealing with an emotionally troubled child, it gives a whole new meaning to 'It takes a village to raise a child.'"

"I imagine." Luke's expression was blank. "Why were the Bauers so set on keeping Janie away from their family?"

Why did they make everything sound so bad and ill intentioned? I tried to keep the annoyance out of my voice. "It wasn't like that. Christopher had read all these books on how to make adoptive children feel comfortable and settled in their first month. He and Hannah had taken time off from work so they could both be home with her during her first month. Lots of the experts said it was best to keep the number of new people to a minimum and to work on developing the parent-child relationship first before bringing other people into the circle. But like I told Christopher, the experts aren't always right."

Luke raised his eyebrows. "Do you consider yourself an expert?"

I blushed. "I . . . I mean, I've been doing this for over twenty years . . ."

Ron nodded, signaling that I could continue. He gave Luke a slightly irritated look.

"I explained to them that sometimes they had to make decisions based on their own situation. I suggested they introduce Janie to their families."

"Why did you push so hard?"

"Because they needed help. They were going to fall apart if they didn't get someone to help them."

SEVENTEEN

Hannah Bauer

I had listened to my married girlfriends complain about their in-laws enough to know how fortunate I was that my and Christopher's families had gotten along since their first introductions. We were lucky that way. Christopher's parents had always wanted a bigger family, so they were happy to welcome mine. Both couples had moved to Florida after retirement like traditional Midwesterners did. They lived two hours away from each other in the southern panhandle. Even when we weren't visiting, they still went out to dinner with each other occasionally. Christopher's dad had passed away three years ago, and my parents were a huge help to his mom, Mabel.

Our parents were excited to meet Janie but had been respecting our request for privacy. Allison had arranged a meal train but made sure everyone understood that the meals were to be dropped off on the porch or delivered by a food service. I called her first to let her know about our change of heart. She was thrilled and couldn't stop squealing. My mom was even more excited than Allison. She took care of calling Mabel for us, and by the end of the night, they'd booked the same flight.

I was nervous when Saturday rolled around, but Janie seemed excited to meet new people. She let me put her in a dress and comb her hair, which she rarely allowed. I kept glancing over at Christopher, both of us holding our breath and waiting for her to revolt, but she sat calmly through the entire process. I even put a red barrette on each side. She looked darling. Christopher wouldn't stop taking pictures, but she didn't mind because getting her picture taken was one of her favorite things, and she never tired of scrolling through them. She smiled and beamed for each one.

My parents and Mabel arrived first since they were always early. They carried wrapped gifts with huge decorative bows. My mom knelt down cautiously in front of Janie, and to my surprise, Janie flung herself into her arms. "Hiya, what's your name?" she asked, all smiles.

My mom was taken aback. She'd been listening to all of my stories about Janie for the past few weeks and hadn't expected such a warm reception. "I'm Lillian, and I'm your grandma. Do you know what a grandma is?"

She shook her head.

My mom pointed to me. "I'm Hannah's mommy. That means I'm your grandma." She reached up to pull my dad down next to her. "And this is Gene. He's Hannah's daddy, which means he's your grandpa."

"Hi, kiddo," he said, ruffling the top of her hair. My heart swelled at his use of my childhood nickname.

Janie shrugged, not seeming to care what any of the labels meant. "Do you want to see my toys?"

"Certainly," my mom said.

"Come on." She grabbed each of their hands and led them to her room, walking between them.

I turned to look at Christopher. He was as surprised as me. "Did you see that?" he asked.

I shook my head in amazement. "Wow."

She bounced out of her room to answer the door each time the doorbell rang and flung herself at whoever it was in the same way she'd greeted my mom. She led everyone into her room. Before long, the party had moved into her bedroom. We'd kept the gathering small, limited to our immediate family and a few close friends, but her room was packed.

Dylan and Caleb sat in the center of the rug with Janie. Even though they were only nine, they looked like teenagers next to her, and I realized how small Janie still was despite the weight she'd gained. She took out toys from her bins and held them up for everyone to see, eliciting oohs and aahs from the adults around her.

"She's loving this," my mom whispered to me.

I smiled. She shined in the spotlight. It reminded me of how people had swooned over her at the hospital.

"Can she open our present?" Caleb asked, looking up at me with his huge brown eyes framed in dark lashes that any girl would kill for. They both had the most beautiful eyes. I didn't know how Allison ever told them no.

I looked at Christopher, and he nodded.

"Sure," I said.

"Mom, where'd you put her present?" Caleb asked.

"It's in the living room," Allison said.

"Why don't we all go into the living room and open presents?" Mabel asked.

Janie looked confused as everyone started moving toward the living room. Dylan reached for her hand. "Come on, Janie. Don't you want to go open your presents?" he asked.

She still looked perplexed. "Presents?"

"Presents. You know, toys?"

She grabbed his hand, and they ran into the living room. The presents were piled on the coffee table. I hadn't expected everyone to bring gifts, but no one had shown up empty handed. The boys loved showing Janie how to rip open the wrapping paper. They were as excited about the gifts as she was, exclaiming over each one with her. Janie bounced over to whoever had given her the present and threw her arms around them. "Thank you. Thank you," she gushed.

Christopher came up behind me and wrapped his arms around my waist. I leaned into his chest, my tension relaxing.

"I've never seen her look so happy," he whispered.

"Me either," I said.

He kissed the top of my head. "Look at our parents."

The grandparents were sitting on the couch, and Janie had climbed onto their laps with the American Girl doll Allison had given her. I'd told her it was too expensive for a gift, but she'd ignored me like always. The grandparents took turns passing Janie around. Everyone was thrilled to have a little girl running through the house. It was so different than the boy energy we were used to from Caleb and Dylan.

I kept waiting for Janie to act out as the day wore on or have one of her meltdowns after something didn't go her way, but it never happened. Not even after we made her stop eating the chocolate cake Dan's wife had brought for dessert. She let me take it from her without a fight and allowed me to wipe the frosting from her mouth without the slightest protest.

Caleb and Dylan adored her. They fought over whose turn it was to give her a piggyback ride and spent over an hour playing hide-and-seek with her in the house before taking her outside. We had hired someone to build a wooden play structure in the backyard as soon as the adoption petition had gone through. It was one that didn't just have the typical swings and slides but had all the extras that Janie's physical therapist had suggested we get to help work on all her motor skills. There was a climbing wall and a clubhouse with a telescope and tic-tac-toe housed inside. They scampered up and down the structure with her.

Allison came up to me while we watched them play. "She's adorable," she said, holding a beer in her hand. I could never get her to share a bottle of wine with me despite all my attempts over the years. She insisted nothing was the same as an ice-cold beer after a long day.

If anyone could understand how difficult parenting was, it was her. She loved to tell people how she hadn't slept for a year after the twins were born, and I didn't think she was exaggerating because I'd never seen her so stressed. There were days she still looked ready to pull her hair out.

"She's definitely not what I'd pictured." She cast me a sideways glance like she was questioning everything I'd told her before about how difficult Janie was.

I took a sip of my wine and laughed. "Maybe she just doesn't like us."

EIGHTEEN

Christopher Bauer

Hannah and I sat sipping our drinks at one of our favorite restaurants downtown. Our parents were only going to be in town for a few more days, and they'd insisted we take a night out for ourselves. It was the first time we'd been out without Janie since she'd come to stay with us.

"Do you feel guilty leaving her?" I asked.

"I should, but I don't. Does that make me a terrible mother?" She giggled. She'd already had two glasses of wine, and she always got tipsy after two.

"I don't either. I thought I would, but I feel good." I scanned the restaurant, eyeing all the other couples in the room—some of them having a great time, others obviously arguing but trying to keep it together since they were in public. "It feels normal, like any other couple with kids taking time to be alone together. I'm so glad things are finally settling down. That was the craziest month of my life."

Lillian and my mom had been taking turns sleeping with Janie. Lillian had suggested it the first night they'd been here, and I'd told her it wouldn't work because Janie only slept if I was in the room. Most nights we all slept together like we were having a big sleepover, but nobody got much sleep. I wasn't sure which was worse—being woken up by Janie's bloodcurdling screams or her staring down silently while we slept, the anger radiating off her. I was convinced she was sleepwalking, but Hannah was sure she was awake. Rhonda said it didn't matter either way because it was common in people who had been diagnosed with posttraumatic stress disorder.

Lillian had begged me to let her try, and I hadn't argued since stubbornness ran in their family. I'd been shocked when Janie hadn't fought it and had gone to sleep easily. My mom had done it again the following night and had been just as successful. A night of sleep had made me feel like a new man.

"I had no idea it was going to be this hard. It's not like people didn't warn us, but I guess you really don't know what it's like to be a parent until you become one, huh?" Hannah smiled at me. It was nice to see her relaxed, the lines on her forehead smooth. "It's getting a little better, right?"

I grabbed her hand from across the table. "It's only going to keep getting better."

Just yesterday I'd prevented a meltdown by getting Janie to use her words to tell me what she needed instead of going berserk. This morning she'd done it with Hannah without even being prompted. The gains were small, but they were happening. All her therapists gave positive progress reports.

"I love taking her outside. It's like Christmas for her every day. I wish we would've known how hard it would be for her to be at home."

She was a different girl when we left the house. She transformed into a sweet, loving child and took in everything around her with amazement. She loved interacting with other people and experiencing new things, always full of questions. Strangers commented on how well behaved and adorable she was.

I flagged down our server for the check, not wanting to stay out too late since I knew my mom wouldn't go to sleep until we were home. "Are you sure you're okay with me going back to work on Monday?"

Our time together had gone by so quickly. Hannah and I had taken an additional month of family leave so we could all be together as a family. Hannah would continue her maternity leave for another two months while I went back to work. We had discussed having me take the same amount of time, but in the end, we'd decided it'd be best for the two of them to have that time alone together so they could bond.

"I wish you'd quit asking me that. We're going to be fine," she said.

She was secretly excited for me to go back, although she'd never admit it. Not even to herself. Janie always came to me first for everything, no matter what. With me gone, it'd force her to go to Hannah for things. Hannah had a list of things they were going to do together and tasks she was going to teach Janie, starting with her ABCs.

I reached across the table and grabbed her hand, squeezing tightly. "I really love you."

"I love you too."

NINETEEN

Hannah Bauer

I texted Christopher again. I was at my wits' end, and he still hadn't responded to me.

Janie won't talk to me.

Christopher had left for his first day back at work two hours ago, and so far, Janie hadn't spoken to me once. She was sitting at the coffee table in the living room coloring in one of her favorite coloring books, and anytime I tried to talk to or interact with her, she ignored me like she was deaf.

"Do you want any help, Janie?" I asked, coming up beside her.

Nothing.

Just like every other time I'd tried to talk to her. She'd been fine at breakfast, chattering away with us about the upcoming day as she'd nibbled on her strawberries while Christopher had eaten his oatmeal and I'd drunk my second cup of coffee. He'd kissed both of us before leaving. I'd expected her to cry or go into one of her screaming fits. I hadn't expected this.

My phone buzzed.

Take her outside. Go to the park.

That was Christopher's solution to everything with Janie—take her outside in the world. She loved the park, but would I be rewarding her behavior by letting her do something she enjoyed? At what point did we stop giving in to her and start holding her accountable? I didn't want her to think she could just ignore me like it was nothing and still get to go about her day like everything was fine, but I also didn't want to sit in the house all day long with her stonewalling me at every turn. The day was already dragging, and it was only ten thirty. One day of giving in to her couldn't hurt.

"Do you want to go to the park?" I asked, not expecting an answer. "Why don't you go put your shoes on?"

She kept scribbling furiously on her paper with a red crayon.

"Janie, I asked you to put your shoes on. I understand that you're not talking to me this morning, but you still have to do what I ask you to do." It was the sternest voice I'd ever used with her, but I was at a loss.

I waited for a few minutes that felt like ten to see if she'd get up and go put on her pink tennis shoes in front of the door. They had Velcro straps, so she could do them by herself, and they were the only shoes we'd been able to get her to wear so far.

I put my hands on my hips. "I asked you to do something. If you want to go to the park, then you have to put your shoes on."

She turned her back so she faced away from me.

Irritation flanked me. I walked into the kitchen to settle myself down. She was only a child and dealing with this in the only way she knew how. I was the adult. I had to be patient and give her the space to process the transition. I took a few deep breaths before walking to the entryway and getting her shoes.

"I'm doing this for you today because I understand you're having a hard time because Christopher went to work, and I want to help you through it. It seems like you're upset, and I want you to know that everything is going to be okay." I talked while I slid the shoes onto her feet. "He is going to be home as soon as he is done seeing all his patients, and then we can all be together again."

There was a neighborhood park only six blocks from the house, so it made for an easy walk. Gene had started taking her there during their last visit. I took her hand like I always did when we walked, and she jerked it away. I reminded myself to stay calm. I pointed out birds and flowers as we went along, but she refused to look in the direction I pointed.

Her face lit up when she spotted the park. It was packed with parents and kids. It always was, no matter the time of day, because it was as practical as it was pretty. The play space was huge, filled with tunnels, different slides, and jungle gyms. There were plastic rocks and walls to climb. Giant yellow canopies shaded the entire space, keeping the kids cool while they played. It was lined with picnic tables and benches so that the parents could watch from the sidelines, and it was completely enclosed, so you could relax without feeling like if you let your guard down, your kid would bolt out of the park.

Janie took off for the playground immediately. I walked up slowly, scanning to see if I recognized any of the moms. I was just starting to get to know the mom crowd and finding it much harder to fit in than I had thought it'd be. Most of them were stay-at-home moms, and they'd met when their children were babies. They already knew everything about each other and their kids. Breaking into the group with a six-year-old was tough.

I waved to three of them that I recognized, and they motioned me over.

"How are you?" Greta asked. She was always dressed in yoga pants, like she'd just come from a class, and today wasn't any different.

"I'm good," I said. All eyes were on me. They always stopped what they were doing whenever I came on the scene. My dad had hit it off with the moms at the park much better than me, but it wasn't that surprising. He was one of the most charismatic people I knew, and people were always drawn to him.

"How's Janie?" Greta's best friend, Sydney, asked. The two of them had been best friends since middle school and did everything together, including having their children as close together as possible. Janie was playing in the sandbox with Sydney's daughter, Violet, while Greta's daughter, Brynn, marched around barking orders at them.

"Things are great," I said. We hadn't disclosed Janie's background and planned on keeping her identity a secret for as long as possible, at least until they'd made an arrest in Becky's murder, but they weren't any closer to an arrest than they'd been when she'd been admitted to the hospital. The women were nice enough not to push for more details, but they always looked slightly annoyed that I didn't say more about Janie, especially when they were constantly talking about their kids.

Janie bounced up to the bench and tapped the other mom, Meredith, on her arm. Meredith had one hand on her stroller, constantly moving it back and forth to keep her baby asleep inside it, and the other gripped her travel coffee mug.

"Hi, sweetie," she said, bending down to kiss Janie on the top of her head, never missing a beat in her stroller rhythm.

"Hiya!" Janie said. "Where's your puppy?"

"He's not here today. I'm sorry. Maybe next time." She smiled down at Janie, who smiled back.

"That's okay. Next time," Janie said. "Bye-bye!" She waved at Meredith and scampered off, calling out to Violet and Brynn to join her on the swings.

My blood boiled. I could barely contain my anger. I'd expected her to talk to the other kids, but I had never thought she'd talk to the other women. She'd spoken to Meredith like it was nothing. She ran up and down the equipment, laughing and squealing, as if she didn't have a care in the world. She never once looked back at me. I could've left, and she wouldn't have noticed I was gone.

I didn't speak to Janie or interact with her the rest of the time we were at the park. I was afraid she'd ignore me, and I'd be humiliated in front of all the other mothers.

I tried again on our walk home, hoping she was over it. "That sure was a lot of fun, huh?" I asked, trying to keep the neediness out of my voice.

Silence.

"Do you want to come back tomorrow?"

More silence.

I dropped her hand and bit back tears. I left her alone for the rest of the afternoon, and she was perfectly content being by herself. She heard the door open when Christopher returned and rushed out of her room.

"Dr. Chris!" she squealed, throwing herself at him.

He wrapped himself around her, laughing and kissing the top of her head. "I missed you, too, sweetheart."

She pulled his head down and whispered something into his ear. His eyes lit up, and he laughed again.

"I have to get groceries," I said, but neither of them acted like they'd heard me. I grabbed my keys and headed to my car. I couldn't stand another minute of it.

"What did I ever do to her? Seriously, what did I do?" I asked Christopher as we brushed our teeth in the bathroom that night. I was still angry. And hurt, but it was easier to focus on my anger.

"You didn't do anything. She's just adjusting to me going back to work," he said as he flossed his teeth like it wasn't a big deal. "She'll be fine in a few more days."

I rolled my eyes. "You don't get it. It has nothing to do with adjusting. She's punishing me."

He burst out laughing. "What is she punishing you for?"

I smacked him on the arm. "Stop laughing at me. It's not funny. I told you that she's mad about being left here with me while you go to work. She's ignoring me to be mean."

He finally stopped what he was doing and turned to look at me. "Do you hear yourself? Being mean? She doesn't even know how to be mean."

"Are you kidding?" I raised my hands in exasperation. "She knows how to be mean, and she knows exactly what she's doing."

He shook his head, refusing to believe it. I stormed into the bedroom. I didn't care what he thought—I was right on this one. She'd been awful to me on purpose today.

CASE #5243

Interview: Piper Goldstein

Luke flipped through the file in front of him like he didn't have a care in the world and could stay here all day. It made me feel more hedged in. He looked up and then back down before speaking. "It says here that you got them help? Why did you feel they needed psychological help?"

I shook my head. It wasn't like that. "Janie had been seeing a child psychologist since the day she was admitted to the hospital. The only thing I suggested was that they see an attachment therapist."

"An attachment therapist?"

"They're therapists that specialize in working with kids who've been abused and are experiencing attachment issues."

Ron jumped in. "So you thought Janie had attachment issues?"

"Anyone in her situation would."

"Did you tell the Bauers that?"

"Of course. And I also told them they needed to have realistic expectations about Janie."

Everyone always acted like I hadn't warned them. I'd warned them plenty. They just hadn't listened.

Luke cocked his head to the side in a way I'd grown accustomed to in only a short period of time. "What do you mean?"

"Parenting a traumatized child is horribly difficult. Most of them suffer from severe attachment issues, and mothers are usually the targets of their rage. It can get pretty awful."

By law, I was only required to check in monthly with the Bauers, but I had stopped by as often as I could. I'd stopped by shortly after Christopher had gone back to work and had gotten to see firsthand how Janie had ignored Hannah.

I had knocked on the door, and Janie had opened it within seconds. She'd frowned when she'd seen me.

"Hi, Janie, how are you?" I'd asked.

"Good," she'd replied.

"Janie, let Piper in," Hannah had called from inside.

Janie had stood there, unmoving.

"Can I come in?"

She'd shrugged. "Okay." Then she'd moved aside.

"It's so good to see you," Hannah had said, coming into the entryway. She'd hugged me. "I'm still trying to adjust to this day schedule. Sometimes I think I still have my days and nights mixed up. Three years of working nights will do that to you."

"I bet it's going to take a while," I'd said.

"I just made tea. Do you want some?"

"Sure." I wasn't a big tea drinker, but Hannah always insisted, and I didn't want to be rude.

"Janie, do you want anything to drink?"

Janie had headed through the living room. She hadn't turned around.

"Janie?"

She'd kept ignoring Hannah and walked into her room.

"Wow, that's harsh," I had said.

Hannah had handed me my cup of tea. “She’s been like that since Christopher went back to work. Ignores me completely. Talks to everyone else but me.”

“But Christopher has been back at work for almost two weeks now.”

She’d forced a smile. “It’s been a long two weeks.”

“Oh my gosh, that’s got to be awful,” I’d said.

“Thank you. It feels good to hear you say that. Christopher looks at me like I’m making a big deal out of nothing. It drives me crazy that he doesn’t see how disturbing it is. I understand that she’s got mom issues, but she’s so hostile toward me now.”

I’d nodded. “Not to mention that it’s manipulative and controlling.”

“I never thought I’d say it, but I kind of miss her tantrums. At least then she was interacting with me.” Her face had been lined in stress. A frown had tugged at the corner of her mouth.

I had placed my hand gently on top of hers. “This has got to be hard on you.”

Her eyes had brimmed with tears. “I’m not sure she even likes me.” She’d struggled to keep the tears from falling down her cheeks. “I’ve never said that out loud. Not even to Christopher.”

“I know I keep saying this, but it’s going to take time. It’s only been a little over two months. We always tell families that it’s going to take about a year before things stabilize. Sometimes it takes even longer.”

“Do you think things will get better? I mean, with me?” She had looked down, embarrassed to even ask.

I had put my arm around her shoulders. “Yes, it will get better, but you’re probably going to need a lot of help.”

Luke’s voice interrupted my thoughts. “And you referred them to Dr. Chandler?”

“Yes. I respected Dr. Chandler, and she was the best at doing early-childhood work with abused kids. If anyone could help Janie, it was her.”

TWENTY

Christopher Bauer

Dr. Chandler's room looked more like a kindergarten classroom than a therapy office. Janie was with Dr. Chandler's assistant playing in an adjoining room so Hannah and I could meet with her alone. There were toys and games stacked everywhere. Comfortable pillows and beanbag chairs were strewn around the room. An entire wall was covered in children's artwork. I felt like a giant and had no idea where to sit because there wasn't any actual furniture in the room. Hannah was eyeing the room in the same way as me. We'd fought in the car on the way over. I could tell by the rigidity in her body that she was still mad at me.

I understood how frustrating it must have been for her, but Janie wasn't treating her the way she was on purpose, even though Hannah was convinced she was. She was only six years old. She was too young to be that manipulative. And besides, Hannah was an adult. She could handle it.

Dr. Chandler strode into the room. "So sorry I wasn't here to greet you. I was at my other office, and traffic was a nightmare getting here."

She was older than I expected, tall and slim with short gray hair piled in loose curls that framed her face. Faint wrinkles branched from the corners of her eyes and mouth. Her face sagged with age and was dotted with sun spots from the era when people slathered themselves with baby oil without any caution of the rays. There was a floral-print scarf tied casually around her neck. She reminded me of my grandmother, in her red cardigan, pleated pants, and loafers with thick soles for support. She plopped down on the floor gracefully and with ease, and she patted the rug in front of her.

"Come; sit. Let's get to know each other," she said.

We sat cross-legged in front of her. Hannah looked comfortable, but I was awkward and stiff. It felt too much like a yoga class, and I hated yoga. Hannah had been into it a few years ago, and she had dragged me to a class with her once. I'd fumbled my way through it and had never gone back. It just wasn't for me.

"I'm Dr. Chandler, but you can call me Anne if that makes you feel more comfortable." She folded her hands on her lap and looked back and forth between us. "Tell me a little bit about what brings you here today."

Hannah and I eyed each other, neither of us wanting to go first.

"We recently became the guardians of a six-year-old girl who we're in the process of adopting, and our social worker suggested we meet with you," I said.

Dr. Chandler clapped. "That's wonderful. Congratulations! Who is your social worker?"

"Piper Goldstein," Hannah said.

She smiled knowingly. "Piper, yes, she's one of the good ones. You should feel very lucky."

Hannah smiled back at her. "We do. Piper's great."

"Are you part of an international adoption, or is it a local foster-to-adopt program?" Dr. Chandler asked.

"Foster-to-adopt," Hannah said.

"Did you hear about the girl who was found in a parking lot a few months back?" I asked. "The one who'd been tied up in her closet?"

Dr. Chandler nodded. "Yes, I read about her case. Is that who you're adopting?"

"Yes," we said in unison, then laughed nervously.

"I imagine you must have your hands full, then. What's it been like?" Her eyes were filled with curiosity.

I chose my words carefully because I didn't want to upset Hannah any more than she already was. "She was diagnosed with child abuse syndrome in the hospital, so parts of it have been extremely challenging, but things are steadily improving."

Hannah snorted.

Dr. Chandler turned to her. "I take it you don't agree?"

"I agree that things are better than when she first came to live with us, but not because she's improving—we've just gotten better at dealing with her," she said.

"Can you tell me more about that?" Dr. Chandler asked.

"Well, bedtime has been bad since the beginning. Nobody slept much because she either got out of bed or screamed her head off from her bedroom. Christopher has to sleep on her floor every night to keep her in bed, or she won't go to sleep. So we've theoretically solved the problem, but not really because she doesn't know how to sleep by herself. I'd like for her to learn how to sleep by herself. It's a skill she needs to have, and I miss sleeping with my husband. Does that make sense?" Dr. Chandler nodded, and Hannah continued. "There're so many other things too. Like, she still eats things that aren't food. Earlier this week I caught her stuffing her mouth with hair she'd pulled out of her doll's head. We had no idea she was going to do that, so we had a few bad accidents, and one of them led to an emergency room visit. We locked everything up in the house after that. Everything is still locked up, and we don't leave her alone because we never know what she'll put in her mouth. And I was okay with all of this in the beginning because having Janie feel safe and secure with us was the most important thing, but I feel like we've done that, so it's time to move to the next phase, which probably means starting to deal with the issues head-on."

"So you feel like you've masked the problems in your home but haven't been able to treat them?" Dr. Chandler asked.

"Exactly," Hannah said, looking relieved. "And there's more. She's really aggressive and violent when she's upset. She's hit, bit, and spit at us. Sometimes she gets up and just stands over us at night—"

I interrupted. "She's sleepwalking."

Hannah shook her head.

"You disagree?" Dr. Chandler asked Hannah.

"Yes. I think she's awake," Hannah said.

"What does she do when you find her standing there?" Dr. Chandler asked.

"She's smacked Christopher in the head with a toy train before. I don't know what she does to him now, but she just stares at me like she's plotting something. I can feel the rage coming off her," Hannah said.

"Oh, Hannah, you're exaggerating," I said.

"I'm not. It's what she looks like," Hannah said defensively. "She's really manipulative too."

"Can you give me examples?" Dr. Chandler asked.

"That's easy. It's why we're here. Christopher went back to work three weeks ago, and she hasn't talked to me since. Not one word." Her eyes flashed with anger before she quickly rearranged her face into a neutral position. "I expected her to struggle when he went back to work, so I wasn't surprised. I even just let it be for a few days, but we can't keep going on this way. It's not healthy for any of us. She talks to everybody else but me, even strangers we meet in stores."

"She talks to you, Chris?"

"Yes." I hung my head, but I didn't want to feel bad. I shouldn't have to feel guilty because Janie had a different bond with me, but Hannah made me feel awful about it.

"Tell her how she talks to you, Christopher." Hannah peered at me.

I let out a sigh. "She whispers if Hannah is around so Hannah can't hear her."

"All the things you are describing are characteristic features of children with child abuse syndrome," Dr. Chandler said. "Maybe—"

I couldn't help myself. I had to interrupt again. "She makes it sound like Janie is this terrible little girl, and she's not. She's incredibly sweet. If she sees a little kid crying when we're at the park, she always runs over and hugs them. She never stops asking questions about things around her because she's so eager to learn. You should see how she is with people. It would melt your heart. I don't want you to get the wrong picture of her."

"Just because she's challenging doesn't mean those qualities you described aren't real. Both things can be true, even though it's hard to wrap your head around. She can be a sweet, charming girl and also mean and manipulative." Dr. Chandler paused, giving her words a chance to sink in. "One of the things you realize pretty quickly about parenting is the number of conflicting emotions you can have about your child. It's a roller coaster of highs and lows. In Janie's case, the highs are likely to be much higher and lows much lower. Why don't you tell me more about Janie's background and history? I'd like to know as much about her as I can before meeting her."

There was little history to give, but we did the best we could. We spent most of our time describing her medical issues, since that was what we knew the most about. We took turns describing the progression from when she had gotten into the hospital and the current status of her issues, making sure not to forget any of the therapy work she was already doing. Dr. Chandler spent a significant amount of time focusing on her rage episodes, asking us to describe the triggers and what we'd done to try to alleviate them.

Time flew, and our session was over ten minutes before the end of the hour. We booked a session for the following week even though I wasn't sure we'd accomplished anything.

"I really enjoyed meeting the two of you, and I look forward to getting to know your family," Dr. Chandler said as she walked us to the door.

We were quiet as we walked to the car.

"Do you want to drive home?" I asked. She hated the way I drove. She said I drove too jerkily, and it made her carsick.

She shook her head.

Hannah stared out the window as we drove, her lips pursed the way they were when she was deep in thought. I knew better than to interrupt. She would come to me when she was ready. I just hoped it was soon. I hated fighting with her. It didn't happen very often, so I was always thrown off by it when it did. I hoped we could find our way back to feeling like we were on the same team.

TWENTY-ONE

Hannah Bauer

I tried to keep my face neutral as Janie kicked the back of my seat while I drove her to her first appointment with Dr. Chandler. I'd asked her to stop twice, but as always, she'd acted like she hadn't heard me. Dr. Chandler had to do something. I was at my limit, especially after what had happened at Target yesterday. It had been the second time she'd pulled a stunt like that.

We'd stopped at Target to grab a few things, and she had skipped in front of me down the beauty section while I had grabbed my conditioner. Suddenly, she had put her hand out and started knocking down the row of shampoo bottles like they were dominoes.

"Janie, no!"

She had ignored me and kept walking. I had scrambled to grab things as they'd fallen. She had walked to the end without stopping, turned, and headed back in my direction. She'd reached out her arm to continue knocking down the bottles on the other side. Bottles had covered the floor.

I had grabbed her arms. "Stop!"

She had jerked away. She'd swatted down more bottles. One of them had popped open on impact, and liquid had spread across the aisle.

"Stop!" I had yelled.

She had paused, and for a second, I had thought she was done, but she had turned and looked at me, challenge written all over her face.

I had done my best to keep my voice calm. "You cannot make a mess in the store." I had pointed to the bottles. "You are going to help me pick these up and put them back on the shelves."

She had stuck her tongue out and bolted before I had had a chance to respond. I had looked at the mess she'd made—horrified that I had to leave it—and run after her. She hadn't been in the main aisle. I had looked left to right. I'd walked fast up and down aisles, eyes continually scanning for her or any sign of her—her purple shirt, the top of her blonde hair, her pink slip-ons. I had almost reached full panic mode when I had spotted her ducking into one of the aisles on the other side. I had bolted after her.

This time she'd been knocking over paper towels. I had scooped them up as quickly as she had knocked them over, but it hadn't taken long before my arms had been overflowing and things had fallen onto the floor. I had grabbed her arm and pulled her back before she could do anything else.

"Mommy, stop! You're hurting me!" she had screamed at the top of her lungs just as a woman had come around the corner. The woman had given me the most horrified look.

I had tried to explain what was going on, but I'd sounded like an idiot. I had been so furious on our drive home that I hadn't said a word, and I'd basically been ignoring her since. It was childish and immature of me, but I couldn't help myself. I hoped Dr. Chandler was as good with troubled kids and families as Piper had said, because we needed help.

She was in her office when we arrived, and Janie rushed over to her like she did with every new person she met. Strangers were some of her favorite people.

"You must be Janie. I'm Dr. Chandler," the doctor said with a smile.

"Nice to meet you," Janie said, smiling in return.

"Did Christopher and Hannah tell you anything about me?"

She shook her head.

"I know you've had lots of doctors before, but I'm a special kind of doctor. I'm a feelings doctor for kids. Do you know what that is?"

Janie tilted her head to the side, puzzled. "A feelings doctor?"

"Yes, my job is to help kids learn about feelings, but mostly we just play. Do you like to play?"

Janie's eyes lit up. "We get to play?" She pointed around the room. "With these toys?"

"You sure do. What do you want to play with first?"

Janie skipped over to the dollhouse in the corner. I hadn't noticed it when Christopher and I had been there by ourselves. It was almost three feet tall with two stories. There was miniature doll furniture in every room, and the bedrooms had actual carpet. Someone had taken a lot of time to put it together and added special touches like knitted blankets on the beds and tiny throw pillows on all the couches. It was every little girl's dream house.

"Do you like the dollhouse?" Dr. Chandler asked.

Janie nodded. Her face was flushed with excitement.

Dr. Chandler walked over and sat next to her on the floor. She pulled out a container. "Why don't you pick the family you want to put in the dollhouse?" The container was filled with every kind of doll imaginable—men, women, girls, boys, even animals. All different shapes and sizes.

I stood rooted to my spot, unsure of my role. Was I just supposed to watch them play? Join in? So far, each therapist had been different. I looked to Dr. Chandler for guidance, but she was intensely focused on watching Janie search through the dolls. Janie carefully pulled them out one by one and studied them before sorting them into piles.

"Why don't we ask Hannah to join us?" Dr. Chandler asked after a few minutes had passed.

Janie didn't acknowledge she'd spoken. She just kept sorting the dolls.

"Janie, did you hear me ask you a question?"

No response.

Dr. Chandler laid her hand softly on Janie's back. "Why don't we ask Hannah to join us?"

Christopher was always trying to get Janie to include me, just like Dr. Chandler was doing. Janie responded now just like she did at home—nothing.

"I'm going to ask Hannah to join us. I want her to play, too, because it's fun to play together, and it might hurt Hannah's feelings if we don't include her." Her voice was sweet but managed to convey authority at the same time. "Hannah, would you like to join us?"

"Sure." I moved over to the dollhouse and plopped down on the floor next to Dr. Chandler. I looked at the piles Janie had sorted. She'd separated the women from the rest of the dolls and put them in a pile all by themselves, away from the others.

"I pick these," she said proudly. She brought the dolls she'd selected to play with into the house. I wasn't surprised when I saw she'd chosen a white male doll with a little girl doll. She set them at the dining room table and announced, "They're going to eat dinner."

I looked over at Dr. Chandler. Had she noticed that Janie had gotten rid of all the grown female dolls? Did she see what Janie was doing?

"What are they eating?" Dr. Chandler asked.

"Hot dogs and ice cream."

"Yummy. That sounds delicious. I love ice cream."

"Me too," Janie said.

"Does Hannah like to eat ice cream too?"

No response.

"Does Hannah like to eat ice cream too?"

Janie started humming underneath her breath.

"Can you tell me about your family in the dollhouse?"

She pointed to the man sitting in the chair. "This is the daddy." She pointed to the little girl in the chair next to him. "And this is the girl."

"Is there a mommy?"

Janie curled her lips in disgust. "No. There's no mommy."

The rest of the session went the same way. I followed them around while they played, and Dr. Chandler asked her questions. Once it was over, she asked her receptionist to take Janie into the waiting room and read with her while she talked to me alone.

"That must've been really hard for you," she said as soon as she had closed the door behind her.

I was on the verge of tears. "It wasn't easy." I forced a smile.

She led me back over to the rug, and we sat down. Her face flooded with concern. "Janie clearly has some attachment issues, but they're not with you." She folded her hands on her lap. "She's acting out her attachment issues with you, but they're not directed at you, even though they seem like they are. They're directed at her mother. Think about what we know about her mother . . ." She held up her fingers as she spoke. "She locked her in a trailer and never let her out. Not once. She tied her up with a leash like a dog and barely fed her. Didn't take care of her. But that barely scratches the surface. We only know the story based on what her body tells us. We can only guess at the rest. It makes perfect sense that she hates her mother. But not just her mother—all mothers. She associates women with mothers, and unfortunately, you happen to be in that role. All her anger and feelings toward her biological mother are directed at you." She took a deep breath. "But that doesn't make it any easier on you. It has to hurt."

I desperately wanted to tell her that her theory only made sense if Becky was the one who had hurt her. There was no way to know if that was true until Janie started talking about it, since there was definitely no asking Becky about it. For a second, I considered breaking the rules and telling her that Janie's mom wasn't missing—she was dead—but Piper had assured us it was the best thing for everyone's safety if we kept it a secret until they had followed up on all their leads. They wanted whoever had hurt Becky to think she was still alive or at least be unsure.

I let out a deep sigh. "Nobody else gets to see how it really is. Christopher acts like it's not that big of a deal, and it makes me feel crazy."

"You're not crazy. She's deliberately avoiding anything and everything that has to do with you."

"What am I supposed to do?" I asked.

"There's nothing you can do right now," she said. "She's had a traumatic disconnect from love and attachment with a maternal figure. In her mind, the world isn't a safe place, and mothers can't be trusted. Think about it—usually when babies cry, they're picked up or fed when they're hungry. But Janie's never had this. She doesn't trust you, so she rejects you even though you're exactly what she needs the most."

I listened as she rattled off therapy goals for Janie. The first thing she wanted to do was teach her how to identify and name her emotions. She explained young children thought abuse was their fault, and our overarching goal would always be helping Janie understand that she wasn't bad. She'd work on developing their relationship and building some of Janie's other skills before she tackled her attachment issues. It all sounded very intense.

I filled Christopher in on the session when he got home that night. He got angry when I described the session, like I'd gone without him to create a secret alliance with Dr. Chandler, even though he'd known all about the appointment. We'd talked about it beforehand.

"You told me to take her by herself," I cried. "We could've rescheduled the appointment if you wanted to be there."

"I just didn't know you'd make all these important decisions together." His forehead was pinched.

I threw up my hands. "We didn't make any decisions. The only thing we decided was that Janie is going to need a lot of therapy, and we already knew that."

He watched Janie thumbing through books on the coffee table in the living room. She hummed under her breath while she looked. "She doesn't even know she's hurting you by ignoring you."

"Oh my God, Christopher. She knows she's doing it, and she's doing it on purpose." I tried to keep the anger out of my voice. Sometimes I caught her sneaking glances at me when she didn't think I was looking, and there was no mistaking the smugness on her face when she talked with someone while I was in the same room or in close proximity.

"It's just not her fault."

"I wish you'd hear what I'm saying to you. I'm actually agreeing with you. It's not her fault. She can't help what her mom did to her, and she doesn't even realize that's why she hates me, but Christopher, she does hate me."

TWENTY-TWO

Christopher Bauer

I listened as Dr. Chandler explained again how Janie's behavior was motivated by attention; it didn't matter whether it was positive or negative. She'd drilled it into our heads since our second session that we needed to ignore her bad behavior whenever we could because she fed off the attention and emotional energy that we gave her when she was acting out. We only praised her and paid attention when she did something positive, no matter how small it was. So far, it was working. We'd had nine fewer tantrums this week.

"I think it's time that we tackled Janie's selective mutism," she said next.

I hated the name and the fact that Dr. Chandler had stuck a label on her behavior. I didn't like labeling children with psychological disorders. They were too young to be slapped with mental health diagnoses. Kids changed constantly. And besides, how could they make any kind of diagnosis about her psychological state when she was so traumatized and far behind developmentally? They needed to give her time to catch up first.

"During your nighttime reading routine tonight, I want you to explain to Janie that you would like her to tell Hannah good night after you finish reading. All she has to say is good night. That's it. Let her know that you're no longer going to tell her good night unless she tells Hannah good night, too, because it's not fair to say good night to you without saying good night to her," Dr. Chandler said with conviction.

"And if she doesn't do it?" I asked.

"Then you don't tell her good night," Dr. Chandler said as if it was going to be that simple.

"It seems really mean." And childish, I wanted to add, but I didn't say it out loud. She was supposed to be the expert.

"Janie needs to learn that the two of you are a unit and if she hurts Hannah, it hurts your feelings, too, because you care about Hannah as much as you do her." Her voice reminded me of how she spoke to Janie—steady, never flying too high or sinking too low. "Children of trauma are experts at triangulation."

"Triangulation?" I asked.

"The child will act a certain way with one parent and a different way with the other parent. They try all kinds of things to drive a wedge in the parents' relationship."

"Janie doesn't do that."

Hannah smacked the pillow she always kept cradled in her lap during our sessions. "Are you serious? She absolutely does too."

"When?"

"When?" Her face contorted in anger. "All the time. Ever since I met her. Remember, she wouldn't even talk to me that day?"

"She was upset. She would've refused to talk to anyone."

Hannah vehemently shook her head. "I used to think that way, but I don't anymore. She's always been threatened by me."

I snorted. "Threatened by you? You act like she's some jealous girlfriend. She's a little girl, Hannah."

"Don't you think I know that?" she snapped.

Dr. Chandler raised her hand. "Okay, I can see I've touched a nerve. This is good."

I looked at her like she was crazy. "How is this good?"

"It illustrates perfectly how she's worked to pit the two of you against each other," she said.

Both Hannah and I looked at her in confusion.

"Right now, Janie thinks you're on her side and that it's the two of you against Hannah."

"But I am on her side . . ." I didn't mean it like I was against Hannah, but I was Janie's biggest cheerleader. I would always be on her side and looking out for her best interests.

"There're no sides. That's the thing." She leaned forward, getting closer to me. "The three of you are a family. Nobody is against anybody. All of you are together, and hurting family members is not okay. That's what we're trying to teach her through this exercise."

I'd forgotten all about the exercise.

"What are we supposed to do if she doesn't say good night to me?" Hannah asked.

"Then you say good night to her, and Christopher doesn't. After that, you proceed to do what you always do. It's not like you're ignoring her completely or anything like that. Stick to the rest of the routine."

"The rest of her routine means I go to sleep on her floor," I said.

"Then that's what you do," she said matter-of-factly.

"I don't think it's a good idea," I told Hannah on the drive home. I hadn't paid attention to the last ten minutes of our session because I'd been trying to wrap my head around purposefully manipulating a six-year-old child, especially one who'd been traumatized, into doing something you wanted them to. Dr. Chandler kept telling us Janie's silence toward Hannah was her way of communicating her anger and hurt toward her mother. If that was the case, and I agreed that it was, then I didn't understand how forcing Janie to talk to Hannah was a good idea. She was communicating her feelings in the only way she knew how, and everything I'd researched stressed the importance of letting abused children make their own choices.

Janie had a right to be angry at her mom. Dr. Chandler was supposed to be working on helping her express her feelings toward her mother during their individual sessions. She said kids often played out what they'd gone through, and Janie was beginning to act out what she'd experienced. I didn't understand why we couldn't just give Janie time to work through her feelings about her mom. Once she'd expressed them, I was willing to bet she'd start talking to Hannah on her own without us pushing her. I was against forcing her to talk to Hannah. Nothing about it sat well with me.

She huffed. "What's the point of going to therapy if you're not going to do what the therapist suggests?"

"Maybe she's not the best therapist for us." There were other therapists who specialized in attachment issues. I'd looked them up on my own after Piper had suggested seeing one. Dr. Chandler had great reviews, but so did many of the others.

"Piper recommended her. She's the best there is." She glared at me.

I dropped the subject, but I was nervous about doing it and grew more anxious the closer it came to bedtime. I didn't disagree with setting boundaries with Janie, but she was too fragile to be pushed. What was wrong with letting her act out until she got it out of her system? Besides, hurting someone on purpose who'd already been harmed so much just seemed inherently wrong. Why couldn't Hannah see that?

We tucked her into bed together like we always did and read *Harold and the Purple Crayon* twice since it was her latest obsession. She knew most of the words by heart. Hannah reached over and gave her a big hug and kiss like she always did despite Janie's unresponsiveness. Tonight was no different. Janie sat stiff as a board with her hands at her sides.

"Good night, Janie," Hannah said.

Janie ignored her. I'd been hoping tonight would be the night she decided to start speaking to her again and I wouldn't have to go through with the plan.

"Honey, Hannah said good night to you, and it's not nice to ignore her. It hurts her feelings when you ignore her," I recited just as Dr. Chandler had instructed me. "We are a family, and it's not okay for you to hurt Hannah's feelings. I want you to say good night to her."

She glared at me.

"I'm not going to tell you good night unless you tell Hannah good night because it's not fair. We practice fairness in our family." It all sounded right but felt wrong in my gut.

She narrowed her eyes to slits. "No."

Hannah slid off the bed. "Come on, Christopher. It's time for bed."

Janie turned to look at her with a murderous glare. Usually, she ignored her completely, like Hannah was an invisible woman. It was the first time in weeks I'd seen her respond to her at all. I didn't know if it was a good sign or a bad one. Hannah held out her hand to me, and I took it. She led me down to the pallet of blankets on the floor like I was a child. Janie leaned over and stared at us.

"I'm going to sleep now," I said.

"No! You have to say good night to me! Say good night to me!" Janie screamed.

Hannah walked over to the light and flicked it off. She left the room, but I saw her shadow hovering in the hallway. I closed my eyes and pretended to sleep.

Janie started wailing. "Say good night! Say good night!" She picked up her stuffed animals and hurled them at me. She ripped her bed apart and threw each piece of bedding at me until she was left with just the bare mattress.

I gritted my teeth, forcing myself not to move. I wanted to comfort her so badly. It physically hurt not to speak or reach for her.

You're doing the right thing. Dr. Chandler said it would help, I recited again and again while I tried to stay strong.

She alternated between screaming and crying for the next two hours. Finally, she was silent. I gave her a few more minutes before I breathed a sigh of relief that it was finally over. We'd made it through whatever weird psyche battle we were going through. I got on my knees and peeked up at her bed to make sure she was asleep.

She was curled up against the wall, rocking back and forth. Her legs were pulled up to her chest, her arms wrapped around them. She'd ripped her clothes off, including her diaper, so she was completely naked. I looked closer. There was stuff all over her mouth, and her chest was covered in vomit. Guilt pummeled me. I'd made her cry so hard she'd thrown up. I jumped up, flicked the light switch on, and ran back to her. The sticky substance wasn't vomit—it was blood.

"Janie!" I yelled. I grabbed her face in my hands. Her bottom lip was gushing blood. Pieces of flesh were missing. Hannah had raced into the room when I had turned on the light, and she stood beside me, staring at Janie in horror.

"How did that happen? I don't understand," she said in disbelief.

"She chewed through her skin," I said.

CASE #5243

Interview: Piper Goldstein

I stared at the picture in front of me. It was the one from Janie's second emergency room visit—the time she'd gotten twelve stitches in her bottom lip. The same one that was in the file on my desk. I should've known it was one they'd use. I didn't wait for them to ask questions.

"I know what you're thinking, but it's not true. They didn't hurt her. She did it to herself. I believed them and not because I'm stupid. I saw Janie get so mad once that she chewed the flesh off her own finger. Not her fingernail. The actual flesh of her finger. So no, I never once considered that the Bauers had hurt her. I called an emergency meeting with them the next day because the social worker from the hospital had reported the incident. I—"

Ron interrupted me. "I read that report. That social worker seemed pretty convinced that the Bauers were hurting Janie."

I shook my head. "It didn't look good. I'll admit that. She'd only been with them for a little while, and she'd already ended up in the emergency room twice, but I spoke with Dr. Chandler, and their story checked out. They were only doing what she'd instructed them to do."

"Did they keep going back to Dr. Chandler?"

"They did."

"Even after she'd suggested a therapy practice that ended up hurting Janie?"

"Yes, they continued seeing Dr. Chandler. Because you want to know the craziest thing about that entire incident?" I didn't wait for either of them to answer. "It worked. Janie started talking to Hannah again."

TWENTY-THREE

Hannah Bauer

Christopher stood holding the trunk open for me so we could set the groceries inside. We were trying to figure out what to grab on the way home to eat for dinner while Janie pulled at his pant leg trying to get his attention. He'd practically dragged her through the parking lot.

"Janie, you have to wait your turn. Christopher and I are talking," I said without looking at her.

She started whining and switched into baby talk while she tugged on him. I looked at him pointedly just as he was about to say something to her. Dr. Chandler was continually working with him on not allowing Janie to interrupt our conversations. He caught himself.

"Go on—what were you saying?" he asked me.

I rattled off our options again, and he nodded as I spoke, but I was sure he wasn't registering anything I was saying.

"Sure, let's just do . . ." He looked down. I followed his gaze. Janie wasn't there.

My heart stopped.

"Janie!" we screamed at the same time.

We took off running in opposite directions, yelling her name. I rounded a corner and spotted her cutting in between two cars. I sprinted after her and grabbed her arm.

I got down into her face. "You cannot do that. Do you understand me? You can't run off in a busy parking lot. You could have really gotten hurt."

She jerked away and looked up at me defiantly. Christopher rushed up behind me. She started crying as soon as she saw him, and he scooped her into his arms. "Sweetie, you can't do that. It's dangerous to run across a busy parking lot. You could've been hit by a car."

She batted her eyelashes at him and wrapped her arms around his neck. "I'm sorry, Daddy."

Calling him Daddy was a new thing, and he turned to mush on the spot every time. She had yet to call me Mommy, except that time at Target when she'd yelled that I was hurting her, and I tried to pretend like it didn't bother me, but of course it did.

He rubbed her back. "It's okay. Just please don't do that again."

"I won't. I promise, Daddy."

He had forgotten all about it, but I couldn't let it go. I replayed the scene all day long. I waited until we were in bed that night to bring it up. I rolled over to face him and said, "You know Janie took off earlier today to get your attention, right?"

He shrugged. "Maybe, but she's also impulsive. You know how she gets."

I shook my head even though he couldn't see it in the dark. "She did it on purpose. You were talking to me and ignoring her. She hates when you ignore her, so she ran across the street so you'd pay attention to her."

"You give her way too much credit," he said. He rolled over, his back to me. "Good night. I love you."

"I love you too," I said. We were always so cordially polite with each other when we were mad—sickeningly polite, really. Maybe things would be better if we got into one of the feet-stamping, book-throwing kinds of fights other couples had, because this way we just ignored anything emotionally uncomfortable without having to ever deal with it.

We still hadn't talked about the fact that Janie was speaking to me again. We pretended like the weeks of silence had never happened, and I might have been able to go on pretending if things had gone back to normal, but they hadn't. It had created a shift in my relationship with Janie, and I didn't like it. I didn't know how to fix it either.

I'd tried to talk to Christopher about it, but he didn't understand my feelings because his relationship with Janie hadn't been affected by the weeks of silence and the stitches incident. Christopher hadn't wanted to go back to Dr. Chandler afterward, but I'd insisted. She'd said what we were going through was one of the most common problems couples experienced when they became parents—figuring out how to do it together. Even though I knew what was going on, it didn't make it any easier.

I was hoping it'd be better when Janie went to school. We had all agreed it was time for her to start. She needed to be around other kids, and I needed to get back to my job. But we had run into a problem when we had started shopping for schools because Janie wasn't potty trained. We had jumped into a crash course of potty training, and we'd been fighting over it all weekend. We had gotten her one of those cute potty chairs with the music and lights, thinking that it might help, but she still wasn't having any of it. She crossed her arms and shook her head whenever we asked her to sit on it.

"Why don't you go together?" Christopher had suggested after we'd spent another three hours trying to get her to go.

"What do you mean?" I had asked.

He'd pointed toward the regular toilet. "Go together. You sit there, and she sits there. Maybe it'll help."

I was an intensely private person about everything in the bathroom. We had been married for six years, and Christopher had never seen me pee. I didn't even like to shower with him. He was the total opposite. He couldn't care less. I was always yelling at him to shut the bathroom door.

"Are you serious?" I'd asked.

He'd shrugged. "Why not? What's more effective than watching someone do it?"

"Whatever. Why don't we try reading her *Once upon a Potty* again? Where'd you put it?" I had flipped through the other books on the floor.

"You're not going to do it? You don't even want to try and see if it will work?" He hadn't moved from his spot in front of the bathroom door.

"Of course I'm not going to do it. You know me. How could you even ask?"

"I would do anything for her."

It wasn't what he'd said. It was how he'd said it, like he'd do anything for her, but I wouldn't.

"We're trying to potty train her, Christopher, not give her a kidney." Normally, he would've laughed. Instead he'd said nothing, just turned and walked out of the room.

I reached toward my nightstand and grabbed my phone, quickly tapping out a text to Allison.

We need to talk tomorrow. When are you free?

She'd had lots of problems with Greg after their boys had been born. They'd almost split up. He'd moved out for a while but had eventually moved back in after they'd sorted it out. Allison liked to say that your chances of getting divorced decreased greatly after your kids turned five. Did that mean we had five more years of this, or did we get to take the accelerated course since Janie was so much older than a newborn?

TWENTY-FOUR

Christopher Bauer

Exploring Times Preschool buzzed with activity. Kids of different ages moved around the room, gathering materials, washing dishes, counting beads, and checking out what their friends were doing. They were the first school on our list, and so far they'd exceeded all our expectations. Exploring Times was a true Montessori school—everything child size. Janie had a lot of catching up to do, and we didn't want her to feel like she was behind the other kids, which was why the Montessori approach was perfect for her. It would allow her to work at her own pace and in her own learning style.

I pointed to a group of kids lying underneath a table, covered in smocks and painting the table above them. "What are they doing?"

The lead teacher, Mrs. Allulo, laughed. "We've been studying Michelangelo's artwork, and they were all fascinated by the Sistine Chapel, so I wanted to give them an opportunity to see how hard it must've been for him to paint the ceiling."

Hannah squeezed my hand excitedly. It'd taken a while, but we'd finally potty trained Janie and had started touring preschools. We'd used a sticker-chart system for the potty training that we'd created during one of our family sessions with Rhonda. We still met with Rhonda once a month for Janie's follow-up care. At one point, I'd almost given up because Janie hadn't had any interest in using the toilet and didn't care when she soiled herself. Then one day, a few weeks ago, something clicked, and she'd been accident-free ever since, even at night.

Potty training was a huge victory in our house and renewed our hope. It rejuvenated us in the same way our parents coming to stay with us had. All the bathroom stuff had brought laughter into parenting for the first time, and it was wonderful—the first glimpse into the fun parts of parenting. Hannah felt it too. There was a new pep in her step, and her old confidence was starting to come back.

"Janie's not going to be that much older than some of the boys in transitional kindergarten. I would recommend having her finish this year in transitional kindergarten since she's had no exposure to school, especially because the program runs through the summer. Then you start her in kindergarten in the fall," Mrs. Allulo explained.

We signed her up to begin the following week. We arranged a special meeting with the director and her teacher to go over her history and background. We'd been on the fence about telling them everything because we wanted people to treat Janie like a normal kid. We didn't want anyone to pity her or treat her differently, but it was too dangerous not to tell them because of all her issues. She was making small gains every day when it came to feeding, but we were a long way from being able to trust her not to eat inedible objects. Those were the things I worried about, but Hannah's biggest concern was that Janie had no exposure to other children besides the ones at the park and would be at a huge social loss.

"I'm so nervous for her," Hannah said on the drive home. "She's going to be so far behind the other kids. She doesn't know her ABCs, how to count to ten—very basic things. Every one of the kids in that class is going to know that stuff. They're going to think either she's really dumb or we're terrible parents." Her face was cinched with worry.

"You know how much she likes to meet new people. She'll probably be friends with half the class by the end of the day, and it won't even matter."

"Are you worried about . . ." She paused, eyeing Janie in the back seat. "You know . . ."

She intentionally didn't finish the sentence. The longer Janie's case went without leads, the more we started getting used to living with ambiguity even if it was scary. We didn't have any choice. Neither of us acknowledged how scared we were to let Janie out of our sight.

I reached over and squeezed her knee while she drove. "She'll be safe. The doors are locked, and they aren't going to sign her out with anyone besides us or our parents."

I was scrolling through golf scores that night when Hannah motioned for me to follow her into Janie's bedroom. She lay down next to Janie on the floor. "What are you playing with?" she asked.

Janie lifted up the necklace she was working on and proudly displayed her progress. My mom had sent her a wooden bead set last week. We almost hadn't given it to her because we'd thought it'd be too hard for her, but we'd been wrong. She loved it and spent hours fitting the colorful beads on the string. It was an excellent exercise for her fine motor skills, and she didn't even know it.

"That is so pretty," Hannah said. "I really like the pattern you're using."

Janie held it up and pointed. "It goes pink, purple, heart."

"I love it." Colors had been the easiest thing to learn. She'd picked them up immediately before she'd left the hospital. One of her favorite things to do was go through her crayon bin, picking out different ones and having us read what they were. Hannah laid out a piece of paper next to the beads. "I made something too."

Janie was immediately drawn to the bright colors. "What's that?"

"It's a map." Hannah pointed as she talked. "This is our house. Then this is the park over here, and this is the grocery store."

"What's this?" Janie pointed to the school.

"That's a school," Hannah said. "Remember how we explained that a school is a place where kids go to learn?"

Janie nodded.

"When kids get big enough, then they go to school. And guess what?"

Janie's eyes filled with excitement. "What?"

"You're big enough to go to school now. This school?" Hannah pointed to the map again. "It's very close to our house, and it's the one that you get to go to on Monday."

The excitement drained from Janie's face. "What about Daddy?" she said.

I plopped on the floor next to them. "I'll be at work while you're at school, but I'm going to be super excited to hear all about it when you get home."

"So just Mommy?" she asked.

I froze. It was the first time she'd called Hannah Mommy. Hannah tried to keep her composure and not make a big deal out of the moment. I reached over and squeezed her knee, knowing how much it meant to her.

"No, Mommy won't be there either," she said. Her voice wavered despite her efforts at control. "School is just for kids and teachers."

Janie shook her head. "I don't wanna go to school."

I planned on going with Hannah to drop Janie off on her first day of school, but I got an emergency call in the middle of the night. There had been a terrible accident on Interstate 10, and I had to rush into surgery. When I finally finished, my phone was filled with Hannah's texts. It was a play-by-play of their morning:

She's refusing her breakfast.

I can't get her to eat anything.

Ugh . . . she's throwing a fit about her clothes.

This is the outfit she chose. Wtf? Seriously?

We're out the door. No food.

Just dropped her off. She was kicking and screaming when I left.

I didn't bother texting. I called her right away, and she answered on the second ring. I could tell she was in the car from the echo in her Bluetooth.

"Sounds like it was a pretty rough morning," I said.

"I'm on my way to pick her up now." There was no mistaking the irritation in her voice.

I glanced down at my watch. "It's only ten thirty. What happened?"

"Mrs. Allulo called because Janie had two accidents and was out of clean clothing. I sent her with an extra set of clothes, but she already pooped in those, too, so I have to come get her. I kept apologizing, and Mrs. Allulo was great about it. She said kids often revert to earlier behavior when they start school and have accidents."

"I'm sure she's right," I said. "Things will get better. It's just another adjustment period for her."

But Janie kept soiling herself at school. She stripped off her clothes and ran around the classroom naked. She refused to follow directions and couldn't be redirected to other activities. At first, Mrs. Allulo was understanding and compassionate. She kept assuring us that it was only a transitional period and Janie would eventually adjust. But then Janie bit another child when he wouldn't give her the toy she wanted, and Mrs. Allulo called us in for an emergency meeting.

She folded her hands in front of her on the desk and didn't waste any time getting down to business. "I'm sorry, but I don't think Janie is a good fit for Exploring Times."

"But it hasn't even been that long. Can't we give her more time to adjust?" Hannah asked.

Mrs. Allulo's face, which had previously been so kind and soft, was firm and unrelenting. "Unfortunately, it's a situation where her behavior problems affect the rest of the class, and I can't have that."

"Don't all behavior problems affect the class?" I asked.

"Yes, but it's different with Janie. She needs constant one-to-one attention, and we just can't provide that because it's not fair to the other kids. And I have to be really honest with you about her toilet issues—it's a health hazard to have her spreading feces. We stressed how important toilet training was during our interviews." She looked completely grossed out.

"She's potty trained. She never has accidents at home," I said.

Mrs. Allulo looked at me with disbelief. I couldn't blame her for thinking we were lying. Janie hadn't made it through a single day at school without an accident. "I've put together a list of other schools that you might want to look into." She handed us a sheet of paper and rose from her desk.

Hannah fumed as we walked to the parking lot and waited until we got in the car until she exploded.

"She did all of that on purpose." Her face was flushed.

"Who?" I asked. "Mrs. Allulo?"

She rolled her eyes. "No—Janie. She got herself kicked out of school on purpose."

I shook my head. "Please don't start."

She snorted. "Start? C'mon, Christopher. She never wanted to go to school."

"Yes, but only because it was too much for her too soon. Something always happens when we push her to do things she's not ready for."

"No, something always happens when we make her do things that she doesn't want to do." Her jaw was set in a straight line.

"I can't get into this argument with you again." I waved her off.

"Fine. It's not like anything I say will make a difference anyway." She pursed her lips and stared out the window.

Dr. Chandler advised us to get Janie into another school and said it might take a while to find a good fit, so we didn't waste any time getting her into the Montessori school that was second on our list. We had to drive all the way across the city to get there, but we didn't have another choice. I sat down with Janie the night before her first day and explained how important it was for her to have good behavior at school. We went over what was expected of her just like we'd done in our session with Dr. Chandler the previous day.

Janie didn't even last a week at her new school. She had the same type of behavior problems that she had had at Exploring Times. They weren't nearly as tolerant as the other school had been, and she crossed the line when she soiled herself, grabbed a hunk of her poop, and flung it at the wall. This time, the director didn't bother scheduling a meeting with us. She emailed us and asked us not to bring her back on Monday.

"Janie, why did you do that at school today?" I asked as we walked out of the school.

She shrugged. "I don't know. Can we play Candy Land when we get home? Please?"

"We're not talking about Candy Land right now. We want to know why you pooped your pants at school and threw it." Hannah looked furious.

"I don't like school." She grinned at us. There was no mistaking the pride on her face. My stomach rolled.

Hannah turned to look at me with the most "I told you so" expression I'd ever seen her wear.

CASE #5243

Interview: Piper Goldstein

"You're saying that all this time Janie never asked about her mother? She never said anything about Becky?" Ron asked.

"She didn't."

He looked at me in disbelief. I wasn't sure he believed much of what I said.

"And you didn't think there was anything odd or off about that?" Luke asked. The two of them exchanged a look.

"No, not at all. Kids who have been traumatized don't talk about what they went through until they're safe. I didn't expect her to talk about it until months down the road."

"You at least tried to talk to her about it, though, didn't you?" Ron asked.

"Of course I tried. I don't know how many times I have to tell you that. I questioned Janie about her mother."

I'd asked all the standard questions. It was one of the reasons our first meeting hadn't gone well.

"Can we talk about your mommy?" I had asked that day.

Janie had stuck out her lip and crossed her stick arms across her chest. "No."

"I can see that you don't want to talk about your mommy. Is it because your mommy is the one who hurt you?"

She had pointed to the hospital door.

"We can talk about something else if you'd like, but it's not time for me to go yet," I'd said.

Her eyes had filled with tears. "You go." She'd pointed to the door again.

"How about we play with your stuffed animals?" I had picked up the dinosaur and elephant she'd been playing with earlier and danced them on the bed.

"No!" she'd screamed. "No!"

I had quickly handed her the toys. "Here you go. You can have them."

She'd snatched them from me, hurling them against the wall, and screamed like she was in pain. Two nurses had rushed into the room and run to her bedside. Janie had thrown her arms around the one wearing her hair in a tight bun and buried her face in her chest. Her frail body had shaken with sobs.

"Make her go. I don't like Piper. She's mean."

Every conversation we'd had about her mother since then had gone the same way. After a while, I had stopped asking because it didn't matter. Not as far as my job was concerned. It wasn't my job to find Becky's killer—it was theirs.

"Did she ever speak with the Bauers about what happened in the trailer?"

"Not as far as I know."

"And they would've told you?"

"I'm pretty sure."

"Did they ask you what was happening with the case?"

"They were more concerned with helping Janie transition into their family and society than what was going on in the case."

Ron rubbed his chin. "I'm having a hard time believing they weren't worried about it."

"It didn't seem weird to me at the time. It just didn't. If it had, I would've done something about it."

"Really? They were just totally fine with Janie's mother being left for dead in a closet? The same closet where Janie was tied up before she escaped? They didn't want the case solved?"

"They didn't think it mattered."

"What?" Luke snorted. "How could it not matter?"

I shrugged. "I don't know. It just didn't."

"So then why did you ask them if they still wanted to go through with the adoption?"

I tried to hide my surprise. Who had they been talking to? Doing my best to appear unmoved, I said, "Yes, I did ask the Bauers if they wanted to go through with the adoption, but only because it's my legal responsibility to do so. I have to let them know there's no going back after they sign the adoption paperwork. Once you adopt a child, you retain the same responsibilities you would have if you'd given birth to the child, and you're legally obligated to care for them until their eighteenth birthday." My voice grew stronger as I spoke. "Foster-to-adopt parents have the option of deciding not to care for a child any longer. Fostering is often temporary or a trial period to see if they are a good match. Sometimes families are matched with children that aren't a good fit, or they discover it's not as easy as they thought it'd be. It's hard work to foster-adopt a child. Lots of foster parents are relieved when we offer them a way out."

"The Bauers still wanted to proceed even with all the difficulties they were already experiencing?" Luke asked.

"More than ever."

I'd never forget the day I had brought them Janie's new birth certificate, proudly stamped *Janie Bauer*. I'd waved it in front of them. "It's official—she's yours!"

The two of them had thrown their arms around each other and jumped up and down, spinning around the living room. Janie had danced with them. Christopher's grin had been so wide you could see what he had looked like as a little boy. He'd grabbed me and pulled me into their circle, twirling me around with them. Their happiness had been contagious, and I couldn't help but laugh.

The memories hurt. I looked down at my hands twisting on my lap. This case would haunt me in ways I would never forget.

TWENTY-FIVE

Christopher Bauer

It'd been so long since Hannah and I had been alone at night, and we didn't know what to do with ourselves. We'd been on a handful of dates, but it was the first time we'd been alone together in the house since bringing Janie home. It was Janie's first night sleeping in her room alone. We'd sleep trained Janie through the SnoozeEasy program that Dr. Chandler had recommended. It was a series of small steps toward sleeping independently that started with me putting a chair next to her bed and getting rid of the pallet on the floor. I sat in the chair while she fell asleep. Gradually, I inched the chair across the room until eventually I was out of her room completely. It wasn't as hard as I had expected. Maybe it was because we took our time doing it or because she was finally ready. Either way, it worked. Tonight, I'd kissed her good night and walked out. Hannah had checked on her ten minutes ago, and she was fast asleep.

We sat on the couch in silence. Part of what I loved about Hannah was how easy things were between us. It was always so natural. I had always thought it was odd how you could go from not knowing someone at all to wondering how you'd ever lived without them, but that's how it was with Hannah. We were two separate people who balanced each other out like a teeter-totter without even trying. But everything felt strange, and I didn't know how to act.

She felt it, too, because she always twirled her hair when she was nervous, and she'd been twisting a chunk around her fingers since I'd sat down. She was afraid to make eye contact; her eyes kept darting around the living room, never still.

"I think we did the right thing keeping Janie out of school for a while longer," she said. "School was clearly too much for her too fast."

I nodded, but I didn't want to talk about Janie tonight. I couldn't remember the last time we'd spent the evening discussing something other than her. Even when we tried, she invariably found her way back into our discussions. "You want a drink?"

She nodded, looking relieved.

I jumped up and headed into the kitchen, grateful for the distraction. I reached for our bottles in the liquor cabinet above the refrigerator. The last time we'd shared a drink in the house was during Janie's welcome-home party. It seemed like ages ago; so much had changed since then. I poured Hannah a glass of her favorite red wine and myself some bourbon. I took a swig from the bottle before screwing the cap back on and returning it to its spot.

Hannah's eyes lit up when she saw me coming back into the living room with drinks. I handed hers to her, and she tried to look nonchalant as she tilted it back, but there wasn't anything casual about her sip. I took a seat next to her. The silence stretched out between us.

"This is nice," she said, her body relaxing as she finally settled back into the couch.

"It is. It feels strange, though, huh?"

"It does." She glanced at me shyly.

I scooted down the couch so I was next to her and put my arm around her shoulder. She nestled up to me like she used to.

"I've missed you," I said, breathing in the smell of her.

"I've missed you too," she said. She rubbed her hand on my leg.

I brought her close and kissed her tenderly. I ran my fingers through her hair, all the way down her back. She kissed me back. I drank in the taste of her before pulling back and gazing into her eyes. She returned my stare with *that look*—the one reserved only for me. I brushed my hand against her cheek.

"I couldn't imagine doing any of this without you," I said.

Her eyes burned with longing and love. She took off her shirt and tossed it to the ground. "You don't have to."

We fell back onto the couch, groping and clawing at each other like teenagers. When it was time to go to our bedroom, we tiptoed in as quietly as we could so that we didn't wake Janie, our hands over our mouths to keep from giggling. We took our time making love, savoring each moment, remembering what it felt like to be close to each other.

It felt so good that we put Janie to sleep early the next night and tumbled into bed with each other as soon as we were sure she was asleep. We lay curled up next to each other after it was over.

"Two nights in a row? When's the last time we did that?" she asked, drawing a design on my chest with her fingers.

I let out a deep laugh. So much of the frustration and resentment between us was gone, evaporated by taking the time to connect with each other. I couldn't forget how important she was to me too.

Our experience wasn't that different than other first-time parents'. We had thought we were giving up on the traditional kind of parenthood by adopting Janie, but we were baptized into parenthood in the same way every first-time parent was. It was all-encompassing. Everything else was pushed aside, and we went into the baby bubble. It didn't matter that our baby was six. It was the same thing, but we were finally coming up for air.

And just like for other new parents, having a child had taken its toll on our marriage. We'd snapped at each other more than we had in our entire decade together. So many of the things that had been the fun intimacy building blocks of our relationship, like binge-watching trashy

TV, putting together jigsaw puzzles on the coffee table, and reading books in bed, had fallen by the wayside.

But there was a certain amount of pride in having survived it together. There were a lot of things that still needed to be said, and some things were still too confusing to put into words, but there would be time to do all that. For now, we were just happy to spend time alone together again and to get to know the new versions of ourselves.

TWENTY-SIX

Hannah Bauer

Pictures of exotic flowers framed each wall. I pulled the thin white gown around me as I shivered. I glanced at the magazines in the stand underneath the prescription drug brochures and nursing home pamphlets, but I was too anxious to read anything. I couldn't believe I might be going into menopause at forty-one. I hadn't had any other symptoms besides my missed periods until I had started feeling exhausted and sluggish, like I could fall asleep at any moment. Lately after we put Janie to sleep, we'd curl up on the couch to watch Netflix, and I was out within ten minutes.

"Lots of women go through menopause early now," Allison had said on the phone yesterday, but it hadn't made me feel any better, seeing as she was almost a year older than me and hadn't gone into menopause yet.

I scrolled through my phone, staring at pictures of Janie while I waited for my doctor to come back inside with the results of my blood work. She'd made so much progress in the last two months. She functioned best in a structured environment, and I'd finally found a schedule that worked well for her. The plan had never been that I would turn into a stay-at-home mom, but I'd had to put in a leave of absence at the hospital since I wasn't going back anytime soon.

Our days were filled with therapy of every kind—speech, physical, occupational, and play. Most of the therapy rooms had two-way mirrors, where I watched from the other side. I took notes throughout all her sessions so I could replicate the exercises at home.

Dr. Walsh tapped lightly on the door before entering. "Your blood work came back fine. It doesn't look like you have any sort of virus. We did find one thing in your urine, though."

My stomach flipped. What could they have found in my urine that they wouldn't have found in my blood? A bladder infection? Sugar? I flipped through scenarios quickly.

"Don't look so scared." Dr. Walsh smiled. "It's great news—you're pregnant."

Everything spun in front of me. For a second, I thought I might pass out. I grabbed the sides of the hospital bed to steady myself. "Are you sure?"

"Positive," she said, smiling at her own joke.

I didn't remember the drive home from the clinic. One minute I was in the doctor's office finding out I was pregnant, and the next minute I was in the kitchen with my mom. She tried to come visit for a few days every month, and it was a huge help. She'd gotten into town the night before. I was as shocked as if I'd found out I had a brain tumor.

"What's wrong? You're so pale," Mom said as she pulled one of the barstools out for me. "Sit down and tell me what's going on."

I slid onto the chair. "Where's Janie?" I asked.

"She's playing out back with Allison and the boys. Allison texted me on their way home from soccer practice, and I told her to stop by," she said. "Those boys just love Janie so much. She was great today. She tied her shoes by herself before they went outside."

"That's good," I said. I fanned myself with my hand, suddenly so hot.

Mom grabbed one of the other stools and pulled it next to me. "What's going on? You're scaring me."

My throat was so dry it was hard to swallow. My head swirled. "I'm pregnant," I whispered.

"What? Did you say you were pregnant?" Her voice reverberated off the kitchen walls.

I grabbed her arm. "Shhh, don't yell it out. I don't want people to know."

"What are you talking about? That's amazing news! I'm so excited for you," she gushed.

I shook my head. "I don't want people to know. I'm sure it's not going to last. I'm just shocked." My mom and I were close, so I didn't need to explain my fertility issues to her.

She looked behind her, making sure the back door was closed, before she spoke again. "How is that possible? How far along are you?"

"I don't know." I still felt like I couldn't swallow. "Can I have a glass of water?"

She jumped up and rushed over to the sink, as comfortable in our kitchen as she was in her own. She poured me a glass and brought it back to me. I gulped it down nearly halfway before stopping, wiped my mouth with the back of my sleeve, and took a deep breath. "I went to the doctor because I thought I was going into early menopause. I missed two periods, and I'm so tired lately, so I figured that's what was happening." I burst out laughing. It sounded weird, not like my normal laugh. "She took some routine blood and urine just to see if anything showed up. Turns out"—I pointed to my stomach—"this."

"And they're sure?"

"The HCG levels don't lie." It meant we had gotten pregnant the first night we had made love since bringing Janie home. I blushed at the memory, glad my mom couldn't read my thoughts.

"God, I can't believe it. After all this time. Did you call Christopher on the way home? What'd he say?"

I shook my head. "I'm not going to tell him."

She snapped her head back. "What?"

"There's no sense getting him all worked up when I'm sure I'm just going to have a miscarriage anyway. What's the point?"

"Yeah, but don't you think he'd want to know either way? Especially if you do have a miscarriage—then he can be there for you."

Piper had always told us it took a year to adjust, and she had been right. It had been almost nine months since we'd become Janie's parents, and even though it didn't look anything like we'd planned, we were reaching a new normal. Over time, three steps forward coupled with two steps backward equaled success. I wanted the miscarriage to hurry up and happen so I could be done with it and we could keep moving forward in our lives.

"Don't tell anyone, Mom, okay? Please? Promise? Not even Dad, because you know he can't keep a secret, and I don't want Allison to know this time." My miscarriages hurt her almost as much as they did me. I couldn't do that to her again. I didn't want any of us going through it another time.

My mom squeezed my arms. "You're not just a teensy bit excited?"

I shook my head. I'd trained myself a long time ago not to get excited. That was when you got hurt.

Nothing had happened by the time I went to my obstetrician appointment the following week, but that didn't mean anything. Just because there hadn't been any bleeding didn't mean I was still pregnant. I'd been down that road before.

"Do you want to wait for your husband?" the obstetrician asked. I couldn't remember her name. I had just picked the first one on the list that took my insurance. I hadn't even checked her credentials. I couldn't help but notice how different it was from the first time I'd gotten pregnant, and I would've laughed if it weren't so sad.

"No, you can go ahead and do it," I said. I turned my head to the side. I'd learned not to look. It made it easier.

She squirted the lube on my stomach and brought the transducer to it. The heartbeat was unmistakable. It pattered along like a train.

"Oh my God," I said, tears welling in my eyes. "I'm pregnant."

CASE #5243

Interview: Piper Goldstein

They kept asking me about Hannah's pregnancy like I was hiding something, but I wasn't. I had never had any clue Hannah was pregnant. None.

"Hannah didn't look pregnant the last time I saw her before she gave birth. She was always so small and tiny, so you'd think I would've noticed, but I didn't." I was usually good at picking up on those things, but she hadn't even looked like she'd gained weight. "I was shocked to find out she'd had a baby."

"Wait." Luke held up his hand. "I thought you told us you were involved with them continuously for two years."

"I was."

"But you didn't know she was pregnant until after the baby was born? So that would mean you didn't see them for at least a few months." He scribbled something in his notebook.

"I suppose."

"So you don't have any idea what happened in their home between November and January, do you?"

I shook my head.

"I'm sorry, Piper. I need you to speak your answers."

"No, but it doesn't matter. That wouldn't have changed anything."

He looked at me like he didn't believe me any more than I believed myself.

TWENTY-SEVEN

Hannah Bauer

"I can't even describe what it feels like to be carrying a child after everything I've been through," I told Allison over the phone. My secret had lasted two days. I'd grieved the idea of having a baby like it was a real death, so it was like finding out your grandfather was alive after you'd been to his funeral. It was that shocking. I couldn't help myself—I had to tell her.

"Have you told Christopher yet?"

"No, I still haven't."

"I wish you'd hurry up and tell him. You have to tell him before dinner next weekend because he's going to take one look at my face and know something's up."

I laughed. She'd always been a terrible liar. "I will."

I was afraid of Christopher's reaction. What if he wasn't happy about it and his negativity affected the baby? Made something bad happen to it? It seemed so silly since all we'd wanted for years was a baby, but I was afraid he might not want it now that we had Janie. I kept putting it off, but I couldn't put it off much longer.

We were in the middle of an episode of *Homeland* that night when I just blurted out, "I'm pregnant."

I wasn't even planning on it. It just came out.

"What did you say?" he asked.

"I'm pregnant." The words still felt strange in my mouth, even though I'd talked about it with Mom and Allison.

"What—how—I just . . . how did that happen? I don't get it . . ." He shook his head in disbelief.

I smiled. "Let me explain it to you. First, the woman has eggs, and the man releases his sperm—"

He cut me off. "This isn't funny. Seriously, how did you get pregnant?"

I flicked the TV off and turned to face him. "I don't know. I just did."

The silence stretched out between us. He stood up and paced the living room, something he only did when he was nervous. I'd watched him do it in the scrub room as he prepared for a big surgery. My stomach churned. I'd been afraid of this. I wasn't a superstitious person, but I was obsessed with keeping things positive in regard to the baby. Somehow, it felt like keeping all the negative stuff away from the baby might be the key to keeping it.

He stopped, put his hands on his hips, and asked, "How far along are you?"

"Almost three months."

"Three months?" His mouth dropped open. "How are you three months pregnant and just telling me now?"

"I just found out. I didn't know."

"How do you not know you're pregnant?"

I narrowed my eyes. "Excuse me? Do you know what it feels like to be pregnant? I just felt really tired."

"What about your period?"

"I didn't get it. I—"

"That wasn't a clue? How do you not get your period for three months and not think you're pregnant?" He ran his hands through his hair.

Anger stiffened my back. "You know what? Quit talking to me like I'm an idiot and acting like I was a teenager hiding her pregnancy. I had no clue. None. I didn't even connect being so exhausted with my missed periods. I thought I was going into menopause."

He let out a deep sigh. "I'm sorry. Really, I am. I'm just shocked. I don't even know what to say."

"You could say congratulations," I snapped. I stomped out of the living room and down the hall to our bedroom, slamming the door behind me.

TWENTY-EIGHT

CHRISTOPHER BAUER

Hannah went from not knowing she was pregnant to walking around the house with a dreamy look on her face and rubbing her stomach, even though it was still flat. She rested her hand on it like she could already feel the baby growing. Her face beamed with the glow of pregnancy, and I'd never seen her look happier.

I tried to pretend I was happy and excited about the baby, but all I could think about was Janie and how it would affect her. She was the child in front of me. It was hard to feel close to a baby that was only real in discussion. Love flooded me the instant I thought about being Janie's dad, and I kept waiting for the sudden rush of love for our new baby, but it just didn't come. It felt surreal, like it wasn't really happening or like it was happening to someone else.

"We still haven't really talked about the baby," Hannah said as we sat around the coffee table putting together our latest jigsaw puzzle. She knew me too well, and despite my attempts to appear excited, my misgivings weren't lost on her.

"Okay," I said slowly. "What do you want to talk about?"

"Really?" She looked perturbed.

"I wish I could be excited about the baby like you are, but honestly, how can I? You know it's throwing a huge wrench in our barely stable life." Normally, I would've grabbed her hand, but she'd been so cold to me lately that she'd probably just pull away anyway, so I didn't bother.

"Lots of people have two kids." Her words were as cold as her body language.

"Honey, you know this isn't the same thing." Any ounce of normalcy and stability we'd created was going to come crashing down. She knew that, too, even though she wouldn't admit it.

"I'm not sure you're connected to the baby, and I'm worried about how it's going to affect things once it's here. I thought it might help to talk about your feelings," she said in her therapist voice. We had both developed them over the past few months. We spent so much time in therapy learning how to talk about feelings with Janie that we'd become minitherapists in our conversations with each other. I was just as guilty as she was.

"I am struggling." There was no use hiding what she already knew. She waited for me to go on. I ran my hands through my hair nervously. I didn't want to upset her, but I had to tell the truth. "I'm worried about how it's going to disrupt our lives. I'm afraid of how Janie is going to react when she finds out."

"She probably won't even care. She doesn't have the ability to think six minutes into the future, let alone six months," Hannah said.

"But what about after the baby's here?" I asked. I didn't know what she'd do when she found out she had to share us.

Hannah laughed. "She's definitely going to struggle. That's a given. She is going to be a nightmare once the baby's here."

"I didn't realize you'd thought about that."

She raised her eyebrows. "Of course I did. It was the first thing I thought about. Janie's always my first thought before anything else." I could tell by the way she narrowed her eyes that I'd upset her again.

"I don't want to fight. I didn't mean to insult you. I'm just scared."

"I don't know why you're so scared. I'm the one who's going to have to be here all day dealing with the drama." Her voice had an edge to it.

I sighed. "Please, let's not get into a fight. We've been doing so well lately."

"I'm not trying to fight. It just bums me out how different you are about the baby. You were so excited when we adopted Janie, and it's been almost three weeks now, and you've barely said anything about the baby." Her lips pulled into a frown. Much like her smile lit up her entire face, her frown darkened it in the same way.

"Come here," I said, motioning toward her. She slid down the couch and into my arms. I squeezed her tightly. "I'll do better, okay? I'm really excited about the baby. I am. Things are going to be just fine." It was the first time in our marriage that I had consciously lied to her.

TWENTY-NINE

HANNAH BAUER

Allison stopped by with more bags of hand-me-down clothes. She'd gone through all Dylan and Caleb's baby clothes and pulled out anything that was gender neutral because we didn't want to know what we were having. My family was thrilled about my pregnancy, which made up for Christopher's lack of enthusiasm. They doted on me constantly.

"I'm so excited for you to be a mom," Allison said. She quickly slapped her hand over her mouth. "Oh my God, I didn't mean to say that." Her eyes darted around the room to see if Janie had heard, but she was too busy playing Uno with the boys to notice. "You're already a mom. I just meant . . . I just—"

I interrupted her. "It's fine. I know what you meant, and honestly, I feel the same way."

She looked relieved. "I know this adoption has been difficult for you, and I hope you know I've always supported your decision, but it's always made me sad that you never got to carry a baby. I'm so glad you finally get the opportunity. No woman should have to miss it. It's so magical," she said.

I giggled. "It is, and I'm loving everything about this because I never thought I'd get to have the experience. I don't even care that I'm gaining weight."

My breasts had already grown two sizes, but when you went from barely there to something to put in a bra, the only one who noticed was your husband. I couldn't wait until my stomach swelled with a pregnancy bump.

"Are you nervous about tonight?" she asked.

Tonight was the night we were going to tell Janie about the pregnancy. I still thought we should wait until we were further along, but as soon as we'd hit the four-month mark and the odds of miscarriage had dropped significantly, Christopher had been ready to break the news to her.

"I'm not worried about Janie because I don't think she's even going to notice or care. It's too abstract for her until she actually has something to see. I'm worried because I think Christopher will be disappointed with her lack of reaction," I said. "Are you sure you guys can't stay for dinner?"

"As much as I'd love to, we're going to see some movie I've never heard of, but Greg says everybody loves it."

"You could've just left the boys with us." She hadn't left the boys with us one time since Janie, and I felt bad about it. "I wish you would've."

"Oh, we're taking them with us. Didn't I tell you? We're letting them see a movie at the same time. Same theater. Different movies. It's happening." She pointed toward the back door, where their squeals and laughter let us know they were still having fun. "Hold on to that one tightly. It won't be long until you guys aren't cool enough to hang out with."

Later that evening, Christopher walked into the dining room carrying a cake. I eyed him curiously. The cake hadn't been part of our plan. He grinned and set it down in front of Janie. There was a giant blue stork carrying a wrapped-up baby in its beak etched in frosting on top.

"Daddy, I like the birdie," she squealed.

"Do you see what the bird is carrying?" he asked.

Janie nodded enthusiastically, always eager to give the right answer. "A baby!"

He grabbed my hand and pulled me next to him, wrapping his arm around my waist. I held the shirt behind my back, waiting for my cue.

"That's right. We have something really exciting to tell you about a baby." He squeezed my side.

I pulled out the T-shirt from behind my back and held it out in front of me. The neon-purple letters proclaimed, **I AM A BIG SISTER**.

"Janie, this is your special T-shirt—"

She grabbed it from me before I could read her what it said. "It's pretty." She started pulling off the shirt she had on.

Christopher laid his hand on her shoulder. "Slow down for a second, kiddo."

"There's a special message on your shirt just for you," I said.

"Really?" She flipped it over and stared at the letters. "What's it say?"

"It says, 'I am a big sister,'" I said.

She looked from me to Christopher and back again, totally lost.

We knelt in front of her. Christopher pointed to my stomach. "Your mommy is growing a baby in her stomach. Once the baby is big enough, it's going to come out of her stomach and become part of our family. That means you're going to be a big sister."

Janie poked my stomach. "There's a baby in here?"

I nodded. "Soon you'll be able to feel it move around inside me. It will kick and do all kinds of other things. It'll be so much fun."

She looked up at me. "How does it come out of here?" She poked me again, harder this time.

"Gentle when you touch my stomach, honey," I said, placing my hand on top of hers. "Sometimes the doctors have to take the baby out of mommies' stomachs, and other times, the baby comes out of a mommy's vagina."

She crinkled her nose. "Yuck. That's gross."

Christopher and I laughed.

"Can we go outside?" she asked. She pulled her arms back into the shirt she'd been wearing previously, the big-sister shirt forgotten.

"Are you excited to be a big sister?" Christopher asked.

She looked at him with confusion, like she wasn't really sure what he was asking and was trying to figure out the correct response because she loved nothing more than pleasing him. "Yes, I'm excited," she said, but her voice was flat.

—

I was determined to get Janie in school before the baby came. We'd given up on school for a while and agreed to give her more adjustment time, but all of that was different now. I wanted to get her settled while I still had the energy to help with the transition. I handled things this time and went with a different approach. I enrolled Janie in a traditional private school, one that was more structured and only a few blocks from the hospital. Part of the admissions process was a half-day visit, and Janie was grinning from ear to ear when I picked her up afterward.

"How'd it go?" I asked, buckling her into her car seat.

"I met a new friend. Her name is Elodie, and she wants to be my friend too. She says I can be the boss of her," she said. "I like this school."

She talked about Elodie until she went to bed that night. We didn't think twice about saying yes when they called to tell us she'd been accepted. Before we'd had to lead her in kicking and screaming, but this time, she went willingly and waved goodbye like she couldn't wait for me to leave.

For the first two weeks, I obsessively checked my phone, waiting for the call to tell me that she'd acted out in some way, had an accident or bit a kid, but the call never came. She liked her new school and seemed happy there. She came home excited to show Christopher and me the projects she'd made, and it wasn't long before our refrigerator was cluttered with her artwork. She called Elodie her best friend and said they were a secret team. Her teacher, Mrs. Tinney, raved about how great Janie was. She said she was one of the brightest kids in the class and had had one of the smoothest transitions she'd ever seen. We beamed with pride.

With Janie in preschool four hours every day, I started planning for the baby. Allison and my mom teased me about it mercilessly, sending me funny texts throughout the day about nesting. I didn't mind. I enjoyed every minute of it. I went through every closet and got rid of anything we hadn't worn in the last two years. Once I'd gone through all the closets, I tackled the cupboards, throwing out old Tupperware and replacing broken sets of pots and pans. I organized all the towels and washcloths in the linen closet and the hallway. I rented a carpet cleaner from Home Depot and spent two days shampooing all the rugs. Normally, I wasn't such an obsessive cleaner, but I loved it. I was getting rid of anything old and getting ready for something new.

I cleaned out everything in the office and moved all the furniture to the garage so that we could make the office into the baby's room. Back when we had thought having a child was a possibility, I had scoured Pinterest boards for baby-room ideas, but I'd deleted all my boards after we'd adopted Janie and had to start from scratch. I spent my evenings sitting next to the fire, scrolling through pictures of baby furniture and accessories. It was hard to believe that in less than two years we'd gone from spending our evenings cuddled up next to each other on the couch with our laptops open, flipping through hundreds of pictures of kids up for adoption, to preparing to welcome our second child into the world.

"We're going to have two kids. Can you believe it, Christopher? Two kids!"

He got up from the couch, walked over to my chair, and perched on the armrest. He gazed down at me. "I've never seen you look happier, and I'm pretty sure there's nothing I love more in this world than seeing you happy."

THIRTY

Christopher Bauer

It was a bad idea to have Janie at the baby shower. I didn't want to be here either. I didn't understand why I couldn't take Janie for the day while they did their thing, but Hannah insisted we come. All the husbands were invited. Baby showers were no longer women-only events, but I wouldn't mind going back to when they had been.

Usually Hannah turned into a basket case whenever we had a big party or event at the house, but since Lillian and Allison were throwing the shower, she didn't have to do much except relax and enjoy herself. She sat in the living room with her feet propped up on our embroidered stool while Lillian and Allison bustled around the house taking care of things. Her feet had swollen up as soon as she'd hit the six-month mark. Janie ran room to room trying to get people's attention.

"Janie, can you go outside and play so Grandma and Aunt Allison can work?" Hannah asked from her position in the living room.

"I wanna help!" She stomped her feet and crossed her arms. I watched from my spot on the couch in the living room to see what Janie would do.

"Sweetie, why don't you go outside and play with your daddy?" Lillian shot me a pointed look.

I'd tried helping earlier in the day, but I'd gotten pushed out of the way just like Janie. I tucked my phone in the back pocket of my jeans. "Let's go swing, sweetheart," I said, getting up and heading toward the back door.

She didn't move from her spot in the kitchen.

"Janie, we don't have time for this. Come on. Let's just go outside and play. We can do whatever you want," I said.

"I wanna help," she said. She stuck out her lower lip in an exaggerated pout.

Lillian handed her one of the balloons she'd just blown up. "Here, take this and play with it outside. You can throw it up and play catch."

Janie snatched it from her. She glared at her, then promptly squeezed her hands together and popped the balloon, making us all jump.

"Janie, that wasn't nice," Hannah said.

"You're not nice," Janie fired back.

We were one step away from a battle. I quickly scooped Janie up and threw her over my shoulder like a sack of potatoes. I tickled her legs while we walked and brought her outside. Sometimes it worked and diverted one of her meltdowns, but her face was still set in stone when we reached the yard.

Her behavior didn't get any better as the day wore on. Janie scowled at people as they filed into the house and greeted Hannah. She barely spoke to my mom when she arrived and refused to respond when people spoke to her. She popped any balloon she could get her hands on, continually startling people. Everyone tried to laugh it off, but it didn't take long for it to become annoying. At first, we ignored her like we did with so much of her attention-seeking behavior, but we had to step in when she went over to the cake. It was a three-layer tower made of cupcakes and almost as elaborate as our wedding cake. It probably cost as much.

"Janie, no!" I yelled when I spotted her reaching for one of the cupcakes.

She pretended like she hadn't heard me. Everyone stared as she grabbed a cupcake from the center and pulled it out. I held my breath, waiting for the cake to tumble. Thankfully, it didn't.

"Stop it!" Hannah said. "If you're not going to behave during the party, then you can go to your room." She pointed down the hallway that led to Janie's bedroom.

I looked at Hannah in surprise. We'd never sent Janie to her room before. It was such a normal way to discipline a child, but what would Janie do in there by herself? It'd been a while since she'd had a full-on meltdown, and I really wanted to avoid it, especially when our house was full of people.

Janie bit into the cupcake, and her mouth filled with yellow frosting. She grinned at Hannah, the yellow staining her teeth. "You're going to be a bad mommy."

Hannah recoiled like Janie had punched her in the gut. She brought both hands up to her face and covered her mouth. Everyone in the kitchen started talking at once to break the tension and pretend like they hadn't heard what Janie had said.

I grabbed Janie's arm and dragged her through the living room. She started screaming as we moved through people. "You're hurting me, Daddy! You're hurting me!"

I just kept going, my face red with embarrassment and anger. I shoved her in the room and slammed the door behind us.

"Don't you ever say anything like that to Mommy again!" I was fuming. I'd never been so mad at her.

She threw herself down on the floor, sobbing.

"Stop it, Janie. Just stop," I hissed. Everyone at the party could hear her, which only made her cries seem louder.

She beat her fists against the floor. Her wails came one on top of another; she wasn't even pausing long enough to breathe. Usually my heart ached for her when she was upset, but I was too angry over what she'd said to Hannah to help. I hurt for Hannah. This day meant so much to her, and Janie had ruined it.

Janie's cries shifted from angry rage to sobs of devastation. "I'm a bad girl. I'm a bad, bad, bad girl!" she cried.

Her self-deprecation tugged at my heartstrings, and my anger started dissipating. This had to be hard for her. She didn't understand that the baby wouldn't take us away from her and that there was enough of our love to go around. She was just hurting. More of my anger drained. She was still curled on the floor, shaking.

I plopped down next to her and reached for her, but she jerked away. She curled into a ball. "You're not a bad girl. You just made a bad choice. That's all. Just a bad choice." I rubbed her back until the sobs subsided. "Everyone makes bad choices sometimes. It's going to be okay."

THIRTY-ONE

Hannah Bauer

My stomach churned as we walked into Janie's school for our meeting with Mrs. Tinney to discuss Janie's behavior. She'd been acting out since the shower three weeks ago. My due date was two weeks away. What would I do if Janie got kicked out of another preschool?

Mrs. Tinney's classroom looked like the classrooms I'd grown up in. There was a huge carpet in the center of the room for the children to gather during circle time. Cubbies lined the back wall with the children's names neatly labeled on each one. Stations were set up around the room for various activities, and the walls proudly displayed the kids' artwork.

I was too big to squeeze into any of the miniature chairs, so I stood while Christopher and Mrs. Tinney sat. It made the situation more awkward and uncomfortable than it already was.

"How are you feeling?" she asked before getting started.

"Ready to have this baby." I smiled, trying to be polite, but I really wanted to know why we were there.

"Those last few weeks seem to drag on forever. Not to mention that all three of my kids were overdue," she said.

"Ugh, let's hope this one comes on time." I rubbed my hand on my swollen bump instinctively, just like I did anytime someone mentioned the baby.

She laid her hands on the desk. "Normally, I would've called you in for a conference as soon as we noticed Janie struggling, but since you were expecting another child, I figured her problems were just part of that transition and would pass. Only children almost always have problems when another member is being added to the family."

Janie was reverting back to behavior we hadn't seen in months. She went into uncontrollable screaming fits almost every day. She refused to eat and threw food at us, yelling for something different and claiming she'd throw up if she had to eat it. She'd started having accidents again, but this time she had them at home and school. She'd always hoarded food in her room underneath her bed, but now she'd started adding all kinds of weird objects that didn't make any logical sense—Christopher's shoes, the remote control, paper towels from the kitchen—and lied when we confronted her about it. Dr. Chandler said we should ignore it like we'd done before, but it wasn't working this time.

"I wanted to meet today so I could let you know that Elodie's mother is expecting a call from you about what's going on between Elodie and Janie at school. I wanted us to have a chance to talk about that conversation before it happened."

"What's going on with her and Elodie?" Christopher asked. His face was lined with concern. Janie referred to Elodie as her best friend. We'd never heard about any problems.

"Elodie started asking to stay inside during recess, which was my first red flag. I couldn't let her do that, since all children have to be outside during recess, but I watched her closely and noticed she cried a lot while we were on the playground. Whenever I asked her about it, she said that Janie was being mean."

"What was Janie doing to her?" I asked.

"Elodie wouldn't say what she was doing—only that she was mean. I took Janie aside and asked her about it, too, but she said she didn't know why Elodie was so upset. It wasn't anything that was unusual; kids fight and get their feelings hurt all the time. But then Elodie started refusing to play with Janie. It seemed like more than your typical spat. Elodie was genuinely afraid of Janie." She looked back and forth between us before continuing, making sure we were digesting what she'd said. "Elodie's mother called me this morning and told me Janie has been hurting Elodie at school. She's been coming home with bruises. Her mother didn't think anything of it at first, but it kept happening, and she grew more concerned. Last night, she noticed Elodie's entire arm was covered in bruises. She finally got her to talk, and Elodie said that Janie pinches her when no one is looking."

A chill ran down my neck. Janie had gotten in trouble at her previous preschools, but she'd never hurt anyone on purpose. It took Christopher a while to speak.

"Are you sure it's her?" he asked.

"Positive. I asked Janie about it yesterday, and she admitted it."

"She admitted it? What'd she say when you asked her about it?" I asked. She hadn't said anything to me about it when I'd picked her up from school. She'd acted totally normal.

"She said she wanted to make Elodie cry. When I asked her why she wanted to make her cry, she said that she likes to see what people look like when they cry." Mrs. Tinney's face was grim. I'd never seen her look so serious.

"Did she say anything else?" Christopher asked.

"No. That was it. I explained to her that it was not okay to make other people cry for any reason." She sat back in her chair and folded her hands on her lap. "As you can imagine, her mother is very angry. She wants Janie expelled from the school. I don't want to expel Janie. I really don't. I tend to think she's going through a rough time with the new baby—"

"She is. We've had all sorts of problems at home too," Christopher interrupted.

Mrs. Tinney nodded. "That's what I assumed. However, because Janie has been violent to another student, if the other parent is uncomfortable with her being here, then we will have to ask her to leave."

"Is that why you called us here? Are you kicking her out?" I asked. My head whirled. What would I do if they kicked her out? Could I get her into another school before the baby got here? What were the other ones on the list?

"Would you be comfortable telling Elodie's mother about Janie's history?" She leaned forward. "The only reason I'm asking is because I don't want to lose Janie. She's a great girl and an absolute joy to have in class. She's just struggling right now, and I want to help her rather than punish her. It might help Elodie's mother be more compassionate if you shared her history."

"So if she doesn't insist on expelling Janie, then you're saying she can stay?" Christopher asked.

"Yes, that's what I'm saying."

"Then that's what we'll do if you think it will help," Christopher said.

I wanted Janie to stay at the school as much as Christopher, even more, but something about telling Elodie's mom about Janie's past didn't feel right to me. I listened as Christopher and Dr. Chandler prattled on about ideas for the conversation, but I grew more uncomfortable the longer they went on.

Our walk home after our session was slow since my feet were so swollen, but it felt good to be outside. Before too much longer, it'd be too cold to be outside. I'd tried to keep it in during the session, but I couldn't any longer. "Telling Elodie's mother feels like we're using Janie's past as an excuse for her behavior."

"It's not an excuse."

"Really? The only reason we're telling her is so that Janie doesn't get kicked out of school."

"That's not true. We're telling her so that she has all the information she needs to make an informed decision." He spoke like he did when he was instructing interns.

"Please, Christopher, come on. We wouldn't even consider telling her unless there was a reason."

He shook his head, unmoving.

"Would you tell another student's mom about Janie?"

"That's not the point," he snapped.

"Just answer my question."

"It's not what we're talking about."

I pulled my hand out of his, irritated by his continual refusal to make Janie accountable for her behavior. "It's exactly what we're talking about. Answer the question."

"No."

"You know I'm right."

"I don't want to fight."

"Oh my God!" I couldn't keep the anger out of my voice. I sounded hysterical, but I didn't care. I was so tired of him backing out of difficult discussions because he claimed he didn't want to fight. "You know what, Christopher? Sometimes you have to fight."

I stomped off in front of him, leaving him trailing behind on the sidewalk. I knew I looked ridiculous—nine months pregnant, huffing and puffing down the sidewalk, clearly fighting with my husband—but I didn't care. He didn't speak to me when we got back to the house. He grabbed his keys and went to pick up Janie from Allison's. I had calmed down by the time he returned, but I still felt the same way about telling Elodie's mom because I didn't want to set a precedent for Janie's poor behavior being excused because of her background.

Christopher settled Janie in front of the TV and came to talk to me in the kitchen. I was chopping up the vegetables to use in the stir-fry for dinner.

"You feeling better?" he asked.

"You mean am I still mad at you?"

He grinned. "Yes . . ."

I set the knife down and looked him in the eye. "I'm not mad at you anymore, but that doesn't mean that I've changed my mind. Hurting someone else is unacceptable, and Janie needs to know that. The only way she'll ever get that is if she's held accountable for her actions. Any other child would be kicked out of school for what she did."

"And letting her get kicked out of school is helpful how?"

"Look, I don't want her to get kicked out of school any more than you do. Trust me. It's the last thing I want right now, but we have to set a precedent for this kind of behavior. All we ever say is that we want her to be treated like a normal child. You can't have it both ways, Christopher."

"You don't know the full story. We haven't even talked to her. How do we know she was hurting her on purpose?"

I slapped my hand on the counter. "Are you kidding me? She pinched her hard enough to leave bruises. More than one time. She absolutely knew she was hurting her."

"We don't know that."

I threw my hands up in frustration. "I'm not doing it."

"Fine. I'll do it. Where's the number?"

I grabbed the contact information from my purse and handed it to him. He tucked it into his pocket.

"I'll call her after we talk to Janie," he said. "I want to make sure we have Janie's story before I have any more conversations about what she did."

He waited until after dinner to talk to Janie about the Elodie incident because she was always happiest after she'd eaten. Allison had sent home fresh-baked brownies, and we each had one for dessert.

"We want to talk to you about school," Christopher said.

"Okay," Janie said, licking the chocolate frosting off the top of her brownie.

"We had a meeting with Mrs. Tinney today, and she told us that you've been hurting Elodie by pinching her. Why are you pinching Elodie?" I asked.

She shrugged. "I already told Mrs. Tinney. I wanted to see what she looked like when she cried."

"But why? Why would you want to make her cry?" Christopher asked.

Her lower lip trembled, and she looked embarrassed. "I'm sorry, Daddy."

"It's not okay to make people cry. You can't do that," Christopher said, trying his best to sound stern. "You're not going to be able to go to school if you keep hurting Elodie. Do you understand?"

She nodded.

He called Elodie's mom, but it didn't matter anyway. Two days later, Janie pushed Elodie off the slide, and Elodie broke her arm in two places. The school had no choice but to expel Janie.

THIRTY-TWO

Christopher Bauer

I listened as Hannah described all the articles she'd read about getting an only child a pet to help with new-baby jealousy and ease the transition. She was fixated on a story from one of her favorite mommy bloggers, because her daughter was the same age as Janie, and they were only a few months ahead of us on the journey.

"They got her a dog, and it worked wonders for everything she was going through. Isn't that amazing?" she asked without waiting for me to respond. She'd already told me the story twice, but I let her tell it a third time since she was so excited about it. "Her jealousy disappeared almost right away because she had something special to take care of that was all hers. I think it really might help Janie if we got her a pet. What do you think?" This time she paused and waited for an answer.

I could tell she already had her mind set on the idea, but I wasn't so sure. "How about we get her a goldfish?" I asked. Unlike her, I wasn't so keen on adding another being to take care of to our list.

Hannah burst out laughing. "A goldfish? What is she going to do with a goldfish? Just sit and stare at it while it swims in a bowl? That will last all of two minutes before she's bored with it. We need to get her something that she can take care of. Something new that's just for her. What about a cat?"

I frowned. "I'm not really a cat person."

She punched me in the arm playfully. "We're not getting the cat for you. We're getting it for her. Think about it. They're easy to train. You don't have to worry about any of the house-training stuff; just plop them in the litter box, and it's done. It'll be something she can sleep with. I think she'll love it."

"As long as I don't have to sleep with it." I smiled.

That weekend we trekked to Petco for their kitten adoptions. We didn't tell Janie where we were going or what we were doing because we wanted to surprise her.

"I don't wanna go shopping," she whined when we pulled into the mall parking lot.

"Just wait," I said, opening her door. "You're going to like it."

"I hate shopping," she said with a scowl, but she got out of the car and followed us inside.

There was a line wrapped all the way through the store. Apparently, everyone had had the same idea as us.

"Wow," I said. "Why don't I grab a number and wait in line while you take a look around? I bet Janie would love to see the turtles in the back. What do you say—you want to see the turtles?"

"Turtles! Turtles!" Janie squealed.

They skipped off while I waited in line. The line went much faster than I had thought it would. Most people just wanted to cuddle and play with the kittens, but they weren't interested in taking one home. I texted Hannah when I was close to the front. They scurried from the back of the store to join me.

"We saw turtles and snakes and puppies! Can we get a puppy? Please, can we get a puppy?" Janie bounced up and down.

I smiled down at her. "You can't get a puppy. Not today. But . . ."

"No puppy?" Her eyes filled with tears. "I want a puppy."

"How about a new baby kitty?" I asked.

Her tears instantly disappeared. "A kitty? I love kitties! I can get a kitty?"

"You can," I said, ruffling her hair.

She stood on her tiptoes, trying to see inside the room where they had the cats. Hannah lifted her up to give her a better look.

"Kitties! I see them! Look, Mommy, look. There's kitties." She pointed to the kittens tumbling over each other in the separate crates. They were so tiny and cute. My heart swelled like it did every time she got excited. I loved experiencing the world through her eyes.

"I see them too. It's almost our turn," I said.

It was only a couple more minutes before they called our number, and we stepped inside the room. There were four different litters. Janie immediately went to the litter closest to the door and started picking each kitten up. She held them up one at a time and looked in their eyes. "Nope," she'd say and then drop the kitten back in the bin before picking up the next one. She picked up one of the black ones with a tiny white spot on the end of its tail. "This one. I want this one."

"Are you sure that's the one you want? You don't want to look at any of the other kittens?" I asked. There were three more crates filled with kittens.

"Nope. This one. This is the one I want." She cuddled it against her chest.

I looked at Hannah and shrugged. She smiled back at me.

Janie and I went through the rest of the store and gathered the supplies we'd need for the kitten while Hannah filled out the adoption paperwork. Janie held the kitten while we shopped and ran through a list of names, changing her mind every three seconds until she settled on Blue.

"Blue. Yep. Her name is going to be Blue," she announced proudly.

"How come Blue?" I asked.

She held her out for me to see. "Her eyes are blue just like me."

She carried Blue on her lap during the drive home, and I'd never seen her look so happy. She was fascinated by Blue, even when she was trying to jump out of Janie's hands because Blue was terrified of the car. I made sure Hannah carried Blue inside, though, because I was afraid she might freak out and jump out of Janie's arms when we stepped out of the car.

Janie spent the rest of the afternoon chasing Blue around the house. I couldn't stop snapping pictures because the two of them were so adorable together.

"It was a great idea," I whispered to Hannah as we watched the two of them together cuddled up on the couch. Blue had fallen asleep on Janie's lap.

"And she didn't get in trouble all day," Hannah whispered back.

Later that night, Janie and Blue were playing in her bedroom when suddenly we heard awful squealing sounds. We rushed into her room. Janie was sitting on her rug. Pathetic meows came from underneath her bed.

"Where's Blue?" Hannah asked.

She looked up at us. "She ran away under my bed."

Hannah was too big to bend over and look under the bed, so I ducked down and lay flat. Blue cowered in the far corner. She scurried away every time my hand got close to her and wouldn't stop whimpering. I finally coaxed her forward and pulled her out. Her entire body shook like she was freezing. I went to hand her to Janie, and Blue arched her back, hissing at her.

"That's weird," I said, looking down. There were bright-red spots on my hands. "What is this?"

"Let me see her," Hannah said.

I went over to Hannah, who touched her carefully. Blue was still shaking. Parts of her fur were sticky.

"She's bleeding," Hannah said. "Janie, what happened?"

Janie held up a safety pin. "I poked Blue."

Hannah's mouth dropped open. "You what?"

"I poked her. I wanted to see if she'd bleed." Janie looked back and forth between us, gauging by our faces that she'd done something wrong.

Hannah's face paled.

"You wanted to see if she'd bleed," I repeated robotically.

"Yep. And she did. Red. Can I hold her now?" she asked.

I held her close to my body, afraid to give her back. "I'm having a turn."

Hannah struggled to regain her composure. She took a seat next to her on the bed, and Janie crawled up on her lap. "You can't hurt Blue. It hurts the kitten when you poke her. Do you understand?"

She nodded. "No poking the kitty."

"That's right. Don't do that again."

CASE #5243

INTERVIEW: PIPER GOLDSTEIN

Ron found the story of Janie poking Blue deeply unsettling. He hadn't shown any emotion during all the other questioning, even when we'd looked at the crime scene photos in the trailer, and they were brutal. But something about her hurting animals really got to him.

"Isn't hurting animals a sign of a sociopath?" he asked, rearranging his face to look unbothered.

"It's one of the signs, but other things have to be present too," I said.

"And none of those things were present?" Luke asked. He wasn't nearly as moved by the Blue story. He was actually starting to look bored. I couldn't blame him. It felt like we'd been in this room for days going round and round in the same circles.

"It's not my area of specialization, and I don't like to comment on things outside my area of expertise," I said just like my supervisor had instructed me to. It's what they'd made us say to the reporters, too, when they'd asked. The police weren't the only ones asking questions.

"But you've got to at least have an opinion. Everyone has an opinion. What do you think was going on with Janie?" he asked.

"She was a little girl who'd been hurt badly, and she hurt other people. It always seemed that simple to me," I said.

Luke set down his file and peered at me from across the table. "But it wasn't that simple, was it?"

THIRTY-THREE

Christopher Bauer

We scheduled an emergency session with Dr. Chandler after the incident with Blue. She listened attentively as we told her the story, then asked us to wait while she stepped into her reception area. She carried papers on clipboards when she came back in the room and handed each of us a pen.

"I want you to take a minute and fill these out," she instructed.

I settled on the floor, and Hannah tried to arrange her body on one of the huge beanbag chairs. She was so pregnant that it looked painful. I skimmed through the paperwork. There were thirty questions about Janie's behavior. We had to read each statement and circle the number that best described her on a scale of one to five. The questionnaire was filled with statements like "my child acts cute and charms others to get what he/she wants" and "my child throws screaming fits for hours" and "my child teases, hurts, or is cruel to animals." It was like someone had created a list of Janie's problem areas. Hannah finished before I did. We handed them back to Dr. Chandler and waited anxiously while she went through them. She set the clipboards next to her after she finished.

"I think it's time we started to talk about disorders that might be affecting her behavior. The questionnaire I just gave you is called the

RADQ, and it's designed to assess the symptoms for reactive attachment disorder. Are either of you familiar with it?"

I'd never heard of it. I looked to Hannah, and she was shaking her head too.

"It's a bit of a controversial disorder in the mental health field, but I'm fairly certain Janie has reactive attachment disorder. I've always had my suspicions, but I was hoping her symptoms would lessen over time. Unfortunately, they seem to be increasing and getting worse."

"What is it?" I asked.

"What's wrong with her?" Hannah asked at the same time.

"It's a disorder caused by a child's inability to form attachments to a caregiver at an early age and results in difficulties forming attachments with other people. It sounds pretty straightforward and commonsense for a child who's been abused, right? Like, of course their relationships with other people are going to be damaged. But in kids with reactive attachment disorder, it goes much deeper than that. Sometimes they're unable to form any sort of connection with another human being. They have problems with empathy, so we see them do things like hurting other children or animals, just like you've been describing. At times, they don't seem like they have a conscience. One of the most common characteristics we hear from parents whose children have reactive attachment disorder is how charming and delightful their children are in public."

I couldn't help but think of all the times Hannah had said that Janie was different when she had an audience. I couldn't deny that she behaved differently. I'd just thought she liked to be out in the real world and interacting with others. Maybe there was some truth to what Hannah had always said. My heart sank.

"These kids tend to be very manipulative and controlling. They're constantly trying to pit people against each other, like we've talked about before with the ways she tries to triangulate the two of you. They can make friends, but they have a hard time maintaining them once their friends actually get close to them. The biggest concern we have is when they start to hurt other people or animals. It's a huge red flag. I'm glad you guys came in when you did."

I felt like she was handing us a death sentence. "What are we supposed to do? How do we treat it?" I asked.

Hannah looked like she wanted to cry. She gripped her stomach protectively.

"Unfortunately, this is where it gets tricky. Treatment is tough, and it's not always effective. There're lots of controversial treatments that exist, but sometimes I think they do more damage than they do good."

"Is she going to get worse? Like, will she keep hurting other kids? What are we supposed to do?" I asked.

A million scenarios whirled through my mind. There had to be treatment. There just had to be. She was too young to be broken for life. Nobody was that damaged. I refused to believe that.

"I'm going to switch the focus of our therapy and move into empathy training. We've touched on that briefly before, but I'd like to get back to it. Sometimes with proper training, kids like this can learn empathy. The good news about Janie is that she does have the ability to develop attachments. She's always had a strong bond with Christopher, and even though she fights you, Hannah, part of the reason she's so hostile toward you is because she depends on you. If she didn't have those skills, I would be more concerned, but I think we can build on what is already there."

"Tell me the truth. Will she get better?" Hannah asked.

"Yes, I believe she can. I won't make any guarantees—nobody can make any guarantees—but she's been doing great for months. The baby has just set her off. It's disrupted her and shaken up her world, so she's reverting to old behaviors and also trying out some new ones. She's afraid the baby is going to replace her."

It was what I'd been afraid of all along. "How do we help her?" I asked.

"I think we should start meeting at least twice a week, maybe even three times, for as long as we can. She's going to need lots of help, but we can get her through it." She smiled at us. "You three have already been through a lot, and this is just a bump in the road."

I looked at Hannah again. She stared back at me. She didn't have to speak to let me know what she was thinking. This was more than a bump in the road. It was a sinkhole.

THIRTY-FOUR

HANNAH BAUER

My eyes snapped open. Searing pain shot through my back. There was water between my legs. I'd wet myself during the night but didn't have any memory of it. I rolled over and threw my legs over the side of the bed, pain gripping me with each movement.

I waddled into the bathroom connected to our bedroom. I pulled my underwear down, and that's when it hit me.

"Christopher! I think my water broke!"

He was up and in the bathroom in an instant. "Are you sure?"

I nodded, in too much pain to speak. I didn't even care that he was seeing me on the toilet.

"Let me get you clean clothes. You just wait there," he said.

The pain slowly subsided, and as it left, I couldn't help but smile. Allison and my mom had told me last week when I'd asked them about the Braxton Hicks contractions I was having that I'd know when it was the real thing. There was no mistaking it—this was the real deal.

Christopher was back in no time, carrying clean underwear and the comfortable outfit we'd picked out months ago.

"Let me help you," he said, bending over to hoist me off the toilet.

I waved him off. "I'm fine at the moment. The contraction stopped."

I got dressed while he called Allison. When I was halfway through brushing my teeth, another contraction seized me in its grip. I breathed through it until it passed.

Allison arrived like she'd been up waiting for our phone call. She was breathless as she ran over to me on the couch, the bags we'd packed weeks ago at my feet. She gave me a huge hug. "It's happening! I'm so excited for you!" She looked like she had on Christmas morning when we were kids and had just run downstairs into the living room to see what Santa had left us underneath the tree. "I'm going to be an auntie."

I burst out laughing.

"Are you in a lot of pain yet?" she asked.

I shook my head. "Not yet."

She gave me another big squeeze as Christopher came out of the bathroom, then pointed at the door. "Okay, go, you two. I've got everything under control here. Don't worry about a thing. Just go have that baby."

—

I'd never felt so acutely alive and present in my body. I wanted to hold on to it and savor the moment before the pain worsened. Christopher held my hand and drove like an eighty-year-old man on the way to the hospital. He knew there was plenty of time to get there, and his biggest fear was someone crashing into us on the way.

They put me on bed rest as soon as they wheeled us onto the labor and delivery unit because my water had broken. I wanted to walk the halls, do something besides just lie there, but I was stuck flat on my back. Christopher flicked through the TV channels trying to find something to watch, but nothing interested me. Time stood still as we waited for the baby to arrive. They checked me every few hours into the night, but I still wasn't dilating. They started me on Pitocin somewhere around four a.m., and that's when everything changed.

I'd heard the stories about Pitocin making your contractions more painful, and they were all true. Within an hour, I was in mind-numbing pain. It was the only thing I could focus on. My entire body shook. Christopher held my hair back while I puked and tied it up in a ponytail for me afterward. My insides felt like they were being twisted apart.

I clung to Christopher. His face was covered in sweat. His hair stuck up haphazardly from him running his fingers through it again and again.

"I can't do this. I need the drugs," I cried.

On my birth plan, I had laid out that I was committed to natural childbirth and didn't want any pain medication. I wanted to experience everything since it was going to be the only time I'd ever do it. I'd also read all the studies about how the drugs could slow down labor and increase the likelihood of having a C-section, and I wanted to have a natural birth.

"Are you sure?" he asked, the doubt written on his face. He'd listened to me rant for hours about doing labor drug-free.

I gritted my teeth against the pain. "Yes."

"I'm going to get the nurse," he said. "I'll be right back."

He hurried out of the room and returned with one of the nurses. He rushed back to my bedside and started rubbing my back.

"Don't touch me!" My entire body felt like it was having a contraction, beginning at my neck and moving all the way down to my feet. White-hot pain at the center. His touch made it worse, not better.

He flinched and stepped back. "Okay, whatever you want. You got this, honey. The nurse is here. She'll help you." His eyes pleaded with her to help me.

"I want the drugs! Give me the drugs!" I shouted at her.

"I understand that," she said. Her voice was calm, unfaltering. "I've called the anesthesiologist. He's with another patient right now, but he'll be with you once he's finished with her." She moved the top of my bed down. "I have to check you again to see how far along you are."

I gripped the side rails as I lay back and almost passed out from the pain. White spots danced at the corners of my vision. I reached for Christopher and dug my nails into him. "Please, please, I changed my mind. Just give me the drugs."

He used his other hand to wipe the hair from my forehead. "You're almost there. The doctor is going to be here any minute."

The nurse pulled her hand out of me, and her face filled with compassion. "I'm sorry, but it's too late for the drugs. I can feel the baby's head in the canal. You're going to have to push soon."

I shook my head like a mad dog. "I can't do it. I'm too tired. It hurts. It hurts so bad!"

"You can do it, honey. You can do it. I know you can. You're strong," Christopher said.

My room filled with more nurses and another doctor in addition to my own. Everyone slipped on gear and surrounded my bed. Christopher lifted one of my legs while one of the nurses lifted another, pulling them back against me.

"Stop! Stop!" I shrieked. "I can't do this. I can't."

"Just relax. Take a deep breath," the nurse instructed. "Breathe. You've got to breathe."

I couldn't concentrate on anything except the searing pain shooting through me again and again.

"Okay, Hannah, push!" she yelled.

They all chanted to ten while I gritted my teeth and bore down. Animal sounds came out of me. They gave me a few seconds to breathe and then made me do it again and again. I didn't think it was ever going to stop.

"It's burning. Something is burning." I wept from the pain.

"Just push," the nurse said.

"I can't. It hurts too much!" But my body ignored me and pushed anyway. "I can't do it anymore."

Christopher looked down at me. I locked onto his eyes, feeding off his strength. "You can do it, honey. Just one more big push."

And just like that, my baby was here. I felt the release immediately as the baby slid out. The doctor grabbed the baby and laid it on my chest.

"It's a boy! It's a boy!" Christopher cried out.

Tears streamed down my cheeks, all the pain forgotten as he let out a wail. He instantly searched for my breast, and a secret space opened up inside me like it'd been there all along, just waiting to be discovered. He latched on to my nipple. I laughed and cried at the same time.

"He's perfect," I said over and over again as Christopher worked with the doctor to cut the umbilical cord like we'd planned.

I fell in love with my baby boy instantly, marveling at his perfection and that he'd lived inside me for so long. My feelings stemmed from the deepest parts of me. He wasn't a stranger in my arms—it was like a missing piece of myself had been returned.

They wheeled us from the delivery room into our hospital room. My head throbbed with exhaustion. All I wanted to do was sleep with my baby cuddled on my chest. We had just gotten settled in our room when he started crying. I'd heard plenty of babies cry, but I'd never heard a baby scream like someone was pulling their limbs off. I tried to nurse him, but it only made him angrier. I tried everything to calm him down—jiggled him, walked him, sang to him, and talked to him—but nothing worked. He screamed for the next eight hours. Christopher and I took turns trying to calm him down.

I was supposed to be resting when it wasn't my turn, but it was impossible in a crammed hospital room. I couldn't relax a single muscle. My body was tensed and hyperalert as he screamed. I was driven to do something, and my body physically hurt from not being able to stop his pain.

As the sun came up, the three of us piled on my hospital bed with the side rail raised on each side. I was on one side of the bed while

Christopher was on the other. We took turns holding the baby. We slept for a few hours, but things got busy in the morning.

We settled on the name Cole. Christopher's grandmother was named Nicole, and we'd already decided to name the baby after her regardless of the gender. Our room bustled with hospital activity, and even though Cole finally slept on and off throughout the day, we were awake as our visitors showed up to congratulate us. Allison called, and we asked to talk to Janie, but she wouldn't speak, not even to Christopher.

"She's had a difficult night," Allison said.

I didn't have the energy to even ask about it.

THIRTY-FIVE

Christopher Bauer

Hannah and I were wrecked by the time we got home from the hospital. We'd barely slept for three days. Janie had refused to come visit the baby and was bouncing with manic energy since she hadn't seen us for so long. I helped Hannah over to the couch and got her settled with Cole. She was still in a lot of pain from where she'd torn during delivery and from getting stitches afterward.

"Come meet your baby brother, Cole," I said, motioning for Janie to join us.

She stood in front of the fireplace, shaking her head.

I tried again. "He wants to meet you. He's so happy to have a big sister. Look how cute he is."

She glared at me before moving to hide behind Allison's legs.

"It's okay, Janie," Hannah said. She looked exhausted. "You don't have to meet your brother right now if you don't want to. You have plenty of time to get to know him."

Janie asked to be picked up, and she clung to me. She stuck her thumb in her mouth, something she'd never done before.

"He's so precious. Look at those tiny fingers." Allison nuzzled Cole's face with her cheek. "Is he still crying a lot?"

Hannah nodded. "It's not as bad during the day, but he screams all night long. I think he's got his days and nights mixed up."

"It usually only takes a few days or so for them to adjust."

"Thank God," Hannah said, looking relieved. "It's pretty brutal. It wouldn't be so bad if he were just awake, but he screams like he's in pain. It's like something is hurting him, and I don't know how to fix it."

Allison hugged her from the side. "He's probably colicky. Mom said I was. Maybe it's a firstborn baby thing. Or he could be hungry because he's not getting enough milk. Has your milk come in yet?"

Hannah shook her head. "I wish it'd hurry up. He's probably starving to death."

I sat down with Janie on the couch next to Hannah and Allison, hoping her curiosity would get the best of her and she'd be forced to look, but she buried her face in my shoulder.

"Why don't you take Janie to the park, and I'll sit with the baby so Hannah can take a nap?" Allison suggested.

The last thing I wanted to do was walk to the park. I wanted to nap with Hannah, but being a parent meant you put your children's needs above your own. Parenting hadn't wasted any time making its demands.

"Go find your shoes, Janie," I said, putting mine back on.

THIRTY-SIX

HANNAH BAUER

Christopher and I arrived at our pediatrician's office for Cole's five-day appointment with a list of questions. Cole hadn't stopped wailing, and we hadn't slept for more than a two-hour period in over a week.

Dr. Garcia checked him over. He was gaining weight and responded to all of the doctor's touches, pokes, and prods just like he should.

"He looks good. Do you have any questions?" he asked.

We pulled out our list, but I jumped to number one immediately. "He cries whenever he gets tired, and he really gets worked up at night," I blurted out before Christopher had a chance to speak.

Dr. Garcia nodded. "Yes, all babies cry when they're sleepy."

"Yeah, but he cries for hours before he goes to sleep. Hours," I said.

"Oh, he might be a colicky baby," he responded nonchalantly, not the least bit disturbed. "It will pass in three to four months."

I wanted to break down and sob in my chair. He might as well have told me it was going to last three to four years, because a minute of Cole's screaming felt like hours.

"Is there anything we can do to help him?" Christopher asked.

"You could try gripe water. Sometimes that works," Dr. Garcia said.

The problem was, we already knew that it didn't work. Christopher was obsessed with finding something to make Cole stop crying. Once while I'd fed Cole, he had scoured the internet, searching for a solution, and gripe water was one of the first things he'd stumbled across. It'd done nothing, much like everything else we had tried.

Thankfully, my mom was coming tomorrow. I couldn't wait to have someone around who knew what they were doing. Christopher tried to help, but his solutions didn't make sense, like suggesting I go shopping while he stayed at home with the baby. Never mind that the baby would starve without me—I could barely walk and hadn't stopped bleeding. Nobody had told me you bled so much after birth. I tried to hide my annoyance with it, but sometimes I couldn't. It'd be nice to have someone around who knew how to help.

THIRTY-SEVEN

Christopher Bauer

Lillian had only been gone for three days, and Hannah was already stretched to her limit again. Cole was a voracious eater and fed every two hours, sometimes sooner, and she wasn't sleeping more than a few hours at a time. Even when she slept, she wasn't completely relaxed. She jolted awake at the slightest sound. Cole was in a bassinet next to our bed, and she obsessively woke up to check and see if he was breathing, terrified of SIDS.

"When he's sleeping, you should just let him sleep," I'd said last night after she'd gotten up to check on him for the third time.

"I'm just making sure he's okay." She'd looked insulted that I'd even suggested it.

The lack of sleep made her jumpy and edgy in a way I'd never seen her act before. I worried what she'd do if Janie gave her any trouble when I went back to work tomorrow. I wasn't ready to go back, but I was out of paid time off since I'd taken so much of it when we'd got Janie. Nobody was ready for it, least of all me.

"I want you to be good while Daddy is at work today," I said to Janie while I poured the milk into her bowl of Cheerios the next morning.

We'd been arguing for weeks about getting help at the house, but Hannah refused to hire anyone. It wasn't that she didn't think she needed it but that she didn't like the idea of having someone in the house with her; she said it would feel like she was under a microscope all the time. I couldn't get her to budge.

I tried not to worry as Hannah paced the living room, jiggling Cole back and forth, treading a path across the room. She'd been up since two. He'd woken up, and she hadn't been able to get him back to sleep. I'd offered to take him from her so she could rest, but she'd insisted she be the one to do it since I was going to work in the morning.

I chopped up strawberries and put them in a bowl next to Janie's cereal. "Mommy is really tired because she's been up all night taking care of baby Cole, so I need you to go easy on her and help her out today. Can you do that for me?" I asked.

She smiled across the table at me. "I'll be good."

The house was trashed when I got home. It was clear Hannah had let Janie do whatever she wanted. Goldfish cracker crumbs formed a trail everywhere Janie had been, leading in and out of the living room and back again. Half-empty juice boxes were strewn around in the kitchen and in her bedroom. Her toys were scattered around the house. She'd created an obstacle course in her room, and it looked like she'd spent most of the day trying to get Blue to run through it like she was a dog. We'd watched the Westminster Dog Show a few nights ago, and she'd been obsessed with it ever since. I kept telling her that cats didn't do tricks as easily as dogs, but it didn't matter. She was determined to get Blue to perform. She was still in her pajamas, and her face was dirty, but she looked happy.

"I was a good girl today," she said.

I gave her a big hug and high-fived her. "I'm so proud of you. Where's Mommy?"

"She's in her bedroom."

"I'm going to go say hi to her, and then I'll make us something to eat. How's that?"

She nodded and went back to trying to loop a jump rope around two of her toy bins.

I walked down the hallway and into our bedroom. Hannah was curled up on the bed with Cole cuddled close to her. At first, I thought she'd fallen asleep, but she jerked her head up when I came into view.

"Shhh, don't come in here. You'll wake him up," she hissed through gritted teeth.

"Okay. I—"

Cole twitched and started to wail.

"You woke him up. I just got him to sleep." She glared at me. "I told you to be quiet." She scooped him up and brought him to her breast.

"I barely said anything. I think he woke up on his own. How long has he been sleeping?"

"I just got him to sleep two minutes before you walked in the door." She said it like I'd done something wrong by coming home.

"I'm sorry," I apologized even though I hadn't done anything wrong. "Do you want me to take him?"

"He's eating," she snapped.

"Maybe we could start trying to get him to take a bottle?" I felt bad that I couldn't help more with feeding him. At least if he took a bottle, I could alleviate some of her responsibility.

"I don't want him to get nipple confusion. Not yet. He's got to get comfortable breastfeeding first."

I didn't dare argue with her about breastfeeding. Lillian had talked to Hannah about supplementing her breast milk with formula, and she'd acted like formula feeding was the same thing as feeding him glass. Hannah wanted to exclusively breastfeed and wouldn't consider any other alternatives. I wasn't used to her being so narrow minded since she was usually so diligent about researching all sides of an issue.

I reminded myself that it had only been a few weeks since she had given birth, and her hormones were wreaking havoc on her; she needed her space to level out. I would wait to bring up leaving Janie alone or unsupervised.

I spent the rest of the night trying to find ways to lessen her load and make things easier for her, so when Cole started screaming again around midnight, I jumped out of bed and ran downstairs to get his car seat.

"What are you doing?" Hannah asked when I came back upstairs with it.

"I'm taking him. You need sleep," I said. As long as he was in the house crying, she would be awake, even if I had him in another room. We'd tried that the other night, and I'd come out to find her listening for his cries outside the guest room door. I took Cole from her, which made him scream louder. I strapped him into the car seat while he wailed.

"Where are you going?" she asked frantically.

"I'm going to drive around with him until he falls asleep." Dan had told me that he used to drive his girls around at night when they couldn't sleep. He'd said there was something about the car that lulled them to sleep. I hoped it worked with Cole.

"But it's two in the morning. I don't want him out. Please, Christopher, please, don't go."

"It's okay. We're just going to drive around for a while so you can sleep. You need to sleep."

She started crying. That's when I knew just how tired she was, because Hannah wasn't a girl who cried easily.

"Please, please," she begged.

I kissed her on the cheek. "Just go to sleep. You'll see. You'll feel better when you wake up."

I strapped him into the back seat and started driving. It frustrated me that Hannah wouldn't consider letting me stay home with the kids while she went back to work. She hadn't always been so traditional, but staying home and bonding with her children during those first few months had been a dream of hers since she was a little girl, and she refused to let it go. I drove slowly up and down residential streets. It took him forty-five minutes to fall asleep, but he eventually did. I drove for another hour to give him and Hannah time to rest before heading home.

I had barely pulled into the driveway when Hannah whipped open the front door of the house. She stormed outside, waving her arms around manically. She didn't even let me shut the car off before she yanked open the back door.

"Don't you ever do that again!" she screamed. She pulled Cole out of the car, waking him up. He immediately started crying.

"What are you doing? He was asleep!" I yelled.

She rushed into the house, and I followed her inside. He quieted once she settled him on her breast. Her face was streaked with tears and blotchy, her eyes wild.

"Did you get any sleep?" I asked.

"Are you kidding me?" she hissed. "I told you not to take him. I was freaking out the entire time you were gone. And you didn't even answer your phone."

"I'm sorry. I forgot it." I tried to hug her, but she pulled away.

"All I pictured were terrible things happening to you guys. I kept seeing you getting carjacked with the baby in the car or getting crushed by a drunk driver. What if a stray bullet hit you?"

"Hannah, calm down. A stray bullet? Where do you think we live?"

Her eyes filled with fear. "I don't care. That's what I kept seeing. Don't ever do that to me again. Ever. Do you understand?"

I nodded. I'd never seen her so unsettled.

THIRTY-EIGHT

Hannah Bauer

I eyed Christopher in the bathroom as he brushed his teeth, trying to pretend like I wasn't spying on him. He'd left the door open while he got ready, something he never did because he didn't want to wake me or Cole. He was trying just as hard to pretend he wasn't trying to keep an eye on me, but it was the reason he'd kept the door open in the first place. He'd looked at me like I was a stranger the morning after a one-night stand when he'd rolled over in bed earlier.

I didn't recognize myself any more than he did. I checked to make sure Cole was still asleep in his bassinet next to the bed before inching my way out and following Christopher into the bathroom. I leaned against the counter for support. I was so tired; it took too much energy to stand. He didn't look up from brushing his teeth.

"I'm sorry. I shouldn't have freaked out like I did last night." Shame burned my cheeks.

"It's okay. You were just exhausted." He spit out the toothpaste and rinsed his mouth.

"It was so weird. Nothing like that has ever happened to me before. I couldn't stop the images. They all just felt so real." This morning it seemed like a strange dream.

"Postpartum pregnancy hormones are brutal, but you've got to be near the end of them," he said. "Things will be better soon."

His words were positive, but they were forced, and he still hadn't looked at me. Why wouldn't he look at me? It made the situation more uncomfortable, and things were already weird enough.

"I really wish you'd let me stay home today."

I shook my head. "They're going to give your job away if you're never there." The last thing we needed was for Christopher to lose his job. I couldn't handle one more stressful event on our plate.

—

The following days didn't get any easier. Janie was determined to make things hard. She started having accidents all the time. She wasn't bothered by the mess or the smell.

"I pooped, Mommy," she'd say in a singsong voice. "Change me."

Sometimes she'd stand in the living room looking right at me and start peeing. I'd yell at her to get into the bathroom, and she'd just stand there, shrugging her shoulders.

I wanted to rest, but as soon as I'd sit on the couch, Janie would call out and ask for help with something. She'd always thrived on being independent and doing things by herself if she could, but suddenly she couldn't do anything without help, and it never failed that she needed something whenever I was nursing. I wanted to crawl into bed and sleep for days. There were moments when I almost gave in and hired a nanny like Christopher wanted, but no matter how tired I was, I couldn't bring myself to do it. If Allison could find a way to manage with the twins all by herself, then I could find a way to manage my family situation too.

I always asked Janie if she needed anything prior to breastfeeding or any other task with Cole that would take longer than a few minutes, but she always said no and then waited until I was in the middle of caring for him to bombard me with requests. So it was no surprise when she slid up to me later that afternoon while I nursed Cole and announced, "I'm thirsty."

I held back the urge to roll my eyes. "Okay, can you grab your cup on the coffee table? I think it still has your milk in it." I'd quickly learned to have snacks and drinks accessible to her at all times. It was one less thing for her to ask me for. The trick was to stay one step ahead of her.

She frowned. "I don't want that milk."

"It's still cold. It hasn't been sitting there that long." She hated drinking milk after it got warm. I hated warm milk too. My mom used to try and get me to drink warm milk when I couldn't sleep as a kid, and I didn't like it then either.

"No. I want that milk."

I looked around. "What are you talking about?"

She pointed to my breast. "That. I want that."

I looked down at Cole suckling my right breast. I tried to pull my shirt over my other breast, suddenly feeling exposed. "Um . . . you can't have that."

"Why?"

I swallowed. "Because . . . well, Cole is a baby, and the milk that comes from my breast is for babies. When he gets older, he won't drink it either. He'll drink milk just like you do."

Her eyes filled with challenge. "It's not fair. I want that milk. It's better."

"It's not better. It's, uh . . . different. It has special things that babies need to keep them healthy. Why don't you give me a minute, and I'll get you fresh milk from the refrigerator?"

"No. I want that." Her voice rose with each word.

I pulled Cole off my nipple. Thankfully, he'd had enough, so he didn't cry. He settled into a milk coma, and I placed him in his infant carrier. I yanked my shirt down, smoothing it in front of me.

"Give me your milk!" She grabbed at my chest.

I pulled away. "Janie, no, stop that."

She grabbed my breast and pinched hard.

I slapped her hand away instinctively. "Ouch. That hurt."

She jumped up and kicked Cole's carrier. "He's stupid. And ugly. Ugly, stupid baby!" She kicked the carrier again, and it fell on its side. Cole rolled onto the floor.

"Janie!" I screamed as Cole started wailing. I scooped him up from the floor. "Shhh . . . shhh . . . it's okay. You're okay." I bounced as I walked. I pointed to her room. "Go to your room now."

She glared at me. "I hate you."

I pointed again. "Go!"

"Take him back!" she screamed before stomping to her room and slamming the door behind her like an angry teenager.

I checked Cole over. Thankfully, he hadn't hit hard, and his blanket had landed first, so he'd fallen on that instead of the wooden floor. He seemed fine.

I texted Christopher at work:

Janie just flipped out and knocked Cole out of his carrier.

It took a couple hours before he texted back:

Just got out of surgery. Why?

She got pissed because I wouldn't let her drink my breast milk.

WHAT????

Yep. She wanted to drink it. Totally freaked out when I said no.

What's she doing now?

She's been in her room screaming and crying for the last two hours.

Ok. Got surgery. Text me later.

Will do.

I carried Cole into the kitchen to get away from Janie's sounds, but no matter where I went in the house, I could still hear her throwing a fit. Cole started fussing, and before long he worked himself up into one of his frenzies. I tried to nurse him, but he twisted away from me. The cries from both of them reverberated off the walls. I paced the house. Neither of them stopped. My anxiety built the longer they cried. I walked through the hallway, pausing at Janie's door. Her screams cut through my brain. Before I knew what I was doing, I pounded on her door and screamed, "Shut up! Just shut up!"

She quieted immediately. I held my breath. The crying didn't start back up. I'd never yelled at her before. All the times she'd pushed me and frustrated me, I'd never raised my voice no matter how much I'd wanted to. I should've felt bad. But all I felt was relieved that she'd stopped. It took another thirty minutes before I got Cole quiet too. I strapped him into his swing and wound it up, grateful for a few moments of peace.

I headed back down the hallway and into Janie's room, hoping she'd cried herself to sleep. I opened the door slowly so I wouldn't wake her in case she had. She was sitting on her rug in a puddle of puke.

"Oh my God, you threw up," I said, waves of guilt crashing over me.

She glared at me through bloodshot eyes.

"I'm so sorry that I yelled at you. I shouldn't have yelled at you," I said. Any relief from the quiet was gone and replaced with shame.

"You're mean," she said.

I crouched next to her. I went to hug her, but she jerked away. "You're right. I said something very mean to you. I should not have done that, and I'm sorry." I rubbed her back. She flinched like I was hurting her. "Come on. Let's go into the bathroom and get you cleaned up."

She walked ahead of me into the bathroom. I peeked into the family room to make sure Cole was asleep before joining her. She was struggling to get her shirt off.

"Here, let me help you." I straightened it and pulled it over her head. "How about we just give you a bath?"

"In the day?"

"Sure. It's not a regular day." I bit my cheek to keep from crying. It was a day I'd never forget. The one where I had crossed the line, made my child so upset she'd thrown up. What kind of a mother did that?

I filled the tub and squirted her with the bath toys. She wouldn't laugh like she usually did, but she finally smiled. It didn't make me feel any better.

"I'm sorry I yelled at you, Janie. Mommy should not have done that," I said.

"It's okay, Mommy." She picked up one of the green toys and handed it to me. "Mommies always yell."

I froze. She'd never said anything about her mother. Never. Not once. What did I do? Was I supposed to say something? Ask more questions? I frantically looked around like Christopher would pop out of one of the walls and tell me what to do. My armpits dripped with sweat. I had to do something.

"Really? They do?"

I didn't want to push her. That much I remembered from the early days. Her team always said not to pressure her to talk about her past, and Piper had said to never ask leading questions. We were supposed to leave it up to her to talk. Did that still apply now?

Cole squawked from the living room. Of course he decided to wake up now. It was only a few seconds before he moved into a full-fledged wail.

"What else do mommies do?" I asked. It wasn't an open-ended question, but I didn't have time.

She shrugged, then squealed, "Poopy pants," before bursting into giggles perfectly timed with Cole's piercing cries. I handed her a towel.

"I'll run and get you clothes while you dry off, honey," I said.

I hurried to her bedroom and grabbed her an outfit. I laid it on her bed.

"Janie, your clothes are on your bed," I yelled above Cole's cries. "I'm going to be in the living room feeding Cole."

He was so worked up it took him a while to settle on my breast, but he finally did. He hadn't been settled for long when Janie plodded into the living room wearing only her underwear.

"Can I have some of your milk?" she asked.

THIRTY-NINE

CHRISTOPHER BAUER

The house was dark when I got home. Stillness enveloped it. I opened the door quietly and stepped over the spot on the wooden floor where it creaked. I tiptoed through the living room and into the hallway. Janie was already sleeping. It was too early for her to be asleep. Hopefully she wasn't sick. Our bedroom door was shut. I put my ear up to the wood, straining to hear anything. I wasn't going to wake them if they were asleep. I'd sleep on the couch. It was worth a terrible night of sleep if Hannah got a chance to rest. My heart sank when I heard whimpering.

I pushed open the door expecting to find Cole fussing, but he was fast asleep in his quilted bassinet next to the bed. Hannah lay curled up in the fetal position with a box of tissues next to her. I rushed over to her bedside and placed my hand on her forehead to check for fever. She wasn't hot.

"What happened?" I asked, leaning down to peer into her eyes. She looked depleted, spent.

"I yelled at Janie today—screamed at her to shut up. I didn't mean to, but she was crying so hard that I couldn't stand it, and I snapped. I yelled at her. Screamed, really. And she cried so hard afterward that she threw up. She's never cried so hard she threw up, and it's all my fault," she sobbed. "I'm a terrible mother."

I wrapped my arms around her and pulled her close to me. Her body was damp with sweat. "It's okay. I mean, obviously, it's not okay that you yelled at her, but everyone screws up. Parents yell at their kids all the time."

An involuntary sob escaped, sending a shudder down the length of her body. "Yes, but not kids like Janie."

"Did you apologize?" It wasn't lost on me that I had asked Janie the same question after she'd hurt Hannah in some way.

She nodded.

"Okay, well, then you taught her a valuable lesson today. You showed her that everyone screws up, even parents, but we apologize when we do. Those things are just as important for her to learn as the other things we teach her." I wasn't saying it to make her feel better, even though I hated seeing her sad; I believed it. There was nothing wrong with Janie discovering her parents were human and made mistakes. I massaged her shoulders. "Why don't I make you some tea? You get in your pajamas while I grab it, okay?"

I didn't give her an opportunity to say no. She'd changed into her pajamas and washed her face when I came back. She looked so worn down. The bags underneath her eyes grew bigger each day. I handed her the cup of tea and said, "So I was thinking about something when I was downstairs . . ." She took a sip. "Do you think it's time we revisited getting you some help with the kids?" I tried to sound as benign as possible to avoid offending her like I had in all our previous discussions about it. She glared at me but didn't say no, so I quickly continued before she could stop me. "I know we always said that we didn't want a nanny, but that was before we had two children and realized how hard it was to juggle everything. I'm having a hard time managing all of it myself." I didn't want her to think it was only about her. I was struggling too. "That's why so many people do it, Hannah. And we don't just have two children—we have two difficult and challenging children. Let's just be honest: our job is harder than most." I saw as she considered the possibility for the first time. I had to spring while there was an opening. "We aren't committing to anything permanently. We can just do it now while everyone is adjusting. Most people have help during the newborn phase."

She shook her head.

Had I read her wrong? "Your mom comes to help whenever she can. How's that any different than hiring someone?" I asked.

"Because it's my mom. It's not some stranger who's going to be judging everything I do. Have you seen how trashed this place is?" Her eyes bulged out of her head as she talked.

Janie's room was the only place in the house that was trashed. Everything else was meticulous. Her frantic cleaning hadn't changed. If anything, it'd gotten worse.

I chose my words carefully, doing my best not to upset her any further. "Why don't you just look at a few profiles online and see what you think?"

"I'm not changing my mind." She crossed her arms on her chest. The door was closed again.

Her stubbornness was maddening, and it didn't make sense. Hiring someone to help her care for the kids was the perfect solution to our problems. I reached out and caressed her back. "Asking for help doesn't mean you're a failure."

At first, I didn't think she'd heard me, but then she announced, "I'm just going to breastfeed her."

I almost spit out my tea. "What?"

It was completely out of the blue. She hadn't said anything about actually doing it when we were texting earlier today. She couldn't be serious. Had she even been listening to me?

"I've been thinking about it all day today. I googled tandem breastfeeding after she fell asleep tonight."

I interrupted her. "Tandem breastfeeding?"

"It's when you breastfeed two different children at the same time."

"Okay, but can we get back to talking about getting help for a while?" I tried to hide my annoyance at her perpetual avoidance of the topic.

She shook her head. "This might work, Christopher. Part of the reason she feels so left out and is acting out is because Cole's attached to my breast for most of the day. There's nothing she hates more than feeling rejected. If she were a part of the experience, she might not feel so jealous."

I stared at her in disbelief. Motherhood had stripped all her former modesty. Women in other countries breastfed older children all the time, but the image of a grown child that I sat with at the dinner table suckling up to Hannah's breast slightly disturbed me. I kept my mouth shut, though. She'd finally calmed down, and I didn't want to say something to upset her all over again. There was no way to know what would set her off these days.

"This could be a bonding experience for us. I'm sure she never experienced it with Becky. I mean, maybe Becky breastfed her, but I doubt it."

"If you're comfortable with it, then I support whatever you want to do." I patted the bed. "Why don't you lie down and close your eyes?"

She yawned at the mention of sleep. I tucked the blanket underneath her chin just like I did whenever I put Janie to bed. I kissed her on the top of her forehead. "Don't worry about anything. Just rest. Tomorrow is a new day," I said.

—

Hannah grinned at me over breakfast the next morning like we shared a secret. She'd told me earlier while we were making coffee that she was still considering breastfeeding Janie. It was good to see the smile returned to her face, but I secretly hoped she'd forgotten about the idea. It wasn't just that it was weird. We had worked so hard at moving Janie forward in her development, and it seemed like it'd be a step backward. What if it made her regress even further?

"I love you," I whispered in her ear before leaving. "Try to be easy today."

Shortly after my midmorning consultation, my phone vibrated with a text from Hannah:

I'm downstairs.

What are you talking about? Did you send this to me by mistake?

No. I'm downstairs.

In the hospital?

Yes.

What are you doing here?

I'm in the ER.

Are the kids ok?

I texted as I sprinted down the hallway. I skipped the elevator and went straight to the stairs because they were quicker.

Kids are fine. I'm getting stitches.

WTF?

She didn't respond. I tapped out a text to Dan, letting him know where I was in case he needed me. I found her in bed 7A. Bags of ice lay across her bare chest. I rushed over to her bedside. "What happened?" I asked.

"Janie bit me."

Anxiety twisted my guts. "Janie bit you? Where? How?"

"How do you think?" she snapped. She shot me a murderous glare.

I threw my hands in the air. I still wasn't getting it. It wasn't registering.

"This morning before I nursed Cole, I asked if she still wanted to try it, and she said yes. She was so excited. I explained to her it was just like sucking on a bottle. I mean, what else was I supposed to say?" Her face was contorted in anger. I'd never seen her so mad. "At first, she latched on like it was nothing. It was pretty amazing. I got a letdown just like I get with Cole. I hadn't expected that. She drank for a few minutes, but then you know what she did?" She didn't wait for me to answer. "She looked up at me. Right at me. And then she bit me. And not just a little nibble. She chomped down on it." She pulled off the bag of ice on her left breast. "See what she did to me?"

Her entire breast was swollen, bruised all around the nipple. Stitches lined the underside.

She pointed. "Six stitches. It took six stitches. She almost ripped it off."

"Oh my God." I didn't know what else to say. My head felt woozy. The room spun. "I have to sit down."

I sank into the chair next to her bed. I put my head in my hands, trying to make sense of what she'd just told me, what I'd just seen. What was wrong with Janie? I'd read about kids with reactive attachment disorder. I hadn't read anything like this. Nothing.

"Where are the kids?" I asked.

"Allison is at the house with them. I told her I was bleeding again and needed to go to the hospital." She shook her finger at me. "Don't you dare tell her what really happened."

I cocked my head to the side, shocked. "What?"

"I mean it. I don't want her to know she did this to me. I'd be mortified."

She didn't need to be embarrassed. She hadn't done anything wrong. I wanted to tell her that, but she was easy to set off these days, and I wasn't taking the chance of getting her more upset, since most of the time it was something I said or did. I couldn't do anything right by her. Nobody had told me having a newborn would be like this.

My phone vibrated again. This time it was Dan. He needed me upstairs. "It's Dan."

She motioned toward the door. "You can go. I'm fine. There's nothing else they can do. They already stitched me up. I'm just waiting on my discharge papers."

"Are you sure? I feel bad leaving you here."

"I'm sure. I don't know what I'm going to do when I get home, though. I don't want to even see her face." Anger radiated off her.

"I'll talk to Janie when I get home." I kissed the top of her head. "I'll call Dr. Chandler on the way back upstairs."

She turned away from me. "Go ahead. I don't want to talk to either of them."

My head spun as I drove home from the hospital. Hannah had texted me when she'd gotten home, but I hadn't heard anything else from her the rest of the day. I'd become a surgeon because I liked to fix people and picked orthopedics because it was an easy fix. Bones were like pieces of glass. When they broke, you put them back together again. That was what I was good at—fixing things. But I didn't know how to fix this.

Things grew worse instead of better every day, and I'd never felt more powerless.

Janie bounced to the door and greeted me like she did whenever I got home—happy, smiling, full of energy and life. I just stared at her, wondering how someone who looked so sweet could do something so awful. It was one of the hallmarks of kids with reactive attachment disorder, but it didn't make it any less creepy.

"Hi, Daddy. I missed you. Did you have a good day at the hospital?" she said like it was just another day.

"It's been a hard day," I said. I'd worry about her later. "Where's your mom?"

She pointed to the family room. "She's in there."

I walked into the family room. Hannah sat in the recliner, holding Cole while he slept. Her face was contorted in pain.

"How are you feeling?" I asked out of habit.

"It's pretty awful," she said, fighting back tears. "I can only feed him out of one breast, and it feels like knives are coming out when I do."

"I'm so sorry." I wished I could do something to make her feel better. "Do you want anything? Can I—"

Janie interrupted. "Daddy, play with me. I wanna play."

"Not right now. I'm talking to your mom."

She tugged on my arm. "But Daddy!"

I jerked it away. "Let go." My voice was louder than I had intended.

She stumbled back as if I'd hit her, eyes wide.

Hannah motioned to her. "Talk to her first. We can talk later."

"Let's go to your room, Janie," I said.

I shot Hannah a knowing look over my shoulder as we headed into Janie's room. I didn't close the door behind us so she could hear our conversation. I took a seat on Janie's bed. "Janie, come sit next to me. We need to talk."

"I don't wanna talk. I wanna play." She crossed her arms on her chest.

"No. We're going to talk first, and then we can play."

She begrudgingly took a seat next to me.

"You bit Mommy today, and it really hurt her. That was a bad thing to do." I wore my most serious face. "I am very upset with you."

"Sorry, Daddy." She grabbed my hand and kissed the top of it. "Can we play now?"

I shook my head. "I want to know why you did that. Why would you do something like that?"

She shrugged, searching my face for an answer.

"Please, I'm trying to understand. How could you hurt your mommy?"

She crawled up on my lap and whispered in her sweet voice, "I like hurting people. Do you?"

CASE #5243

Interview: Piper Goldstein

Ron stopped me midsentence. "How did Hannah seem to you during those early days?"

This time there was nothing I could do to keep the red from burning my cheeks. I shrugged.

He leaned forward. "How was Hannah after the baby was born?"

I cleared my throat. "I told you before—I didn't see much of them during that time period."

"No, you made it sound like you were around when the abuse happened, but that's not true, is it?" Luke peered at me from across the table.

I looked away; his gaze was too intense.

Ron rubbed his chin. "It's true, isn't it? You hadn't seen them in months until you got called to investigate at the hospital."

"I—"

He cut me off. "You weren't there for months. You have no idea what happened in that house, do you?"

"I didn't have to be in the house to know what happened. I knew them."

"Answer the question. You don't know what went on in that house for three months after Cole was born, do you?"

I didn't want to say the words, but I had no choice. "I didn't have any contact during that time period." I hung my head.

"And anything could've happened. Anything." Ron pounded the table. "You didn't know anything was even wrong until you got the call to go to the hospital, did you?"

"I didn't know there were any problems in the home."

"And by then it was too late, wasn't it, Ms. Goldstein?"

I couldn't take it anymore. I burst into tears.

FORTY

HANNAH BAUER

I could only feed Cole with my right breast because my left one was in stitches. He was a voracious eater, and one breast didn't suffice. I still got a letdown in my left breast, which meant it was constantly engorged and I had to find a way to express it. I couldn't use the breast pump because of how it pulled on my stitches, so I had to sit and do it by hand.

It only took two days before blood and pus oozed from my nipples, and it felt like fire coming out of me whenever Cole latched. I gritted my teeth and held back the urge to scream each time. He cried when he was finished because he was still hungry. I refused to quit, though, because breast milk was too important for development. I rushed to see my doctor, hoping she could fix me.

"It's probably time for you to stop breastfeeding," she said after her examination. "You have a horrible infection in your left breast."

I'd expected as much. "I'm not ready to stop. Can't you just prescribe an antibiotic? I know there are ones that are safe for nursing."

"I can, but it will only be a temporary fix. I'm fairly certain the infection will come back."

"I want to at least give it a try." I wasn't willing to give up that easily. Not on something that was so important.

She looked irritated, but she wrote me a prescription anyway. "I highly doubt these will work, but give them a try."

—

The pain grew worse every hour, so bad it kept me up all night. My left breast was swollen and engorged. The right one was supposed to be healthy, but by morning, it'd grown hard, painful lumps and was just as red as my left. I couldn't touch them; even the skin brushing against my shirt sent white-hot pain searing through my body until I was nauseous. I sobbed as I filled Cole his first bottle of formula later that evening.

"I feel like such a failure as a mom," I said through my tears.

"Just give it a few days," Christopher said, rubbing my back in wide circles. "It will probably clear up soon, and you can go back to breastfeeding. Formula isn't going to hurt him, and I promise, he's not going to forget how to do it."

I glared at him. He didn't understand what I was going through. Breastfeeding was the one thing making Cole's crying bearable. I loved lying with him as he coiled his body around mine and staring at his tiny clasped fingers. In those moments, it didn't matter that he cried all night long, and it made my utter exhaustion worthwhile. Feeding him a bottle wasn't going to be the same experience. It just wasn't. I didn't care what anyone said.

"Here, why don't you give him to me?" Christopher scooped him from me and took the bottle with his other hand. "And you go to sleep. You've been up for almost forty-eight hours. You've got to be exhausted."

I stumbled back into our bedroom, my eyes burning with exhaustion. I curled underneath our comforter but couldn't get warm. My entire body ached. I alternated between feeling like I was freezing to being so hot I felt sunburned.

"Christopher." It hurt to speak. "Christopher."

He rushed into the room, bouncing Cole on his chest in one of the baby wraps we'd gotten from our shower.

"I feel really awful. Can you take my temperature?"

He looked back and forth between the baby and me. "What do I do with him?"

"Take him with you."

"I can't take him with me and get the thermometer." He looked overwhelmed at the task.

"Are you serious? Give him to me, then."

The handoff startled Cole, and he started shrieking. His screams pierced my brain. Christopher just stood there, not knowing what to do.

I motioned toward the door. "Go!"

I was too weak to get out of bed and in too much pain to hold Cole. I laid him on his back next to me. He screamed and writhed like he was being tortured. I could tell by how worked up he was already that it was going to be a bad crying episode and last for hours. I covered my ears and sobbed.

Christopher returned with the thermometer and stuck it under my tongue. He picked up Cole, but it didn't make any difference. Sometimes he cried even harder when Christopher picked him up. He said it didn't bother him, but it did. The thermometer beeped, and I looked down.

103.4. I hadn't had a fever that high since I was a child. No wonder I felt so terrible.

"You need to go to urgent care." Worry lined his forehead. "Your fever shouldn't be that high. Not on antibiotics and Tylenol." His voice sounded like he was speaking at the end of a tunnel. "You're not driving yourself either, so don't even think about it."

I couldn't think. It hurt too much. I just wanted to go to sleep.

It wasn't long before Allison shook me awake.

"Come on, hon. I'm taking you to urgent care," she said, leaning down by the side of the bed, her face in front of mine.

I nodded. She slowly peeled the covers off and helped me to my feet. I sat on the side of the bed while she rummaged through my closet for a pair of shoes I could slip on easily. Cole's screams reverberated from down the hallway.

"Why doesn't he ever stop crying?" The room spun. I gripped the side of the bed.

"He will. Sometimes it just takes time for them to get used to being born." She came out holding a pair of old tennis shoes and plopped them on the floor for me. We hobbled into the hallway.

"Chris!" she called out.

"Yeah?"

"I'm taking Hannah now. I'll text you when I know anything."

"All right. Love you, Hannah."

I didn't have the energy to respond. Allison helped me to the car, and I fell back to sleep as soon as I sat down. I nodded in and out while we waited to see a doctor. Finally, it was our turn, and we shuffled down the hallway. Allison helped me into the room and went to shut the door.

"I'm okay," I said.

She looked at me, baffled.

"Just wait for me in the waiting room. I'm okay from here," I said again, desperately trying to keep it together. She edged her way out and shut the door behind her. I gasped and stumbled to the table. I couldn't let her see what Janie had done. I slid out of my shirt and into the gown and lay back on the table, suddenly feeling nauseous. Putting my hands on my stomach, I took deep breaths.

I didn't have to wait long for the doctor. His name tag swerved in front of me: Dr. Flynn. He tried to touch my right breast, and I yelped as soon as his finger made contact. "I'm sorry—it just hurts so bad," I cried.

He looked at both of them. "You have a nasty infection surrounding your wound, and it also looks like you have mastitis in both breasts."

"It's so painful; I don't know what to do."

"I'm sorry, but you're going to have to stop breastfeeding. I've got to put you on a strong dose of antibiotics, and they're not safe for the baby. I'm afraid if we don't aggressively treat this, you're going to become septic."

I cried the entire way back to the house.

"Don't let me forget to call Greg and let him know I'm staying over to take care of you tonight," Allison said as she helped me out of the car.

I shook my head. She looked surprised. Any other time, I would've gladly accepted her help, but the doctor had instructed me to shower in order to massage the milk out. She'd insist on helping me, and I couldn't let her see my breasts. Not that I was embarrassed for her to see them—she'd helped me fit my first bra—but she couldn't see what Janie had done to me. I hadn't told her. I hadn't told anyone. I was too ashamed.

"What's going on, Hannah?" she asked.

"Nothing. I'm fine," I said just as Christopher opened the front door to greet us. He wore Cole in the same sling as earlier.

"Hi, Auntie Allison!" Janie waved from behind him.

Anger burned my insides like it did whenever I looked at her. All of this was her fault. She'd never said anything about biting me. She'd never apologized. Never asked me how I was doing or how I felt.

"Come here and give me a hug, sweetie pie," Allison said. She opened her arms, and Janie ran into them. "Do you want to come home with me?"

Janie jumped up and down. "Yes! Yes!"

Allison looked up at me. "Why don't I just keep her overnight? That way Christopher can focus on taking care of you and Cole without having to worry about her. It's one less thing to worry about."

"Sounds great to me," I said.

Christopher didn't look so sure. "I don't know. She's never stayed overnight anywhere before."

"She'll be fine. Don't worry about it," Allison said. "It'll be good for her."

"I don't know . . ."

"Christopher, just let her go," I said, moving past him into the house. I needed to lie down.

—

I wasn't ready for Janie to come back from Allison's. Things were worse, not better. Both breasts were filled with knotty lumps. I tried to massage the milk out in the shower like my doctor had instructed, but the water felt like knives on my swollen skin. Percocet barely touched the pain. I couldn't keep anything down. I lay in bed with a bucket next to me. It was devastating not being able to nurse Cole. Every time he cried, my breasts instinctively filled with milk. Not being able to go to him broke my heart again and again.

Allison had kept Janie for four days, and it wasn't fair to make her keep her longer when she already had so much on her plate, even if I wanted her to. She looked frazzled when she brought Janie home later that afternoon. Janie threw her stuff on the floor and took off for her bedroom without speaking to me or Cole.

"How are you feeling?" Allison asked. She fluffed the pillows behind my head. I'd been camped out on the couch since Janie had left. We didn't have a TV in our bedroom, and I needed the distraction.

"Better than this morning," I said. I'd thrown up three times before ten and hadn't been able to keep any coffee down, so I had a raging headache on top of everything else. "Thanks so much for taking her. I hope she didn't give you too many problems."

She plopped down on the couch next to me, propping her legs up on the coffee table just like Christopher. "Honestly, it was a little rough. Promise you won't feel bad if I tell you something?"

I nodded. Nothing could make me feel worse than I already did.

"You always talk about how difficult Janie is, and I've never seen it. She's so well behaved and sweet whenever I'm around. Part of me thought you were overreacting." She glanced at me before continuing, making sure I didn't look hurt or defensive.

I waved her off. "It's fine. Don't even worry about it."

She looked relieved that I wasn't angry. "She can *really* be difficult."

I burst out laughing. "Um, you think so? What'd she do?"

"First she insisted on being carried everywhere, which lost its cuteness almost immediately. Then I couldn't get her to use the toilet, and she kept going in her pants." She wrinkled her nose. "Even the boys started to get annoyed with her because she kept acting and talking like a baby. You know it must've been bad if her two biggest fans were annoyed. But the weirdest thing was how she kept getting up during the middle of the night and coming into our bedroom. She'd just stand over us and stare. Does she always do that?"

"She used to do it all the time, but she hasn't done it in a while."

"Probably just part of the adjustment period." She squeezed my knee. "Can I get you anything before I leave? I have to go get the boys from soccer."

"I'm good. Thanks for taking her."

She nodded and looked away. It wasn't lost on me that she didn't say "no problem" or "anytime" like she normally would.

"Bye, Janie! I'll see you soon," she called out. She waited a second to see if Janie would respond and shrugged when she didn't. "Text me later, okay?"

Janie came into the living room as soon as she heard the door close.

"Did you have fun with Auntie Allison?" I asked.

She stuck out her lower lip. "I don't like Allison."

"What? Since when don't you like her? You love your aunt."

She shook her head. "No, I don't. She's a big meanie." She looked around. "Where's Daddy?"

"He's at work."

"Will you play with me?"

"Why don't you go play with Blue? I'm sure she missed you." I turned away. Her presence was unnerving.

"You never play with me. You're mean too. Just like Allison." She stuck her tongue out at me and stomped back to her room.

There was something about having her in the house again that sucked the air out of the room. My heart hammered. I grabbed Cole from his swing and squeezed him against my chest, hoping his heartbeat would calm mine, but it did nothing for the panic surging through my body. I had to get air. There wasn't enough air around me. I stumbled toward the door as waves of heat coursed through my veins. I was so hot, drenched in sweat.

I pushed open the front door and stepped outside onto the porch. The cool air hit me and felt good against my face. I sucked it in, trying to pull myself together.

She's just a girl. There's nothing to be afraid of.

FORTY-ONE

Christopher Bauer

I was happy to see Hannah up and moving around but was a little concerned as I watched her bustling with frenetic energy through the house. She'd been obsessively cleaning the house for three days, ever since Janie had gotten back from Allison's. She kept Cole wrapped tightly against her chest while she worked.

"Hey." I came up behind her as she arranged the picture frames on top of the fireplace. "You've been busy all night. Why don't you take a break?"

She pushed me aside. "It's just a mess in here. It's too dirty."

"How are you feeling?"

"Good. I feel good."

"Do you want me to take him?"

"No, but can you do something with Janie?"

Janie stood behind the baby gate in her room like she was an animal in a zoo, looking bewildered. We'd never made her stay in her room like that before, not even when she was at her worst.

"Mommy made me go to my room," she said as I unlatched the gate.

Hannah ignored us for the rest of the night. She kept Cole on her chest and moved through the house like she couldn't clean fast enough.

Our house sparkled and shone. You could smell bleach when you walked in the door. It looked like we were about to put it on the market. It was staged to perfection—everything in place, proportional—except Janie's room. Hannah wouldn't touch it.

I didn't know what she did with Janie all day while she cleaned and didn't dare ask. Ever since the biting incident, Hannah had avoided talking about her or doing anything with her. I understood how hurt she was and gave her the time she needed to work through her emotions, but then I came home and found Janie in soiled clothes.

Her poop had been in her pants for so long it had hardened against her skin like a rock. I couldn't even scrape it off. She was still in the pajamas she'd been wearing for the last two days. Her hair was a tangled mess, there was food all over her face, and her breath smelled foul, which meant she hadn't brushed her teeth either. I waited until she was in bed to talk to Hannah about it.

"Can you put the broom down and talk to me for a second?" I asked.

"What? I can talk while I clean."

"Hannah, that's the third time you've swept the floors since I got home. I'm pretty sure they're clean. Are you getting ready to adopt another kid that I don't know about?" I joked to lessen the tension. The only other time she'd cleaned like a madwoman was when we were getting ready for Janie's home visit.

"I just don't like dirt. You can't see it, but I can. Besides, Blue sheds everywhere. I don't want Cole breathing all that in. We never should've gotten a cat. He might be allergic."

"I don't think he's allergic to cats. He would've had some reaction by now." I massaged my forehead. "Can we sit down, please?"

She shook her head. "I ordered a carpet cleaner on Amazon today."

I raised my eyebrows. "We don't even have any carpets."

"We have rugs," she said like that explained everything.

"Can we please talk about Janie?"

"What's there to talk about?" she asked, immediately defensive.

"Honey, I know you're still upset because of what she did to you, but you can't treat her the way you've been treating her."

"The way I've been treating her?" She laughed sarcastically.

"Yes, you can't let her sit around in poopy pants all day."

"She knows how to go to the bathroom when she needs to go. I'm done playing her games. Done." She stopped sweeping, walked over, and locked eyes with me. "If she's going to be a brat and poop in her pants, then she can sit in it."

"Dr. Chandler said it's totally normal for her to revert to babylike behavior."

"She also said Janie is manipulative."

I sighed. "What about the fact that she's filthy? She was still in her pajamas when I got home tonight and hadn't even brushed her teeth."

"I tried to get her to brush her teeth and change her clothes. Do you know what she did?" Her jaw was set in a straight line. "She stuck her tongue out at me and said she wished she had a different mommy. I'm tired of pretending like she's ever going to like me. That girl hates me."

"She doesn't hate you." It broke my heart to hear her talk about Janie that way.

"Really?" She laughed. Bitterness lined every word. "The only person she cares about is herself. And you," she added as an afterthought.

"That's not true."

She gave me a pointed look, daring me to argue with her.

"It's just rough right now. Everyone's emotions are on edge. This happens to all families when there's a new baby. You've still got to take care of her even when it's hard."

She opened her mouth but quickly shut it again, changing her mind. She turned on her heel and stormed away, taking Cole into our bedroom with her and slamming the door behind her.

—

Hannah met me at the door the next day when I came home. She started screaming immediately. "Tell her to give it to me!" Her eyes were wild. Her hand shook as she pointed to the hallway leading to the bedrooms. "She's in there. Tell her to give it to me."

I set my stuff on the end table next to the couch. "Whoa, calm down. What are you talking about?"

"My phone. She took my phone and hid it somewhere. She won't give it back." Her voice trembled with anger.

"Your phone? Why would she take your phone? Are you sure you didn't just misplace it somewhere?" I eyed the room, expecting to spot it.

"She took it! You said I needed to take care of her, so I did. She wouldn't go to the bathroom today when I asked her to or brush her teeth, so I told her she couldn't watch any cartoons until she'd done what I asked. You know what she did? She looked right at me and took her pants off. She walked over to the rug in the dining room and peed on it. Then she laughed like it was the funniest thing in the world."

I'd never seen her so unhinged. "That's not okay, but what does that have to do with your phone?"

"Oh, the phone? The phone happened when I took away her Barbie dolls. Ask me why I took away her Barbie dolls. Ask me." She moved in front of me, smashing Cole between us like a sandwich.

"Why did you take her Barbie dolls away?"

"I set Cole down. Just for a second. That's why I never set him down. Never. You want to know why I carry him around all the time. That's why. That's why."

I put my hands on her shoulders and moved her back from me. "Hannah, please calm down. You're not making any sense. None of this makes sense. Why don't we sit down just for a second?"

She jerked away. "I don't want to sit down. I want you to make her give me my phone."

Janie stood in the doorway of her bedroom, watching everything play out with a blank expression on her face.

"Janie, did you take Mommy's phone?" I asked.

She shook her head.

"Yes, you did! You took it!" Hannah screamed.

"I did not! You're a mean mommy!" Janie yelled back.

Cole started to wail.

"Now look what you've done!" Hannah said, red faced and furious.

"Everybody, calm down. Just calm down." I motioned to the couch. "Sit down while I get him a bottle."

I walked into the kitchen and took some deep breaths while the water heated up. The beginnings of a headache throbbed behind my temples. I didn't care what Hannah said anymore. I couldn't live like this. None of us could. Dan had given me the number of the woman they had used when their girls were young, and I was calling her tonight as soon as I got a chance. Enough was enough.

"I'm going to call your phone," I said.

"I already did with the house phone. It must be dead because I didn't charge it last night," she responded from the living room.

Her phone immediately went to voice mail. I pulled up the Find My iPhone app just in case she'd gone out and left it somewhere. The pin showed it was in the house. I shook the bottle on my way back into the living room, bracing myself for a fight. I handed the bottle to Hannah, and she stuck it in Cole's mouth. He settled on the bottle and stopped crying.

"Okay, let's see if we can get to the bottom of this. Janie, can you come out here?" I asked.

She walked out of her bedroom, hanging her head. "I'm sorry, Daddy. I don't know why Mommy is so mad. I tried to get her to calm down."

Hannah glared at her.

"I'm going to ask you again, and I want you to tell me the truth. Did you take Mommy's phone?" I asked.

"I didn't," she said adamantly.

"Yes, you did," Hannah said through gritted teeth. "You told me you took it."

"She told you?" I asked.

"Yes. I took away her Barbies. Then later on this afternoon, I needed my phone and couldn't find it anywhere. When I asked her about it, she said, 'Give me my Barbies, and I'll give you the phone.'"

Janie crossed her arms on her chest. "Did not."

Hannah looked like she was one second away from screaming again.

I put my hand on Hannah's shoulder, trying to calm her. "How about this? Why don't we all look for the phone just to make sure?"

Hannah glared at me, but she got up and went into our bedroom. I took all the cushions off the couch and searched underneath the furniture. It wasn't in the living room. I checked on the toilet paper stand in the bathroom because she'd misplaced it there before, but it was empty. Janie scurried through the house, and every few minutes she called out, "It's not here, Daddy."

I emptied out everything in Hannah's purse even though I was sure it was the first place she'd looked. It wasn't there either. Finally, I moved into Janie's room.

Her room was a mess—a sharp contrast to the rest of our put-together house. Her toys were everywhere. The bed was rumpled and unmade. Her books were strewn across the room. Broken crayons were ground into the floor. I picked up the chunks as best I could and threw them in the trash. I picked up a few toys and tossed them into the plastic toy containers. Her stuffed animals were scattered around the room, and I scooped them into a pile. I straightened out the covers at the end of her bed, and Hannah's phone rolled out onto the floor when I tugged on one of the blankets.

"Janie! Come here."

"What, Daddy?" she asked.

I crouched down in front of her. "I found Mommy's phone in your bed. I thought you said you didn't take it from her."

"I didn't take it. Mommy put it there."

Hannah had been so spacey that she could've easily put it there and forgotten about it. She'd left the stove burners on twice last week.

"And you're sure you didn't take it?"

She nodded.

I walked into our bedroom. Hannah was on all fours peering underneath the bed.

"You can get up," I said. "I found your phone."

She leaped up and snatched it from me. "Where was it?"

"I found it underneath the couch cushions in the family room."

"But I took out all the cushions twice and never found it."

I shrugged. "I guess you just overlooked it."

FORTY-TWO

Hannah Bauer

I stormed into Janie's room and towered over her with my hands on my hips. "Where did you hide Cole's blanket?"

Her hoarding was out of control. She'd always stashed stuff in her bedroom, but now she was making it personal. In the last week, she'd stolen my favorite coffee mug—the one I used every morning that said **I LOVE CHOCOLATE.** I'd found it in her tub of Legos. She took my T-shirts and stuffed them in her drawers, buried underneath her clothes. I didn't usually confront her about it because she'd only lie, but I didn't have a choice this time. It was Cole's blanket that he rubbed against his cheek to soothe himself. He couldn't fall asleep without it.

Janie ignored me and kept working on her puzzle. She'd been busy with it most of the morning.

I tapped her on her shoulder. "I asked you a question. Where did you hide Cole's blanket?"

"I didn't do it." She turned her body so her back faced me. Some days I fought her, but I didn't have the energy today.

I checked underneath her bed first since it was her most used hiding space. At least she wasn't very creative about her hiding places, but there wasn't anything under her bed except cookie wrappers and empty toilet paper rolls. I stood and rifled through her sheets and comforter. It wasn't there either. I scanned the room, hoping I wouldn't have to go through every toy bin like before, and that's when I spotted the yellow tuft of his blanket poking out of her garbage can. I stormed over and snatched it out.

I flung the blanket in front of her face. "How did this get in your garbage can?"

"I don't know," she said. She looked up at me, doe eyed, and smiled all innocent and sweet, but I didn't believe her for a second.

"We're going to give Blue back if you don't start behaving." My patience had run out. I'd use Blue if I had to. She'd left me no choice.

She shrugged. "So?"

"No more taking my stuff and hiding it in your room either. Or Cole's. You leave our stuff alone. And you are going to stop having accidents in your pants, or else Blue's gone." I figured I might as well add things on since I was delivering the ultimate threat. "Do you understand me?"

She looked at me with no expression on her face. I stared back at her, a blunt refusal to look away first, like a dog establishing dominance. Cole's fussing in the other room broke our stare-down.

I shook my finger at her. "I mean it," I said before marching away to tend to Cole.

I fed him and fixed our lunch afterward, reheating the spaghetti from last night and cutting up fruit to go with it. Sometimes I missed the days when my life wasn't centered on food.

"Janie, it's lunchtime. Come eat."

She skipped into the kitchen with a big grin on her face and took a seat at the table, our spat forgotten that quickly. She wolfed down her food while I barely touched mine. I hadn't had an appetite in weeks. The thought of food made my stomach churn.

"I want to show you something," she said after she finished her plate. She walked over to my chair and grabbed my hand. She led me into the bedroom and pointed to the spot on her floor next to her rainbow-colored toy bins. Blue lay there motionless, her paws sticking straight out. Her head was cocked to the side at a funny angle. Alarm bells went off inside me.

"I don't care about her," Janie said.

I knelt down next to Blue and turned her head. Her eyes bulged out of the sockets. Blood leaked from her nose. Her chest wasn't moving. There was no air. No movement. No life. The hair on the back of my neck stood up. I slowly turned to look at Janie. Time stilled.

She smiled down at me with the same grin she'd worn when she'd come out of the bedroom. "She's dead."

Blood pooled in my insides. My stomach heaved. Jumping up, I pushed her out of the way. I ran down the hallway and barely made it to the toilet in time, where I heaved again and again.

Cole.

I leaped up and ran to the living room, where I'd left him napping in his swing. Janie stood next to the swing, staring down at him.

"Get away from him!" I screamed as I ran over to them. I grabbed her by the arm and pulled her away. "Don't you ever go near him! Ever!" I shook her, flinging her small body back and forth. "Do you hear me? Don't you touch him! Don't you even look at him!"

FORTY-THREE

CHRISTOPHER BAUER

"Send her away. Please send her to Allison's. She'll take her for a while. Or my mom. She can go to my mom's. Please, I just can't have her here. Not right now." Hannah was sobbing so hard it was difficult to make out her words.

I hugged her tightly. "It's okay. It's going to be okay."

"No, it's not. How can you even say that? She's evil. She killed an animal. Killed an animal." She kept saying it over and over again.

My brain reeled. I never would've believed it if I hadn't seen it myself, but I had. I was the one who had put Blue's body in a plastic bag and laid her in a cardboard box. Janie had sat on the outside steps by the back door observing it all like she was watching a movie. I had sat down next to her after I'd finished.

"Did you hurt Blue?" I had asked. I'd still been hoping it had been a weird accident, like maybe Blue had had a seizure and died. Or a stroke. It was possible. Maybe Janie had just happened to be there when it had happened, so she had thought she'd done it.

"Yep. I hurt her real bad," she'd said without an ounce of emotion in her voice.

"How?" The question had come out without thought.

"I put my pillow on her and sat on her head. She really meowed. She didn't scratch me though, because I had the pillow, so she couldn't get me." She said it like she was proud that she'd thought it through.

I didn't ask any more questions after that.

Hannah hid in our bedroom with Cole until after I put Janie to bed. "I want you to put a lock on her door," she said when I came into the bedroom. "She has to be locked in there at night."

I grimaced. "A lock on her door? We can't just lock her in her room."

"What if she gets up in the night while we're sleeping and kills us?" Her voice was hysterical. Her arms shook as she held Cole close to her chest.

"She's not going to kill us," I said with more calm than I felt.

"How do you know that? She killed Blue." She started sobbing all over again.

Killing an animal was one thing. Killing people was another—sociopathic. Sociopaths didn't have any feelings toward anyone, animals or otherwise, so Janie couldn't be one because she had feelings. I'd seen them. She cried when she was afraid and laughed when she was happy. She was proud when she did something right, like the first time she'd learned how to swing without a push or had gone down the slide by herself. She was just a damaged girl—a severely disturbed girl, too, but she wasn't a sociopath.

Hannah wasn't going to rest unless I did something, though. I went out to the garage and dug through my tools until I found rope. I brought it back inside and started wrapping it around her doorknob.

What would we do if there was a fire? How could I get her out of her room quickly if there was an emergency? Or what if she got sick and needed to wake us in the middle of the night and couldn't get out of her room? I unwound what I'd done and headed back to our bedroom.

"I can't tie her in there. Something might happen, and we wouldn't be able to get her out in time. Even if it's for one night, I don't feel right about it. I'll just sleep on her floor."

Hannah's face crumpled. "Why? Why do you always pick her?"

"I'm not picking her. I would be responsible if something happened to her, and I'm not taking that chance. It's not right," I snapped. "I'll get an alarm system for her room tomorrow. A proper system that we can set and program so that if anything goes wrong or there's an emergency, she can easily get out."

"Fine," she huffed.

But nothing was fine. We both knew that.

FORTY-FOUR

Hannah Bauer

I hadn't been able to sleep since it had happened. I saw Blue's face every time I dozed off, the way her eyes bulged out, and Janie sitting on top of her with that stupid grin on her face. I'd made Christopher tell me how she had killed her. He'd tried to pretend like he didn't know, but he wasn't a good liar. I could tell by the look in his eyes that she'd told him, so I had forced him to tell me. Afterward, I'd wished I hadn't.

A sense of impending doom filled every room in our house. The smell of urine hung in the air no matter how much I cleaned because Janie peed everywhere like a dog that wasn't housebroken. I couldn't even be in the same room with her, and just the sound of her voice made my skin crawl. Waves of fear pummeled me. As soon as my heart sped up, so did my breathing. It was only a matter of seconds before I was gasping for air. It didn't matter that I was a nurse and knew I was hyperventilating; I still felt like I was going to die.

I was putting away the leftovers, trying to keep it together, when Janie came into the kitchen.

"Can I have a cookie?" she asked.

I took one look at her and started sobbing. Christopher ran into the kitchen. I gripped the counter with both hands.

"What's going on, Janie?" he asked.

"I want a cookie," she said, unsure of herself or what she'd done to upset me.

He grabbed a cookie and handed it to her. "Why don't you go eat this in the living room while I talk to Mommy?"

"What happened?" He knelt beside me and ran his hands through his hair.

My finger shook as I pointed to the other room. "Her."

"What did she do?" His face blanched; he braced himself for what was to come.

"Nothing. She's already done enough. I can't be around her any-more. I can't do it."

He lowered his voice so Janie couldn't hear in the room next door. "Be quiet. She might hear you."

"I don't care if she hears me."

"I do."

"Of course you do," I said under my breath.

"What did you say?" he asked, then quickly shook his head. "Never mind." He reached out to take Cole from me. "Why don't you give him to me and go lie down for a while?"

I turned away, pulling Cole tighter against my chest. I only put him down to change him. Besides that, I wore him on me at all times.

"I don't want her here." I spit the words out.

"She's our daughter. Where else is she supposed to go?"

"She's not really our daughter."

He recoiled like I'd slapped him. "Don't you ever say that again." His eyes flashed with anger. "We knew what we were getting into when we adopted her. We knew she would have problems. We signed up for this."

"Problems? You call these problems? She's a killer!" I shrieked.

He threw his hands up in disgust. "She hurt an animal because she was mad at you. There's a big difference."

"She's a killer!"

He grabbed my arms, his fingernails digging into my skin. "Stop saying that."

I jerked away. "Get your hands off me! Don't touch me!"

He let go but stepped closer. His face was in mine, wearing an expression I'd never seen before. "She is our daughter, and she's only seven years old."

I folded my arms across my chest and looked at him without flinching. "I don't want her here."

"What are you talking about? We can't just give her back—we're her parents. Her parents, Hannah. Whether you like it or not, that's what we signed on for." His body shook as he tried to control his anger. "You can't just give your kids away when it's rough."

"You can if your kid is a monster."

CASE #5243

INTERVIEW: PIPER GOLDSTEIN

Ron cracked his knuckles like he'd been doing all afternoon. I cringed. I didn't know what was worse, their relentless questioning or the silence that made me so uncomfortable I wanted to start talking just to fill it. "What I'm having a hard time understanding is why Christopher went back to work if things were so bad and he was supposed to be such a good husband. What kind of a husband leaves his family at a time like that?"

"What else was he supposed to do?" It was the first time I'd challenged him, but I drew a line with the direction he was going. I didn't like what he was implying.

Luke jumped in, always on Ron's side. "He could've stayed home, got her a nanny, called one of their parents. There were a lot of options."

I glared at them. "You can judge them all you want, but you weren't in their situation."

"Neither were you." Luke didn't try to hide his smirk.

Anger rose in my chest. They were never going to let that go. "He had to go back to work. They couldn't afford for him not to."

Luke snorted. "Really? You're trying to tell me that an orthopedic surgeon needed money?"

"That's exactly what I'm saying. The Bauers had sunk all their savings into buying their house and spent the last five years paying off all their student loan debts." I wanted to point out that he'd know all of that if he knew the Bauers like I did, but I held myself back. "Do you have any idea how much it cost to pay for all Janie's therapy? Medical insurance didn't pay for her psychological care, and her medical costs were thousands of dollars each month. So Christopher couldn't lose his job. Imagine how much stress that would've added to the situation. He was just trying to keep their family afloat."

Ron finally jumped back in. "It dawns on me that there's no record of the incident with the cat anywhere."

"It wasn't intentional."

"Was there anything else you may have unintentionally left out?"

FORTY-FIVE

Christopher Bauer

Hannah refused to come with me to the session I'd scheduled with Dr. Chandler. She said she was done going to therapy because Janie was never going to change, and she was sick of talking about it. She'd come around eventually. She just needed a few more days.

We had thought we'd be able to meet with Dr. Chandler twice a week after Hannah gave birth, but we hadn't been to her office since Cole was born, and he was going to be two months old next Monday. Just because we hadn't been there didn't mean I hadn't thought about what we'd talked about last time. I'd done plenty of research on reactive attachment disorder since then. I kept getting drawn into morbid documentaries about kids adopted from Russian orphanages who turned into mini–serial killers.

There were all these online tests you could take, too—the "Answer these twenty questions and get a diagnosis" kind. I knew I shouldn't, that there wasn't any validity in those kinds of test, but I couldn't help myself. I'd taken them all: *Does Your Child Suffer from RAD? Is Your Child a Psychopath? Should You Institutionalize Your Child?* I'd taken the same test online that Dr. Chandler had given us in her office, and Janie had scored even higher than she had then. Her scores on the others were in the clinical range too.

Dr. Chandler was a stickler for staying within her allotted fifty-minute sessions, so I didn't waste any time on small talk once we were alone in her office. There was so much that had happened since Cole had been born, and I didn't want to leave out anything. I talked so fast my words tripped over each other. She kept telling me to slow down.

"It's like walking into a war zone every day," I said after I'd filled her in on everything. "And it just keeps getting worse. I don't know what to do. I've tried getting Hannah help, but she refuses. Her mom comes to stay sometimes, and that always makes a difference, but everything goes right back to where it was after she leaves."

"I share Hannah's concerns about Janie," she said. She rarely took sides on any issue, so she had to feel strongly about it. "I'm really worried about Janie's potential for violence." She paused. "But I'm not just concerned about Janie. I'm also very concerned about Hannah and the toll this has taken on her."

I'd told her how Hannah had lost so much weight that her clothes drooped on her, her T-shirts sliding off her shoulders and sweatpants dragging on the floor. Her pale complexion looked pasty, sallow, and almost gray now, like she was sick. I couldn't remember the last time her eyes weren't sunken and rimmed in black.

"Is she sleeping?" Dr. Chandler asked.

"Not really. I expected her to start sleeping once Cole did, but her sleep got worse. It was bizarre. I'm not sure if she's slept at all this past week." When she wasn't pacing throughout the house, I felt her tossing and turning next to me in the bed.

She frowned and looked down at her notes. "I can't imagine how tough insomnia must be on top of everything else that's going on. Has she tried to take anything to help?"

I shook my head. Hannah hated any kind of drugs. She didn't even like to take Tylenol unless it was absolutely necessary. It was weird for a nurse, but she said she didn't like putting foreign chemicals into her body.

"And you already said she wasn't eating. What's her mood like?"

"Her mood?" I rubbed my forehead. "It's all over the place."

She folded her hands together and placed them on top of her notebook. "It sounds like everyone in the family needs help, and the best way for everyone to get it might be putting Janie into a residential facility for a while."

I sat up straighter. "What do you mean by a residential facility?"

"It's a facility that provides care for emotionally disturbed youth like Janie. They're therapeutic homes designed to provide a more structured environment for the kids to learn new skills. They'll also keep them from harming themselves or someone else. Some facilities are better than others." She reached out and patted my hand. "I'd make sure we got her into one of the best."

"You mean she stays there? Like, lives there?" An overwhelming sense of defeat washed over me. Sending her away felt like we'd failed her.

Dr. Chandler nodded.

"For how long?"

She shrugged. "It depends. Some kids stay for a few weeks or months. Others stay for years. At this point, there's no way to know how long it would be for Janie. The first step would be completing an assessment for mental health services. I do them all the time and could easily do it for you. Then, based on my findings, we'd look for the best therapeutic placement for her. I know you guys have been against medication, but it might be time to consider it as an option to stabilize her impulse control, and a residential facility would be a great place to try it. The doctors there would be able to monitor her medication and adjust as needed."

"It just feels like we're giving up on her." Emotions filled my throat.

"I know it feels like that, but you're not giving up on her. You're giving her what she needs right now. It's not always going to be this way, but she needs help. More help than either of you can give her right now." She squeezed my hand. "And Hannah needs an opportunity to rest and recover. She really does. This will provide her with a chance to regroup herself." She tilted her head and smiled. "And you might find out that you needed the break too."

I looked away so she couldn't see the tears moving down my cheeks. "She's going to feel like we abandoned her."

Dr. Chandler's eyes filled with compassion. "You'll be able to visit her. Initially, things will be very strict, and she won't have many privileges, but once she adjusts, you'll be able to take her on outings. Eventually, you'll even be able to bring her home for overnight visits. Some kids flourish in residential settings. She might be one of them."

Normally, I wouldn't have considered making such an important decision without discussing it with Hannah first, but I already knew what she'd say. There was no need to ask her.

I took a deep breath, whispering a silent apology to Janie as she played in the waiting room with Dr. Chandler's assistant. "Okay, how do we start the process?"

Hannah was agitated when we got home. She looked ghoulish. She'd started losing clumps of her hair. I wasn't sure if it was from the post-pregnancy hormones or stress. Either way, it added to her appearance of being ill. She paced the house, back and forth. As soon as Janie and I came in, she scuttled to our bedroom and shut the door behind her. I settled Janie in front of the TV and went to talk to her. I knocked before entering.

"Who is it?" she asked. Her voice was filled with paranoia.

I jiggled the doorknob. It was locked. "It's just me."

She opened the door a crack, peering out to see if Janie was hiding behind me, like maybe I was trying to trick her into letting Janie into the room. Once she was satisfied that I was alone, she opened it wide enough for me to slide through. She slammed it shut as soon as I was inside.

"Look what I found today. Look what I found in her room while you were gone." Her voice was pressured, rushed, like she couldn't get the words out fast enough.

Our bed was covered with photo albums and pictures. She grabbed my hand and pulled me over to it. She picked up one of the albums and thrust it at me. "Look! Look at this! Look at what she did."

It was our wedding album—the one we'd lovingly put together after we'd gotten back from our honeymoon. The first page was our engagement photo, taken by a professional photographer; it was the one we'd used on our "save the date" cards. We were in front of the café where we'd had our first date with our arms wrapped around each other. I stared in horror at Hannah's scratched-out face. I flipped to the next page. It was the same thing. My smile shone from the pages, while Hannah's face was destroyed. Janie had used black crayons on some of the pictures to make a big *X* on her face. Others were just scratched out.

Hannah grabbed pictures off the bed, all of them ripped up and torn. "There's more. All of this. Do you know how long it must've taken her to do this?" She slapped them dramatically back on the bed one by one. "And look." Her hand shook as she pointed to a different set of pictures on the bed.

I looked down at the spread of pictures I'd printed out a few weeks earlier—the ones I'd taken in the hospital of Cole and his first day home. His face was as destroyed as Hannah's. Any doubts I had about sending Janie to residential treatment vanished.

Hannah threw the scraps of pictures on the bed and collapsed on the floor in tears. I sat next to her and held her. The bones poked out from underneath her shirt.

"It's going to be okay," I said in my most soothing voice. "She's not going to live with us for a while."

FORTY-SIX

HANNAH BAUER

Christopher's eyes peered into mine. "Where's Janie?"

I rubbed my eyes. I must've fallen asleep. Cole stirred next to me. What time was it?

He shook my shoulder. "Where is she?"

My heart pounded. He wasn't supposed to be home yet. I hadn't had time to clean up.

"In her room."

He stopped in his tracks when he got to her closed door and noticed the alarm was engaged. "She's in here? We agreed if I put the locks on the door that we would only use them at night."

I didn't dare tell him I'd been doing it for weeks. It was the only way I felt safe. Instead, I said nothing and waited for him to unlock the door.

"Oh my God," I heard him exclaim.

Janie must have smeared her feces again. I walked over to join him and stood in the doorway. This time it was on the walls. She'd finger painted with her own poop. Christopher stared, taking it all in—Janie naked in the center of the room surrounded by toys, her food smashed all around her, empty juice boxes and broken toys.

Christopher turned to look at me, the reality registering on his face. "Do you leave her in here all day?"

I nodded.

"Wh—what? I don't . . . I don't understand . . ."

"I clean everything up before you get home." I was surprised he hadn't smelled the poop whenever he was in there. Her room permanently smelled foul no matter how hard I scrubbed.

"How long has this been going on? How long?" His fists were clenched at his sides.

"Ever since she killed Blue."

He came at me, his face contorted in anger. "How could you? How could you do this to her? After everything she's been through?"

"How could I?" I pointed to her. "She's evil. That's what her grandmother said. Remember? She said we didn't know how terrible she was. Did you ever think that's why her mother had to lock her up like an animal? It's because she is one!"

I saw the pink blur of his hand as he slapped my face. My skin stung as my teeth cut through the soft, wet flesh of my mouth. My head jerked back. I stumbled from the force of it, bringing my hand up and pressing it against the sting, shocked.

Janie let out a piercing shriek.

Christopher's eyes filled with horror. He came toward me again. I backed up. "Don't." I held my hand up. "Just don't."

CASE #5243

Interview: Piper Goldstein

Luke slapped the picture on the table. "What kind of a husband does this?"

Who had told them about the incident? I knew the way they would look at Christopher now—the same way I looked at men who hit women.

"He only hit her that one time."

"Let me guess—he'd never hit a woman before?" He couldn't keep the disgust off his face.

I hung my head like I was the one who'd been hit. "Yes."

"And he was so ashamed, right? Promised to never do it again? Probably even brought her some beautiful flowers too." He snorted. "Seriously. You know better than that."

He was right. I couldn't deny it. Men didn't hit women no matter what. Period. It didn't matter if a woman was beating up on a man—he took the hits. There was nothing that justified hitting a woman. It was what I taught perpetrators in all of my domestic violence education classes.

FORTY-SEVEN

Christopher Bauer

I was doing my best to calm down on the short drive to the house. A few minutes ago, Hannah had called me while hysterical again. I couldn't understand anything she was saying because she was sobbing incoherently. There were few words, mostly just sounds. I was so tired of leaving work to calm things down between Hannah and Janie. Dr. Chandler had put Janie's name on the waiting list for a place called New Horizons, but she'd said it could take weeks. I didn't know what I was going to do until then. I hadn't even bothered giving Dan an excuse this time.

It'd been three days, and we hadn't talked about what had happened. I couldn't believe I'd slapped Hannah. I'd never laid a hand on a woman. Ever. I wasn't that kind of man. I had just reacted. I would never look at myself the same way, but I couldn't bring myself to apologize, even though I knew it was the right thing to do.

The house was still when I walked inside.

"Hannah?"

No answer.

"Janie?"

Nothing.

I walked through the living room and into the hallway. It was eerily quiet. I checked in both bedrooms, but they were empty. The bathroom door at the end of the hallway was ajar. Something was wrong. I could feel it. I rushed down the hallway and into the bathroom, throwing open the door.

Hannah sat in front of the bathtub with her feet straight out, holding Cole's body against her chest and staring into space. Janie was on the other side of the room against the wall, rocking with her legs pulled up to her chest. Her clothes were drenched. Why was she soaked? I looked back and forth between the two of them.

"Hannah?" I said cautiously, taking a step toward her.

She didn't even blink.

"Hannah?"

Nothing.

I moved toward Janie. "What's going on?"

Janie looked up and started crying immediately. Heaving sobs shook her body. I walked over and put my arms around her. She crumpled in my arms, her body trembling.

Hannah sprang to life. "Get away from her! Get away! She'll infect you with her evil. It's everywhere. Her evil is everywhere."

"Hannah, stop. Enough. Sit down," I ordered.

She inched her way across the tiled floor, never letting go of the baby. "Cole. My baby Cole." She started sobbing. Her wails joined Janie's and reverberated off the bathroom walls.

I scooped Janie up and carried her over to Hannah. I crouched next to them. That's when I looked at Cole's face. His eyes were open wide and unblinking. His lips were blue.

"Oh my God, what's wrong with him?"

"My baby. My baby Cole." Hannah only sobbed harder.

"Give me the baby." I tried to grab him, but she jerked away.

She hugged him closer to her. "My baby. My baby Cole."

I grabbed her and pulled her toward me as she struggled against me. She tried to hold on, but I pried him out of her arms. His body was cold. His chest wasn't moving. I set him on the floor, felt for a pulse. No heartbeat. I pushed on his small chest with my two fingers.

"Call 911! Call 911!" I didn't recognize the sound of my voice.

Breathe. One. Two.

Breathe. One. Two.

I pushed on his chest again.

"Hannah!"

She sat motionless while Janie sprang into action. She sprinted out of the bathroom and came running back with Hannah's phone. She handed it to me. No way I was stopping CPR. I tossed it to Hannah. She missed, and it clattered to the floor.

"Hannah! Hannah!"

She picked up the phone, still moving slowly. "I can't. I don't know. I can't."

"Call 911!" I grabbed her by the shoulders and shook her, holding back the urge to smack her again. "Do you hear me? Call 911!"

CASE #5243

INTERVIEW: PIPER GOLDSTEIN

Why did we have to talk about everything? Couldn't they just read all the medical reports? The clinical case summaries? It was all there, written down in black and white. I didn't know why the words had to come out of my mouth.

It wasn't like I hadn't thought about those days. I couldn't stop thinking about them. I ran through them like movie clips playing out over and over again, always starting with my trip to the hospital.

I had recognized the nurse at the nurse's station from one of my previous cases. She'd been busy typing into her computer when I had approached her.

I had cleared my throat. "Excuse me."

She'd looked up. She had a long, narrow face and dark hair tucked behind her ears.

I had flashed her my badge. "I'm here to see Cole Bauer."

She'd pointed to the narrow hallway on her right. "He's in room 10E."

"Thanks," I'd said, but she'd already gone back to what she had been doing before I had interrupted her.

It didn't matter how many times I'd been in the NICU; each visit felt like walking onto another planet. Time crawled underneath constant movement and manic activity. I had steeled myself for what I'd find. All I had known from the file was that there'd been a terrible accident at their home. Nothing more. I had knocked before pushing through the door.

The telltale Isolette with its hard plastic walls and holes on the side had stood in the center of the room. Thin, flexible tubes had wound in and out of the small bed, attaching themselves to various monitors. The ventilator had moved up and down, breathing for him. Not a good sign. I hadn't wanted to look at him. For now, I hadn't had to because there had been nurses scuttling around him, and I would've been in the way, so I had gratefully stepped aside to let them do their work.

Hannah had sat in a vinyl recliner next to the bed, clutching a blanket to her chest. Christopher had stood rigid next to the chair, his arm on her shoulder. He had looked up when he had seen me, his face white. Tunnels of emotion in his eyes. I'd just nodded. There weren't any words. I had knelt in front of Hannah and placed my hands on her knees. She hadn't blinked. My presence hadn't registered.

"Hannah?" I had prompted.

Still nothing.

"They had to sedate her with something because she wouldn't stop screaming. She's in shock," Christopher had explained. "She's been sitting like that for the last hour. Barely talks. Won't move."

I had tilted my head in the direction of the bed, still too afraid to look. "How is he?"

His manner had been clenched and rigid as he had desperately tried to keep it together. "Alive. That's about all they know for now."

"What happened?"

His Adam's apple had moved up and down with the emotions caught in his throat. "I'm not sure. I ju—just . . . I can't—"

I had put my hand on his back. "Don't worry about it. We can talk later."

We had stood together, watching the nurses work and listening to Cole's machines beep. The room had felt even smaller with all of us in it.

"Where's Janie?" I had asked.

Christopher had frantically shaken his head, then looked at Hannah and mouthed the word *no*. I had looked at him in confusion, but he'd just done it again. I had stood quietly next to them until the hospital case worker had knocked on the door and asked to meet with me outside. I had stepped into the hallway, shutting the door tightly behind me.

She'd looked fresh out of college, like she might've just taken her licensing exam last week. She had a rounded, heart-shaped face under pulled-back dark hair. Her lips had been thin and compressed by thought. She'd looked quiet—not mousy quiet, just pensive. She had moved the iPad she carried underneath her left arm and stuck out her right. "I'm Holly."

I had shaken her hand. "Piper. Nice to meet you."

She had taken a few steps away from the door just in case Hannah and Christopher might overhear, and I had followed. We had stood in front of one of the food carts waiting for someone to take the empty trays down to the kitchen. The smell of old food had wafted up my nose.

"I'm the social worker assigned to Cole and Janie's case," she had said, even though it went without saying.

"Where is Janie?" I had asked.

"She's on the fourth floor with her aunt."

I had nodded and waited for her to continue.

"I don't want to waste time giving you details that you already know, so why don't you let me know what you know, and I can fill in any of the gaps." Her green eyes had been piercing and intense.

I had smiled, trying to ease some of the tension. "Honestly, I didn't even know they had a baby, so I'm a bit out of the loop. I was really involved in their lives for a long time but haven't been since the adoption was final. I thought things were going well."

"Hmmm . . ." She had looked down at her iPad. "It looks like things have been bad for a while. They've been in the emergency room twice before this?"

"Yes, but both those incidents were accidents."

Her face had filled with doubt. I would've thought the same thing if I'd only read the files, but I knew the Bauers.

"Have you spoken with them recently?" she'd asked.

I'd shaken my head. "Can you fill me in on what's happening?"

"That's really what we're trying to figure out. The paramedics were called to the house around eleven this morning. The father was performing CPR on the infant when they arrived. There was a faint heartbeat, but the baby was unresponsive. He was intubated and brought here. We are still waiting for the results of his CT scan."

I'd read all that in his chart. It wasn't anything I hadn't already known. "Yes, but what happened?"

She had hesitated, as if it had been some kind of secret.

I had raised my hands, open palmed. "Look, I'm not sure you're aware, so I just want to be really clear with you—we are on the same team. I want what's best for these kids as much as you do."

Her face had flushed with embarrassment. "That's not it."

I had raised my eyebrows. "Really? It sure feels like it."

She had shaken her head. "I'm sorry if I gave you that impression. I've never worked on a case this serious before." She'd dropped her voice to a whisper. "I just want to make sure I don't do anything wrong."

I'd smiled. She was new, really new. "I've been exactly where you are. So why don't you take me through what you know, and we can start working on this thing together?"

She'd smiled back. The intensity had lessened. "Cole suffered a head injury. They're worried there might be blood on his brain, so they ordered the CT scan. The doctors aren't sure if he was shaken or if he fell."

"But they're positive it's a head injury?"

She had nodded. "He has a soft, swollen spot on the side of his head. There's also pinkish fluid draining from his ears."

My stomach had flipped. "I still don't get it. Why is there all this confusion over what happened? What do Christopher and Hannah have to say about it?"

Her brow had furrowed. "That's the thing. Christopher wasn't there when it happened. It was only Hannah and the kids."

"So what does Hannah say?"

"She's not talking."

"That doesn't make any sense."

She had shrugged. "Christopher found them all in the bathroom. The tub was full of water, and everyone was soaked. He says Hannah was incoherent when he got there and started screaming when the paramedics arrived. The paramedics didn't even let her ride with them in the ambulance because she was such a mess. She created a scene when they got to the hospital, and that's when the doctors gave her Valium to settle her down. They weren't going to let her into the NICU otherwise."

None of what she had been telling me had fit with anything I knew or had experienced with Hannah.

"Christopher doesn't know what happened." She'd added as an afterthought, "Or so he says."

"What about Janie? What happened to her?" I had asked.

"We're not sure about that yet either. She has a dislocated shoulder."

"What room is she in?"

"Room 29c." She had tapped her screen and scrolled through the file. "Her aunt's name is Allison."

Allison's height had surprised me since Hannah was so short, but you couldn't miss the similarity in their faces. They had the same angular jaw and thin lips. Both had huge green eyes framed by dark lashes. She had looked stricken.

"Hi, I'm Piper Goldstein, Janie's social worker," I had said, standing in the doorway of Janie's room.

Allison had motioned for me to come in. "Christopher texted that you were on your way up."

Janie had sat cross-legged on the bed. Her left shoulder had been in a blue sling. The TV had been on in front of her. I had walked over to her first. "How are you doing?" I'd asked.

She'd looked lost. Her face had been blotchy, and snot had been dried on her face.

"I know this is really scary for you right now, but things are going to be okay. I'm going to make sure you're taken care of."

She'd nodded, her lower lip sticking out like she might start crying again at any minute.

I'd straightened up and looked at Allison. "I'm so sorry that you and your family are having to go through this."

"Thank you." Her eyes had brimmed with tears. "I just can't believe this is happening. It's so horrible."

"Let's step out in the hallway for a minute." I hadn't wanted Janie to overhear anything. "Janie, me and your aunt Allison are going to be in the hallway right outside your door if you need us, okay?"

She'd nodded.

Allison had followed me into the hallway and started talking immediately. "What were they doing in the bathroom? You don't bathe babies in the regular tub. I never did. Hannah didn't either. She was hysterical at the hospital. Did they tell you that?" She hadn't waited for me to answer. "I've never seen her that way before. She was completely unhinged. It was awful. She kept letting out these animal-like shrieks, and I couldn't calm her down. Nobody could. I've never seen anyone act that way before. Is that normal? I mean, what's normal? It just doesn't make sense. None of it. Hannah tried to attack Janie when she came into the room. She went after her. Did they tell you that?"

"Nobody has told me much of anything yet."

She had grabbed my arm. "Cole's going to be okay, though, right? I mean, he's going to make it through this, isn't he?"

There had been too much desperation in her face to tell the truth.

"Absolutely," I had said.

FORTY-EIGHT

Christopher Bauer

Every time one of Cole's monitors sounded, I was sure we were going to lose him, even though the doctors assured me his scans looked clear. He was no longer intubated and was breathing on his own, but he still hadn't woken up. His CT scan showed he'd suffered a seizure after hitting his head. They assured me infants often had difficulty breathing when they came out of seizures, but their words did nothing for the fear surging through me.

I paced the room. Six steps from the back wall to the door. Four steps across. My head swirled with questions. What had they been doing in the bathroom? Why had the kids had their clothes on? How had they gotten so wet? If only Hannah would talk. She held all the answers, but she still wasn't making sense or acting right.

I was as worried about her as I was about Cole. The effects of the Valium had long worn off, and she'd barely moved from the chair. Every now and then, she'd get up and robotically move to Cole's enclosed crib. She'd stick one of her fingers through the hole and stroke his arm, tears streaming down her face. I asked her what happened twice, but she acted like she didn't hear me. She'd disappeared somewhere inside herself, and I couldn't reach her. Nobody could.

"What's wrong with her?" I kept asking the doctors.

But none of them cared all that much about her. Their primary concern was Cole. His was the life in danger, not hers. The only one who paid attention to her was the hospital social worker, Holly.

The first time she entered the room, she washed her hands at the sink like she was one of the doctors, serious faced and all business. She introduced herself to us with her back turned, blotting her hands with the paper towels above the sink. Since there was only one chair in the room, we stood facing each other in front of Hannah.

"Hannah, I'd like to ask you a few questions about what happened today." She turned toward Hannah and peered down at her, taking in her disheveled state.

Hannah didn't make eye contact. She twisted her hands on her lap.

Holly didn't waste any time getting down to business. "Can you tell me how Cole got injured?"

Hannah didn't respond.

"How did Cole get hurt?"

Hannah's hands trembled. Something registered on her face, passed through her—a memory—and then it was gone. That was more than I'd gotten from her, so maybe we were going to get somewhere.

Holly knelt in front of her. Hannah kept her head down. "Your son is seriously injured, and we need to know what happened. I understand you've been through a lot today, but we need answers."

A lone tear escaped from Hannah's eye and traveled down her cheek.

"Hannah?" Holly prompted.

I jumped in to save her. It was cruel to push her like this. "The doctors gave her Valium to help settle her down, and she always has strong reactions to drugs," I explained.

Holly didn't acknowledge me. She kept her attention focused on Hannah. Nobody had pushed her to talk yet. What would happen if Holly pushed her too hard? My heart twisted in my chest.

"You can ignore me all you want, but eventually you're going to have to talk, and the sooner you talk, the better." Her gaze never wavered. "I'm having a difficult time understanding what kind of mother wouldn't do everything she could to help her child."

"It was an accident." Hannah's voice was barely audible.

Holly nodded, pleased she'd broken through. "Go on."

But Hannah didn't know how to go on. I watched helplessly as she struggled to find words. "It was an accident."

"Yes, you said that. Tell me more about the accident."

She waited for her to answer. Hannah's body trembled. She gripped the armrests with both hands.

"Please, stop," I said. I couldn't take any more. By the looks of it, neither could Hannah.

Holly finally shifted her gaze to me. "She seems very upset."

"Are you serious?" My finger shook as I pointed to the crib. "Have you seen our son? Read the reports?"

She stood up, facing me. "Yes, I have, and that's why I'm here." We stood in an awkward stare-down. The silence stretched out between us until it was uncomfortable. Finally, she spoke. "Were you angry when you got home?"

"Me? Why would I be angry?"

"It's understandable that you'd be angry about having to leave work again for something going on at home. I mean, that can only happen so many times before it starts getting on your nerves."

Who had she been talking to?

I forced myself to stay calm. "I wasn't angry."

"Was Hannah angry?"

"No." My voice was clipped.

"Did Hannah ever get angry with the baby?"

"Cole?"

She cocked her head to the side. "Is there another baby?"

"Can't we do all of this with Piper?" I asked.

Piper would never talk to us like this. I was sure it had something to do with Holly being so young. She compensated by being cocky and arrogant, trying to establish some kind of authority over me, but I didn't like it.

She glanced down at her iPad. "Piper Goldstein?"

I nodded.

"Piper will be involved as well. We'll be working as a team. She'll work more directly with the Department of Children's Services, and I'm the social worker assigned by the hospital."

"Why do we need two social workers?" I asked.

"We always assign two social workers in cases like these."

I raised my eyebrows. "Cases like what?"

"Investigations of child abuse."

FORTY-NINE

HANNAH BAUER

I wanted to speak, but I was locked in the background of my head and had lost the ability to communicate with the world outside me. The world pulsed and thrummed around me, warping my vision into blackening fear. The hospital lights were too bright and jarring. My thoughts moved so fast I couldn't discern any particular one except the constant desperate begging of my psyche to every god in the universe: *Please don't let my baby die.*

I could see and feel everything. I felt the prick of the needle and the wetness of the cotton swab when they shot me full of Valium. I heard everything the doctors and nurses said as they swarmed the room like bees. Their discussions about the CT scan not showing blood on Cole's brain and how they would do an MRI to catch anything the CT scan might have missed. Their assurances that his brain just needed to rest after what it'd been through.

Everyone kept asking me what had happened, and I wanted to tell them. My mind told my body to speak the words, but it refused. The connection between the two was unplugged, severed. Parts had folded into blackness and created a void. All I could do was listen helplessly as Holly drilled Christopher with questions. I'd never seen him look as furious as he did when she mentioned child abuse.

"Child abuse? Are you serious?" The anger radiated off him.

Holly didn't skip a beat. "Weren't you questioned the last time Janie was in the emergency room?"

"Yes, but that was different."

"How was that different?" She crossed her arms on her chest. "Didn't a hospital social worker interview you then?"

He unbuttoned the top two buttons of his shirt and loosened his collar like it was choking him. "He did. He asked us what happened to Janie, and we told him. End of story. He never accused us of child abuse."

She balked in mock surprise. "I didn't accuse you of child abuse either."

"Yes, you did." The cords on his neck stood out.

She shook her head. "No, I said we are investigating the possibility of child abuse."

"How is that any different?" He glared at her.

"Mr. Bauer, I understand that you're upset. Today has been a very difficult day. I'm just trying to do my job." She took a step back from him, creating more space between them. Christopher took a deep breath and ran his hands through his hair.

Relax, Christopher. Just relax.

We needed him to be strong. All of us.

He cracked his knuckles and stretched. "So what do you need from me?"

"We need to know what happened at your home today. Is there anything you can think of that might help us figure it out?"

He let out a deep sigh. "I wasn't there."

"Who was there?"

"Hannah and the kids."

"And you're sure of that?"

He nodded.

The questions went on and on. They spoke around me like I wasn't there. I couldn't keep up with the plot or process the information correctly. The sound of Cole's skull as it cracked against the side of the porcelain tub interrupted everything they said, everything that was going on around me. It forced its way in unbidden. He was never supposed to get hurt.

CASE #5243

Interview: Piper Goldstein

"Is it common for parents to act the way Hannah did in the hospital?" Luke asked.

"Yes."

"So you'd seen it before?" He and Ron exchanged another glance like they'd been doing all afternoon.

"I have." Previous cases flashed through my mind in snippets. The teenage mother who'd given birth in the locker room after hiding her pregnancy from everyone and hadn't spoken for two weeks afterward. The nine-year-old boy who'd gone into catatonic depression after being removed from his mother's care. And the Vaughn baby. "Sometimes the brain shuts down after trauma for a while."

"That's what everyone believed was going on with Hannah? Some kind of traumatic shock?"

"We had no reason not to."

"But not Holly. She filed a Child in Need of Protective Services order given the nature of Cole's injuries." He tapped his pen on the table.

I understood Holly's concerns even if I hadn't agreed with filing the report because I'd seen the type of injuries Cole had had before. They were rare in babies who hadn't been shaken, but just because it was unlikely didn't mean it was impossible, and he was missing all the other signs. Nothing else pointed toward abuse. He didn't have any of the rib fractures, seizures, or bruises that you typically saw. But mostly, I knew it wasn't abuse because it was the Bauers. There was no way Hannah had hurt Cole. Not even a chance.

"Take me through what happened after the Child in Need of Protective Services order was filed."

"Because of the Child in Need of Protective Services order, Janie had to be removed from her home during the preliminary investigation. Cole would've been removed, too, but since he was in the hospital, it was basically the same thing. It's standard practice when there's been more than one report made on the parents."

"How long does it take to complete the investigation?"

"It usually only takes a few days to determine whether there's probable cause for child abuse. They automatically remove children from their home until they can determine they're safe from any harm." I looked at Luke because he was the one I'd spoken to about it earlier. "I told you before that we always try to place kids with relatives first rather than in foster care, and Janie's case wasn't any different. It made the most sense for her to stay with Allison."

"Did she go home from the hospital with Allison?" Ron asked.

"Yes."

"Allison agreed to take her?"

"She did."

"And you felt comfortable with that? You didn't have any concerns?"

"None."

FIFTY

Christopher Bauer

The neurosurgeon and pediatrician walked into the room together still wearing their green scrubs from surgery. Their faces were blank, unreadable. I gripped Hannah's hand. The neurosurgeon wasted no time getting down to business. "We were able to find the brain hemorrhage and stop the bleeding."

Relief flooded my body. Cole had had another seizure, and they'd rushed him into surgery afterward when the MRI had shown a bleed the CT had missed.

His neurosurgeon went on, his hands in continual motion as he spoke. "His brain stem reflexes are working. His pupils are reacting to light, and he reacts appropriately to external stimuli. I expect him to experience a full recovery."

Hannah's hand shook in mine.

Two other nurses wheeled him in from the recovery room. Hannah and I shuffled to his side, afraid to look. His eyes were closed. His head was wrapped in bandages. He was pincushioned with needles. Hannah stuck her finger through one of the holes and stroked his leg. He opened his eyes.

"I'm so sorry," she whispered. The pain in her voice was so thick it was tangible. I wrapped my arms around her shoulders and brought her close to me. Her body was stiff, unmoving, like a pile of bones next to mine.

"We'll watch him overnight to make sure everything continues to be okay and probably for the next twenty-four hours, but if he continues to do well, we can start talking about discharge plans."

His pediatrician spoke up. "We'll watch him closely for the next few months, but it was only a cranial bruise, so we shouldn't expect to see any long-term damage."

I squeezed Hannah. "Did you hear that? He's going to be okay."

CASE #5243

Interview: Piper Goldstein

"It says here that your colleagues expressed concern that you were too close to this case. That there were important signs you could've missed. What do you think about that? You think there's any truth to their claims?" he asked.

"Absolutely not. I'm good at what I do because I care about the people I work with." I'd never apologize for it.

"But you missed the bruises on Janie's neck, didn't you?"

Dread crept into my throat.

He motioned to the tape recorder in front of him and asked the question again.

"Yes, I did, but only at first."

"Was there anything else you could've missed at first?"

I winced. "No."

"When did you finally notice the bruises on her neck?" he asked, emphasizing the word *finally* for effect.

"By law, you have to check on the child in the new home within twenty-four hours, so I stopped at Allison's house the next day."

Allison had looked like she'd aged overnight. No amount of makeup could hide the bags underneath her eyes. She'd offered me tea just like Hannah, and I'd said yes to her in the same way. We'd sat in the breakfast nook in her kitchen.

She had rubbed her temples. "How is Cole?"

"He's still doing well," I'd said. "He took a bottle this morning, and the doctors said that was a really good sign."

"That's great. And what about Hannah? What are they doing to help her?"

"I'm not sure what the plan is."

"Have you seen anyone turn into a zombie like this before? Why is she still out of it?"

Janie had run into the kitchen screaming and waving a toy truck while one of the twins had chased her from behind. The boys looked so much alike that I couldn't tell them apart.

Allison had raised her voice. "Stop running in the house."

They'd ignored her, and their footsteps had thundered through the kitchen and into the family room.

"Greg?" Allison had called out. "Greg?"

"What?" a male voice had responded from somewhere in the house.

"Can you please take them outside? They need to run off their energy, and they're giving me a headache."

"On it," he'd said. I'd heard footsteps on the wooden floor in the next room.

Allison had sighed. "I don't know what I'd do without him these past few days. I'm so glad he's home."

"I bet." I'd shifted into the reason for my visit. I hadn't wanted to, but I'd been pressed for time. "There have been some changes in the kids' case, though, and that's what I wanted to talk to you about." I'd paused, giving her a minute to settle back into the conversation. "The Department of Children's Services works as a team, and different social workers have different roles. There're social workers that work within the hospital setting and workers like me who work outside the hospital setting. It gets confusing because I often visit families in the hospital but only if I'm already working with them or if one of the hospital social workers files a report. Does that make sense?"

She had nodded.

"A hospital social worker was assigned to Cole's case. Her name is Holly, and she filed a Child in Need of Protective Services order given the nature of his injuries." Allison had looked as confused as I'd expected. "Any children that are in the home have to be removed until the preliminary investigation is complete. Basically, it's an emergency order designed to keep the kids safe until they rule out child abuse."

She'd held up her hand to stop me. "Wait. They think Cole was abused?"

"Not necessarily, but they have to make sure because of the factors surrounding his injuries. Unfortunately, his injuries and the circumstances surrounding them are what we typically see in kids who've been abused—the kind of head injury, his age, the mother being alone with the child, no identified accident, and previous emergency room visits due to injury with other children in the home. I—"

"That's absurd. Hannah would never hurt anyone, let alone a child. Are you kidding me?"

"I agree, but you have to understand where the hospital is coming from. They are liable if they miss child abuse, so they always err on the side of being overcautious. I can't blame them for it, and honestly, if I didn't know Hannah so well, I'd have my suspicions, too, and probably do the same thing."

"Really?"

"Yes."

"So what happens now?"

"That's what I was hoping you could help with," I had said. "Janie has to be in emergency care until the report is finished. It will probably take about two to three days for them to determine that it's not a case of child abuse, and then the protective order will be lifted. In cases like this, we like to place the child with a family member, so I wanted to ask if you would act as Janie's guardian during the investigation."

She hadn't even paused before responding. "Of course. I'll do anything for Hannah."

"It won't just be Janie. If Cole gets out of the hospital before it's complete, he'll need to stay with you too."

Her face had flooded with worry at the mention of Cole's name. "That's fine."

"Thanks so much for doing this. I know Hannah appreciates it, too, and she'll thank you once she's feeling more like herself." I had looked around. "Can I talk to Janie before I leave?"

"Certainly. I'll get her." Greg had herded all of them into the backyard for a game of tag, and now Allison had walked to the back of the house and called her inside.

Janie had stomped into the kitchen. She hadn't looked happy to see me. She never did.

"Are you having a good time playing with your cousins?" I'd asked.

She'd nodded, looking annoyed. "Can I go play now?"

"I just wanted to talk to you about something before I left. Have you ever had a sleepover before?"

Her eyes had lit up. "I love sleepovers."

"Good, because you're going to have a sleepover here for a few nights while your parents are in the hospital with Cole." I'd stared at her, making sure she understood. That's when I had noticed the fingertip bruises on her neck. My legs had gone weak. I'd needed to sit down. How could I have missed them? In all my twenty-five years as a social worker, I'd never missed something so important.

Luke's voice broke into my memory. "Did you report it that day?"

"I had back-to-back client meetings, so I wasn't able to." It was true, but we both knew it didn't matter.

"For the record, you didn't report the incident that day?"

"I did not."

He locked eyes with me. "In fact, you didn't even note it in her chart until three days later, did you?"

FIFTY-ONE

Christopher Bauer

We were waiting on Cole's discharge papers. The doctors had finally cleared him to go home, but that had been two hours ago, and we still hadn't gotten any of the paperwork we needed.

I stared at Hannah as she paced the room, treading a path across the linoleum. She was in the same clothes she'd been in since we had gotten here. Her shirt was filthy now. She held Cole against her chest as she walked, babbling underneath her breath. I needed to get them both home. I had understood her being this upset when we hadn't known if he was going to be okay, but she was worse now than she had been before, and the doctors said he was going to be fine. Dan's former nanny, Greta, was coming to our house tomorrow for an interview. I hadn't told Hannah, but I didn't think it would matter all that much because she spent most of her time lost somewhere in her thoughts. There was no way I was leaving her alone with either of the kids. Not until she was better.

Someone knocked at our door. Everyone always knocked before coming in, but it was more of a formality than anything else. No one ever waited for you to invite them inside. Piper walked in with a man and a woman dressed in civilian clothes. I'd never seen them before.

"Hi, Hannah," Piper said.

Hannah gave her an almost imperceptible nod.

"Hi, Christopher," Piper said.

"Hi."

We stood there awkwardly. Why wasn't she introducing me to the people with her?

Piper cleared her throat. I'd never seen her look so nervous. She kept clearing her throat like there was something stuck there before she finally worked up the nerve to speak. "This is a very difficult conversation for me to have, and I'm not sure how to get started, so I think I'm just going to cut to the chase." She looked at me since it was impossible to make eye contact with Hannah, who still paced the room. "Given that Cole sustained a head injury in the way that he did, the hospital social worker made another report to the Department of Children's Services that they suspected child abuse was going on in your home. This is the second time the hospital has made a report, and by law, we have to investigate it."

I understood child-protection laws. I'd made similar reports before. We all had. It was always better to be safe than sorry.

"During the investigation, the children have to be removed from the home." Her voice got softer with each word.

"What? Why? Where would they even go?" I looked to Hannah to gauge her reaction, but it didn't look like she was even paying attention. How could she ignore this? I wanted to shake her, get her to snap out of whatever stupor she'd been in. I couldn't go through all this without her.

"I spoke with Allison this morning, and she agreed to take the kids until this all blows over. I'm sorry, Christopher. I really am," she said. The two individuals with her moved forward to stand beside her. "These are my colleagues, Marilyn Fragick and Josh Hoff. They are going to transport Cole to Allison's."

"What? We can't even bring him to Allison's? You have to take him there?"

She nodded. Tears filled her eyes. "I know this is hard, and if there was anything I could've done to prevent it, I would have."

A knot of anxiety balled in my stomach.

She placed her hand on my back. "You can follow us there if you want." She shrugged at my confused expression. "I know. Some of the policies don't make any sense. We have to be the ones to make sure he gets into proper custody—"

"And they don't trust us to get him there?"

"Of course I trust you, but they don't know you. It's just policy. You understand that."

I turned to Hannah. "Do you want to follow them there?"

She'd moved back against the window, cradling Cole against her chest with both hands. Panic filled her eyes, her body tense.

"Hannah?" I took a step toward her. "Hannah?"

She shook her head. Her eyes flitted around the room.

"I know this is hard, hon, but it's only like ten minutes that we'd be away from him. It's just for the drive."

She shook her head again.

I reached for her.

"No!" she screamed and jerked back.

I stopped, stunned. Piper came up behind me. She reached her hands out toward Cole. "Hannah, give him to me," she said gently.

"No!" she screamed. "Get away from me! You can't have him! You can't take him! He can't stay there!"

"Hannah, calm down. They're just taking him to Allison's. It's not like they're taking him to a stranger. She'll take wonderful care of him." I reached for her arm, but she moved too quickly, stepping out of my reach. She grabbed the nightstand and shoved it at us. The empty tray on top flew across the room and slammed into the wall before clattering to the floor.

"Get away from me. I'm warning you. Don't come near me. If you come near me, I'll jump out this window." Her eyes were wild, her body tense, ready to fight. Cole let out a wail. "Shh . . . shhh . . . it's okay." She frantically jiggled him.

"See, you're scaring Cole. Just stop now. Give him to me." I motioned for him. "Hannah, please. Hannah . . ."

She plastered herself against the window. Her nostrils flared in and out. She clawed at the window behind her while staring at each of us, daring us to move. "I'll do it. I swear to God, I'll do it, Christopher. Get away."

A voice from behind me said, "Somebody call psych."

FIFTY-TWO

HANNAH BAUER

I wanted to scream, but it was caught in my throat. There was water between my legs from wetting myself. My eyes snapped open. I tried to move. I couldn't. My hands and legs were restricted, strapped down. I fought against the restraints. It was no use. I couldn't break free. My spine throbbed all the way through my tailbone.

I scanned left to right and back again, searching for someone—anyone—to help me. There was nothing but four cement walls surrounding me and fluorescent lights above me. No windows. No door. The smell of hospital assaulted me. My heart pounded, threatening to explode. I was covered in sweat. Panic clawed at my throat.

It's just a dream. You're having a nightmare.

I willed myself to breathe.

None of this is real. Wake up. Just wake yourself up.

And then it all came flooding back. Memories shoved their way into my consciousness in random flashes—Cole in the hospital, my screams, strange faces shining lights in my eyes. I shook my head, trying to clear the cotton from my thoughts. My throat was so dry it hurt to swallow. My muscles screamed; my body ached to move. How long had I been here?

Tears moved down my cheeks, unbidden. I cried myself back to sleep.

—

Nothing had changed when I woke up. The fluorescent lights above made my head hurt. I turned to the side. That's when I noticed a small red light in the upper corner I had missed before. Someone was watching me.

I started to yell but stopped myself as quickly as I started. What would they do to me when they came in the room? My body flooded with panic again. Not being able to move was excruciating. The straps cut into my ankles.

I was so thirsty. I'd never been this thirsty. My teeth stuck to my lips, and pieces of skin came off when I tried to separate them.

A door opened behind me. I froze. The sound of footsteps moved around me. And then she was hovering over me, peering down at me—a woman I'd never seen before, and I'd remember if I had because she was stunningly beautiful. She had a face you didn't forget—high cheekbones, lashes so long they looked fake, and perfect round lips.

She laid her hand on my forehead. "How are you feeling?"

I tried to talk, but my voice was gone; I was so thirsty it'd dried out.

"Would you like to sit up?" she asked.

I nodded eagerly.

She took the restraint off my left arm. I wiggled it around, so glad to be free. Then she took off my right restraint. She grabbed my arms and pulled me into a sitting position on the table. Angry red scratches lined both arms.

"You did those to yourself," she said as if she could read my mind.

She released the straps around my ankles. Her scrubs were white—so bright they hurt my eyes—and perfectly pressed; there wasn't a fold or a crease. Even her tennis shoes gleamed. She was spotless.

"I've let Dr. Pyke know you're awake and out of your restraints. Once she clears you, we can have someone show you around the unit and to your room. Everyone has their own room here." She spoke like a schoolteacher.

Another woman strutted into the room and moved past the nurse to stand beside my bed.

"I'm Dr. Pyke," she said. She had a prominent nose and thin lips. Her short hair was clipped back. "How are you feeling?"

"Thirsty," I managed to squawk out.

She motioned to the nurse. "Can you get her some water, please?" The nurse nodded and scurried away. "It's frightening to wake up this way, and I apologize for that, but you had to be restrained and sedated for your own safety. Most patients find it very disorienting when they come out of it. Again, my apologies. We wouldn't have done it if it weren't absolutely necessary."

I nodded, even though I didn't understand or remember. What had I done? The nurse returned with a Styrofoam cup filled with water. I took the water from her and gulped it down. "Thank you," I said.

"You're welcome," Dr. Pyke said, taking the cup from me and tossing it into the trash can underneath the sink. Her face exuded a neutral warmth. She grabbed the stool and slid it beside the bed, taking a seat next to me. "You got pretty upset earlier today. Why don't you tell me what's been going on with you?"

I stared at her, willing myself to talk, but I couldn't. There were just images. Flashes. Pieces. I tried to focus—remember—but my memory had too many holes in it. Pain leaked out of me like a bad smell.

She stood. "Okay, well, if you don't want to talk, then your nurse, Maureen, will take you to the unit. I'll check in later to see how you're settling in, and we can discuss your medication." She pointed toward the door. "Go."

The world spun when I stood. Maureen held open the door, and a long, narrow hallway greeted me. The obnoxious fluorescent lighting was gone and replaced with dull, barely visible light casting a murky gray on all the walls. A series of metal doors flanked the sides. Maureen held my arm and helped me forward, my legs still wobbly underneath me from whatever they'd given me. I stumbled through the hallway. The door to my left opened, and a nurse brushed against me. I stepped back instinctively as if I had a contagious disease.

We followed the hallway through another series of twists and turns—a sense of impending doom mounting with each step—before arriving at another set of double doors. Instead of using her key card to unlock the door, Maureen pressed a red button next to it. There was a loud buzz, and the doors opened into another hallway. People shuffled around with vacant eyes, some of them talking to themselves. The door clicked shut behind me. The lock engaged.

"You have to keep moving. You have to stay in front of the red line," Maureen said as she nudged me gently forward.

I hadn't realized I'd stopped. I looked down. A thick red line stretched across the hallway in front of the doors. Maureen nudged me again. I stepped over it.

"You can't go past this line without a staff member. If you do, it will sound an alarm. Do you understand?" She spoke slowly, enunciating each syllable like I had difficulty hearing.

I nodded.

She pointed to the tape again and repeated herself like I still didn't get it. "Patients can't go past this line."

I breathed a sigh of relief. I was safe now.

FIFTY-THREE

Christopher Bauer

The smell of spoiled milk assaulted me when I walked in the front door of our house. Everything was exactly like we'd left it, including Janie's cereal bowl from breakfast in the sink. I rinsed it out, but the place still smelled foul, so I walked through the house searching for other culprits. Our house wasn't big, but it felt huge without my family.

I found the sippy cup Janie used each morning for her snack on the coffee table in the living room. The leftover milk was turning into cottage cheese. I didn't bother to clean it but just threw it in the trash. I filled the dishwasher with the remaining dishes in the sink and added detergent before pressing start. I leaned against the counter, crossing my arms against my chest.

What had happened that morning?

It was the question that chased itself around and around like a snake trying to catch its tail. I'd spent the last three days racking my brain for anything I might have missed, but there wasn't anything unusual. It had been a rough morning, but most of our mornings were difficult. That wasn't anything out of the ordinary, so it never gave me any cause for concern, at least not any more than it did every day when I left for work.

I walked aimlessly through the house searching for clues as if they were hidden in the walls somewhere. I moved from room to room, picking up things as I went. I couldn't remember the last time our house had been messy, and I missed when Hannah hadn't cared so much about cleaning. Who was I kidding? I missed Hannah, period. But I missed the old Hannah. Not this new one who had taken her place. What if I never got her back?

I moved into the bedroom and sat on the edge of our bed. How would I fall asleep tonight? It didn't feel right without them here—the kids at Allison's and Hannah at the hospital in Columbus.

When the psychiatric response team had arrived at the hospital, I had begged them to take her to Worthington Presbyterian. It was twenty miles away from Clarksville, but she couldn't stay at Northfield Memorial. There was no way her admission to the psychiatric ward would stay a secret, and she'd be mortified that she'd been institutionalized once she felt better. I had to protect her reputation and career. She would've done the same for me.

Our bedroom floor was covered with family photos and various albums. They were arranged in neat piles that Hannah had constantly gone through, getting just as worked up as she had the first time. She didn't need them staring her in the face when she came home. I grabbed an empty box from the garage to store them in. I would go through them when things calmed down. Maybe there was a chance I could salvage a few, but for now I needed to get rid of them. They were the last thing she needed to see when she got home. I started sorting through the mess.

There were so many of them, all of them damaged, defaced in some awful way. They were too sad to look at. I began to toss them into the box, quickly moving through the piles. The fancy baby book Allison had given us at our baby shower was buried underneath the last pile. I hadn't realized Hannah had been filling it out.

The cover was beautiful, with the telltale title "Your First Year" and a picture of Cole in the hospital in a see-through slipcover on the front. I thumbed through the first couple pages, the dates starting the day we had gotten home from the hospital. It was the usual stuff—weight, height, length—coupled with his little footprint from the hospital and the ID bracelet he'd worn. She'd written everything in swirly handwriting, and even that looked happy. She'd added notes and comments next to all the factual information: your hands were your biggest part, you didn't like the hearing test, the nurse named Judy made you cry. The next page was a letter she'd written to Cole. It was one that only a new mother could write after she'd just fallen hopelessly in love with the life she had created.

But it wasn't long before things turned. Her handwriting changed. The big spiral curls were gone, replaced with messy, hurried scrawls. Each page had a small spot to journal, and the space was too small for all her words, so she'd scribbled between and around the designs or fact sheets on the page. She'd made herself disjointed lists, writing the same things over and over again.

Pregnancy weight is all gone. Some women would be happy about this. Me? It's just more proof that I'm wasting away. Today Christopher told me I need to be more loving toward Janie. I can't. I just can't anymore. I don't have it in me. I'm depleted. So empty.

I am in the background of my head. How did I get here?

The next few entries were more of the same:

I'm a prisoner in my own home. I feel her watching me everywhere I go. She's just waiting. She wants to hurt him. I know she does. I can see it in her eyes. Those black eyes. Today when he was crying she screamed at me to take him back. I wanted to slap her. Tell her she's the one who needs to go back.

I never used to cry. Now? It's all I do. It washes over me like an unwanted wave, flattening me. I don't try to stop the tears anymore. There's no point. I just let them come. Something is eating me up inside, telling me I'm not good enough. I fake smiles for him. Can he tell?

She told me she hated me today. It's not the first time. It used to hurt. Not anymore.

At first, her entries were cohesive and put-together paragraphs describing her struggles, but it wasn't long before they derailed. She'd been obsessed with creating a detailed calendar of the things Janie had done, but she'd never quite got it right because she'd constantly been crossing them out and starting over. And then her writing took a turn I had never expected:

I feel the ice-cold breath of her demon. It blows on my neck while I'm feeding Cole. I can see the demon in her eyes when I look at her. The twisted grin on its face. It licks its fangs like it wants to hurt Cole.

I heard her talking to it again today. In a different language. Latin? She thinks he's funny. She says he's the one who told her to put her poop on the walls. When the devil takes over, there's nothing you can do.

I stopped there, stunned. Hannah wasn't a religious person, never had been. Her parents hadn't brought her to church, not even on the holidays.

His talons. Those ugly claws. They reached out from inside her and tried to grab Cole. They want him too. They aren't going to be satisfied until he joins them. I screamed at her to stay away from him, and she just laughed.

I have to do something. I can't let them have him. I won't. I'm his mother. I have to protect him. No matter what. No matter what it takes. That's what you do. I can do it. I'll do it if I have to.

She wrote down websites about children who were demon possessed. Each of the websites was circled multiple times.

Keep track. Must keep track of her.

Called again. Answers. None.

Then she stopped dating the pages.

Today I met the angels. I'm so glad they're here. I'm not going to be able to do this without them.

Their voices are so kind and soft. Not like the demon. Cole hears them too. He giggles when they whisper in his ear. I'm glad he likes them.

Her last entry was four words:

Today is the day.

Hannah always barged into Allison's house without knocking, but it felt weird without her, so I knocked instead. Allison opened the door just as Janie came barreling down the hallway.

"Daddy!"

I swept her up in one swift movement. I kissed her and squeezed her tightly, wishing I could grab her and take her to the park for the day instead of what we were about to do, but there was no way around it.

"I missed you," I said, kissing her again and straightening out her ponytail in back.

"Come in," Allison said just as formally as I felt.

Dr. Chandler and Piper stood in the entryway with her. They both held coffee cups. I was early, which meant they'd been even earlier. Had they met without me beforehand? Why would they do that? What weren't they telling me? All of this was making me paranoid. I needed to calm down.

The Department of Children's Services needed Janie's statement, and Piper had worked her magic so that Dr. Chandler could do the forensic interview. She was the perfect choice, since she'd served as an expert witness in numerous child abuse cases, and Janie already trusted her. She was more forthcoming with her than with anyone else. Greg had taken Dylan and Caleb to the batting cages so they would be out of the way for the interview. I appreciated his thoughtfulness.

Allison ushered us into the dining room. Their taste in decor was completely different than Hannah's and mine. We used to joke about it all the time. We favored homey craftsman looks, while Allison's house was sleek and contemporary. The windows were draped in matching white fabric, and professional family photographs lined the other wall. The first time we'd visited, I'd been afraid to sit on the dining room chairs in case I wrinkled the white fabric or spilled on the floor.

Dr. Chandler scanned the room. "Do you think we might have this discussion with Janie in another room? I want her to be as comfortable as possible. Maybe a playroom or family room?"

"Sure," Allison said.

Janie held my hand as we followed Allison into the basement. Unlike the rest of the house, the family room was a wide-open space, perfect for children. The concrete floors were covered in sidewalk chalk, and the place was big enough for them to race their scooters. Toys lined the floor, and beanbag chairs were scattered everywhere. An *L*-shaped sectional was pushed against the far wall.

"This is the kid zone. I let them do whatever they want down here," Allison said.

"This is perfect. I love it," Dr. Chandler said. She took a seat on the couch, and we all followed suit, even Janie, who seemed to have sensed there was something different and important about the day. "I'm so glad to see you, Janie. We have some important things to talk about." Janie leaned forward, listening intently to what she was about to say. "Remember how we've talked about the difference between a truth and a lie?"

Janie nodded.

"It's really important that you answer my questions with the truth and no lies. Okay?"

Janie nodded again.

Dr. Chandler looked at Piper to see if she had anything to add. Piper motioned for her to continue. "I wasn't there the day that Cole got hurt, and I don't know what happened," Dr. Chandler said. "Do you think you could help me understand what happened?"

Janie's eyes lit up. She was always eager to help. "Sure."

Dr. Chandler smiled at her. "Why don't you start by telling me where you were when Cole got hurt?"

"I was in the bathroom."

"What were you doing in the bathroom?"

"Taking a bath."

Dr. Chandler kept her face expressionless. "Do you usually take baths during the day?"

Janie shook her head. "It was a special bath."

"A special bath? What's that?"

"A bath with my clothes on, silly." She giggled.

Allison looked at me, her face stricken. Tension radiated off her.

"Of course, a special bath. Now I understand. Do you take special baths a lot?"

"Sometimes." Janie nodded. "Mommy said she wanted to play a game with me."

"She did?" Dr. Chandler feigned excitement. "Was it a fun one?"

Janie narrowed her eyes to slits and crossed her arms. "No, Mommy was mean. The mean mommy came out to play."

All the color drained from Allison's face.

Dr. Chandler didn't miss a beat. "Oh, you have a mean mommy? What's Mean Mommy like?"

Janie wrinkled up her face. "She does bad things."

Dr. Chandler didn't press. "What did Mean Mommy do during the special bath?" Dr. Chandler moved from her spot on the couch and knelt in front of Janie. She looked straight into Janie's eyes. "Sometimes it's hard to find the words to use when we want to talk about something that's happened to us. Remember how we played with my dolls?" Janie gave a barely perceptible nod. "Would you like to use the dolls and show me what happened?"

Janie's eyes lit up at the idea. Dr. Chandler reached into her bag and pulled out a container. She took off the lid and handed it to Janie. She pulled out two dolls—a grown woman and a young girl. Dr. Chandler watched as Janie held on to them for a few seconds. We all sat and waited for her to do something. Allison was on the edge of her seat, looking like she wanted to stop her.

Suddenly, Janie's screams pierced the air. "You can't have him! I won't let you take him!" She smacked the little-girl doll with the other doll. Allison jumped up and ran upstairs.

Dr. Chandler looked at me to see how I was holding up, and I nodded for her to continue. I was glued to my seat like I was witnessing a horrible car accident. She placed her hand softly on Janie's back. Her voice was even as she spoke to her. "Janie, I like how you are using your words to tell us what happened. What's the Mean Mommy doll doing?"

"She's fighting with the girl." Her lower lip trembled.

"Why is she fighting with the girl?"

"Mommy says the girl is a bad girl. She has to go away." Tears filled her eyes and threatened to spill down her cheeks. "The girl doesn't want to go away. She's not bad."

Dr. Chandler pulled her close and cuddled her against her chest. She rocked her slowly and gently. "The girl is not bad. She doesn't have to go away. She's a good girl." Janie's shoulders shook with sobs. I reached out and stroked her back even though Dr. Chandler had instructed me to not intervene during the interview.

"Is that enough?" I asked.

Dr. Chandler looked at me, annoyance written all over her face, and shook her head. I quickly scooted back on the couch and folded my hands on my lap before she banished me from the room. Janie's body trembled, and I couldn't help but remember all the times Dr. Chandler had talked about trauma being stored in the body. It made sense in a way that it never had before as I watched Janie twitch and fight as she struggled with her secret.

"Mommy tried to push me down in the water," she said between sobs in the baby voice she only used when she was upset. "I said, 'No! No! No! Mommy!'" She flung her body back and forth in the same way I was sure she'd done that day. "Mommy didn't care. She just pushed me down and pushed me down. Then Mommy fell and gave Cole a boo-boo on his head."

My stomach rolled. Silence filled the room with the enormity of her words.

"What happened next?" Dr. Chandler's gaze never wavered from Janie.

"I cried."

She was crying again now. My heart squeezed within my chest. I sat on my hands to keep from reaching out and pulling her close. Thankfully, Dr. Chandler rested a comforting hand on her back.

"That must have been very scary," she said.

Janie's lower lip trembled. "I wanted my daddy."

"Janie, I—"

Dr. Chandler put her hand up to stop me. "Christopher, why don't you go get Janie some water while I finish up the interview?"

"You're doing great, Janie," I said. I reached over and tousled the top of her head. "I'll be back in just a minute. You be a good girl and finish talking to Dr. Chandler, okay?"

She nodded.

I hurried up the stairs and almost ran into Allison in the kitchen. She'd been crying. "You couldn't take it either?" she asked.

"More like I couldn't stay out of it. I just kept trying to jump in and save her. I understand that they need her statement, but it was excruciating to watch Janie have to go through it again."

"I don't know how Dr. Chandler does her job. I never could. That was too much." Allison shuddered. "There's no way Hannah hurt Cole or Janie on purpose. No way. She just wouldn't." She jutted her chin forward. "She brought every sick animal home with her when we were kids. And not just cute animals like the stray cats in the neighborhood." She smiled at a memory. "She brought home a litter of baby rats once. Rats. Can you imagine? Our mom was totally freaked out and wanted her to bring them back to where she found them, but Hannah refused. She kept them hidden in a shoebox in her room and bottle-fed them. That's the kind of person she is. I just don't understand." Her eyes welled with tears again.

"Come here," I said. She fell into my arms sobbing. I held her while she cried and gave her a moment to gather herself when she was finished. She splashed water on her face from the kitchen sink and patted herself dry with a paper towel.

"Do I have to go back down there?" she asked. "I'm not sure I can handle any more."

I motioned toward her breakfast nook, her favorite spot in the house. "Why don't you make yourself a cup of tea and take a seat until they're finished."

She looked relieved. "You want a cup?"

"I'd love a cup. Just give me a second." I didn't wait for her response. I grabbed the baby journal from my car and headed back inside. Part of me had considered keeping it. I'd been trying to convince myself that just because Hannah had written those things down didn't mean she'd acted on them or done anything wrong. But after what I'd seen and heard, the only explanation that made sense was the one contained within its pages.

I hurried back inside and downstairs. Dr. Chandler was huddled on the floor with Janie, busy playing with dolls. Nobody was speaking. Piper sat in the same spot on the sofa where she'd been when I'd left her. I handed the journal to her. "I found this in Hannah's things. You need to read it."

FIFTY-FOUR

HANNAH BAUER

"Do you have any kids?" I asked the chief psychologist, Dr. Spence, as I hugged my knees to my chest and shifted in my seat. Our positions never changed during our sessions, even if we met more than one time in a day.

"Do you think it's important that I have kids?" She sat in her straight-backed chair, legs always crossed at the ankles, notebook balanced on her lap, ready. She was always straight faced. I'd never seen her smile. Was she that way with everyone or just me?

"You don't know what it's like to be a parent unless you have kids," I mumbled underneath my breath.

Our sessions were painful, but I liked being in her office because it had a window. Very few rooms on the unit had windows. I didn't care that most of my view was blocked by the building across the sidewalk because I could see the sky, and there was hope as long as I could see the sky. When I first got here, all I did was stare out the window at the sky. She used to let me do that. Not anymore.

"Anyway, you were telling me about Cole's crying. Do you want to continue with where you were at?" She had wide-set champagne-colored eyes and a flat face, perfect for masking her emotional responses.

"I just wanted him to go to sleep. For so long that's all I wanted." It had seemed like his crying and sleeplessness would never end. The days had been long, the nights even longer. "And then he did. He finally slept."

She smiled. "That must've been wonderful."

"It was awful."

She looked surprised. "Why was that?"

"I couldn't sleep." My voice cracked, barely audible. "It was brutal. All I wanted was rest. But I couldn't sleep. I just couldn't."

I had tossed and turned all night long. Even if I'd managed to nod off, it had been only a matter of minutes before I jolted awake. I could never sleep for more than an hour at a time. It had been torturous to be bone tired but unable to sleep.

"Is that when the images began?" she asked.

She knew about the images? When had I told her that? My memory was filled with too many blank spaces.

I nodded. "Cole was only a week old the first time. He might've been two weeks old. It's hard to remember. Things are still pretty cloudy."

My mind was coming back in the same way it'd left—slowly and in pieces. It had been one of my hard days. That part I remembered clearly. I hadn't slept at all, and Cole had been crying on and off for hours. Janie had been in the living room screaming. There had been a pair of scissors on the dresser next to the changing table. Suddenly, I'd been acutely aware of their presence. I had never experienced anything like it.

A strange voice had interrupted my thoughts and whispered, "Grab the scissors," and it was quickly followed by the image of me stabbing the scissors into Cole's chest. It had felt like the scissors were controlling my thoughts. I had chanted "Don't look at the scissors" as I stepped over to the dresser, holding the scissors in front of me at arm's length like they'd burn me if they got too close. I had slowly walked into the kitchen and put the scissors away. I hadn't felt safe until they were tucked in the drawer.

"Was that the last time anything like that happened to you?" Dr. Spence asked.

"No, I saw Cole hitting his head on the doorframe whenever I walked through one with him. I was terrified that I wouldn't give myself enough space to make it through and would bash his head on the side of the frame. There were other times I saw his head exploding while Christopher held him up in the air in a strange attempt to calm him. I'd watch as Cole's spine snapped and folded backward. Eventually I couldn't take it, and I'd yell at Christopher to stop."

The images had played themselves out like unwanted movie clips. The harder I had tried to stop them, the more they had come.

"Did you tell anyone what you were experiencing? Christopher? Allison?"

"No."

How could I have told anyone what I was seeing? Having images of stabbing your baby wasn't consistent with being in love with your baby, and I loved Cole with all my heart. I'd been terrified of something happening to him. Utterly terrified. I'd mentally walked through every possible danger, each one a graphic novel in my head. I hadn't trusted anyone to keep him safe, not even Christopher.

"Have you thought any more about your diagnosis?"

I shook my head. The psychiatric team said I'd had a psychotic break from postpartum depression. They told me there was nothing I could have done to stop or prevent it and assured me it resulted from a combination of biological factors beyond my control—my sleep deprivation, dramatic hormone shift, and genetic predisposition—but I knew I was still responsible for what I'd done. It didn't matter how much therapy they gave me or what kind of drugs they pumped into me. I had tried to drown Janie.

"My psychiatrist told me everything I felt or saw was delusional, but he was wrong. Some of it was right. It was real." I took a deep breath before going on. She needed to know the truth. "Janie was the only person who scared me more than my thoughts. I didn't want her anywhere near Cole. Christopher thought I was just irritated and frustrated with her because I was so tired, but Janie would've hurt Cole if she ever got the chance. That part was never delusional, and I don't care how much medication you put me on; I'm not going to change my mind."

She interrupted me. "But that's the problem, Hannah. You can't trust your mind anymore."

CASE #5243

Interview: Piper Goldstein

Luke slid the album across the table. I didn't have to look at the cover to know what it was. I'd been through it many times. "Is this the journal submitted into evidence?"

"It is."

"And what did you think when you read it?"

How could he understand that nothing I had read fit with the woman I knew? All he saw was the woman from the last few months, and that person was a stranger. She wasn't Hannah. But this time I didn't have to try and explain myself.

"I can't discuss records in an open child-protection case," I recited exactly as I'd been told by my supervisor.

He had no choice but to switch tactics. "What did you do with the journal?"

"I handed it over to the authorities investigating the Bauers' case."

"Did you tell Allison about any of the things you read in the journal?"

"No."

"Why was that? Didn't she have a right to know?"

"I assumed Hannah had told her because the two of them were so close. They weren't just sisters. They were best friends, and best friends tell each other everything, even stuff that's horrible, so I just figured she knew everything."

"But she didn't know everything, did she?"

I shook my head. "No, she didn't."

Would it have made a difference?

FIFTY-FIVE

Christopher Bauer

In all my years as a doctor, I had never been on a locked psychiatric ward before, and I was horrified by the place. It must've been designed to be as grim as possible because there was nothing warm about it. The rooms were in desperate need of a paint job. Their whitewashed walls had become a grimy yellow. There weren't any windows. Nothing that spoke of life. Just stale recycled air and a complete sense of isolation. How was anyone supposed to feel better in a place thick with depression?

There were all these plainclothes orderlies who were paid to watch the patients like glorified babysitters. One of them led Hannah into the room, and she shuffled in, her head hanging low and her hair haphazardly falling forward. It was matted and had a big ball in the back. I couldn't believe they'd just let her walk around like that. Why didn't someone brush her hair? Her pajama pants dragged on the floor. She wasn't allowed to be alone, so the orderly guided her into a seat, then grabbed one of the chairs for himself and plopped down in the doorway, leaving the door open so he could listen.

I barely recognized her when she looked up. Her eyes were clouded and hazy with all the drugs they were pumping into her. She stared at me like she wasn't seeing me. I wasn't sure she was.

"Hi." I didn't know what else to say.

She put her hands on the table, nervously wringing them together, and looked down.

"How are you doing?"

Still no response. The silence was so thick you could reach out and touch it.

"Do you want me to leave?" I asked.

She mumbled something, but I couldn't understand.

"Excuse me? Can you say that again? I didn't hear you."

She refused to answer. We sat in silence. I could hear the orderly breathing in the doorway. Hannah played with her hands. I stayed for another few minutes, but it wasn't long before I couldn't take any more.

"I think I'm going to go," I announced.

She didn't flinch. I stood up and left without saying goodbye.

She'd brushed her hair, so she didn't look quite so ragged at our next visit. She shuffled into the room in the same manner she had before. It was a different orderly in the doorway this time.

"Hi." I tried again.

"Hi." Her voice was raspy and hoarse.

We sat in the same spots as before. She put her hand in her mouth and anxiously chewed on her fingernails. She'd never chewed her fingernails before.

"I didn't think you'd come . . ." Her voice stopped.

I bit back tears. "I couldn't leave you here alone."

Her eyes were vacant; she wore a thousand-yard stare.

"You look better today," I said. I talked to her doctor every day, and she kept me updated on Hannah's progress. They'd recently added a new medication to her cocktail of antipsychotics.

"You were here before?" she asked.

I nodded. "Yes. You were pretty out of it."

"I hate the drugs. You know how I feel about drugs." Her voice was flat, devoid of emotion.

I cleared my throat, nervous to ask. "Do they help?"

She shrugged.

"Are you eating?" I didn't know what to talk about.

"Not really. The medication makes me nauseous."

"Is there anything that sounds good? Maybe I could bring you something."

"You'd bring me food?" Her eyes filled with tears.

I reached across the table and pulled her hand out of her mouth. I put it in mine. Her hands were dry, scaly. I rubbed my finger gently on top of hers. "Yes." It was hard to speak around the lump in my throat.

She jerked her hand away. "Don't touch me."

I dropped her hand. "I'm sorry. I just—I just . . ."

"Please go. Just go." Tears streamed down her cheeks. "Don't come back."

"I'm not going to go, Hannah. I'm not just going to leave you here. I love you. That doesn't change because you're sick."

Her voice trembled as she spoke. "I am more than sick. I tried to kill a child. Don't try to make this better for me."

"We've all done some horrible things during this." I lowered my voice to a whisper so the orderly sitting in the doorway couldn't hear. "I hit you, Hannah."

FIFTY-SIX

Hannah Bauer

Our meetings blended into each other like one never-ending session. Twice daily. Sometimes three if it was a really bad day. Dr. Spence didn't have a time limit. Not like Dr. Chandler. No way to tell if they were going to go twenty minutes or three hours. This one felt like it'd been going on forever. We might break our record.

"Do you remember when you started hearing voices?" she asked.

"Remember those images I told you about earlier?" I asked.

She nodded.

"The voices worked the same way. From out of nowhere, a voice started whispering, 'Janie's possessed by a demon.' At first they were murmurs, just whispers that made me wonder if I'd heard them at all. I kept telling myself they weren't there. That it wasn't real. I felt my mind snapping, going somewhere it'd never gone, but I couldn't stop it. I was outside myself watching it happen."

The investigators had shown me my journal and all those things I'd written. Allison had given me the journal at my baby shower. She'd used the same one with her boys. I remembered my first few entries, but most of it was like reading a story about someone else. It was hard to believe it was me.

"You never sought help?"

"I didn't." I hung my head. "It's different when it's happening to you. I kept telling myself that it was normal because of everything going on and I'd adjust in a little while. But then I didn't . . ."

"And then what happened, Hannah?"

"You already know what happened. Everyone knows what happened."

"It might help you if you talked about it."

That's where she was wrong—where everyone was wrong. Nothing was going to help me. And I didn't care how many times doctors told me I had had a psychotic break. It didn't justify what I had done. It never would. I had walked into the bathroom that day intending to drown Janie. That part was crystal clear. So was how hard she'd fought as I'd tried to hold her under the water.

FIFTY-SEVEN

Christopher Bauer

Janie screamed in the background of my phone. It'd only been twenty minutes since I had left Allison's house after my visit with the kids, and it was the same routine every time. Janie sobbed and clung to me when it was time to leave, and Allison had to pry her off. Sometimes it took her thirty minutes to calm her down. Other times it took three hours.

"She bit me again," Allison said.

I turned my Bluetooth down as I drove; it made Janie's piercing screams in the background lower. "I'm sorry," I said.

I'd lost count of how many times I had apologized to her in the past few weeks. Even though Hannah had confessed to hurting Janie and Cole, the Department of Children's Services treated me like I was a criminal, too, as if I'd been in on some conspiracy with her. They didn't understand that I had been as blindsided as they were when I had discovered the baby journal. The shock had dulled over time, but it was still there. Hannah's story corroborated everything Janie had said—she'd been trying to drown Janie when she had slipped and Cole had hit his head as she'd fallen. None of that mattered, though. Janie and Cole still had to stay with Allison until they cleared my name. Piper said it was standard practice, but it didn't make me feel any less like a criminal.

"She actually drew blood this time. Blood, Christopher. Do you know how hard you have to bite someone to draw blood?"

"Have you tried distracting her?" I asked. Janie wasn't making any of this easier on anybody. Every time I talked to her, I told her she needed to behave better, but she never listened.

"Of course I've tried distracting her. We've tried everything. Nothing works." She sighed. "I don't know how much longer we can keep doing this. She's still stealing food. That hasn't stopped. And today? She smeared feces on the bathroom wall." I could hear the disgust in her voice. "I don't know how you deal with her."

"It's not easy. You might have to lock up the refrigerator. I can send you the link for the locks we used."

"I refuse to lock up the refrigerator like we're in some weird prison. I'm sorry, I know you guys do, but I just don't feel right about it. It's not fair to my boys either. None of this is."

Janie usually loved her cousins, but she'd started being mean to them. She snuck into their rooms and broke their favorite toys. She took their homework out of their backpacks and scribbled all over it. The other day, she'd locked Dylan in his closet.

"This has all been very hard on her," I said. "She's trying to work things out. Remember how Dr. Chandler said she's probably going to act out for a while? That it's really common for kids to do in these types of situations?"

"It's more than that, though. She scares me, Chris. She really does. I'm afraid she's going to do something awful to my boys. I'm probably just being paranoid, but sometimes when she looks at me, it's like she's plotting something. Just waiting to get her chance. I don't want to keep pushing this, but how long until the kids can come back to you?"

"Believe me, I want them home as much as you do. I can talk to Piper again and see if she can move things any faster. Hopefully, we'll know something for sure within the next week or so. I—"

She stopped me. "Another week? Oh my gosh, I can't take another week of this. Greg goes back to work on Friday, and they have to be gone by then. This was never supposed to be this long. It was only supposed to be a few days. I can't do this by myself."

"But there's no way they'll let them come back home in two days. I can call later tonight after she's calmed down and talk to her again about having good behavior."

Allison snorted. "Christopher, how many times have you talked to her? It never does any good."

"I'll bribe her. I can promise to bring that new outfit she wants for her doll if she's good."

"That never works either."

I was running out of options. "Please, Allison, I know this is hard, but it's only temporary. Just a little bit longer, and you'll get your life back."

"I'm sorry, Christopher. I can't do this."

"What are you saying?" The seriousness of the situation suddenly became clear.

"She drove Hannah over the edge. I know my sister, and that girl is what drove her crazy, and I'm not going to have the same thing happen to me. I was horrified when I found out what Hannah did. I couldn't even imagine it. But you know what? Now I can. I've only had Janie in my house for a short time, and I'm already starting to not feel like myself. She makes me nervous and on edge all the time. Don't you feel it? She doesn't make your skin crawl just being around her?"

Waves of fury passed through me. Janie was family. Nobody seemed to get that besides me. Just because Janie wasn't the same as her perfect little boys didn't mean we could throw her away. She couldn't help what she'd been through.

I did my best to sound calm and avoid pushing her any further away. "There's no place else for them to go. They'll put them in foster care if they can't stay with you."

"I have to protect my family," she said.

"But she's your family."

"No, Christopher. She's not. I didn't adopt her—you did."

"She's serious, Piper. She wants them gone by Friday. What am I supposed to do?" I'd called Piper as soon as I had hung up with Allison. She already knew there was no place else for them to go. Dr. Chandler was working as hard as she could to get Janie into a program, but there wasn't much she could do on such short notice, and I was unwilling to send her anywhere that wasn't top of the line. "I could probably talk her into taking Cole, but that doesn't solve anything for Janie. And besides, how traumatic would that be for her?" I lined my voice with sarcasm. "'I'm sorry, Janie, but you can't stay at your aunt Allison's house, but your brother can.' Do you really think she'd get over that?"

"I know this isn't what you want to hear, but there's no way I can push anything through by Friday. The system doesn't work that way," Piper said.

"But you have to do something. What's going to happen if Allison refuses to keep the kids?" I asked even though I already knew the answer.

"We have to place them in foster care until the hearing."

"They can't go into foster care. Cole's just a baby. And Janie? Imagine what that will do to her. We have to do something. Piper, please."

"Is there any way you can talk her into one more week?"

"I don't think so. She was pretty adamant." I'd spent the last five minutes begging her, but it hadn't made a difference.

"What about your parents?"

"My mom's diabetes is completely out of control right now. She's been in and out of the hospital herself. Lillian just left last week. She'd turn around and come back in a heartbeat if I asked her, but Gene took a bad fall while she was gone. His hip is still bothering him. The timing on all of this couldn't be worse."

"Look, why don't I give Allison a call and see if I can change her mind?" Piper asked.

"You'd do that?"

"Of course. I'd do anything for you guys."

CASE #5243

Interview: Piper Goldstein

Luke paused before continuing, "You seemed more involved with Christopher than with Hannah. Any particular reason why?"

It was no secret that Christopher and I were close. We talked every day, sometimes multiple times. I wasn't going to lie about it. Besides, they probably had the phone records anyway.

"I helped Christopher navigate the legal minefield once everything started falling apart," I said.

"It wasn't a conflict of interest?"

"No. My role is very different. I'm not involved in the specific legalities of criminally prosecuting parents for abuse. My job is to determine the best placement in situations like Janie's and Cole's and then to provide recommendations to the family court."

"And did you do that?" Luke's eyes had grown bloodshot as the hours had passed, and he spent most of his time sitting down now instead of animatedly pacing around the room, but Ron looked like he could go all night.

"I did."

"And you felt the best placement continued to be with Allison?" Ron asked.

"Yes. That's why I called her."

I knew they had that record. Everyone did. Besides, I had nothing to hide.

—

I had called Allison immediately after I'd gotten off the phone with Christopher. I'd known from her voice that the decision had been set in stone before I had said anything. She hadn't wasted any time on small talk.

"I'm sorry. I know you're calling for Christopher, and I wish I could keep the kids, but I just can't. Greg leaves on Friday, and he'll be gone for ten days on business. I was hoping Janie would've settled down by the time he left, but her behavior keeps getting worse. I have to watch her like a hawk and can't leave her alone with my boys, which makes it almost impossible to take care of Cole."

The last part had taken me by surprise. "You don't leave the boys alone with her? How come?" I asked.

"Hannah didn't tell you?"

"I haven't seen them much since the adoption was complete. Technically, I'm on the case until the end of the year, but I haven't had an active role since we got the birth certificate."

"Oh . . . okay . . . well, I don't leave her alone with the boys. Ever."

"Can I ask why?"

She'd lowered her voice. "She tried to be sexually inappropriate with them. My mom caught her. Who knows what else would've happened if she hadn't."

Nobody had said anything about it.

"I can only do this if Greg is here. Once he's gone, there's no way to keep an eye on her at all times and manage the other kids." She'd let out an exasperated sigh. "Normally, my mom would be able to help out, but my dad just took a bad fall, so she has to take care of him. Did Christopher tell you that?"

"He did."

"If I knew for sure that it would only be another week, I would do it, but that's what you said the last time, and look where we are. I'm sorry, Piper. I really am. But I have to look out for my family too. I can't let my boys get lost in this."

"You don't have to apologize. I get it. Taking on two other kids is a huge responsibility, especially kids who've gone through so much," I'd said.

"What happens to them now?"

"They'll go into emergency foster care until they're returned to Christopher."

She'd been silent. My last shred of hope had vanished when the threat of foster care hadn't changed her mind.

"How is Janie doing?" I had asked. "Christopher said she had a really hard time when he left tonight."

"She's fine now. As soon as I got off the phone with Christopher, she turned down the hysterics." She'd paused before continuing. "She's only worried about Christopher. She never asks about Hannah. Don't you think that's odd?"

"She's young. Who knows what she understands about what's happening. Or maybe she's denying the whole thing."

"I just think it's weird after, well . . . you know . . ."

"I'm sure she talks about it in her sessions with Dr. Chandler." I hadn't had time to get into it. "Look, Allison, I've got to run. Thanks so much for helping out."

I'd been on my phone the rest of the night calling in every owed favor, hoping for a miracle. I'd even had a lawyer friend talk to the judge, but nothing had worked. There'd been no way the Bauer kids would be allowed home without a hearing, and it would be another week before it would happen. Maybe two. Christopher had been my last call.

"They can't go into foster care, Piper. They can't." His voice had wavered with emotion.

"I'm sorry, Christopher. I wish there was something I could do, but my hands are tied. They can't stay at Allison's, and they can't come home. The only option is emergency foster care." I had tried to find a silver lining. "Not all foster homes are terrible. Some of them are really good. Look at you guys. They might end up with someone like you."

"Why don't you take them?"

I had laughed. "Me?"

"Why not? Are you certified to take in foster kids?"

"Technically, I could, but it's frowned on, and I never have before," I'd said.

I'd worked with hundreds of children, and I'd never once thought of taking one of them home with me. Most of my colleagues made comments about wanting to do it, but I had never liked the idea of having kids in my home. It was one of the reasons I didn't have them.

"Would you do it? Please, could you do it for us?" He'd never sounded so desperate.

"I don't know, Christopher."

He'd jumped in before I could say no. "Janie knows you, so at least you're not a stranger. And if anyone can handle her right now, it's you, Piper. Please. You don't have to decide tonight. You can think about it for two days since we have until Friday. Just think about it, okay? Promise me you'll think about it?"

I'd called him in the morning before I'd had my first cup of coffee because I'd known he'd be anxiously waiting for my call. I hadn't wanted to take the kids but couldn't bear the thought of saying no to

Christopher. I wouldn't have been able to sleep knowing I could've done something to ease his burden and chose not to. Surprisingly, his phone had gone straight to his voice mail. I had left him a message to call me whenever he got the chance. I'd been halfway to my first appointment when he'd returned my call. His voice had been even more frantic than the day before.

"Piper? Where are you?"

"Driving to a home visit. What's going on?"

"It's Allison. She—"

I had interrupted him. "You don't have to worry about Allison. I'll take the kids until the hearing. I can come get them this afternoon."

"You have to come now."

"What? No. I can't. I have an appointment. They will be fine there until this afternoon. Allison said they could be there until Friday."

"Now, Piper. You have to go there now. Please."

"Christopher, what's going on?"

His voice had broken. "It's Allison. You have to come. It's Allison." He'd let out a sob. "She's dead."

FIFTY-EIGHT

Christopher Bauer

"What are you doing here?" Hannah asked. She grew more and more coherent every day, and it wasn't lost on her that I was there outside of visiting hours. They'd finally found a medication combination that worked, one that muted her psychosis without turning her into a zombie. Her eyes were still lifeless from grief, but they were no longer dead from the drugs they'd been pumping into her.

"I have something to tell you," I said. They'd allowed me to see her given the circumstances. I rubbed my hands anxiously up and down my face. I hated to be the one to tell her about Allison, but the thought of the police telling her was worse. "It's awful."

She pointed to the barren walls around her. "What could be worse than what I did to get here?"

"I'm sorry, Hannah. I'm so sorry." I fought for composure.

She took my hand from across the table. "I understand, Christopher. I do." She rubbed the top of my hand like she used to. Those days felt like a lifetime ago. "I wouldn't be able to stay with me either. Not after what I've done, who I've become."

I'd give anything to be breaking divorce news to her instead of what I was about to do. I felt so much responsibility for the moment of telling her. When she looked back on things, she'd remember everything I'd said, how I'd said it, and probably hate me for it. I thought about the scripts they taught us in medical school, the coined phrases to use when telling someone a family member or loved one had died:

I'm so sorry. We did everything we could, but he didn't make it.

Despite our best efforts, we weren't able to save her.

I flipped through all of them. None of them were appropriate. None of them would lessen the bomb I was about to drop on her already-fragile self. I couldn't believe I was the one breaking her heart another time.

"Christopher, what's going on?" Her face was stricken.

My stomach churned. The room spun. My heart hammered in my chest.

"It's Allison . . ." I couldn't get any further.

Her eyes widened instantly. "What about Allison?"

"Something terrible happened."

"Is she okay?"

I shook my head.

She jerked her hand away and pushed her chair back from the table. "What happened?"

How could I? How would she ever find the strength to go on?

"Christopher, what happened?"

"She's dead."

My words splintered inside her. I saw it happening. Her hands clutched her shirt, pulling on it. She shook her head frantically, staggering backward into the wall like she'd been hit.

"No. No. No." Her voice was quiet, barely a whisper.

"I'm so sorry." It was all I could say, over and over again.

"How?"

I took a deep breath, bracing myself. "She fell down the stairs. It was a terrible accident."

"Down the stairs? How do you die falling down the stairs?" Her voice shook.

"Her neck snapped on the landing."

Her face paled. She covered her mouth with her hand. I stood and stepped toward her cautiously. "I'm so sorry."

"Stop saying that. Please stop saying that," she cried.

"I don't know what to say. What to do . . ." My voice trailed off. There were no words left. Nothing that could make this better. She sank to the floor, pulling her knees up to her chest. I slid down next to her.

"I don't understand. What happened?"

"I told you. She fell."

"But how? How did she fall down the stairs?"

I shrugged. "The police are at the house now."

She snapped her head up, locking eyes with me. "Why are the police there? I thought it was an accident."

"It was. It is."

"Who found her?"

"I don't know why any of this matters right now. It's only going to upset you more."

"It matters to me." Her jaw was set with determination.

"Caleb."

"That poor thing. What about Dylan? Where was Janie?" Her brain raced to connect the dots, the questions tumbling over each other. "Was Greg home?"

I put my hands up to stop her. "Hannah, no. Not now. I can't. It won't help things."

"You're hiding something. I can tell." Her eyes narrowed. "I can see it in your eyes. What are you hiding?"

I shook my head.

She sprang up from the floor and shook her finger at me. "Yes, you are, Christopher. You're lying to me about something. I can tell."

I shook my head again. The truth would only make it worse. "You—"

She clenched her fists together at her sides, her eyes narrowed to slits. "Tell me what happened to Allison." I took her hands in mine. She jerked away and moved to stand behind the table. "Tell. Me. Now."

I struggled to gain control of my voice. "Janie overheard Allison telling Piper that she couldn't stay there any longer. She was really angry, and they got into a fight after Allison got off the phone." I paused, struggling to speak the words. "It looks like there was an altercation on the top of the stairs and Allison fell."

Hannah let out a howl. She picked up a chair and threw it against the wall. "I should've killed her! I should've killed her!"

The orderly outside the door rushed into the room and pressed a button on the wall. She tried to grab Hannah, but Hannah shoved her away. The nurse flew back, hitting the wall behind her.

"She's a monster! I should've killed her!" Her eyes were wide open—manic. Spit was flung from her mouth as she screamed. Her entire body shook.

Two huge men rushed into the room. She clawed at her neck, raking her hands against it like she wanted to tear off her skin. They each grabbed one arm to keep her from hurting herself. She writhed with incredible strength. Her grief and anger had turned her into a beast. It took both of them to wrestle her to the floor, pinning her arms behind her back. That was when she unleashed the most primal screams I'd ever heard. They echoed down the hallway as they carried her away.

CASE #5243

Interview: Piper Goldstein

"Were you there for the altercation after the funeral?" Ron asked.

I nodded. I had gone to Allison's visitation to pay my obligatory respects even though I hated being in the house of someone who had just died. I had since my uncle had passed away when I was nine. I didn't like the way the house filled with people aimlessly moving from room to room like there was anywhere to go or how everyone was afraid to talk loudly, so it sounded like a steady hum of insects. Allison's house was no different that day.

Luke raised his eyebrows. "Do social workers usually go to funerals for the relatives of their clients?"

Of course we didn't. He knew that as well as I did, but the Bauers were like family. I ignored him and kept my attention focused on Ron.

"What was Greg like before the altercation?" Ron asked.

"He was a wreck," I said.

I'd never seen a man cry like he had. There was something especially devastating about watching a man fall apart. He had sat at the dining room table with his head buried in his hands as his shoulders had shaken. His sobs had been deep, guttural. His family had surrounded him.

"And the Bauers? How were they?"

"They weren't doing much better. Hannah had gotten a day pass from the hospital, but I'm not sure it was the best thing for her. She was so racked with grief she could barely stand."

Christopher had found her a chair in the living room, and I had made a beeline for them. It was one of the few times I'd ever seen them without the kids. I'd helped check Janie into New Horizons yesterday, the residential treatment center that Dr. Chandler had gotten her into. The waiting list was one of the longest in the country since they were one of the few private facilities that treated children under eight, but Dr. Chandler had done her fellowship with the new director, so he'd found Janie a bed once Dr. Chandler had told him about her situation. I'd arranged for Cole to stay with Christopher's mom.

I'd laid my hand on Hannah's knee. "I'm so sorry," I had said.

"This is a nightmare. An absolute nightmare. I keep thinking that it's not happening." The full weight of despair had shone on her face. "I don't know if I can do this."

I had put my arms around Hannah. Her body had been rigid and stiff, full of unspent emotion. Words had failed me. She'd been right. In all my twenty years of work, I'd never seen anything like this. I probably never would again. The case haunted me in ways I'd never imagined.

"What set Greg off?" Luke asked, bringing me back to the present.

"I don't know. I'm not sure anyone knows. One minute he was crying in the other room, and the next minute he was lunging at Christopher and Hannah."

"He wanted to fight them?"

I shook my head. "He wanted them out of his house. He kept screaming that it was their fault Allison had died."

Ron held up a nanny cam. "He'd seen this?"

"He had."

We'd all seen it by now. It was set up above the fireplace in their basement and provided a full view of the stairs, ending at the landing. There wasn't any sound, but you could tell by Allison's and Janie's movements that they were fighting, even though you couldn't see their faces. They scurried back and forth across the screen. There was a split second when Janie's feet rushed forward, and in the next, Allison plummeted down the stairs. She lay on the bottom, all her last moments captured in painful detail. Janie's feet never moved from their spot—not for seven minutes and thirty-two seconds.

FIFTY-NINE

Christopher Bauer

I hadn't realized when they'd referred to New Horizons as a residential home for emotionally disturbed youth that it would look like a big house. I parked in a driveway behind a wooden gate. Trees dotted the property. A concrete sidewalk wove up to the front door, cutting through perfectly manicured grass. The house was nondescript, made of smooth gray concrete that gave no clue to what was hidden behind the door.

Flowers lined the porch, and there was an old-fashioned swing on one end. I took a moment to compose myself so I could give all my attention to Janie. I was still trying to shake my conversation from earlier this morning. The director of the Department of Children's Services had called and informed me Piper was no longer going to be Janie's social worker and was being replaced with someone named Elaine, effective immediately. She'd refused to say why, only that switching social workers was common and we were lucky to have been with the same one for so long. But I could tell by Piper's voice when I had called her afterward that she was lying when she said it didn't mean anything and that it happened all the time. She'd had no idea she'd been removed from Janie's case.

Normally, I would have debated the scenario with Hannah, but we didn't debate much of anything these days. I hated what all of this had done to her, and the medication only made things worse. It was her fifth day home, and she moved through each one like she was sleepwalking. Her doctors assured me it was only a matter of time before she was herself again, but she was forever changed.

She'd chopped her hair into a short bob framing her chin, and it made her look less skeletal. There was finally life in her skin again. But the way she carried herself had changed too. Her eyes bore the weight of what she'd been through; she seemed more like a soldier who'd been to war and returned home.

I took a deep breath and lifted my hand to knock, but a large woman wearing a flowing printed skirt opened the front door and stepped outside before I made contact with the wood.

"Welcome," she said. "I'm the house manager, Viviane." She stuck out her hand. Her eyes were framed by dark lenses. She had thick black hair that she wore in a braid falling down the middle of her back. "Come in." She motioned me inside.

I scanned the foyer quickly, trying to take everything in all at once. A long staircase rose in front of us. Two hallways split from the foyer, one on each side of the staircase. Viviane veered to the hallway on the left, and I followed. She didn't speak while we walked. The house was quiet despite the ten girls living there.

"Where is everyone?" I asked.

"Things are very different here on the weekends. Many of the children go home because they've earned weekend visits." She squeezed my arm. "I know it must seem like it will be forever before you get there, but I tell all my first-time parents that visits will happen before you know it."

First-time parents? Children came here more than one time? I swallowed the anxiety creeping its way up the back of my throat.

"Normally, you would be in the common areas because it's where we do supervised visits, but Janie's been lying down all morning because she hasn't eaten since yesterday."

"Nothing?"

She shook her head. "Unfortunately, no. I saw you've already spoken to the doctors about it."

We'd spent over an hour on the phone yesterday. Janie was refusing food again. Last week, she'd gone three days, and they'd had to hospitalize her. Somehow, I had to find a way to convince her to eat today.

Viviane stopped when she came to the third door on her right. She knocked before entering, announcing her presence, not asking permission.

"Daddy!" Janie squealed, flying off the bed and into my arms in record time. I wrapped my arms around her and twirled her around as she giggled. I smothered her with kisses all over her face.

Viviane took a seat on the bed against the other wall. Janie's room was arranged much like my college dorm room during freshman year—a twin bed pushed against each wall. I wished I could meet with her alone, but the judge had ordered supervised visitation only. He'd promised to revisit the issue at our next court date.

Janie tugged on my hand. "Daddy, look. See?" She pointed at her walls. They were covered in a collage of her artwork. Drawings and paintings with bright colors and thick, solid lines brought life to her room. Most of them were done in purple and pink. Smack in the center was one of a man and a little girl holding hands underneath a rainbow. My eyes filled with tears. I struggled to contain them.

I'd never been blinded by love before. I'd thought that was reserved for romantic love, but it wasn't. I loved Janie in ways I couldn't describe or understand. I probably never would. Even after everything she'd done.

I carried her over to the wall and tapped the picture. I grinned at her as she smiled back. "This one is my favorite."

Cole had fallen asleep early, something that was so rare. He had been with my mom since the funeral, and we had finally gotten him back into our custody. Piper had worked out an agreement with the judge after Hannah had pleaded guilty to child abuse. There was no way our new social worker would be able to get things done as quickly as Piper.

It was his second night home, and last night had been rough. He'd screamed for most of it, but unlike before, when Hannah had tended to him all night long and woken at his slightest sound, last night she had put in her earplugs and rolled over to go back to sleep. I'd taken him into the living room until he had calmed down. It had looked like it had physically hurt her to watch me walk out of the room with Cole, but allowing me to take care of him during the night was part of her treatment plan, since sleep was one of the most important factors in her recovery.

It was like Cole had sensed we needed him to go easy on us tonight. It usually took him over an hour to fall asleep, but he'd been out within ten minutes. Hannah and I had been sitting at the kitchen table ever since, just staring into our tea. It had long grown cold, but we stayed rooted to our spots. Everything between us felt strange and forced. We moved around each other in the house like awkward roommates. We'd barely spoken since I had gotten back from my visit with Janie. She'd asked how it had gone but then had walked away before I could answer.

My phone buzzed in my pocket. It'd been going off for the past hour, but I had been ignoring all my calls. I could do that now that I didn't have to worry about getting called in to the hospital. Dan had put me on administrative leave last week. He'd said it was only temporary, but I wasn't sure I believed him.

Suddenly, the house phone rang, and we both jumped. No one called on our house phone unless it was an emergency. Most of the time

I forgot we had it. I looked at Hannah. She shook her head. Neither of us moved.

It cut off only to start again a few seconds later. What if something was wrong with one of our parents? I felt like throwing up. The room spun when I stood. I grabbed the phone from its spot on the counter. "Hello?" I said.

Piper's voice was hurried, breathless. "Christopher, I'm two minutes away from your house. Don't pick up your phone if anyone calls, and don't answer your door. I'm going to come around the back."

The line went dead.

I hung the receiver up slowly. She never called this late. What was going on?

"That was Piper," I said.

Nothing.

Were we even supposed to talk to her now that she wasn't on the case? What was allowed? How was Hannah not burning with curiosity? Didn't she have questions?

"She's on her way over," I said.

Still nothing. Hannah's shoulders were hunched together like she was trying to disappear inside herself. She wore the stare that meant she'd slipped away. The one that made me want to beg her to talk to me, to just let me inside again. But I didn't. She'd come to me when she was ready. I fought against the fear that she never would. I took her hand in mine. She didn't jerk it away; at least that was something.

It wasn't long before there was a tap at our back door. Nobody ever used that one. Piper stood on the step, panting and sweating like she'd run a mile. "I hopped the fence," she said.

I motioned for her to come inside. I peeked around the corner of the door, half expecting someone to be chasing her.

"Do you want a glass of water?" I asked, locking the door behind us.

"That'd be great." She took a minute to gather her breath while I poured it. Normally, Hannah would've asked her if she needed anything else, but she didn't have enough energy to say hello. I was surprised I'd gotten her out of bed today. Yesterday, she'd refused.

"I had to get here before they did," Piper said after she'd taken a drink.

"Who? Who's coming?"

"Probably the police."

"Why are the police coming?" I asked.

This got Hannah's attention. She smoothed her hair back away from her face and sat up straight in her chair.

Piper nodded and furtively looked around the kitchen like someone might be spying on us. "Or the lawyers. I'm not sure. But they're going to come for you, Christopher." She sounded like a paranoid junkie who'd been up all night smoking crack.

"Me? What did I do? I don't understand."

"Greg's attorney filed a motion to charge you with reckless manslaughter for Allison's death."

Her words fell like lead on the table.

"What? You can't be serious."

"I am. And apparently, the judge agrees with him. At least enough to issue a warrant. One of my colleagues on the police force gave me the heads-up. I came as soon as I found out."

"How am I responsible for Allison's death? I wasn't even there."

"His lawyers reviewed the footage from the nanny cam. They're claiming Janie intended to kill Allison when she pushed her down the stairs and that you should've known she might do something like that given her history of violence."

"What?" I shrieked. "There's no way they can claim any of those things based on that video."

I'd seen the same footage they had. I'd probably been over it as many times. Piper too. There was no disputing that there had been a struggle at the top of the stairs and that Janie had pushed Allison down them, but it was impossible to know anything else besides that.

You could speculate all you wanted, but there was no sound, and you couldn't see anything above the shins.

"Just because she pushed Allison doesn't mean she was trying to kill her. That's absurd." I shook my head, opposed to the very idea of it. "Janie didn't try to kill her. Not on purpose. She'd never do that."

I didn't doubt Janie had been angry when she'd found out Allison wanted her to leave and had pushed her down the stairs, but she'd done it because she'd been angry and frustrated, not with any murderous intent. I could guarantee she hadn't given a thought to the consequences. It was common in children who'd experienced trauma. They had very little impulse control. I'd read all about it in one of Dr. Chandler's books.

Piper shrugged. "It might be absurd, but it's happening."

"Janie went to get help. Why would she go for help if she wanted her to die? How come I'm the only one who sees that?" I threw my hands up in the air.

"I understand what you're saying, but she waited a long time before she did." Piper's breathing had finally slowed. She slid into a dining room chair next to Hannah.

"Seven minutes isn't that long for a traumatized child to freeze. She doesn't even have any concept of time anyway." I was running out of steam. No one would ever see Janie through my eyes. "Am I going to jail?"

"Whether it was intentional or unintentional doesn't really matter. You're focusing on the wrong thing." Piper downed the rest of her water before speaking. "His lawyers claim it was your duty to warn them about Janie's problems. He says if you'd told them the things Janie did, like killing the cat or biting Hannah, then they never would've taken her into their home, and Allison would still be here. Greg is determined to make someone pay for Allison's death, and he's putting the responsibility on you. His lawyer hired a hotshot private investigator from out East to dig up as much dirt as possible."

"Do you know anything about the private investigator?" I asked. "What could they possibly be looking for? There's nothing hidden. Nothing." I laid open my palms. "We've been up front about everything. Always have."

Piper stopped me before I spiraled further. "It's not that uncommon to hire a private investigator. Lawyers do it all the time. It's easier for them if someone else does their dirty work. I don't know anything about the guy he hired other than that his name is Ron and he used to be a homicide detective."

Hannah looked stricken. "He can't do this to Christopher. He just can't."

"Unfortunately, he can. And Greg's serious about the lawsuit."

"What about Hannah?" I didn't mean to sound so angry.

"I guess they figure she's not responsible for any of it given her mental state. You need to get ahead of this. Do you have a lawyer?"

Of course I didn't have a lawyer. I'd never even had a speeding ticket. I shook my head.

"Then you need to get one, and now. I'll send you a few referrals—people that I trust who've helped out parents in sticky situations."

"You've had this happen before?"

"Not this. I've never even heard of something like this before. I've seen parents get charged with violating parental-responsibility laws, but never on a manslaughter case." She scanned the kitchen. "We're not going to answer the phone or the door until we get you a lawyer. Where's your computer?"

"My laptop is on the coffee table," I said, already walking into the living room to get it.

I brewed a fresh pot of coffee. The three of us pored over lawyers, trying to find someone from Piper's list who specialized in parental-responsibility laws. I kept sneaking glances at Hannah while she worked. It was the first time she'd looked like her old self in a long time. She still nibbled on her lower lip while she read. I smiled despite the awfulness of the situation.

Shortly after ten, there was a knock on the door. We all froze. It had to be the police. No one visited us this late. We didn't speak for thirty minutes just to make sure they were gone. It wasn't long until Piper's source emailed her the affidavit for my arrest.

"Aren't you going to lose your job for that?" I asked, pointing to the report opening on her screen. We'd been so wrapped up in my legal drama that we hadn't even talked about her removal from our case.

"It's a matter of public record once it's filed. He just got ahold of it as soon as it was filed. He knows how much you guys mean to me." She smiled warmly. I'd never appreciated her more than I did at that moment.

We plowed through the document. Greg's lawyer claimed I'd had a duty to warn them about Janie and failed to fulfill my parental obligation in exercising responsible care, supervision, and control over her. He went on to say that I'd ignored Janie's violent behavior and failed to provide the proper mental health treatment for her issues. He claimed I should've known there was a possibility that Janie would hurt someone, even kill them. He sealed his order by laying out how my lack of action and proper care contributed to Allison's death and how I was therefore criminally responsible for it. He cited penal code after penal code and ended with something called Autumn's Law, which I'd never heard of before.

I instinctively reached for Hannah's hand, but it wasn't there. Her hands were clasped tightly together on her lap.

SIXTY

Hannah Bauer

I startled awake. There was a moment every morning when, for a split second, I didn't remember everything I'd lost, and in the next instant my changed reality came rushing back, flooding me with memories. The grief pummeled me, making it take too much effort to roll over. But I didn't have a choice. My outpatient therapy was a requirement if I stood any chance of ever getting my nursing license back. They hadn't taken it yet, but they would as soon as they found out about my felony child abuse charge. It was only a matter of time.

I stared at Christopher while he slept. The trial judge had thrown out the manslaughter charges against him. He hadn't wanted to be the first one to set a precedent for something like that, but Greg wasn't willing to let go that easily. His lawyer had filed for the lesser charge of reckless endangerment, hoping they'd stand a better chance. Our lawyer assured us it was only a matter of time before that one was thrown out, too, but it didn't matter. The damage had been done. Our story had been featured on the nightly news twice.

Cole was sprawled sideways across Christopher's chest. Christopher had been bringing him into bed with us at night after he calmed him down. He said it was easier to keep him asleep that way. They'd been up three times during the night. I faked sleep when he came back to bed. My body refused to allow sleep until Cole was content. That part hadn't changed, but I let Christopher take him at night when he fussed and said nothing. That's how I was supposed to parent now.

I carefully slid Cole from his arms, doing my best not to wake Christopher, and carried him with me downstairs so Christopher could have an hour to sleep by himself. Cole stirred, and I bounced him on my chest as I heated his bottle. I'd spend the rest of my life making up for what I'd done to him, how close I'd come to irreversible damage. The images of him in the hospital would never leave.

I grabbed my pill container and carried it with us into the living room. Cole eagerly latched on to his bottle and settled on my chest. I lifted the tab for Tuesday. Two pinks in the morning. One white at lunch. Two pinks again in the evening. Blue octagon right before bed.

I'd expected coming home would be difficult, but it was harder than I had imagined. Our situation hung over us at all times. The walls were heavy with our story. Having Cole with us again didn't make it any easier, even though I was grateful to have him back.

My panic attacks had waned at the hospital, but they were back in full force. The first one had happened as soon as I had walked in the front door. Everything about the house was a trigger. I felt like I was underwater, struggling to reach the surface for air, and each time I made it, I didn't get enough air before I was shoved under again. I'd stopped counting attacks yesterday after I'd gotten to eleven.

I'd called Dr. Spence three times after they had started making me feel like I was going to throw up and have diarrhea at the same time. None of the techniques we'd practiced at the hospital worked in the real world. All I could do was hide in the bathroom until the feelings passed. The only things that made an impact at all were these stupid pills. I threw the two pink ones in my mouth, washing them down with the water I'd left on the end table last night.

Christopher and I still hadn't talked about Janie. We tiptoed around her like she was a bomb that might explode if we got too close. I had asked him how their visit had gone yesterday because it was the right thing to do, but as soon as he'd started talking, panic had flooded me, and I'd barely made it to the bathroom in time.

Her presence was everywhere. I wanted to pack it up in boxes and put it all away. I closed my eyes whenever I walked by her room. I was never letting her back in my house. Ever. I didn't care if there wasn't a way to prove what had happened on the stairs—she had killed my sister. I wasn't ever going to visit or see her again. I hadn't told Christopher yet, but I would when I was strong enough for the fight I'd be up against. He'd still trade his life for hers.

CASE #5243

Interview: Piper Goldstein

Ron slid the evidence bag across the table and pointed to it. "Do you know what this is?"

"Someone's phone," I said.

"Becky's phone," he said.

"The one they recovered from the trailer?" I asked.

They'd found a phone in Becky's bedroom in the trailer, but it had been locked and illegal to open without establishing probable cause. It was a complicated legal process, and as far as I knew, nobody had gone through the proper channels to access it.

"We want to show you some of the videos on Becky's phone." He turned to Luke. "Can you set up the computer?"

My curiosity got the best of me. "How'd you get into her phone?"

"We got her Fourth Amendment rights waived," Ron said.

I nodded like I understood, but that was the first time I'd heard of someone doing that. I jiggled my leg nervously while we waited for Luke to come back with a laptop. He set it on the table in front of me, sliding into the aluminum chair next to me. A video was queued up. He hit play.

The closet in the back room of the trailer came into view. The silhouette of Janie's body curled into a ball in the corner. I'd never forgotten the picture of the ties, but seeing them in use—tightened around her ankles and wrists, the dog chain around her neck—burned them into my memory in a way that I knew meant they'd never leave. It was dark, but there was no mistaking her face when she turned around.

"Janie, it's time to eat," a woman's voice said.

Janie uncurled herself and stood slowly, head down, shoulders hunched forward like she wanted to disappear inside herself.

The woman continued. "Like I was saying, she been good lately. Earned her some time out of her ties."

My eyes were glued to the screen. The woman shuffled toward Janie. She held her phone in one hand and unlatched her collar with the other. Janie smiled up at her lovingly. I could barely breathe. Janie held her stick-thin arms out for her next. The woman easily slipped those ties off; the picture never wavered. She took a step back, then knelt in front of Janie, the angle bringing her into frame. She placed a small bowl of dog food on the ground. Suddenly, blood sprang from the side of her neck.

"Don't!" I screamed for them not to show me, just like I'd refused to look at the dying part in the Allison video, but it was too late. I saw it happen. The slice. The sound as the phone clattered to the concrete floor. I covered my ears so I didn't hear the sounds of the sixteen stab wounds that I knew came next.

Luke pressed pause. Ron slowly walked to our side of the table, leaning back against it. He crossed his arms on his chest. "Disturbing stuff, huh?" he asked.

All I could do was nod. No words.

"Quite a violent attack for such a little girl."

I swallowed the fury in my throat. "She must've been terrorized beyond belief to have been able to fight back with that much strength. Was that Becky's voice?"

"It was," Luke said.

Ron cocked his head to the side, opened his mouth like he was about to say something, then shut it quickly and turned to Luke instead. "Why don't we show you the next part?"

"Wait." I put my hand up. "If she was tied up, then how did she get a knife?"

Ron shrugged. "We don't know."

"Maybe there was someone else involved," I said. That had been my suspicion all along. "Was there ever anyone else in the videos?"

"There's a man's voice in one of the videos, but we haven't been able to identify him, and nobody has come forward," Luke said.

"What does he say?"

"He asks one question." He paused for effect. "'Is this the devil child you were telling me about?'"

Hannah had called her the same thing. A chill filled my insides.

He pressed play. The videos had been cut and spliced together to form a series following Janie's activity, all of them within the confines of the trailer, most in the back bedroom. There were scenes of Janie smearing her feces on the wall in the living room like she was finger painting and flinging it at Becky when she got upset with her. Other scenes showed Janie screaming and crying like she was being tortured even though no one was touching her. Times when Janie bashed her head against the floor until she passed out. All the neighbors had claimed not to hear anything, but there was no way that was true. Time and time again during the episodes, Becky tried to get close to her to comfort or calm her down, but Janie rejected each attempt, sometimes spitting at her, other times biting her arm.

Luke paused it again.

"There're hundreds of video snippets just like this. Becky goes on to record all the things she did to try and control Janie. She started with starving her and using food as a reward for good behavior. She gives her plenty of old-fashioned spankings that escalate into beatings before she moves on to tying her up in the corner for time-outs. Finally, she works her way into the closet. Do you want to see the progression?"

I shook my head.

He moved the slider. This time the video swelled with Becky's face. Her skin was pale and spotted with pockmarks, pieces of flesh that had been removed and scabs that were still healing—the telltale sign of any meth addict. Her eyes darted back and forth; her voice was hurried and pressured.

"I need your help. Please, I need your help. I keep calling. Nobody answers. But okay, okay. Here's what I'm going to do. This is it. This is what I have to do to show y'all what I'm talkin' 'bout. Otherwise, y'all just look at me like I'm the crazy one. But she the bad one. She pure evil, this child. I tell you. What'd I tell you? How many times?" She worked her jaw as she spoke. "I want you to see for yourselves what I'm talkin' 'bout. You'll see how she acts. I'm gonna record her. You'll see. I can't keep doing this. You gotta help me. Somebody gotta help me with this child. Please. I call and call, but nobody comes. None of you ever want to help me."

The video stopped on its own. We'd reached the end. My emotions moved quickly from panic to sadness and back again. Ron took a seat. They each turned their chairs inward, fencing me between them. Sweat dripped down my neck.

Luke leaned forward as he spoke. "Becky reached out for help. More than once. In fact, quite a few times. Do you know who she reached out to?"

I shook my head, my throat too dry with fear to speak.

"Ron, why don't you tell her who she called?"

"Certainly." Ron pulled the file across the table and flipped through it before he found what he was looking for. "It says here that Becky called the Department of Children's Services seven times in the year leading up to her death. In fact, she started making these videos the day one of the social workers was supposed to come by the trailer and help her." He pulled out a piece of paper and held it in front of me. Our agency letterhead was in bold letters at the top. "Do you know which social worker was assigned to visit Becky?"

I felt like someone had punched me in the gut. Words were impossible.

He set the paper back on the table. "It was you, Piper. You were the worker assigned to follow up on her phone calls. But you never did, did you? You never went. Never even called." He shook his head in disbelief. "Imagine if you would've. What would've happened if you'd gone all those months ago when she called the department clearly distressed from trying to parent a child who we all know is sick. Really sick. That must be a lot of weight to carry on your shoulders."

Every wisp of air was stolen from my lungs. "I didn't know anyone had called the department. I'd never heard of Becky Watson until I met Janie in the hospital. I swear."

He leaned so close our heads nearly touched, the smell of stale coffee on his breath. "Then what happened? Who dropped the ball? Because it says right here that you were assigned to do the visit."

"I didn't know about any of this."

"Stop!" He slammed his fist on the table. I jumped. "Allison might be alive today if you'd done your job the way it was supposed to be done."

My voice shook. "I had no idea Becky contacted the department. Nobody ever said anything. I was never assigned to do a home visit, but that doesn't mean I'm not responsible." Tears spilled over, and once they had started, I couldn't hold them back. "You don't understand. The Department of Children's Services gets so many calls every day—parents, teachers, friends, police, even elderly people who are just bored and have nothing to do with their time. We are so short staffed it's impossible to handle every complaint that comes across our desks. So we prioritize. Claire weeds through the complaints and handles my schedule." I struggled to speak. "Becky Watson's case never made my list."

"How is it possible that something like this never made your list?"

Was he serious? Didn't he know how broken our department was? "The Department of Children's Services is a revolving door. The same files come across our desks again and again. We see the same faces, meet the same families. We take one child out of the home and are forced to leave the other children behind or send children back to the families that abused them in the first place. I've been called to investigate abuse in foster homes almost as much as birth-parent homes. We have to operate within the system. Every social worker knows it's broken, but it's the only one we have, so we have to make do with it."

Luke raised his eyebrows. "So you're saying you failed Becky?"

"I'm saying the system failed them both."

We'd failed all of them. Christopher was never going to be the same again after he heard this. He had to believe that children were born good and pure, that no child was beyond repair, in order for his world to make sense. This would shatter his core belief.

"What will you tell the Bauers?" I asked. It went without saying that they had to know. I couldn't begin to imagine how this would change things.

Ron didn't need time to think about his answer. This was what he'd been waiting for all day. "The only thing I can tell them—the truth. Their daughter is a killer, and until she's an adult, they're responsible for making sure she doesn't hurt another human being."

"When?"

"When what?"

I cleared my throat. "When will you tell them?"

Ron glanced at his watch. "It's too late now, but we'll be there first thing tomorrow morning."

"Can I come with you?"

He frowned. "I'm not sure that's a good idea."

"Look, if I wanted to, I could go over there tonight and tell them myself. I'm not on the case anymore, and I already told you that we're more like family than anything else now. So I'm doing you a favor by waiting to go with you in the morning." I did my best to sound threatening.

I couldn't bear the thought of Christopher hearing the news without someone to support him. Hannah was barely hanging on herself, and she would be relieved. Elaine had confided in me that Hannah had spoken with her about relinquishing her parental rights and rehoming Janie. I hated the term because it made children sound like pets, but there were instances where the state allowed adopted children to be returned to foster care. There was no doubt in my mind Hannah would push for that now.

And I didn't blame her. Unlike Christopher, I knew there were children who were too damaged to be fixed. It was an awful fact of life and my job, but that didn't make it any less true. You couldn't fix what Janie had, but he would spend his life trying. That much I knew for sure, and he would do it alone unless I was there for him.

Luke folded his hands on the table. "You should know that Greg's attorneys have filed a civil lawsuit against the Department of Children's Services." He paused, letting his words sink in before continuing. "You should be aware that you are named in that suit." He exchanged a look with Ron, then turned his attention back to me.

"I don't care," I said.

They needed a friend. The charges against them had made their situation public, and people were avoiding them like everyone avoided tragedy, afraid they'd catch it if they got too close.

They exchanged another look. Ron nodded before Luke spoke.

"Meet us here at eight tomorrow."

SIXTY-ONE

Hannah Bauer

The toilet flushed, signaling Christopher was awake. His feet plodded down the hallway, and he grabbed a cup of coffee before joining us in the living room. He stood behind the couch.

"How'd you sleep last night?" he asked like he'd done every morning since I'd been home.

"Good," I lied.

He'd worry too much if I told him the truth. No matter how hard he tried to hide his worry for my sake, deep lines of it were carved in his forehead. I hated what Greg's charges had done to him. The case had stripped every shred of confidence he'd had left.

He planted a kiss on my forehead. "Can I take him?"

I nodded. He scooped Cole from me tenderly, and I struggled with the emotions in my throat. Sometimes his kindness hurt too much. I wanted him to hate me. That's what I deserved.

Christopher held him up, and Cole cooed, his eyes dancing with joy. He added new sounds every day. We both grinned as he babbled. I burst out laughing when he blew a spit bubble, then was immediately swallowed up by guilt because happiness felt like a betrayal to Allison. Mom kept telling me we needed to give it time, but time wouldn't heal this wound. I'd miss Allison just as much in ten years as I did today, but time would move forward regardless of our loss. That much was a given, and Cole would be the force pulling us along. He was the reason we got up in the morning. For now that was enough. It had to be.

Christopher and I didn't speak about how hard things were, but we didn't speak about much these days. Our suffering was too big for words. But it was better that way. I preferred it over the clichés we got from other people. One of my coworkers had sent me a card that said you needed to find beauty in the broken. I wanted there to be beauty, but I could only see broken.

He laid Cole on his lap. The two of them fit together perfectly. Cole favored him more every day. Their lips even turned up the same way when they smiled. Christopher tickled Cole's stomach until he squealed with laughter. My heart swelled with love for them.

This. This is how it was supposed to be. Me, Christopher, and our baby.

I pushed the thoughts away. Thoughts like that only destroyed me. I didn't need any therapist to tell me that.

"Do you want to take a walk after breakfast?" he asked.

I nodded.

Our walks were new. We'd only started them last week. I hadn't been able to hide my panic attacks from him for long, and he'd quickly learned to recognize the signs. I'd balked when he'd suggested going for a walk on the brink of one of my attacks, as my biggest fear was having an accident in public because I couldn't get to a bathroom in time, but he'd promised we would only go around the block. I had started feeling better by the time we'd been at the end of the sidewalk, so we'd just kept going. We worked them into our day as often as we could, and our first one was after breakfast. We rarely spoke, but something about the outdoors made it okay even when it felt suffocating in the house. Yesterday we'd walked two miles without saying a word.

Cole was happiest when we walked. Christopher strapped him to his chest in the Baby Bjorn, facing him forward because he liked to see what was happening. Once we'd walked in the direction of the park and had run into a few mothers who had recognized us. We hadn't made that mistake again. All our miles were in the opposite direction of the park. We'd gotten to pass through neighborhoods we'd never been in before.

Cole stirred in Christopher's lap, and I let out the breath I hadn't realized I was holding. I leaned close and inhaled the smell of his vanilla-mint baby shampoo. I would get through this for him. I had to. I made myself concentrate on what Christopher was saying, doing more than nodding my head at the appropriate time and faking interest like I did most days. He was in the middle of telling me about Janie's new social worker, Elaine.

"I can already tell I'm not going to like Elaine, and I'm not just saying that because she's not Piper." He took another sip of his coffee, pausing to nuzzle against Cole's cheek.

We both knew it wasn't true. No one would measure up to Piper. She'd taken the time yesterday to check on me even though I should've been the one calling to support her since she was the one on her way to be grilled by the private investigator, Ron. He'd interviewed Christopher, too, and Christopher had said it was more intense than the medical malpractice deposition he'd been part of a few years earlier. Neither of us had heard from her last night. I had no idea if it meant things had gone well or terribly wrong. My appointment with Ron was next week. I would be happy when this entire thing was over.

Greg wouldn't let me near my nephews, and I missed them terribly. My heart ached, especially since I knew Allison would've been furious with him because she would've thought this entire lawsuit was a joke too. If the roles had been reversed, she never would've done something like this. Ever.

But I wasn't mad at Greg. He was in unimaginable pain and not thinking straight. I wanted to be there for him. Christopher felt the same way. He'd told me he wanted to take Greg out for a beer and just let him talk until he ran out of words or sit in silence until the sun came up. He'd almost called Greg the other night, but our lawyer had told him he had to wait until all the paperwork was finalized.

"I'm ready for another cup," he said. "Do you want me to fill up yours too?"

"Yes, please," I said, instantly mad that I'd said *please*. I was working hard at not sounding so formal. He handed me Cole and headed into the kitchen with our mugs. I laid Cole on my lap just like he'd been on Christopher's since it was one of his favorite positions. He smiled up at me when I looked down, and I beamed back. I never got tired of looking into his sweet face.

"Hi, little buddy," I said, taking one of his hands in mine. He wrapped his fingers around mine and tried to pull himself up.

"Ma-ma-ma-ma . . . ," Cole cooed.

Christopher raced in from the kitchen. "Did he just say *Mama*?" he asked.

I leaned down, and Cole patted my cheeks with both hands. "Ma-ma-ma-ma."

Of course he wasn't saying *Mama*. He was too young. They were just sounds. But it sounded like it, and there would come a day when he would say *Mama* in reference to me. He would say *Daddy* too. I let the tears fall down my cheeks. I looked at Christopher. His eyes were wet as well.

The doorbell rang, interrupting our moment. I looked at the clock above the fireplace: 8:10. I glanced at Christopher. He shrugged. "Do you want me to get it?" he asked.

"Let's see who it is first," I said. I peeled back a corner of the curtain and peeked out the window.

"Who is it?" Christopher whispered.

"It's Piper," I said. "And the police are with her."

ACKNOWLEDGMENTS

Each book has its own journey. This one was particularly unique. It marked the step into a new and exciting partnership. First and foremost, I want to thank Megha Parekh for continually pulling me back to a normal level of what most people consider "disturbing." She's the one who let me know that a child and pet can't die in the same book. Thanks to Charlotte, who helped me bring the story to another level and pointed out blind spots. Both of you have been amazing to work with. To my husband and son, who give me the space to write and create—thank you so much. I promise someday I will write a story with a happy ending. Just not yet.

ABOUT THE AUTHOR

Photo © 2017

Dr. Lucinda Berry is a trauma psychologist and leading researche childhood trauma. She uses her clinical experience to create disturb psychological thrillers, blurring the line between fiction and nonficti She enjoys taking her readers on a journey through the dark rece of the human psyche. If she's not chasing after her ten-year-old s you can find her running through Los Angeles, prepping for her r marathon. To hear about her upcoming releases, visit her on Faceb or sign up for her newsletter at https://about.me/lucindaberry.